Once Upon a Time

Siren Fairy Tale Collection

Emma Wildes
Lara Santiago
Tonya Ramagos
Gracie C. McKeever
Samantha Lucas
Sage Burnett
Morgan Ashbury

EROTIC ROMANCE

Siren Publishing, Inc.
www.SirenPublishing.com

A SIREN PUBLISHING BOOK
IMPRINT: Erotic Romance

ONCE UPON A TIME

Print Book ISBN: 1-60601-036-0

First Printing, April 2008
Cover design by Jinger Heaston

Printed in the U.S.A.

PUBLISHER
Siren Publishing, Inc.
www.SirenPublishing.com

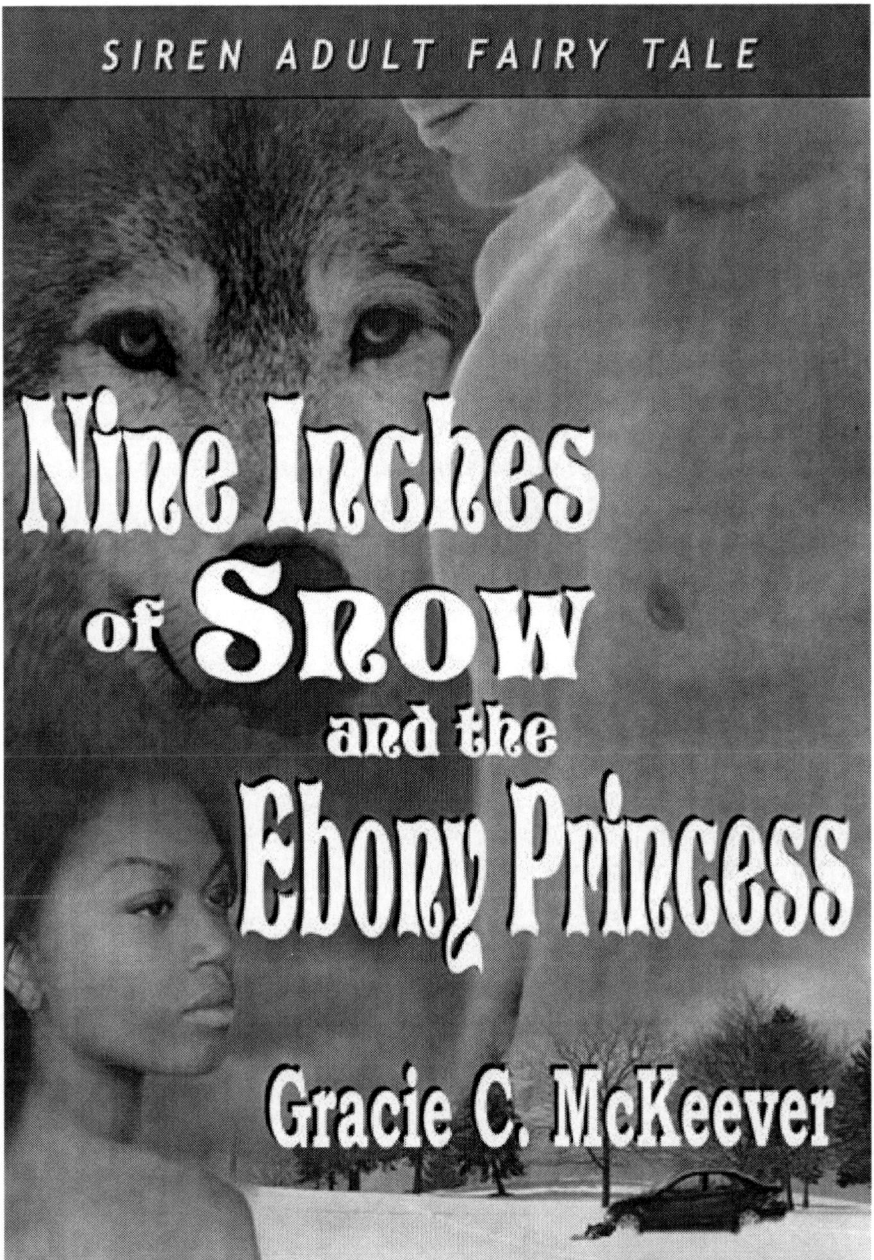
SIREN ADULT FAIRY TALE
Nine Inches of Snow and the Ebony Princess
Gracie C. McKeever

Nine Inches of Snow and the Ebony Princess

Erotic Paranormal Fairy Tale (Urban Fantasy, Light BDSM, Interracial, Shape-shifting)

An empathic young nurse driven to help and heal others since childhood after watching her mother languish for months before finally succumbing to cancer, Aziza Lopez abhors cruelty and suffering in any form. When she is assigned comatose patient David Healey, Aziza is confronted with the depth of her abilities for the first time since her mother's death and has a chance to contribute to a patient's recovery when modern medicine fails. But can she convince anyone else outside of David's family that she knows who is responsible for his injury when she's finding it hard to deal with the knowledge herself?

The youngest of five brothers, David Healey comes from a close-knit, no-nonsense family of psychics and shapeshifters. He has never suffered fools—or demanding, jealous girlfriends—lightly. But on the eve of a bitter break-up he realizes he is about to suffer a woman scorned when he glimpses his ex behind the wheel of a car careening towards him.

Now Aziza and David are in a race to pull him out of his coma before Aziza's vengeful stepmother can get to him and finish the job she started on a dark road.

NINE INCHES OF SNOW AND THE EBONY PRINCESS

The Fairy Tale Collection

GRACIE C. MCKEEVER

Chapter 1

Healey Pavilion, St. Frances Hospital, Winter Fundraiser

From the moment the guest of honor arrived, Aziza Lopez had to keep telling herself tonight was all about business, her job to keep the elite full and happy with hors d'oeuvres and champagne, and otherwise stay scarce.

Her stepmother would certainly never let her forget her place.

Homegirl needed to take a chill pill and get a life, if anyone asked Aziza, but, she was just the hired help, and no one was asking her.

She gave her hair one last pat, took a deep breath, and prepared to rejoin the party when the door swung inward, and the man of the hour stepped through.

Aziza's pussy muscles instantly contracted at the sight of David Healey standing just inside the door. She'd never had so carnal and instant a reaction to a man before, had been told by her father she would only feel this way when she found her soul mate.

But if this were so, that would mean that David Healey was—

"So here's where you're hiding."

He was way more gorgeous up-close and personal, his countless pictures in the society pages of the city's various newspapers not doing homeboy a bit of justice. He was also a lot taller than she remembered from the dining hall, wide-shouldered and towering over her 5'8 by at least six inches.

He stepped into her path when she tried to leave and made her temperature go skyward.

Overwhelmed, she held the tray of hors d'oeuvres up between them, tried to maintain some distance, but it didn't do much good. His essence surrounded her.

Aziza had been trying to keep her distance all evening, knew homeboy could be her downfall if she allowed him in her personal space. But she refused to allow him in, despite craving his touch from the first moment she'd seen him, awareness a sharp knife edge to all her female senses.

"I'm not hiding. I'm doing my job." She flicked her gaze up and down the long length of him, taking in the black formal evening wear that sensuously melded to his physique and made her feel like a ragamuffin in her waitress uniform. "What are *you* doing back here?"

"Looking for you." He stepped closer.

The scent of his cologne washed over her in one engulfing wave, and her pussy moistened at the piquant smell. Subtle, yet intoxicating, it reminded her of the woods after a hard rain, fresh and musky. Totally masculine.

"You've been avoiding me since I arrived."

She would have wondered how he knew, but Aziza had felt him watching her all evening, his azure gaze hot and tactile like a touch. "Didn't you get the memo? I'm not supposed to fraternize with the bigwigs, and the bigwigs aren't supposed to fraternize with the help."

He plucked a caviar-laden cracker from her tray and popped it into his mouth, chewing slowly and licking his lips with relish when he was done. "I'm no bigwig. And you're certainly more than the help to me."

Despite his nonchalant manner, making him seem approachable and efficiently closing the gap in status between them, Aziza said, "I'm nothing special."

"See, now that's where you're wrong." He reached out a hand to caress her face. "You're more than special."

Aziza's heart stuttered at his persuasiveness, something in him touching the core of her in a way nothing ever had, something about him speaking to her even when he didn't open his mouth.

She closed her eyes and reveled in his touch, had to stop herself from leaning into his palm and falling any more under his spell than she had already. "What is it you want?"

"One dance."

"Here? Now? You must be tripping."

He chuckled, took the tray out of her hands, and placed it on the table to his right. "I assure you I'm not…tripping."

Oh, but she was, heartbeat doing a happy dance in her chest already. If she stepped anywhere near his outstretched arms, she was sure she would implode.

Everything about him tempted her. His straight white smile beckoned like a lighthouse beam on a foggy night. His arms looked inviting and full of warmth and security.

She knew he wouldn't hurt her or do anything to her that she didn't want, and for the first time since her father's untimely death, Aziza felt like someone really cared about her for her and not for the fortune she was worth.

Scratch that. She used to be worth, before Philomena weaseled her way into Daddy's good graces and trust.

Her stepmother had had dollar signs glowing out of her eyes from the moment she met Aziza's father until he'd died a few months ago. And now, the woman was on the hunt for another rich husband.

What made David Healey any different, any less mercenary? He had money of his own, loads of it, so what did he want from her? True, the Healey fortune made Donald Trump seem like a pauper and could buy her self-made father's small fortune a million times over, but everyone was out for something.

Aziza hated to be such a cynic, and up until a few years ago, before her father married Philomena, she hadn't been. "What do you really want?"

"One dance," he repeated, his rich, butter-melting voice seeping into her bones, simultaneously liquefying them and hardening her nipples.

One dance. What harm would it do? Except maybe wet her panties even more than they were already?

Her feet closed the small distance between them of their own accord, and before she knew it, she was swept into his strong arms and against his hard-muscled chest.

He felt like she'd thought he would—firm in all the right places, solid, and so damn sexy, he made her mouth water and her pussy throb with anticipation.

"I've thought about holding you like this from the first moment I saw you tonight. Thought about making you mine."

She tilted back her head to stare at him, momentarily hypnotized by the intensity shining out of his blue eyes before she found her voice. "Making me yours? Let's get one thing straight, homeboy. I'm not looking to get hooked up or *belong* to anyone." It was a weak attempt at defiance, but the best she could muster under the circumstances. She needed to assert herself now before he took total control, the way she sensed he was capable of doing. Bad enough Philomena acted like she owned her free and clear. Aziza let her think it, because as long as she herself knew the truth, Philomena didn't need to know how little attention Aziza really paid her.

He was chuckling again, the sound not insulting or mocking at all, just self-assured. "But you will."

She knew without asking, but did, anyway. "Will what?"

"Belong to me," he murmured and bent his head.

Aziza had an instant to close her eyes and suck in a breath before his lips made contact with hers, reminding herself not to like it too much, not to feel too much for him, that her stepmother had already claimed and dug her claws into him.

Resistance and logic, however, were impossible once his lips touched hers.

They were at once demanding and firm, even fuller than she'd expected when he slowly slid his mouth across hers, as if searching for the right entry point. Finding it, he thrust in his tongue, brushing against hers with a low growl before completely foraging inside her mouth.

This wasn't exactly the dance she had imagined, but it would do, the wild beat of her heart the perfect accompaniment to his darting tongue.

He slowly rocked against her, and Aziza didn't know if it was to some music in his head or the slow song playing outside the doors in the ballroom. She no longer cared when his erection pushed against her abdomen and sent hot tingles surging to her core.

Warm moisture flooded her pussy, vaginal muscles contracting at the idea of his hard cock sliding inside her, to the hilt, his naked body pressed against her as she squeezed his well-muscled ass cheeks in her hands to motivate deeper penetration.

Aziza arched her neck and moaned, one leg automatically curving up around his hip.

She rubbed her slit against the large, rigid bulge in his pants, and he bent his knees to accommodate her desperate need to fill the emptiness and ease the sudden ache inside.

She burrowed her fingers in his longish chestnut hair, reveling in the waves and surprising silkiness, but when she pushed out her tongue to deepen the kiss, he pulled back, catching her around the shoulders as she stumbled forward.

Aziza wasn't sure if he was trying to steady himself or her, and the look in his vivid eyes told her he wasn't sure, either.

He leaned forward, panting and pressing his forehead against hers. "Damn, you are hot."

Only for you, she wanted to say, but just mutely gawked at him, wondering why he had stopped and why she had lost control so easily. She'd never lost herself like that before, had never been so instantly turned on.

But let's face it, sister-girl, your self-control was compromised the minute he walked into the room earlier in the evening.

"You want me," he murmured.

She avoided gaping with a monumental effort. "You're pretty sure of yourself."

"I'm sure of us because I want you, too." He reached down a hand to cup her pussy, stroking her engorged clit with his thumb as he grinned. "Don't you believe in lust at first sight?"

Inflamed by his touch and all-knowing smile, she closed her eyes and gritted her teeth to keep from whimpering. She was relieved he hadn't asked if she believed in *love* at first sight. That would have been too much to resist, with his seductive tandem assault on her senses. She was already too close to caving, wanting to believe in him and romantic platitudes, even though she had lost all sense of romanticism the minute her father said 'I do' to Philomena.

"I believe in lust and desire more than love," Aziza whispered.

"At least we have something to work with."

She almost asked him what he was doing with her stepmother, but didn't want to let him know she cared already, or that she was jealous so early in the game. Instead, she asked, "Why'd you stop?"

"Because if I didn't..." He took a deep breath and shook his head, looking impossibly sly like a fox and innocent as a boy when he murmured, "Let's just say I don't want our first time to be rushed in a hospital kitchen."

He said it like they were a done deal, and she couldn't dispute him. She felt like she already belonged with him, to him, from the first moment he stepped into the ballroom.

How could that be when he was with Philomena?

"I want to see you again."

"I don't think that would be a good idea."

He frowned and tilted his head, like he was unaccustomed to having his wishes questioned.

Aziza silently stared at him, reaching out with her mind to feel the echoes of her own ecstasy and confusion from their kiss, trying to slip further below the surface to read him more thoroughly, but her consciousness slammed against a barrier. It was unlike anything she had ever encountered and couldn't have been more substantial had he erected a physical wall against her.

She read people's feelings on the regular, naturally and easily. Reading their thoughts was admittedly much more difficult and involved a lot more effort, depending on an individual's will and resistance, but was still doable.

Was David Healey consciously blocking her, or did he have some sort of natural barrier?

He brushed her cheek with his fingers. "I think you think too much."

This was eerie. She wasn't sure if he was addressing her last spoken words or her most recent thoughts.

"Tell me your name," he murmured.

Aziza had a feeling he didn't need to ask, that he could easily get it if he tried, either by conventional or unconventional means. It was the unconventional means that had her ready to bolt, despite her own gifts. "I have to go." Aziza turned to pick up her tray and stepped around him to leave when the kitchen door swung open again.

"There you are! I've been looking all over for you." Philomena gaped when she noticed David standing just behind Aziza. "Has this young woman been harassing you, David?"

"Quite the contrary. I couldn't wait for her hors d'oeuvres and followed her in here to filch a couple." He reached for another caviar cracker and winked at Aziza when he brought it to his mouth.

"Oh…well, I suppose that's fine." Philomena caught Aziza around the arm and led her towards the doors. "Don't make me regret doing you a favor in hiring you for the night. Socialize less, and do your job more. You have guests to tend to," she said through her teeth.

Aziza grinned, stopped just short of blurting "I told you so" to David over her shoulder when Philomena shooed and ushered her out of the kitchen. Her heartbeat kicked up another notch when she caught David's answering wink before the doors closed behind her.

* * * *

David watched Philomena's fingers dig into his kissing-buddy's upper arm, wincing as he just barely held his anger at bay.

He hated cruelty in any form, and if he hadn't already made his decision to let Philomena go, he would have after that display.

He had gotten glimpses of her malice before, especially in the way she treated her staff and those she thought beneath her. Her elitism was the major reason he kept his distance with her emotionally. Physically was another story. He was a man, after all, at least for the most part, and unabashed when it came to his appetites.

But even a stunning blonde ice queen like Philomena VanWizer couldn't hold his attention indefinitely, especially not when he just found the woman he intended to make his mate.

The couple of weeks he and Philomena had been seeing each other so far was unprecedented for him, and her clinging possessiveness made it seem even longer. He couldn't imagine Philomena boldly declaring her independence as his kissing-buddy had. She was too eager to please, too afraid of risking a fat payday.

David wasn't about to be husband number two, despite what Philomena thought.

"Are you sure she wasn't harassing you?" she asked and hooked an arm through his. "I can have her disciplined for insubordination."

David just barely bit back a curse. "That won't be necessary." If there was anyone who would be doling out discipline and pleasure to that lush chocolate body he'd just held in his arms, it would be him. The sooner, the better.

He closed his eyes at the memory of her face—the prominent, high cheekbones, those intoxicating onyx eyes and the seductive, smoky voice—as a sudden wave of need washed over him. He just barely held a shiver at bay, took everything in his power not to make Philomena aware of his reaction to the girl. "What's her name?"

She looked at him askance. "Why do you want to know?"

"Just curious." He'd tried getting it himself, but came up against a psychic barrier almost equal to his own. Reading someone and maintaining his shields wasn't the easiest thing to do. It was something only his grandfather did with complete effortlessness. He'd gotten just a glimmer before the girl had shut him down, something with an A.

"You are so sweet, wanting to be friendly with the help, but it's really not a good idea. In fact, I think it's much more preferable to keep up formal barriers between myself and my employees. Less chance of any emotional attachments or misunderstandings."

He understood the tenets of good business better than most, thanks to his tycoon father and grandfather, and the rules of good manners thanks to his mother. There was no question Philomena would have benefited from the lessons he'd learned under his parents' tutelage. "I'm well aware of business etiquette, Philomena."

"You're not still upset at the way I talked to that waiter earlier, are you?"

"It's your party."

"David, he was dreadfully incompetent. He had to be firmly put in his place."

He removed her hand from his arm and held it. "We need to talk."

"Certainly, honey. What is it?" She turned to him with a confident expression, and David had a feeling she was expecting something from him he would never be able to give, at least not to her: commitment.

"We've had a nice couple of weeks together, but this isn't something that can go any further."

She blinked. "What is it you're trying to tell me, darling?"

He gritted his teeth at her term of endearment. It made him uneasy. Always had, as it presumed a love affair that did not exist, never could. "I'm telling you it's over."

"That's simply not possible."

"I'm sorry, but it is."

"But I was expecting you to pro—"

He stared at Philomena as she cut herself off, realization dawning.

Jesus, she was expecting him to marry her after two weeks? They barely knew each other—not that brevity of courtship would stop him from pursuing his kissing buddy. He knew her as well as he knew himself. He knew her *soul*—but what he knew of Philomena, he wasn't too enamored with.

David should have cut this off a lot sooner, but decided dragging it out any longer to soothe her wounded psyche would be even crueler than she.

"It's my stepdaughter, isn't it?"

He blinked and looked at her. Surely he hadn't heard her right. "Your stepdaughter? I've never met—"

"The waitress who just left!"

"She's your *stepdaughter?*"

"Are you scandalized because she's my stepdaughter, or because I know what's going on between the two of you?"

He was still dealing with the shock of discovering who his kissing buddy was when he met Philomena's glare with his own. "I'm scandalized because you're a cold and uncaring witch who doesn't deserve to have a young woman like her in your life."

"I see she has you fooled, too." Philomena sneered. "Don't you know you should never trust a big butt and a smile?"

"I'm sure I don't know what you're talking about." Her stepdaughter, and she never said anything, not one word. Didn't even introduce them. She'd treated the girl worse than an employee or servant. She'd treated her like a stranger off the street.

"She'll only use you. But you would know about that, wouldn't you? Being a user?"

David grinned and silently shook his head.

Another man would have been chastened at the tacit indictment, but David had never been one to worry about what other people thought of him, had never let barbs get to him. Years of growing up the youngest of five brothers and beneath the glare of family success and the public spotlight had inured him.

David made allowances for Philomena's hurt feelings, knew they were behind her insult, but he had no doubts about the nature of her character, or that he was doing the right thing in breaking things off now.

"So you have nothing to say for yourself?"

"This may surprise you, but despite my sharing your bed on occasion the last couple of weeks, I don't answer to you."

Her reaction was instantaneous, but so were David's reflexes. He would have had a nasty red handprint across his cheek had he not caught her hand mid-strike, the force behind her blow was that potent.

"How dare you!"

"Stop being so melodramatic." He held her wrist fast when she tried to jerk out of his grip. "If you'll calm down, I'll release you, but not before."

"Let me go," she said through her teeth.

"Can I count on your cooperation?"

"Who do you think you are to order me around?"

If she really knew him the way she thought she did, she wouldn't ask the question. And she would never have dared to strike him. "It's up to you." David tightened his grip just enough to get his message across, but not enough to cause any real pain, and just barely holding in a growl.

Philomena grew still beneath his grip, seemed to sense he was on the edge. "Fine. You have my cooperation."

Once he released her, she whirled on him, pointing her forefinger like a weapon. "I'll make you sorry you ever crossed me, David Healey. That's a promise."

"If I didn't know any better, I'd say you were trying to live up to my earlier name-calling by putting a curse on me."

"Mock me if you wish." Philomena turned on her heels and pushed the doors open before tossing a glower over her shoulder. "But you and your precious ebony princess will never be. I will see to this."

Chapter 2

Philomena decided she wouldn't cry. She had spent the better part of her life shedding tears over one slight or another, over one man or another. She would not spend her time or energy so unproductively. There were better ways to let David know he had irrevocably hurt her: revenge.

She glanced at her face in the rearview mirror—the flawless ivory complexion, the green eyes, the long, blonde hair framing her finely sculpted face—searching for one flaw that could have caused David's sudden defection, searching for something that certainly wasn't there.

Philomena caught movement out the corner of her eyes and followed when David exited the hospital through the emergency exit, most assuredly in search of her hussy of a stepdaughter.

Always proactive, she had quickly taken steps to ensure the little lovebirds didn't see each other again tonight, immediately dismissing her stepdaughter and sending her home. That took care of the immediate problem, but there was still the matter of Philomena's wounded pride.

She swallowed against the bitter taste in her mouth while she watched David, so handsome and regal in his evening wear and long wool overcoat, the epitome of class and money, born with a silver spoon in his mouth and a symbol of everything she had ever come to covet and loathe over the years.

Why would he choose that wretch of a girl over her?

She was perfect, far prettier and with much more class than any Aziza Lopez. She had done everything in her power to ensure her irresistibility to the male species as soon as she could afford to leave her old life as Phyllis Lipinski behind and become Philomena VanWizer.

Philomena frowned at the memory of her own wretched past, but quickly changed her expression to neutral, if not quite happy. She did not want to get wrinkles, after all. She spent entirely too much money to maintain a standard of physical perfection deserving her station and would not lose everything she'd worked so hard for now.

Most of her life, Philomena had been a misfit, rejected by the mainstream, the popular kids, because she didn't have the right clothes, the right shape, the right *look*.

She'd buried herself in her studies, wallowing in her geekiness, convinced smarts would get her what she wanted until she realized that brains and personality would only get her so far with a man. If she really wanted to catch a man's eye, wanted to snag her prince charming, she needed to act *and* look the part. She needed to be the entire package.

With the help of a boob job (an eighteenth birthday present to herself), liposuction (a twenty-first birthday present to herself), contacts, and a dye job, she'd become ultimate trophy-wife material and was ripe for the picking when Aziza's father came along.

She had gone through all that work and all that money, and for what? For David to dump her for a buxom and overly curvaceous younger woman at the first sign of go? Dumped for her stepdaughter?

Philomena would not have it.

She watched now when David crossed the street, sauntering in the general direction of Aziza's apartment building, a confident and determined bounce to his step. She had a sudden bad feeling about where he was going.

Was it possible he knew where the girl lived? That one of those meddling guests or hospital staff members told him? She knew how those nurses and orderlies all stuck together, and Aziza had ingratiated herself with each and every one of them, even the egomaniacal doctors, with that bubbly personality and easy smile of hers.

Was that all it took to lure a man like David Healey nowadays?

No matter. Aziza would only have him over Philomena's dead body. Or David's.

She started her Benz and slowly followed him, trailing at a good distance and waiting as he got several blocks from the hospital for the right moment to strike, until she was sure of his destination.

She would repay him for his insult.

When David stepped off the snow-encrusted curb onto the damp blacktop, Philomena revved her engine and careened towards him.

She saw the look of shock on his face, emphasized by her headlights and instantly replaced with a look of recognition.

No matter. He would not live to tell.

Philomena's heart pounded with excitement when she plowed her car into him. She heard the satisfying thud of his body when it flew into the air, skidded across her hood, up and over the roof, bouncing off the trunk and onto the pavement behind her as she sped away.

That would show him she was not to be toyed with.

* * * *

"Someone call 911!"

"Did you see that? The car just ran right over him and didn't even slow down!"

"Is he dead? He has to be after that."

"Did anyone get the license plate?"

David saw and heard everything clearly—the people hovering over his body, their words of concern and cries for help. He just could not respond.

He was trying to figure out whether or not this was a bad thing when he realized he was in wolf form and outside of his body.

Oh, fuck.

Something had gone wrong, something he'd never encountered or heard of before.

He'd started to shift when he saw the car coming at him and recognized Philomena behind the wheel. It was a natural reaction, his body instinctively changing to another form to avoid maximum damage, or at least trying to change. She'd come at him so fast, it was a wonder he'd had time to react at all. It was a wonder, too, that he'd seen her face. But he had. There'd been no mistaking that long, platinum blonde hair or hateful green-eyed glare.

She'd meant to kill him.

David trotted over to his body to see if she'd succeeded, nuzzling his neck and releasing a howl at the non-response. He gaped up at the spectators and realized when none of them reacted to his presence that they couldn't see or hear him.

Double fuck.

Either he was dead, or he wasn't. Either he was wolf, or he was man. He couldn't be both, could he? David had never heard of a split or bilocation of this nature. He needed to get to his father or grandfather to find out what was going on.

Would either of them be able to hear or see him any better than the spectators could?

David barked two times in quick succession, trying to get someone's attention, but no one flinched—not even his brother Matthew, whom out of all his brothers, he had the closest bond.

How was he supposed to find out how to get back into his body and wake up if he couldn't communicate?

David refused to feel sorry for himself. First, it was behavior too unbecoming of a Healey, and second, he would never hear the end of it from his Grampa. He couldn't help, however, feeling regret at being snatched away from Aziza and deprived of spending quality time with her when he had only just met her.

He glanced up at his Grampa and loudly howled.

His grandfather glanced in his direction, frowning at the same time that Peter sneezed and pulled a handkerchief from his jacket pocket to blow his nose.

"Did anyone hear that?" Grampa asked.

"I think the entire floor heard that sneeze," Richard grumbled.

Matthew finally woke from his doze and asked, "Hear what? Did the doctor come out with word about David yet?"

"Between, grumpy, sneezy and sleepy…" Thomas chuckled and shook his head at his younger brothers.

"And who does that make you?" Richard asked and Thomas playfully brandished a fist.

"It makes me the oldest brother with rights to clobber you accordingly." He arched a brow at his still-drowsy brother Matthew. "Another late night?"

"I can't help it if I'm popular." Matthew gave him a wolfish grin and shrugged.

Thomas pointed his chin at Peter. "What about you? I don't see any furry creatures or vegetation in the vicinity."

"It's the damnedest thing. My sinuses all of a sudden feel like they're under attack."

"I think you're allergic to yourself, Pete. Have been since you were a pup," Richard muttered, and his brothers laughed, even Peter.

"This is different. I know it sounds weird, but there's an animal nearby. A big one."

David's heart sped at his family's reactions. It was obvious they sensed him on some level. The problem was to up the level and make them clearly hear and see him, not just vaguely sense him.

"Shh. The doctor's coming," his mother said, and though no one appeared in the room for several long seconds, David didn't doubt someone was on the way.

A minute later, a doctor came in from the hall, pausing on the threshold as he took in the Healey clan one at a time before making his way to David's parents. "Mr. and Mrs. Healey?"

"Yes," they chorused.

His mother pulled out of his father's arms to confront the doctor as David's brothers and Grampa converged and presented a united front.

"How is he?" Dad asked.

David almost zoned out at the litany of ailments the doctor outlined ... compound broken bones ... internal bleeding ... torn spleen ... bruised liver .... yadda, yadda, yadda.

He had faith that his unique anatomy was healing and taking care of the physical problems well enough. What concerned him more was mention of a deep coma and ventilator.

"There was brain swelling and intracranial pressure that we alleviated in surg—"

Mom gasped. "He's not brain-dead, is he?"

"There is brain activity, so no; he's not brain-dead, but—"

"Thank God."

"*But*, I'm not going to lie to you, Mr. and Mrs. Healey. Your son's condition is critical, and the next twenty-four hours are going to be crucial in telling whether or not he'll recover."

"Oh, horse pucky."

"I'm sorry?" The doctor turned to Grampa, who pointed an accusatory finger at the medical man.

"You youngins with your highfalutin education and degrees and jet age medical breakthroughs think you're God and know so much. Well, you don't know my grandson."

You tell 'em, Gramps.

Mom threw Grampa a chastising look.

The old man returned it with a wide-eyed, what-did-I-do-wrong expression and said, “Well, it’s true.”

“I know this is a difficult time for you all, but I’m only telling you the facts. The longer David stays in a coma, the less likely his chances are of coming out of it.”

“We understand.” Mom, ever the mediator in the family, grabbed the man’s hands in hers, gently squeezed, and held them. “Thanks for your time and patience.”

“No problem.”

“Can we go in to see him?”

“He’s being moved into a room from recovery as we speak. Once he’s settled, a nurse will come out to get you, but only two of you at a time, and only for ten minutes a visit.”

Mom thanked him again and shook the doctor’s hands before finally releasing him.

He gave her a sympathetic smile, then left.

David paced about his family, weaving between them like a human obstacle course before finally standing still to stare up at all of them in turn.

He had to reach them somehow, either in this form or human form.

That was it! He’d just shift back and merge with his body. Non-responsive, his ass!

He trotted away to follow the doctor down the hall, where he soon found his body lying peaceful, still and on a ventilator.

Oh hell, this was bad.

He’d never once been sick or injured in his thirty-two years of life, aside from that one rebellious incident as a pup when he was determined to forage in the woods and see if he could survive on his own in wolf form.

He has been brought down by a hunter’s bullet, and had it not been for the superior healing abilities naturally built into his DNA, and the doctor the Healey family had on retainer to discreetly take care of such matters, his previous injury could have been much more disastrous—both personally and professionally.

David went closer, heart pumping, as if he had just done several wind sprints.

Seeing himself flat on his back, unresponsive and in such serious shape, shook him more than he was willing to admit.

He leaped into the chair beside the bed, noticed the wave patterns accelerate on the monitors and wondered if his human self was reacting to the proximity of his wolf form.

David watched himself for several long moments, wondered if he should try to shift. He hadn't since the accident—accident, ha, that was a laugh!—and it would definitely be a test on this plane.

Only one way to find out.

He leaped out of the chair back onto the floor and took a deep breath. He closed his eyes, mentally blocked all distractions, concentrated on his own heartbeat and the change.

He'd done this a thousand times, natural and often as blinking, and didn't think he should have a problem, until he suddenly felt woozy and stumbled back onto his haunches.

Okay, he'd just have to try a little harder. He was used to challenges.

As the youngest, he'd learned at an early age to fight for everything he got, especially his clan position. He still wasn't where he wanted to be and knew the only way to achieve breeding status was to disperse, leaving his natal pack to find his mate and start his own pack. As much as he loved his family, biding his time had never been his strong suit. He was a prime at heart, too impatient to work his way up the dominance hierarchy, especially not when he had four older brothers ahead of him, with more rank and so far biding their time, too.

David stood now, started the process over again, meeting with some success.

His comatose self hadn't changed however. He'd thought with all the energy he'd expended to change back to human form, it would have affected his corporeal self. Not the case.

David got into the bed to join with his body and for an instant, felt like he was falling into a bottomless pit. His body surrounded his recently shifted spirit like an empty shell.

This wasn't merging. This was just filling a void, unable to affect change in it, unable to make his body respond to his commands. Not even the simplest one of wiggling a toe or finger, much more moving a limb.

Damn, he wasn't comfortable with this situation at all, felt too vulnerable like this, especially considering who had been behind his injury: a woman dumped and scorned.

In addition to his many dubious attributes, Johnny was better than average looking, handsome in a rough-hewn sort of way. He fucked pretty well, too. At least she had attained the prerequisite orgasms during their sundry times together.

Philomena might have considered Johnny her perfect foil except for several serious drawbacks. He wasn't the sharpest tack in the box as far as IQ went, and personality-wise, he was a pretty dull boy. He could never touch David Healey in the witty banner or intelligent conversation department, and he certainly wasn't sophisticated or rich like David.

Pity.

Johnny did have his uses, but playing sugar daddy to an already rich and pampered socialite wasn't one of them. He was good for sex and grunt work in Philomena's book. It was for the latter reason she might have enlisted his help in taking care of her little problem at St. Frances, but she didn't think Johnny was clever enough to pull it off.

Philomena wouldn't totally discount using him if the need arose, however. She just preferred finishing what she'd started wherever possible.

Besides, she wanted the pleasure of being there when David took his last breath.

Chapter 4

When Aziza reported to work on the ICU the next evening, the nurses' station was abuzz.

In addition to three sets of nurses present during the shift change jawing about the club scene the evening before, or the amazing thing their two-year-old did, or the silly thing their significant other did that morning, the main topic of discussion was the hit-and-run that had occurred several blocks away and the esteemed patient now in their midst as a result.

Aziza punched in at the nurses' station and checked the roster, surprised David Healey was one of her two patient assignments for the evening shift.

She would just have to switch with one of the other nurses, plead a conflict of interest, even though she barely knew him. Well, if one didn't count a little tonsil hockey and dry humping in the hospital kitchen as knowing each other.

Normally, she wouldn't have been so doubtful of her ability to care for a patient and competently carry out her duty, but David Healey was too much of a distraction. She was sure a coma would have little effect on the power of his aura, or his ability to unnerve and turn her on in equal measures.

And what did that say about her morals, lusting after a comatose man? Maybe that she was just one sick sister?

Gloria Goodwich, the supervising nurse and something of a maternal figure to all the nurses in the ICU and under her direction, caught Aziza's eye from the center of the gathering at the nurses' station and waved her to the side.

"I'm sure you're already aware of what's happened and who our most recent patient is."

"I heard about the hit-and-run on the news, yeah."

"I don't have to tell you that Mr. Healey is to receive the utmost VIP treatment during his stay at St. Frances, like all our patients." Nurse Goodwich went on to brief her on the basics of David Healey's condition. She stressed his unresponsiveness since the ambulance brought him in last night and the doctor's bleak prognosis for improvement. Though the patient's body seemed to be undergoing a miraculous recovery, he yet remained in a coma.

"Nurse Goodwich…"

She arched a brow. "Yes, child?"

Aziza swallowed, took a deep breath. "Surely there have to be other nurses more qualified and experienced to take care of Mr. Healey while he's here than me?"

"Oh, don't be ridiculous!" Nurse Goodwich waved a dismissive hand. "There's no one more qualified for this job than you." She put the same hand on Aziza's shoulder and squeezed. "You'll do fine. Just go in there and do what you were trained to do."

"Is there anything else I need to know?"

"His family's here and has been since last night. But they're a wonderful group of people and shouldn't give you any trouble. A little eccentric, especially that grandfather. Oh, he's a pill, by the way. But like I said, they're all nice folk."

He shook his head and leaned in. "Hedonist," he murmured against her throat, firmly sank his teeth into the soft skin connecting her shoulder to her neck before gentling his stroke, nipping and licking his mark.

Aziza shuddered beneath him. "When I'm free, I'll—"

"What, sweet Aziza?"

She growled. "Don't start no trouble and there won't be none."

He laughed at her barely veiled threat, nibbling a trail from her shoulders to her hips before pausing at her core, need barely contained when her musky-sweet scent wafted to him.

He nuzzled her pussy and inhaled deep as she moaned. "I've waited all my life for you. Aren't you willing to wait a little for me?"

"Don't make me…" She gasped and pitched her hips, offering herself. "Please, David."

She was too much to resist, even for someone like him, who prided his self-control. She made his mouth water with want, and the only way to stop it was to satiate himself—in her body, in her essence.

David nudged her engorged clit with just the tip of his tongue, garnering a tremor that rocked through him before she bent her knees to brace her feet against his ass.

He slowly opened her with his thumbs, tracing her vulva before plunging his tongue inside her like a rapier.

"Ahhh, yes, yes…" She dug her heels into the small of his back while he alternately sucked and licked her cunt.

He stopped after several minutes, only long enough to come up for air. He tongued and nibbled her clit, maintaining the internal pressure when he slid two fingers inside her and rhythmically stroked her G-spot.

Aziza stopped just short of squeezing his head between her knees, brutally pushing herself against his mouth, begging and calling his name until he curved one finger around the soft sex gland and massaged it with abandon.

"Oh man…oh God…David!" She stiffened beneath him, her juices hot and copious when they gushed and coated his fingers.

He pumped his fingers and sucked her in concert, bringing her to a frenzied orgasm that shook her entire body before he slid his fingers out of her to lick them with relish. The idea of prolonging their encounter flew out the window the minute he enjoyed the intense taste and whiff of hot female in heat. His female.

David instantly willed his pants and boxer briefs away, rising up between Aziza's legs and spreading her thighs wide with his knee. He poised at her entrance for just a second, the tip of his dick moist with pre-come and mingling with her cream as he experimentally circled his hips and teased her opening.

Impatient, Aziza wrapped her legs around his waist and drew him forward, wiggling beneath him in an irresistible sensual rhythm that had his heart pounding in his ears and fired his entire body from the inside out.

He bent his head to nip her earlobe, pulling it into his mouth and sucking hard before drawing back to lick the tender spot. He circled the shell of her ear with his tongue and murmured, "I'm going to have to teach you the virtue of restraint."

"Not before I teach you the virtue of wild abandon," Aziza purred, nestling her face close to his chest and biting a flat male nipple.

The low sound that escaped his lips was a hybrid of a grunt and gasp, emphasizing his approval and surprise at her intense instruction. He thrust into her on a roar, scorching a path through her hot, wet canal, stretching her slow and deep.

She welcomed him inside her with a long moan, tightening her legs and pitching her hips to meet his steady thrusts.

David lowered his head to kiss her, alternately drawing her voluptuous lower lip between his teeth and plunging his tongue to the rhythm of his hips.

Aziza pulled back long enough to whisper against his mouth, "Make me come again, David. Make me come hard and fast."

She had a point. Fuck restraint!

David pumped harder, speeding his thrusts and nipping her shoulder in his excitement.

Aziza whimpered and bucked her hips in response, sinking her teeth into his chest right above one nipple when he sank into her one last time and ground his pelvis against her so fiercely, he no longer knew where he began and she ended.

For one infinite moment, their world balanced on a knife edge of ecstasy and pain while David staved off coming only through sheer force of will and wanting to see Aziza come again before he allowed his release.

He eased away from her just enough to allow his hand to squeeze between them, thumbed her clit and circled his pelvis until Aziza cried out and vibrated beneath him.

She pulled against her bindings so roughly, David half-worried about her bruising her wrists. The other half of his brain was occupied with the climax that suddenly crashed down on him and shattered his remaining senses.

Wordlessly, David gathered her close and held her the length of his shuddering and release.

Chapter 6

"Untie me, baby," Aziza panted, nuzzling his ear and moving suggestively against him.

His cock was semi-erect inside her, showing signs of life when she squeezed her pussy muscles around his hot flesh, still hungry for him. She wondered if there would ever come a time when she wouldn't be.

Chiding her nosiness and jealousy beforehand, she wondered too if David had tried half the stuff with Philomena that he had done with her, especially the rough sex and bondage. She couldn't imagine it. Despite the other woman's cruelty and calculation, Philomena had low self-esteem, was just a damaged and fragile little girl deep down.

Not that she didn't want to see her stepmother punished, and good, for what she did to David, but Aziza felt sorry for the woman.

David lifted his head and frowned. "Why?"

"Why what?" She played dumb, hoping he hadn't caught her last thought. She'd been working hard to keep him out of her head, the same way she worked to get into his.

"Why do you want me to untie you?"

"You'll see." She wanted to taste him, the need so urgent, she licked her lips in anticipation.

David leered. "You don't need your hands to taste me."

"I want to touch you, too, smart-ass."

He chuckled, closing his eyes and lifting up to move away from her.

It took Aziza a second to realize he had done her bidding before he took her hands in his and gently kissed each wrist.

"Wild woman," he murmured.

"I'll show you wild." She sat up and flipped him beneath her, full knowing he had let her, especially when he laughed and pulled her down on top of him with one powerful arm.

"Now what?"

Aziza straddled him, bent her head to kiss a path from his chest to his hard, sectioned abdomen, swirling and zigzagging her tongue around his navel before moving further down. She glanced up at him once before she lost her nerve, watched him lift an eyebrow and fold his hands behind his head, looking supremely relaxed and satisfied.

She lowered her head again, determined to knock him off his haughty little throne.

His erection jutted straight up, a big tasty treat, beckoning her. Aziza couldn't resist.

She began at his balls, sucking them into her mouth before licking a path from them up his enormous, hard shaft. She circled the head of his penis with the tip of her tongue before finally licking the pearl of liquid from the tip, closing her mouth over him and sucking hard.

David shifted and moaned beneath her, hands automatically burrowing in her hair.

She descended further, reached the base of his cock, and licked his balls. Then, she sucked her way back up to the purple mushroom head, loving the moist surface with her tongue before starting over and repeating the process again and again.

For several minutes, she worked up a steady rhythm that had David writhing before a hoarse shout ripped from his throat. His fingers tightened against her scalp.

Needlessly, he held her in place, and Aziza coaxed every drop of come she could out of him, savoring the down-to-earth taste of him when she swallowed.

"Damn." He caught her around the shoulders and pulled her up against his chest.

"Don't get too comfortable."

"Why not?"

"I have to go."

"My gramps will keep the rest of my family out."

"It's not your family I'm worried about." She had shirked her duty long enough and didn't want to give Nurse Goodwich any reason to doubt her reliability.

Reluctantly, he released her and sighed. "If you insist."

He sounded like a little boy who'd just had his favorite toy taken away from him, and Aziza giggled at the picture before jerking up on her haunches, eyes wide.

"What is it?"

"Someone's in the room. We have to get out of here, David. Now!" She jumped from the bed, and David instantly willed her scrubs back on before she bumped into his solid chest on the way to where she thought a door should be.

"Calm down. I'll get us out."

"Um, your clothes?" Not that she wanted him to cover up that gorgeous naked body.

"Don't need them."

"Wha—"

"C'mon." He grabbed her hand, and darkness instantly enveloped them when he dragged her forward.

She thought she was prepared, but the trip out was a little rougher than in.

One minute, Aziza was standing in David's mental bachelor pad. The next, she was sitting in a chair and blinking her eyes open back in his hospital room.

The moment she glanced around and spotted Philomena with her back to Aziza on the other side of the bed, she knew her earlier alarm had been warranted.

Silently, she stood and peered around Philomena to confirm what she was doing: trying to pull out the plug to David's life support systems.

The woman didn't know it wasn't that easy.

"Trying to finish the job?"

Philomena yelped and turned to Aziza with a start. "Where did you come from?"

"I think the question should be, what are *you* doing here, Philomena?" Aziza came around the bed to confront her.

"I have more right to be here than you do."

"Even if you were still his girlfriend, you're not his family."

"What do you mean, 'if'? Has he said some—" Philomena snapped her mouth shut when she realized her mistake.

Aziza approached, grabbed Philomena around the arm. "I work here, and I have every right to be in here. You, on the other hand, are impersonating hospital staff." Aziza gave Philomena's white coat and stethoscope the once-over. "I'm sure security will have some questions regarding your attire."

"You can't prove anything."

Aziza didn't need to. She had David's memories and would bluff a confession out of her stepmother if she had to. "I saw what you did, Philomena. I know your car."

"Even if what you say was true, it's your word against mine. Who would believe *you,* anyway?" Philomena sneered. "And as for this little visit, I'm just a concerned girlfriend desperate to see her injured boyfriend. Now let me go!" She tried to jerk her arm out of Aziza's grip, but Aziza held fast.

Philomena brought up her hand to strike when a low growl rose up from the opposite corner of the room near the door.

Both women turned at the same time.

Aziza smiled when she saw her furry friend from the night before. Now she knew who and what he was—a manifestation of her desires, but so much more than her father could have ever predicted.

"That…that's a wolf."

"You can see him?"

"Of course I can! What kind of hospital is this?" Philomena pulled her arm again, and this time, Aziza let her go.

She didn't know how, but David would stop her stepmother.

Philomena ran for the door, but not before the wolf leaped through the air and landed on her back with a resounding thud.

Philomena crashed to the floor beneath the animal's weight, turning on her back to ward off his attack and screaming for help when the wolf stood on all fours on top of her, baring his teeth.

When David's grandfather burst into the room trailing two police officers and another man Aziza didn't recognize, Philomena was wildly flailing her arms and screaming for help.

To everyone else in the room she looked like a woman suffering from delirium tremens, but Aziza knew the wolf was still on top of Philomena. Only now, he was lapping at her face like a domesticated dog.

It took everything in her to keep from laughing and giving herself away.

"Get this wild beast away from me! Get it away before he kills me!"

The two policemen stepped forward, one on each side of Philomena. They each took an arm and dragged her to her feet. "Is this the woman who dropped off the damaged Benz at your shop, Mr. Lemeauix?"

Philomena glared at the man standing behind the two uniformed policemen and spat, "You treacherous bastard!"

He just smiled while the two police officers dragged her out of the room past him.

One of the officers stopped in the door as his partner waited for him in the lobby. "We'll need you to come down to the precinct to finish giving your statement, Mr. Lemeauix."

David's grandfather spoke up, grabbing one of the younger man's hands in both of his and vigorously shaking. "I can't thank you enough for contacting the authorities with your information." He handed the man a business card and slapped him on the back. "Call me when you're ready to receive your payment."

"I'd have done it for free, just to see the look on that uppity bitch's face when they took her away." Lemeauix took the card, jerked a thumb at the door and smiled before bidding David's grandfather good-bye and heading out in the hallway behind the two policemen.

Before the door could close, Nurse Goodwich popped her head in, a wide grin on her face. "Coast clear?"

"All clear." David's grandfather smiled, went to the door, and pulled her into a one-armed embrace. "I'll be out with you in a minute."

Aziza noticed the proprietary way he held Nurse Goodwich before guiding her out the door, felt a tingle between her legs at the memory of David handling her the same way and wondered just what was going on between the two older people. Whatever it was, she thought they were two of a kind that made a perfect couple, both protective decision-makers.

David's grandfather came back to the bed, where she was standing beside David. "I gave the rest of the family instructions to stay out in the waiting room. You won't have any interruptions from them. And that fine Nurse Goodwich has taken care of things on her end."

"Her end? Interruptions?"

He put an arm around her, the same way he had done with her supervisor. "To keep you from doing what you need to do."

"Oh yeah. That." Whatever *that* was.

*Lead our David out of the darkness...*How was she supposed to do that?

David's grandfather gave her arm a squeeze before releasing her. "Just follow your heart," he whispered, then left.

Aziza stood at David's bedside, looking down at him. After a long moment, she reached out a hand and ran her fingers through his silken waves.

He looked so serene, she almost didn't want to wake him. Like his grandfather seemed to think she could.

Follow your heart...

Right. God, if she was wrong about this…

Aziza disengaged the ventilator and waited a beat as she watched his chest. No movement. No spontaneous respirations.

She didn't panic, simply bent over the side rails, closed her eyes, and sent up a quick prayer to forgive her folly when she pressed her lips to his.

She opened her eyes to stare at him. Nothing. Not a blink.

She'd just try it again and again and again until it worked.

Aziza pressed her lips to his, firmer this time. After an endless moment, she felt his tongue thrust into her mouth, stroking hers. She jerked up her head with a gasp, stumbling back and almost falling into the chair behind her. "David!"

"Who else were you kissing?"

She lowered her face for another kiss, this one deeper and longer, and when she came up for air, she whispered, “You scared me.”

“Didn’t mean to.”

“Were you…you know, outside your body watching me when I disconnected your ventilator?”

He nodded.

“And you weren’t worried?”

“I knew you wouldn’t let anything happen to me.”

She wished he had said something, because she hadn’t been half as sure as he sounded. “Between you and your grandfather…”

“He’s a smart man, and I’m learning more from him every day.” David cupped her face and drew her closer. “Kiss me again so I know I’m really alive and that you’re mine.”

Aziza kissed him, becoming more alive beneath his lips when he claimed hers. She wondered what it would be like to make love to him after they both shifted.

She felt him smile against her lips once she completed the thought and pulled back to ask, “What’s so amusing?”

“You won’t have to wait long to find out what it would be like.”

“What—” She snapped her mouth shut, almost afraid to ask.

He took her hand and held it. “Your father told you what you needed to know about your soul mate. He didn’t tell you what you needed to know about yourself.”

“You mean—”

“Once we consummate our relationship in the real world, your first shift will occur.”

She gaped, too stunned to speak.

He laced his fingers through hers, held her wide-eyed gaze. “Don’t ever be frightened of me, Aziza. Don’t be frightened of what you are.”

“No. Never.”

“Tell me you want this.”

“I want this. I want *you*.”

"Good." He nodded. "Rest assured, if Philomena ever gets out of prison—and knowing my Dad and Gramps, that's a remote possibility, but if she does—we'll both have something waiting for her. She'll never hurt you again."

Aziza liked the sound of that.

NINE INCHES OF SNOW

AND THE EBONY PRINCESS

THE END

WWW.GRACIECMCKEEVER.COM

SIREN ADULT FAIRY TALE
Beau and the
Lady Beast
Morgan Ashbury

Beau and the Lady Beast

Erotic Contemporary May-December Fairy Tale / BDSM

Indecent proposal, or merely business?

Isadora MacLean gave up on a personal life after a disastrous and costly early marriage. She worked hard to build her company, earning the nickname Lady Beast. No one crosses her. So she's totally unprepared for Beau Brannigan's offer: He'll return shares in her company in exchange for a weekend spent as his 'hostage.'

Dubbed The Most Beautiful Man in advertising, Beau Brannigan can have any woman he chooses, but the only one he wants seems out of reach. When shares of her company unexpectedly come into his hands, he knows he's found the key to lure Isadora to his country estate, certain that once he has her, he can win her heart.

Sexy as sin and twice as tempting, can this much younger man unlock the heart of the Lady Beast?

BEAU AND THE LADY BEAST

The Fairy Tale Collection

MORGAN ASHBURY

Chapter 1

"You want me to *what*?"

Beau Brannigan took a moment to appreciate the sight of Isadora MacLean in full temper. Living up to her reputation for having a beastly disposition, she'd surged to her feet, her breath heaving in a way that showcased her lovely silk-covered breasts.

Her scowl told him she'd noticed him ogling her chest. He flashed her a grin and answered, "Become my hostage for the next three days. It's a small enough price to pay for fifteen percent of your company. Let's see…going with the most conservative estimates, fifteen percent of twenty million dollars is three million. Divide that by seventy-two hours, and that's damn near forty-two thousand dollars an hour."

"That's absurd!"

Beau watched the shock wash through her and waited while she slowly lowered herself onto her chair. He wasn't going to point out this deal could effectively make her the most expensive courtesan of all time.

She'd certainly looked stunned when he revealed he'd purchased the stocks from one of her largest single shareholders. He understood the step she'd taken more than a decade before with her ISO had been, in her mind, a necessary evil. He also knew that ever since, she'd been buying up shares when they became available. Some had referred to the process as the *Lady Beast's Holy Grail*. The fifteen percent he'd just waved under her nose represented one hell of a big chunk of her company. Vital to her and valuable to him only because it gave him what he'd craved for the last year—the chance to get his hands on Isadora. It didn't matter, her being a dozen years older than he. He wanted her, and by damn, he was going to have her.

"Are you out of your mind? You want me to give you seventy-two hours of my time? To do what?"

"It isn't your time so much I want. It's *you.* And to do, Isadora, whatever it is I tell you to do."

Beau's plan was risky, that was certain. He understood her well enough to know she'd be suspicious of any overt attempt on his part to court her. Better to keep her off balance by way of an indecent proposal. When she was in his home, when he'd spent some time with her, would be soon enough to reveal his heart. He smiled. Sliding forward slightly on his chair, he put his elbows on her desk.

"Tomorrow at noon, my car and driver will arrive at your home. You'll be driven to my country estate, about an hour outside of town. Once inside the gates of my property, you will become a voluntary hostage, completely subservient to my every whim. Oh, and you don't need to pack a bag."

"You want me to come to your home in the country for the weekend and not pack anything? Not bring a change of clothes? That's totally ridiculous. You're not making any sense at all."

"Of course I am. *If* I require you to wear any clothes while you're my guest, I'll provide them."

He could tell by the look on her face she finally understood what he wanted.

"You…me…you…*if* I wear clothes? You want me to be *naked*?"

"In my experience, having sex is easier if the parties involved are naked."

"Sex. You and me. Are you crazy? You think I'm going to have sex with you?"

"In exchange for fifteen percent of your company? Yes, I think you will. You look a little piqued, darling. Why don't I make you some tea?"

She was, he mused, a woman who obviously liked to have her creature comforts at her fingertips. A tiny service area took up one corner of her office. Beau blessed all those years spent in front of a camera when he'd been dubbed the most beautiful man alive. The skills he'd acquired then allowed him to affect a relaxed pose. She wouldn't see his nerves. He could hear the sound of her sputtering, but not her actual words.

Using the hot water dispenser, it took only moments to make a cup of tea and set it before her. He resumed his seat, and his bravado.

"You want me to sell my body to you in exchange for those stocks. You want to turn me into a…a…whore? Are you out of your ever-loving mind?"

Her choler captivated him. Red slashes of fury decorated her cheeks and icy darts shot from her electric blue eyes. Her voice rivaled the thunder and he wondered why her assistant hadn't come running in response. She was, quite simply, the most stunning creature he had ever seen. He could admit that, and the fact that he likely needed therapy.

"Don't look at it that way. It's not my intention to make you feel like a whore."

"Then I don't understand. Is this…some sort of payback, or something? Did I do something to piss you off? Seizing the opportunity to cage the *Lady Beast* and humiliate her? Humiliate *me*?"

"Is it so hard for you to understand that I simply want you? You're a beautiful woman. This has nothing to do with payback or humiliation, and everything to do with pleasure. You're not currently in a relationship, are you?"

"No."

"Then there really is no reason why you can't give yourself to me for the weekend, is there?"

"You can't be serious. You're going to…to…*for seventy-two hours*?"

Beau chuckled. Her temper had cooled as quickly as it had fired. Now, her face had gone pale, and she seemed to be having trouble putting sentences together. Her eyes had dilated and her nipples hardened. Two signs, he hoped, of arousal and not just extreme shock. He wanted to hug her and assure her all would be well, but he needed to maintain the role of roué. "I may allow you some time to eat. To sleep. Shall we make a small contract, just between the two of us? You have a printer here, which is handy. Two copies, and we'll both sign them. From noon tomorrow until noon Monday, you will be a willing hostage to my every whim. I'll absolutely guarantee your safety, but not necessarily your comfort. In return, upon completion of your, shall we say, 'personal service', I will sign over to you the stock in MacLean Cosmetics I've so recently purchased. Or you can say no, and I keep the stock. I'm sure you're aware fifteen percent is enough of a base for a canny manipulator to engineer a hostile takeover. I can be exceedingly canny, when the situation calls for it. The choice is entirely up to you."

In all the rumors about Isadora he'd heard, there'd been no talk of a personal life. She lived, slept, and breathed her company. She'd earned the nickname *Lady Beast of Bond Street* because her office was her lair from which she guarded her empire ruthlessly. Beau believed that the tough exterior of the Lady Beast hid a warm and compassionate woman, and if he had her to himself, even if just for three days, he could set that woman free.

But he had to get his hands on her first.

Beau tramped down the arousal that began to grow when she licked her dry lips. He noted the fine quiver in her hand when she picked up her tea and sipped.

"I've never…what you're asking is that I give up all control. I've never *not* been in control. Never thought I would ever be."

"Nervous?"

"Very."

"Good. I can offer you a safe word. We could include in the contract between us that I won't hurt you. But then, once you're my hostage, I can do what I like, can't I? You'll just have to trust me. If you say yes." He sat back and let his eyes roam her body, much like he planned to let his hands roam as soon as he had her under his roof. "Can you do that? Can you trust me, put yourself into my hands? Do you accept my proposal?"

He watched the emotions play over her face and felt his heart surge in triumph when he saw her answer before she spoke it.

"Yes. I, ah, accept."

"Let's get it written up then, darling. One copy for me, and one you can place wherever you like, for safekeeping."

* * * *

Isadora hadn't expected a chauffeur-driven limousine. Settling herself into the back seat, cut off from the driver by a glass partition, she wondered if she had finally lost her mind. The moment the chauffeur closed the car door, she began to tremble. She wasn't certain if she felt terrified, furious, or excited.

The bizarre agreement had been written up, signed, and a copy locked in her desk drawer before she'd allowed herself time to reconsider. Now, of course, it was a matter of honor.

She was stunned that Beau Brannigan could really want *her*. Black hair and green eyes, with the kind of sinfully sexy good looks that had sold millions of dollars of whatever merchandise he'd been hired to model, Beau could easily have any woman at all. She recalled the first time she'd set eyes on him, in person. He had absolutely taken her breath away, and when he'd smiled at her, she'd felt the clutch of sexual attraction deep in her belly. The arousal had shamed her, even as it had intrigued, for he was nearly a dozen years younger than she. She'd done her best to ignore the sizzle, but as the months passed, and she came to know him, she wondered about the sense of connection she felt, and wondered if it was reciprocated. If it could *be* reciprocated. Then she'd remember the years between them. She'd very nearly convinced herself that her attraction and growing feelings for him were completely inappropriate.

Truthfully, her sex life had been nothing to brag about. She understood—intellectually, at least—that part of the reason for that was how badly her one and only waltz down the matrimonial aisle had burned her. It might be unfair to paint every man she'd dated with the same brush as Neil MacLean. But that was life.

Her cell phone rang, pulling her out of her memories.

"Yes?"

"Tyler here, Isadora. Just stopped by the office to see you and your assistant said you were going away for the weekend."

Disbelief laced the voice of oldest friend and lawyer, Tyler Parkinson.

"What, I can't take a weekend off?" Isadora smiled, looking out the window of the limo at the passing scenery.

"Well, you haven't for a long time, Dory."

"I'm entitled to have a life after all these years of hard work and no play. But then, I believe I already mentioned my intention to change things." She couldn't keep the laughter from her voice, and could easily picture her old friend's scowl.

"Please don't remind me. It was that sentiment that led to your completely irrational and foolhardy decision which had me tromping all over the city earlier this week."

"You're a good friend, and a good lawyer, Tyler. Thank you for doing what I asked you to do, even when you didn't agree with it."

"That little piece of business made me feel like neither. I really don't think you covered your ass very well. Have you had any response yet?"

Tyler sounded so aggrieved, she wanted to laugh. If only he knew.

"Some," she wanted to change the subject before he got too curious. "Was there something in particular you needed to see me about?"

"No, just wanted to drop off copies of the injunction I filed on your behalf yesterday."

"No problems?" she asked. The small matter of an unfaithful employee had prompted her to get Tyler working on another front.

"No. All straight forward. Theft is theft. I left the copies of the court papers with Charlene."

"Excellent. Thank you, Tyler."

"You're welcome. So, where are you going for the weekend?"

Looking around, she could see only trees and fields. "The country," she replied.

"You? In the country? What the hell are you going to do there?"

"I think I'm going to get my feet wet. I'll see you next week, Tyler."

Not giving him a chance to respond, she hung up. Then, considering, she turned off the phone before she tossed it back in her purse.

Sitting back, she let her mind travel over her meeting with Beau, and her current situation. Something he had said—or intimated—flooded her thoughts. He wanted her completely under his command. Control wasn't something she'd surrendered to any man, ever.

She wondered what he was going to do when she declined to surrender it to him.

Chapter 2

Isadora perked up when the car paused at the entrance to a gated country lane. The gate swung open slowly, and she had to suppress a nervous laugh. The car eased through, and she turned, the sight of the gates swinging closed again knotting her stomach. Trees canopied the long and winding lane. The brush was so thick on either side, she could see nothing beyond a few feet. Then the lane curved sharply to the left. Before her, a stone-and-glass building, immense, seemed to stretch to the sky.

Far from the 'country home' of a well-to-do corporate executive she'd imagined, this was more like a magical castle from the heart of a fairy tale. It lacked only a moat. Then the car stopped, and the driver opened her door. Thirteen steps led up to the massive wooden door. Ascending, she counted them and chided herself for being foolish. Beau Brannigan was a flesh-and-blood twenty-first century man, not some spellbound recluse from the pages of a fairy tale. Despite his choice of words, she would certainly be no hostage, voluntary or otherwise, but a businesswoman visiting an associate for a weekend in the country, to cement a business deal. There, that felt a lot more calming and reassuring.

It was an illusion she held onto until the door opened.

* * * *

Beau hadn't been entirely certain she would come. Until the moment when he knew the limousine had driven onto his land, he'd hoped, but hadn't been sure.

He opened the door abruptly, catching her off guard, and watched with admiration while she got herself under control.

"Isadora. I've waited a long time to have you in my home. Please, come in."

"Your home is unexpected," she said, turning her head this way and that to look around.

Beau smiled when she faced him.

"The expected would be boring, wouldn't it? Actually, this is a forty-room reconstructed castle. My grandfather, who had more money and whimsy than sense, brought it over, stone by stone, from England several decades ago."

"That must have cost a fortune and been logistically complicated."

Beau laughed out loud and then impulsively hugged her. It didn't matter that she was a bit stiff in his arms. He needed the contact right then and there.

"Grandfather didn't care. If he set his mind to something he wanted, he let nothing—certainly nothing inconsequential like cost or logic—get in his way. In this, my pet, I take after him."

"I'm not your pet, Beau."

He'd anticipated that response. "My darling, this weekend, and starting right now, you're whatever I choose to make you."

He cupped her face, caressed her lip with his thumb. His heart beat just a bit faster when he saw her eyes widen, when he understood that, just so simply, he'd aroused her. Carefully, he dipped his free hand into his pocket to take out his first surprise. In an instant, he had it secured exactly where he wanted it. Quick, unforeseen, and over before Isadora could even have guessed what he intended.

He watched her reach up, her fingers touching the jewel-encrusted leather collar now encircling her neck.

From his other pocket, he withdrew a leash. One quick flick attached it to the collar.

"See? You wear my collar and my leash. So you must be my pet. Ah, ah," he added when mutiny clouded her face, "you did agree. *My every whim.* Considering the liberties I'm about to take with your lovely body, a collar and leash are small things."

"Bastard."

"Remember our deal. Behave…and submit." He enjoyed watching her struggle to get her temper under control.

Finally, she lowered her hand.

"That's better."

"It's only for seventy-two hours, after all." Her words emerged from between clenched teeth.

"Ah, but what fun we can have in seventy-two hours." He took a moment to look at her body, making his stare lascivious. "I've a pot of tea waiting in the front parlor. Just to show you how magnanimous I can be, pet, I'll let you drink from a cup instead of lapping from a saucer."

The room he indicated was just to the left of the entrance hall, across from the stairs. Taking the first few steps, he noticed Isadora standing her ground. The color in her cheeks was high, and he bit back a smile. That saucer comment had been spontaneous and obviously a direct hit. He judged the distance. One more step, and the leash went taut.

"Did I misjudge your integrity, Isadora?" Unable to resist, he punctuated his question with a small tug on the leash.

Her hands clenched and unclenched, and he could almost hear her mentally counting to ten.

"No one questions my integrity."

He could have relented, let the leash go slack, but he wanted her to submit. For a long moment, she held his gaze, and defiance filled her eyes. Then, without the tiniest sign of giving way, she walked toward him.

"This can be a pleasant interlude, or a nasty one. It's entirely up to you," he said, careful to make his tone amiable, his voice soft.

"You said this had nothing to do with humiliation." The edge in her voice was more than temper. If he hadn't made such a point of paying attention to her during their many encounters over the last year, he would have missed the hurt.

"It's not my intention to humiliate you, pet. I'm just trying to demonstrate the parameters of what's expected of you. Don't think of it as humiliation, and it won't be. Think of it as…training."

Temper fully eclipsed the hurt in her eyes, and he smiled, satisfied. He'd much rather have her mad than pained. "Come, our tea will get cold."

He saw her seated on the love seat, casually draping the leash over the arm of it. Then he served her tea and set a plate of cookies on the low table before her.

"It's Earl Grey," he said, sitting across from her.

"My favorite."

"Yes, I saw that in your office yesterday. I hope you didn't have any trouble getting away?"

"I had no plans to change."

He wanted to know how that could be, but he didn't ask. Instead, he enjoyed his tea and watching her. Interesting that she looked everywhere but at him. When she did finally meet his gaze, he grinned.

"I don't know what I'm supposed to do." Genuine confusion laced the words.

"And in any given situation, you always know what to do."

"Yes."

"Because you're always the boss."

"Yes."

He wondered if she'd heard that grudging tone in her voice. He was touched by the sadness she seemed to always carry with her. Usually, she kept it more deeply buried. He'd hoped this weekend might bring it, and much more, to the fore.

"Always being the boss carries with it a burden of responsibility. I know you meet that responsibility head-on. But everyone needs a break, pet. This weekend is yours. You don't have to be responsible. You don't have to worry. Just be co-operative, that's all I require. Are you finished with your tea?"

"Yes, thank you."

"I'll show you to your room, shall I?"

He used his hand at the base of her spine to guide her so that she walked beside him, rather than employing the leash. He escorted her up the stairs and then turned right, stopping at the first door on the right.

"Here's your room. Mine is just next door. You can rest and have a nice long bath, if you like, and yes, before you ask, you'll have complete privacy behind this door. Since you're bound to obey my every command, I don't need to stoop to voyeurism to see you naked. Dinner will be at six, sharp. I'll come and escort you." He opened the door, then unsnapped the leash. "Oh, and darling? Leave the collar on. I don't want to have to punish you so soon into our time together. Your garment for the evening is hanging on the armoire."

He had to give her a small nudge to get her to move into the room. Then he pulled the door closed and locked it.

* * * *

Isadora froze, the sound of the second "click" echoing off the walls. A lick of fear, instinctive and female, shivered down her spine when she realized he'd locked the door. She waited a moment, unsure, and then tested the handle. The test turned into a furious, vigorous assault.

The door remained stubbornly closed.

Her hand went up to the collar. It felt as if it had been made for her, sitting comfortably around her neck. She reached back to unfasten it. Panic fueled her fingers searching for the clasp.

There was none.

Her eyes scanned the room. Bars on the window and a locked door. Good thing she understood she wasn't *really* a prisoner.

A single garment hung on the outside of an antique armoire. The ivory silk robe, long and beautiful, begged for her touch. It boasted no buttons, zippers or Velcro, just a silk sash. A folded piece of paper stuck out of one of the pockets. She pulled it out, opened it, and read.

The deep V neck of this gown should show your collar off to perfection. As it is made of the finest silk, I'm looking forward to seeing how this robe caresses your breasts, ass, and thighs. Wear this for dinner, tonight, my darling Isadora. The robe, the collar, and nothing else.

Reaching forward, Isadora caressed the robe with fingers that weren't quite steady. She wondered how it could be that locked in, wearing a symbol of a man's control, she felt seduced.

Chapter 3

Beau had to restrain himself from taking her on the spot.

She'd put her hair up so that curls tumbled half down. The effect—the long, white column of her neck adorned by his collar, unhampered by red tresses—was very arousing. The silk caressed her sensuously. He'd known it would. Held closed only by the belt, he imagined reaching forward, giving one tug.

The game he'd chosen to play was proving to be hell.

"You're beautiful, Isadora."

"Thank you. So are you, but then, I've always thought you wore a tux very well."

He couldn't resist chuckling. "And you're feeling underdressed?"

"Maybe just a little."

"Well then, perhaps I can offer one more item." He held up the end of the leash, his thumb resting on the catch, and waited to see what she would do. He watched her eyes focus on the shiny metal, and he wondered at the emotions chasing across her face. She shuddered slightly, just once, and tilted her head, giving him free access to the small ring dangling from the leather.

"Good girl," he said softly. Unable to resist, he stroked his hand over her shoulder and down her back, finishing with a gentle caress across her bottom. His touch not only fed his arousal, it told him she wore nothing under the gown but flesh.

"That was very clever of you, demanding I not remove the collar, knowing I'd need a key to do so."

He didn't mind the bite in her words. He simply smiled at her. "You're an intelligent woman. I half expected you to have picked the lock."

"I thought about it. I very nearly did."

"What stopped you?" he asked, escorting her down the stairs.

"The realization that I *did* sign a contract. In essence, giving you my word. I'll have you know I've never reneged on a contract in my entire life. Well, except for that marriage one, but that was years ago and hardly counts."

Beau stopped at the bottom of the stairs and turned to her. "Was that all? Your honor? My promise of punishment didn't factor into your decision at all?"

Her face reddened slightly, but she looked him dead in the eye when she answered. "No."

"Liar."

He ran his fingers up and down the leash, then casually caressed her collar. "When the time comes, I'm going to enjoy taking you. I'm very much going to enjoy hearing you scream my name when you come." He leaned toward her and filled his lungs with the scent of her. "Lilacs. I see you availed yourself of the Jacuzzi. I trust everything in your room met with your approval?"

"How could they not? My favorites, every one."

His eyes drew to her nipples, beaded and poking out under the silk. "Yes, they were." Turning, he led her down the hall to the dining room.

He'd had the long table set for just the two of them, with a place setting at each end. The food had already been brought in, kept warm with silver domes and warming trays.

He saw her seated, then taking up the open and waiting wine bottle, poured her a glass. "I hope you enjoy the meal." He couldn't resist a light caress of her cheek. This kind of touch he knew he'd lavish on her constantly, and he wanted her to get used to it. Though she looked startled at the tiny familiarity, she didn't jerk back or jump. She blushed, and that delighted him.

"It smells wonderful."

He treasured her surprised smile when she lifted the cover to her plate. He'd had his housekeeper grill the fresh Pacific Salmon with a honey garlic glaze. The rice pilaf and fresh green beans also numbered among her favorites. He'd chosen a nice, crisp Chablis to accompany the main course of their meal.

"You're at my table, wearing only the robe I've allowed you and the symbol of my possession I've bestowed upon you. You've pleased me, pet."

He enjoyed the confusion that crossed her face. Time to switch gears.

"I hear you've had a brush with corporate espionage recently." He watched her mentally follow the segue and wondered what she thought about as she nibbled so delicately on her food.

"My V.P. in charge of advertising thought she could cut a better deal by taking herself—and the ad campaign she'd designed for MacLean—to a competitor."

"I hope you skinned her greedy ass."

"Well, it's a clear case of theft. My lawyer has initiated proceedings. Poor Mary Ellen doesn't really know who she's messing with. The little bitch."

Beau smiled when she stabbed a fork full of beans for emphasis. "Good for you. You can't let people get away with theft—whether it's product or ideas."

"Don't worry, I don't."

"Neither do I. Tell me about your ex-husband."

She stopped her fork halfway to her mouth. "Why?"

Shifting gears was a good strategy. "Because I want to know."

"Not much to tell. I made a mistake. I never repeat them."

He didn't mind the acid in her tone. After all, it wasn't him she was remembering with such venom. "There must have been something good about him to attract you in the first place."

"It happened a long time ago."

He simply waited, his head cocked slightly to one side.

"I was so impossibly young," she said softly after a moment. "Looking back, I find it hard to believe I ever could have been so young. I'd just started my company, with an inheritance from my grandmother. I approached each promotional opportunity with the enthusiasm only the young can manage, and at one of the functions— a concert, I think—I met Neil. I didn't know at the time that he'd been watching me for a couple of months. That I was at the top of his 'list.' I didn't know he planned on courting me, marrying me, and then cleaning me out, financially, that he'd done just that to at least two other women before me. I only saw what he let me see. He appeared cultured, smooth, and seemed to be infatuated with me, and I fell for it. I fell for him."

Beau didn't like the sadness in her voice. She'd stopped eating and seemed far away. He knew better than to offer her pity, though. There was only one way to pull her out of her funk. He needed to rile her.

"You annoy me, Isadora. How can you still blame yourself for the dishonesty of another, after all these years?"

Her eyes focused on him with a fierce scowl. "Well pardon me all the way to hell and back. The bastard betrayed me. Not just with his dick, which doesn't strike me now as being a particularly memorable one. He took my money, my self-respect, and broke my heart. At the time I loved the asshole. So excuse me for *hating* that I fell for him."

Pissed was better than vulnerable in his opinion. "And he wasn't worth even one of your tears, sweetheart. I bet he's still looking for marks, and it burns his ass to know how well you've thrived without him."

The look on her face spoke volumes. He wondered how she'd managed to cut herself off from people so completely that simple words of support floored her.

"Whenever I think of him, I feel stupid."

He rewarded her candor with a gentle smile. "And you haven't let anyone get really close to you since." He heard the gentleness in his own voice and hoped she did, too.

"No."

"Until me."

He waited patiently, the silence between them lengthening. He waited and felt his heart kick once, hard, at her whispered response.

"Until you."

Chapter 4

She'd never been more churned up and confused in her life.

The echo of the door being locked still reverberated in her head. The taste of Beau's kiss, their one and *only* kiss, still clung to her lips.

After dinner, he'd led her into the library, a wonderful room filled with books and the rich scent of leather. A fire burned in the hearth, and the gentle warmth of it filled the room. By the fireplace, a chessboard had been set up, and once she was seated, he brought her an after-dinner liqueur. That it was her favorite, peach schnapps, didn't surprise her in the least. It appeared he'd done his homework, and she truly didn't have any secrets from Beau Brannigan. Settled comfortably in the chair, her drink at hand and the game underway, Beau threw her off balance yet again.

"Isadora, open your robe. I want to look at you."

She hadn't consciously decided to grant his request, but her hands reached for the belt and untied it. Then, when he just sat there with that maddeningly sweet smile on his face, her hands had gone that one step further, folding back the fabric, baring herself to him.

"Very nice. You have beautiful breasts, pet. Yes, and your nipples stand out quite a bit when you're aroused. Good. The nipple clamps will work well. They're silver, in the shape of small rings. If you like the look of them, I'll consider making the look permanent. Two rings, one in each nipple. Perhaps with a tiny silver chain on each, running from the rings to the center of your collar. Would you like that, pet?"

She wanted to scream no, of course she wouldn't! Picturing what he described, she felt arousal stir in her belly and moisture gather between her thighs. She couldn't hide her reaction or bluff it off, either. Somehow, he'd known.

"I'm glad that turns you on. I bet there are a lot of things that will turn you on. I'm going to enjoy discovering each and every one. It's your move."

Not in their personal tango, she knew, but in the chess game. "How do you expect me to be able to concentrate when I'm naked before you, and you're looking at me like that?" When you have me so horny, she meant. She couldn't say it, but she couldn't hide it, either. He knew.

"By relying on your competitive streak."

He pushed his chair back from the table just slightly. Unplanned, her eyes moved to the very obvious erection tenting his trousers.

"If I can do it, then, pet, so can you."

She couldn't seem to remember the difference between a rook and knight. Before she was ready for it, the game, and the evening ended. Nearly midnight, he escorted her to her room. She'd felt the air caressing her breasts, her belly, and her mons as she walked with the silk robe gaping open. The shivers coursing down her back came from more than the cool breeze.

At her door, he turned her. And he kissed her. He touched only her face, cupping it between his hands, his thumbs tracing an invisible pattern over her cheeks. His touch gentle, as if she were precious. His mouth avid to sample and taste. She couldn't stop herself from responding. No, that was a lie. She hadn't even thought to refuse him. His tongue stroked hers in a strong, almost forceful rhythm, touching and tasting every part of her mouth in a single instant. All she could do was hold onto his wrists with her hands and return the kiss. How often had she wondered what it would be like to have his mouth on hers? Reality outshone imagination. She could taste the brandy he'd had while she'd sipped her schnapps. She could taste him, his flavor more intoxicating than any alcoholic drink could ever be. On and on the kiss went, and she nearly stumbled when he pulled back slightly.

"You'll be awakened at seven. We'll have breakfast at eight."

It had taken her long seconds to understand that this kiss wasn't a beginning, but an end. Before she could comment, he'd opened the door, unclasped the leash.

"If I'd wanted just a quick lay, you can bet I'd have had you flat on you back with you legs spread before now. So think about that, pet. Oh, and sleep naked tonight, Isadora, wearing only my symbol of possession. Sleep naked, and dream about all the delicious things I'm going to do to you tomorrow."

Now, standing alone in the center of the bedroom, she shook her head slowly. Sleep? How was she supposed to get to sleep when every inch of her felt painfully wired? She looked around the room and felt her face heat when she saw the bed had been turned down. An envelope rested on her pillow. Beau hadn't left her, which meant he had staff in the house.

She'd walked through the place with her assets hanging out, and he had staff in the house!

"At least he put it in an envelope," she muttered, picking up the thing and pulling out the folded single sheet within.

Your clothing is being laundered. In the armoire is your outfit for the morning. After you've been awakened, shower and dress. By then, your door will be unlocked. Join me in the dining room.

Curious, Isadora opened the armoire. The storage space held but two pieces of clothing: a pair of white slacks and a matching white tee shirt, both of summer-weight cotton. If they fit, they would be snug, and very nearly transparent. Then she realized there truly were only two items in the closet. A quick search of the room revealed what she'd suspected. No underwear of any description could be found.

She never slept naked. Just one of those things she'd never done. But Beau had asked her...no. Isadora closed her eyes, inhaled deeply. He hadn't asked her anything. He'd *ordered* her to sleep naked. Before that, he'd called her his pet, and *ordered* her to bare herself to his sight.

Thoughtful, she got to her feet and approached the wooden closet. She slowly removed the robe and hung it up, then slid into the bed. Turning off the light, she lay in the dark and wondered why being commanded by Beau had felt so right, and why obeying him had become the only thing she really wanted to do.

* * * *

"It's beautiful."

"I think so, too." He'd brought her outside for a walk on his land, and now they overlooked his favorite place, on the banks of a large pond. "This piece of property belonged to the farm my great-great-grandfather established when he came from Ireland in the eighteen hundreds."

"No longer being farmed?"

"Well, I have a few acres devoted to corn and hay. But no, for the most part, the Brannigans moved from rural environs to the city in my father's childhood. But I've always loved it here."

"It's so quiet. I've been a city dweller all my life. I grew up in an apartment, never even lived in a house until just after I started my business."

She fell silent, and Beau knew her thoughts had turned back to less pleasant memories. Stepping behind her, he wrapped his arms around her, cradling her against his chest. He couldn't help but speak from his heart. His respect for her had always been huge, and his love for her was growing. He wondered when she would recognize the feelings he had for her.

"Now you have a beautiful home in the middle of the most exclusive area in the city. You've furnished it with the best of everything from all over the world, and you did it all through your own brains and vision and guts. Your company is one of the most solid, most respected cosmetics companies in North America. This, too, is the fruit of your hard work, planning, and determination. That's a hell of a lot to be proud of, love. The rest that came before? Maybe you had to go through that to get where you are. To be *who* you are now. I happen to have very fond feelings for who you are now."

Beau closed his eyes in pleasure when she folded her arms over his.

"Thank you. That's...that's the nicest thing anyone has ever said to me."

"You're welcome." He resisted the urge to cup her breasts, to slip his hands under her shirt and pinch her pretty pink nipples into erection. It was absolute hell, being this close and not having, but he wanted her for more than a quick tumble. He could have her body now. He knew he could turn her in his arms, pull the clothes from her, lay her down, and plunge. But all he would have would be her body, and he'd decided, even before he'd brought her to his home, he wanted much more than sex. The time he'd spent with her so far only reinforced his determination.

Reluctantly, he released her and stepped away. "Come, pet. We've not finished our walk." He tugged on the leash and smiled when she didn't bitch or tug back. She blinked once, as if just now remembering the collar and leash. She tilted her head and looked at him, her expression serious.

"As you wish."

"Now you're getting it," he couldn't resist saying.

Chapter 5

"You want to play another game?" They were back in the library, but the chessboard wasn't set up.

"I do. Please, pick a seat."

Looking at the Scrabble board, Isadora shook her head. She could remember playing it as a child. The thought came out of nowhere that some things endured.

She'd brought her after-lunch tea with her and sipped it while Beau set the game up. He handed her a large pile of tiles.

"I thought I was supposed to pick them blindly, a few at a time," she commented idly, turning the letters over and arranging them.

"My board, my rules, and I get to go first."

"You like being in control."

"I do, but I know when to let go, pet. Never fear. Ah, here's an excellent first word."

Isadora knew her eyes widened when he laid four letters on the board. F-U-C-K, never a word she'd used for points before.

"I thought profanity against the rules."

"Like I said, my board, my rules."

Isadora found herself returning his smile, though she was sure hers wasn't as heart-melting as his. Examining her letters, she picked a single one, an "S," and put it at the end of his word.

"Ooh, you went for simplicity, I see. Let me just tell you what I think of that."

She watched avidly while he picked up four tiles and used her already placed "S" for another letter. She laughed. He'd spelled the word 'pussy'.

"I think you have a one-track mind. At least, when it comes to words. Aren't you going to keep score?"

"Who says I'm not?"

Shaking her head, she picked up two letters and placed them after the "P", adding the innocuous word 'pan' to the mix.

Quick with his next contribution, he placed an "S" at the beginning and a "K" at the end of her word.

"Spank. Is that a threat?"

"I don't make threats, only promises."

"Beau Brannigan, you're a very confusing man," she said, studying the board and her letters.

"I don't know what you're talking about. I'm an open book."

She shot a look of disbelief. Deciding two could play the same game, she used his "K" for the last letter of her word.

"Cock," he said, smiling. "That's more like it."

Too engrossed with enjoying his playful expression, she didn't immediately notice the word he formed next. He had gone back to the original two words and added four more letters.

"Fuckslave. Is that even a word?" she asked, and could have cursed when the slight tremor entered her voice.

"You'll be in a better position to answer that question, personally, after dinner. Your turn."

His remark had been without that bantering tone she'd come to enjoy. The expression in his eyes told her he was quite serious.

Over the last twenty-four hours, he'd pulled more out of her than anyone before. Enough that she spoke without thinking. "You keep me off-balance. I came here prepared for what I believed would to happen. I thought we'd have a few laughs, maybe…and a lot of sex."

"And I invited you here to share intimacy. Tell me, Isadora, have you ever been so intimate with another man?"

Isadora couldn't lie. "No." She couldn't pretend not to understand what he'd been doing to her, systematically, since she arrived. Looking down at her letters, she scooped up five and lined them down under the "A" in his last word.

"I know you're afraid. You don't have to spell it out for me."

She laughed, loud and sudden in the silence of the library. She felt an extra bond form between them when he smiled and winked at her. She watched him place one more word on the board, beginning with an "S" that fit onto a word already there.

"I win."

She read the new words: fuckslaves submit. Becoming aware anew of the collar around her neck and the leash attached to it, she understood in that moment he spoke nothing but the truth.

* * * *

She hadn't heard the lock turn or the door open. That was her first thought when she awoke and saw the box.

Plain white and decorated with a red ribbon, it waited at the foot of the bed and hadn't been there when she'd drifted off for an afternoon nap.

After their word game, Beau announced he would return her to her room so she could have that nap.

"I never nap in the middle of the day."

"You will today, because I order it. I want you fresh for tonight."

That had certainly been imperious of him, and she let him know it by the frosty look she sent him. She'd felt quite proud of that tiny rebellion, all things considered.

And hadn't she just ruined it all by being sound asleep when he'd made his delivery?

Tossing the blankets aside, she got to her feet and stretched. The second time she'd crawled into bed naked, she'd done so this time, automatically. She felt a bit more at ease with the concept, but not with standing awake, totally nude. She opened the armoire, unsurprised to find the outfit she'd worn that morning gone, but very grateful the silk robe still hung in place.

Feeling more secure with the robe on and belted around her, she approached the box. There was, of course, a brief hand-written note attached:

Your attire for the evening. I'll collect you at seven.

It took her a few moments after opening the box to understand what she was looking at.

"Oh, you have got to be kidding!" She pulled each item out one at a time, examined it carefully, set it aside. She removed six items in total from the box. When she had them on the bed, she arranged them, as they would be worn, and she picked up the item that had been at the very bottom of the container.

If she put *those* on, she'd be…what? Giving in to Beau Bannister's prurient fantasies? Well, *duh*, she'd done that the moment she'd accepted his proposition. No, if she put on this last item, she'd be telling him he really was in control. That she submitted to him and his self-proclaimed right to dominate her.

And what had giving up that precious commodity netted her so far? Isadora licked suddenly dry lips. The answer came to her with no effort at all. She'd never felt more pampered, more cherished, or more *special* in her entire life. She'd certainly never been so intimate with a man—hell, with anyone—as she had been with Beau. Before this weekend, she'd believed herself infatuated with the man, and curious if that infatuation could become something more. Now she knew she was falling in love with him, and here she stood, on the very precipice of crossing into totally unknown territory.

Could she continue being submissive? So far, it had been simple and, she acknowledged, superficial. Tonight, when he opened her door, if she wore everything he'd provided for her, it would go far beyond the superficial.

Tonight, if she wore this outfit, the real submission would begin. Her hand went to her stomach. It felt like she'd swallowed an entire hive of bees. She had no idea what plans Beau had in store for her. She felt a little bit afraid and a whole lot nervous.

The only question was, did she trust him—and herself—enough to do obey him?

* * * *

He unlocked the door and knocked.

She'd been his "guest" for just thirty hours. It seemed longer, somehow. Forever—that's how long he'd been waiting for her. Waiting for her to come into his life and into his bed.

Tonight, he was taking them just one step deeper into intimacy, and closer to his ultimate goal. He hoped. It all depended on what he saw when she opened the door.

The door swung inward, and his breath caught.

"My God, woman, you're hot."

"Thank you."

Touched that her cheeks turned pink, Beau couldn't resist reaching out to stroke them lightly. Neither could he resist continuing the caress down her body. The bra he'd chosen for her, French cut and siren red, displayed the top of her breasts and nipples. With his fingers brushing her flesh, nipples already pebbled poked out even more. His gaze swept down, noting with approval she wore the thong panty over the garter belt. She'd understood he intended to remove the one, but not the other. At least, not right away. The stockings and shoes showcased her long, sexy legs.

He'd left looking at the best for last.

The felt-lined black restraints he'd included with the ensemble encased her wrists. Ordinary handcuffs made of metal invariably connected the wrists together. He'd chosen these ones not only to match the collar, but for their versatility. He could restrain her with her wrists together, or her arms spread wide. Also, like the collar, these could only be opened with a key. He'd included no key in the box.

"I didn't know how you wanted me to wear them. I snapped them together, figuring if you didn't want them that way, you'd change them."

"You've pleased me, pet. Are they comfortable?"

"Yes."

Beau cupped her face, his thumbs stroking either side of her mouth. "Take that last step, Isadora. You've come so far already, and you're safe. You know that. Take that one last step for me, pet, and answer me again."

He felt the slight tremble and smiled when she lowered her eyes.

"Yes, they're comfortable. Master."

"Good girl." He kissed her, his tongue thirsty to drink from her, his lips firm and demanding. The taste of her, honey and ambrosia, shot straight to his groin. He felt her surrender in the tilting of her neck, in the widening of her lips. He pulled her tight against him so she could feel the strength of his erection. He used one hand, pressing on her ass, and was rewarded with the feel of her pussy grinding against his cock. He loved her, and at this moment he knew his goal within reach. Wanting her more than he'd ever wanted a woman, stepping back was hell.

He broke the kiss, smiling in response to the dazed and passionate haze in her eyes. He stepped back and handed her the clasp-end of the leash. She didn't hesitate, but attached it to her collar in one move.

"My grandfather wanted this castle to be identical to an actual medieval castle. He included a few features the rest of the family thought over the top. I've been a negligent host in not giving you the complete tour. So tonight, I make amends. First, we'll have a small snack in the dining room. Then, I believe we'll take our party to the dungeon."

Chapter 6

The dungeon was real.

One wall held what appeared to be medieval weapons. Daggers and swords, a mace, a large club, and a shield decorated the old stone. At the base of the weapon display stood a table, with a wheel at one end.

Isadora tilted her head and realized, with some shock, the table was a rack. A small cage, mid-room, hung suspended above the floor by a heavy chain.

She couldn't suppress the shaking that had begun when she stepped into this room.

"Now you understand why I only fed you a light snack. Are you afraid, my pet?"

And he had fed her, Isadora acknowledged. She'd sat on a low stool beside him in the dining room. He'd unhooked her handcuffs, fastening them behind her back. He fed her, one small mouthful at a time, from his own plate. He allowed her a few small sips from his wine glass. He even dabbed her lips delicately with a napkin, and then he brought her here.

Was she afraid? Isadora examined the emotions swirling within her.

"No, Master. I'm…nervous. And excited."

"None of these tools have been used. They're all replicas, for decoration only. But over here," he put his hands on her shoulders and turned her to face the other direction, "is where we're going to play."

Chains hung from the ceiling and wall. A black leather medical exam-type table, complete with stirrups, waited innocuously in the corner. A shelf held various items, some of which she couldn't identify. Those she recognized included a riding crop, a flail, a paddle, and a strap.

"None of these have been used before, either, but we won't be able to say that after tonight, will we, pet?"

"N...no, Master."

Her belly jittered when he disconnected her handcuffs from each other and massaged her arms.

"Sore?"

She didn't think she could speak, so she just shook her head. Her arms weren't sore, even though they'd been manacled behind her back for nearly a half hour.

"Hold your hands out in front of you so I can attach these chains."

A part of her wondered why the hell she obeyed his every command, calling him "master"—that tiny part of her that was a stubborn, foot-stomping shrew. And yet the rest of her, fascinated, wondered *what would come next?*

When he'd attached both chains, one to each cuff, he stepped behind her. She heard the rattle of metal, and then her arms, lifted by the chains, rose above her head, and away from each other.

"There."

Stretched to the maximum, her feet still touched the floor. Barely. She tested her bounds and found she couldn't lower her arms one bit.

"Rest your eyes now, pet."

The blindfold was soft, and he had it in place before she could take a breath. She felt him fastening it, the way one would fasten a watchband or a belt. It fit snugly, and she could see nothing. Blind and immobilized, she waited, totally at Beau's mercy.

She felt his body press against her back and she gasped for his hands came around her, touching her everywhere. It wasn't until she felt him cup her naked breasts she realized he'd unfastened the bra.

"I've wanted my hands on you for so long. I would see you across the room at cocktail parties and imagine you here, naked, mine to take. I would be trading snappy repartees with you at those functions and dream of the day I would have you hot and needy, writhing under me. Wanting only me."

Heat washed through her, and she could only moan in response. Her head fell back, and she heard his chuckle, low and deep, felt it roll through her belly. She was completely seduced, and if only he knew it, completely his already. Despite her nervousness, despite the situation, she knew she could trust Beau Brannigan, as she had trusted no other man. Completely and absolutely.

"You like having your breasts played with? They're luscious. Plump and ripe…and mine. How do they taste?"

He stole her breath when he moved around and suckled her. His hands stroked her ass and up and down her back. He used teeth and tongue and lips on one breast, then the other. His movements varied in speed, slow at first, then, unexpected, he'd feed ravenously. Unable to see, suspended, she felt disoriented, and emotionally off-balance. Sometimes breath-soft, other times sharp, almost painful, he doled out delicious torture.

"Please." She couldn't stop the plea, which came from her soul.

He moved his mouth up her body, then settled on her lips in a totally carnal kiss. She wanted to give everything and take even more. Her tongue met his, stroked and danced and tasted. Her arousal blossomed in the pit of her stomach, spreading out in all directions. Her hips moved convulsively, and she cried out when he moved himself out of their reach.

"Yes, you like your tits sucked. Let's see how you like this."

Isadora heard movement, something sliding, and then something soft and gentle caressed her. Whatever it was floated softly back and forth across her breasts, making her nipples pucker even more.

"The strands of this flail are velvet. Gentle, but they aren't always."

She heard him step back, and a whistle in the air. She nearly shrieked when the lashes of the flail streaked across her breasts. It hurt, but only a little. She clenched the lips of her pussy when it struck her again, and then a third time. She couldn't believe how the light pain increased her arousal. A fine electric current seemed to run from the strands of the flail through her entire body. She couldn't hold back the moan of pleasure.

Beau laughed softly, cupped her breasts, and placed gentle kisses on each. "A bit pink, but no real marks," he whispered, just before he suckled her some more. "And you liked it. I can tell. Let's see if you like this, too."

He stepped away, and she heard a tiny bell-like clang. Then, she sensed him step close, felt his cool breath on her still-damp nipple. The bud puckered even tighter.

The metal felt cold against her hot flesh. Two pieces, on either side of her nipple. She whimpered when the metal tightened, pinched, and knew these were the nipple clamps he'd spoken of.

"Can you take a bit more?"

"Mm…yes, Master." What previously secret nerve ran from the end of her nipples to her pussy? She was so hot, so wet. Moving her hips, she gave herself over to the sweet, stinging arousal that this man stirred in her.

"There, that's tight enough for the first time. Now, we'll do the other one."

Tiny, desperate mewing sounds echoed off the stone walls of the small room. *Was that needy, begging sound coming from her*? She didn't care. She just cared about, needed more.

The sound and feel of fabric tearing preceded the wonderful sensation of his hand brushing against her slit.

"I bought them, I can ruin them. Oh, baby, you are so wet for me."

"Please." She didn't care if she begged. She wanted more, and she wanted it now. Her hips moved, helping her pussy follow his hand.

And the stinging smack of something hard and flat on her ass made her jerk in shock.

"How many, pet? How many times should I spank your ass with this paddle?"

He struck her again, and the smarting pain, accompanied by the brush of his fingers against her mound, brought more arousal than she'd ever known, certainly more than she believed she could bear.

"Don't come," he ordered, his voice hard.

Don't come? She wanted to come so badly. Only a few minutes, and already, she wanted to come.

Her thoughts scattered, then focused. That's what sex had always been for her—get hot, get off. Wham, bam, no fuss, no muss. And no importance, really.

As if he read her mind, his next words cut to the very heart of her. "That's right. You want to come, but I'm not going to let you. It's only Saturday night. We have until noon Monday. I'm not going to be fast and clean and over. I'm going to be long and messy and enduring. I'm going to *matter*."

Oh, God. You already matter, more than I ever thought anyone could. But she couldn't tell him that, not when every nerve ending in her body was crying for orgasm.

"Now…how many more times shall I spank you, pet? Ten more?"

She cried out when yet another blow stung her ass. She could feel the flesh of her bottom getting hot and tight. She never would have imagined being spanked could turn her on like this.

"Yes, yes. *Please*!"

His tongue swirled in her ear, one hand stroking the lips of her pussy, back and forth, and the paddle fell in hard, fast slaps. Never the same place twice, unpredictable, the blows covered every inch of her ass. The pressure on her nipples added to the fire burning deeply within her. The sounds coming from her throat as she felt her wetness on his hand turned almost feral. She hadn't counted, but knew the spanking finished when she heard the paddle drop to the floor.

"Kiss me, sweetheart."

She needed to kiss him more than she needed to take her next breath. He hadn't just stimulated her body, he'd stimulated her heart. Opening her mouth, she devoured him. Such heat, such hunger ran through her it was a wonder she didn't melt. Barely aware her hands had been freed, she wound her arms around him. He was everything she'd ever wanted, everything she'd ever needed, and she had to have more. She'd die if she didn't get more.

She closed her eyes for a moment in the harsh light when he took off the blindfold. He kissed her lightly, then stepped back. He had the clamps off her nipples in mere seconds. The sudden cessation of stimulation made her feel almost drunk, certainly bereft, and oddly uncertain.

She hadn't even seen the lush velvet robe he bundled her into. When he gathered her into a hug, she clung hard and fast.

"Come on, sweetheart. Let's go upstairs."

Yes! Upstairs, where the beds were. Horny enough to take him now, she'd prefer a bed. She wanted Beau more than she'd wanted any man in a long, long time—probably ever.

She blinked in bewildered confusion when he opened her door, unsnapped the leash, and stepped back.

"I don't understand."

He bent down and kissed her, his lips and tongue both gentle. He tasted good, and she wanted more. Trying to take more, she tried to wind her arms around him, but he gently set her away from him.

"Inside, you'll find your clothes, the key to the collar and cuffs, and a notarized letter, dated today, confirming the terms of our agreement have been met, and that the shares in MacLean will be turned over to you Monday at noon. When you awaken in the morning, your door will be unlocked. Downstairs, there'll be a car with the keys in it. You can go home, if that's what you want to do. Or, you can come next door to my room. And we'll make love. Tomorrow. Your choice."

"I...I really don't understand. What was that downstairs? Just...playing?" She felt her temper climbing and didn't care. Damn this man all to hell and back, he really messed with her head! Not to mention what he'd just done to her body. No man set her on fire like that and then just walked away!

"No, darling. *That* was foreplay."

"It worked!"

"For me, too."

She felt some satisfaction when he grabbed her hand and pressed it against his engorged cock. She obviously wasn't the only one in need.

"But I need you to choose me when you're not high on arousal, when you're not flooded by submissive urges to please your master. I need us both to be certain that if we make love, it's because we have both chosen to."

He kissed her lightly, just once more. Then closed the door in her face.

Chapter 7

Everything was exactly as he said it would be.

Isadora stood at the window, looking down at the late-model sedan parked by the base of the steps. Her clothes had been returned to her, cleaned and pressed and ready to wear. She held in her hand the document Beau had mentioned. Those stocks were hers.

She could walk, and she knew instinctively that Beau, the next time she met him at a party or business function, would be charming, and witty as he'd always been. He wasn't a man to hold a woman's choices against her. There wasn't a petty bone in his body.

Pity she couldn't say the same about herself. She could be small-minded and mean-spirited when pissed. She had a temper second to none. Despite the fact that being called *The Lady Beast* sometimes hurt her heart, she knew she'd earned that name down to the ground and would likely continue to be more than worthy of it.

She should go back to the city and chalk the entire weekend up to temporary insanity.

The sun broke from behind the clouds, sparkling like diamonds on the stone and glass house. The green of the forest shimmered, as a soft breeze caressed the leaves.

Temporary insanity, her mind echoed, while her finger reached down to stroke the collar that lay on the dresser.

* * * *

Beau wanted coffee, but he couldn't bring himself to move away from the window to go get it. He knew she'd awakened. He'd heard her shower come on.

He wondered if leaving her high and dry last night had been the wisest course. Sure, he felt noble, if frustrated, but what if she made the wrong choice today?

He could court her. Flowers, candy, whatever it took to convince her she belonged with him—to him. Or he could make her his hostage for real. Refuse to unchain her until she vowed to spend the rest of her life with him. Until she accepted his love, and gave hers in return.

Fuck this. The waiting was driving him nuts. He'd waited long enough. The time had come to claim what belonged to him.

He spun away from the window and froze.

He hadn't heard the door open, but it had, of course, opened and closed. Isadora stood with her back against it. She wore his collar, and nothing else.

* * * *

"You didn't leave."

"I nearly did. I thought of all the reasons why I should just go. There were a lot of them." Isadora amazed herself. She didn't feel self-conscious standing naked before him. Now with the pretense of master and slave gone, there was nothing to figuratively hide behind any more. She had chosen to be here, her pride stripped as bare as her body.

"What reasons?"

She wished he'd come closer, rather than lean against the window frame. She shot a quick look around the room. The massive bed showed definite signs of a restless night. It was the only sign she had that he felt as she did, and she clung to it stoically as she answered him.

"To begin with, I'm too old to be thinking about changing my life, taking on a man for the long haul. My business eats up a lot of my time. I've gotten rather used to doing things my own way and not having to think about pleasing anyone but myself."

"Those sound like some pretty solid reasons for you to go."

"Hm. That's only some of them, but only one reason I could think of to stay." If he didn't do something soon, she was going to scream.

"And that reason would be?"

Finally, he took a step toward her. "Because I want you. It doesn't matter if it doesn't make sense, if people laugh behind my back because I'm so much older than you are. Nothing matters but being with you. You've already touched me as no one has. You *get* me as no one has. Damn it, man, put your hands on me!"

He could move fast when he wanted to. He scooped her up and brought her to the bed.

"I'm going to put my hands, my mouth, and my cock all over you, pet."

"Less talking. More action."

"Yes, ma'am."

She'd known. Somehow, she'd known that it would be like this. Even through his clothes she could feel the heat and the strength of him, and that heat and strength warmed not only her flesh, but her soul. Fast, hot, give and take. She tore at his clothes, greedy for the feel of his flesh under her hands. He seemed to be just as greedy for her if the speed with which he feasted was any indication. She had his shirt open in a heartbeat. He was beautiful, his chest broad and firm, dusted in brown hair. Then her mouth fastened on a male nipple, biting, licking, sucking. He tasted of salt and sin, musk and man. His was a taste she wanted never to do without again.

A hard hand cupped the back of her head, fingers tangling in her hair, guiding her closer. "More, baby. Give me more. Take more."

Her mouth explored his chest, then found his lips as three hands—one of hers and two of his—worked frantically to free him of his pants. She crawled on top of him before he got them all the way down his legs. And cried out when he lifted her off and set her on her back again.

"Beau!"

"In a minute, baby. I want to feel you. Let me."

She knew she drenched his fingers when they so easily slipped into her. She was so hot, so ready, that his hand was nowhere near enough. She wanted his cock, and she wanted it now. She felt him reaching into the bedside table drawer even as he fastened his mouth on her right nipple, nipping it sharply, then sucking the swollen bud into his mouth.

She loved the feel of his mouth at her breast, but it wasn't what she needed most right now. Pulling away, she said, "Give me the damn thing." Ripping the condom packet from his fingers, she had it open and on him in a heartbeat. Then, using all her strength, she pushed his back to the mattress and mounted him.

His cock, long and thick, slid inside her and she groaned. This is what she'd been missing all her life. He was what she'd been missing, and to have him now, a part of her, filled her soul with joy. Her pussy, hungry for him, took every last inch, squeezing tight, then releasing, and doing it all over again. He felt hard and slick and *wonderful*. He completed her.

Beau sucked in a sharp breath, his fingers digging into her hips. "That's it. Fuck me, baby."

"You feel so good inside me. Mm, yes, I need more."

"More?" he asked.

He was incredibly strong to be able to wrap his arms around her, lift them both, and change positions without taking his penis out of her.

"More, then."

He spread her legs wide, and she felt the muscles in them straining. He shifted his position and…oh lord, he pushed so much deeper now, moving harder and faster so that he hit her cervix. It hurt, but the pain just rolled itself into the arousal, taking her higher and higher. She could feel the flesh of his shoulders and back straining, and ran her hands over the hot silk-covered muscles, her fingers drinking of the feel of him. A fine sheen of sweat glistened his skin. Leaning up, she tasted his salt, the flavor of his sweat going straight to her sex. The scent of him, all man, swelled her senses until she thought she might explode.

"Yes, yes, keep taking me, pet. More."

His voice, no longer smooth, no longer velvet, conveyed his tension. The animal in him emerged, and Isadora loved it. She tilted her pelvis, wrapped her arms around him, and added fuel to his fire.

"Fuck me harder, master! Fuck me harder." Her orgasm gathered as he did exactly that. The sound of labored breathing, of his balls slapping against her flesh echoed in the room. Primal sounds, they tore away the pretense of civilization.

"Now, sweetheart. Come on my cock now. Come with me now"

"Beau!" She screamed his name, her orgasm exploding through her. Wave after wave of pure rapture convulsed her pussy and rippled from her belly to her fingertips. She wrapped herself around him and held him, just held him through the convulsions of his own orgasm, absorbing the energy, the emotion and the intimacy. On and on it went until, finally, drained and replete, she fell back on the bed. Beau collapsed on top of her, and she wanted him to never leave her.

* * * *

"I knew it," he panted. "I knew it would be beyond good with you. Shit, lady, I think you wrecked me."

Her laughter was music to his ears. He managed to roll to his side, bringing her with him, tucking her close.

"I love you, Isadora. I love you."

"I think I figured that out when I kept finding my favorite things all over the place, but mostly when you went to so much trouble to show me I didn't have to worry that a relationship with you would hurt me."

"I knew you were smart enough to figure that out." He held her closer, nuzzling her neck. "I like the way you taste, right here."

"I like the way you taste, too. Everywhere."

"You haven't tasted me everywhere yet," he teased, and laughed in delight when she blushed.

"I will."

"Good. I've been gone over you since the first moment I laid eyes on you, more than a year ago. I kept trying to get you to see me as a man, one who wanted you, but you wouldn't."

"Oh, I saw you all right. You turned me on, more than I'd ever been turned on in my life, but I thought myself foolish. An older woman in mid-life crisis lusting after a young stud."

Beau couldn't help it. He laughed and hugged her tighter so she'd know he wasn't really laughing at her.

"Sweetheart, you're only forty-two, not sixty-two. You're too young for a mid-life crisis." More seriously, he stroked her face. "I'm going to be forever grateful to Cyrus Carmichael for deciding to sell his stock in your company. It was perfect timing, and the perfect lure. I knew that if I could just get you alone …what?" Her face colored in a light blush, and her eyes skittered away from his. Intrigued, he scooped her up and laid her on top of him.

"About that stock. It wasn't Cyrus' idea to sell it to you. It wasn't even his stock. It was mine."

"Yours? I don't understand. I got a call…"

"From Max Kessler, who said he'd been speaking to Cyrus, who wanted to sell his fifteen percent in MacLean. My lawyer arranged it all, at my request. Gave me grief over it too. He called me irrational and complained I didn't cover my ass."

"I like your ass uncovered. But why, sweetheart? Fifteen percent is a pretty hefty chunk. Why did you want me to buy it?"

"Because I wanted a *life*. I wanted something more than just my business. I had it all planned out. You'd buy the stock, then take an interest in the company, come to meetings, and get involved, and then I'd find a way to get you to make a move on me."

Beau felt his smile spread. "Yeah?"

"Yeah."

He watched her fingers play with his chest hair. He could feel his erection growing, and knew they wouldn't be talking for much longer. "When I came to your office, you seemed so shocked."

"I *was* shocked. You moved a lot faster than I dreamed you would. What you suggested was way over the top. I thought."

"The reality of it turned you on, though." He couldn't get enough of the feel of her under his hands. He stroked her, back to thighs, lingering on her ass.

"Yeah. Enough to suggest that we take this party to the dungeon later."

"Later. You know I want you to be my sub only when it comes to this, don't you?"

"I figured that one out, too."

"That's why I gave you that document. Those shares are yours, that company is yours. I respect that. I honor that." He enfolded her within his arms, hugging her lightly.

She kissed him lightly, then said, "But I really want you to be a part of it. That's why I tore up that document you gave me."

He knew he looked stunned. He had been certain nothing meant more to her than her company. His hope had been to come to mean as much to her, in time. "Is that your way of telling me that you love me?"

She looked up at him quickly and he cursed himself for sounding so insecure. But then she smiled, the most beautiful smile he'd ever seen.

"No, that's my way of saying I'd like us to work together. Maybe even, you know, merge. But I do love you, Beau Brannigan, and that's a miracle I never thought to have."

"So maybe, since you love me and all, you wouldn't mind merging more than our companies."

"Maybe."

He flipped her onto her back. One finger stroked the collar—his collar—that she'd worn, just for him. He kissed her, taking her deep, drinking in her unique flavor.

"Brannigan MacLean International has a nice ring to it." He knew his smile was smug.

"I like MacLean Brannigan, myself."

"We'll negotiate."

BEAU AND THE LADY BEAST

THE END

WWW.MORGANASHBURY.COM

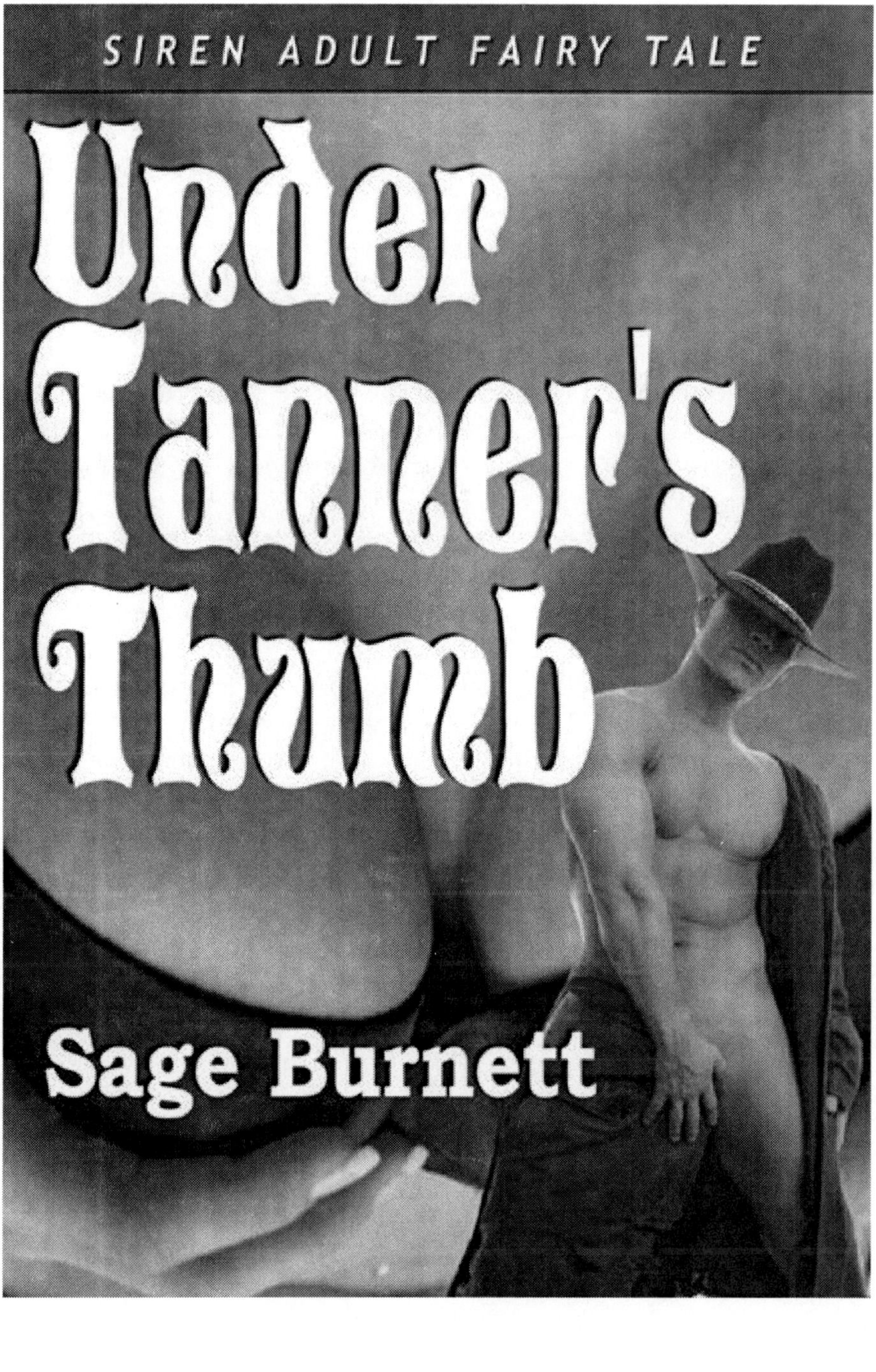
SIREN ADULT FAIRY TALE
Under Tanner's Thumb
Sage Burnett

Under Tanner's Thumb

Erotic Contemporary Fairy Tale

Tanner Clinton plays along with his nephew, Jeremy, when the little tyke casts a spell on him over the phone. Believing he turned his uncle into Tom Thumb, Jeremy tells Tanner he needs to kiss a fairy princess and nuzzle her neck before he'll be six foot tall again.

While sipping a glass of wine, Camille Barton knows she's losing it big time when a two-inch naked man suddenly appears on her porch one evening. The wine is supposed to tamp down the anger brewing inside her system that her no good boyfriend caused, not make her hallucinate. The voice that vibrates from the tiny man is rich and seductive. Camille wishes that deep irresistible voice accompanied a normal-sized man instead of one the size of Tom Thumb. When the man asks her if she can put him up for the night, Camille figures she's already a case for the psychiatric journals, so why not?

And when she wakes up in the morning with a six foot hunk of burning love...

UNDER TANNER'S THUMB

The Fairy Tale Collection

SAGE BURNETT

Chapter 1

"I bet I can turn you into Tom Thumb," Jeremy said.

Tanner Clinton chuckled before he took a swig of beer. "Sure you can." He lifted his long legs and plopped his bare feet on the coffee table. He got a real kick out of listening to his five-year-old nephew chatter on about his life.

"I really can, Uncle Tanner. I been reading *lots* of stories. Magic stories."

"Okay, cast a spell on me and we'll see what happens." He shifted the phone to his other ear.

"I'm gonna turn you into Tom Thumb. 'Cause that's a good story."

"Go for it." He drained the last swallow of beer from the bottle, sliding it on the end table next to his couch. Yawning, he waited for Jeremy to throw some hocus-pocus at him. Glancing at the wall clock across the room, he saw that it was past ten. His sister, Ann, let Jeremy stay up late on Friday nights.

When his nephew didn't rattle off any magic words at him, he wondered if the little guy has drifted off. True, it was only nine in Seattle. "Hey, buddy. You still with me?"

"Shhh...I need to be quiet."

Another minute passed. So what if his only nephew was burning up the long distance air waves between Washington and Montana?

"Done," Jeremy finally said. "I know you're real short now."

"Holy sh—" He caught himself in the of nick time. No cursing in front of his nephew. "I mean, holy cow. I'm about two inches tall now. Heck, I can't even hold onto the phone."

Jeremy responded with loud squeals of laughter.

"I'm so short I had to crawl up on the phone so I can talk to you."

More laughter bubbled over the line. "Told you, Uncle Tanner."

"How about shooting me back up to six feet again because I have lots of work to do on the ranch tomorrow."

"Can't do it, Uncle Tanner."

"Why not?"

"A fairy princess has to kiss you before you'll be tall again. And you have to, um....nuzzle her neck like Mama does to me."

"Okay, then, Send me a fairy princess."

"I'll work on it. I gotta go to bed now. Night, Uncle Tanner."

"Night, buddy."

He sure as hell could use a fairy princess in his life since he had gone so damn long without a woman. The family jewels felt slightly tarnished. They needed a good and thorough polishing. Tanner stood up, scratched his bare chest before he walked around his house switching off the lights.

Maybe he'd get lucky tonight and at least dream about making love with a beautiful fairy princess. A man had to take what he could get in times of drought. Inside his bedroom, he stripped off his jeans and briefs, kicking them aside before he climbed into bed.

He definitely needed some good loving. Stacking his hands behind his head, he stared up at the ceiling. Since his ex-fiancé Jenny, had called off their engagement a year ago, he hadn't seen much action in the female department. Jenny had been right about their relationship. They didn't have what it took for the long haul.

After turning off the night light, he rolled onto his side. It wasn't just the sex he missed, he also missed the companionship of a woman. Maybe Jeremy's magic spell would work and he'd meet his fairy princess.

Yeah, right. If only it was that easy...

* * * *

Camille Barton sat on her back porch, listening to the creak of the ancient wooden rocking chair as she sipped her wine. The cool, April night air soothed the anger still brewing inside of her. Of course, the red wine helped, too. Another one bites the dust.

Stood up again. How many times did that make for her now? Todd Wilson would never set foot inside her house again or in her bed for that matter. She was certain of that after the message she'd left on his answering machine an hour ago. No more dangling by her fingertips from a cliff waiting for him to show up for their dates. One of these years, she might learn.

Ready to take another sip of wine, she nearly leaped out of her skin at the sound of a deep, masculine voice.

"Do you think you could help me, lady?"

Her eyes quickly scanned her backyard. The porch light over her head only illuminated so far into the yard. Springing up from the rocker, she walked to the edge of the porch and searched for the source of that deep, husky voice.

"Careful. You damned near stepped on me."

"What?"

"Look down by your left foot."

Bullets of fear shot through her at the bizarre request and the fact she couldn't see the man. Since she hadn't even finished her first glass of wine yet, there was no way she was falling down drunk. Besides, she didn't do falling down drunk. The bulb near the door afforded enough light for her to see the entire porch clearly. Goose bumps popped out on her flesh, but that could be because she didn't have on a jacket. Her instincts warned her to bolt inside the house and quick, but when she heard that seductive male voice again...

"Can you please just look down?"

The masculine voice held a richness to it, reminding her of a decadent two layer dark chocolate cake. Sucking in a deep breath, she slowly lowered her eyes.

"Ohmigod!" She jumped back, and the wine glass slipped from her fingers, shattering into a dozen pieces across the porch boards.

"Jesus, you could have killed me."

Staring down at the tiny creature standing on her porch, she couldn't believe what she was seeing. Camille blinked and shook her head simultaneously. She'd skipped dinner because Todd was supposed to have taken her out to dinner. Still, there was no way that one glass of wine could make her hallucinate.

She blinked several more times more to make sure her eyes weren't playing tricks on her. Sure enough, a tiny naked man about two inches tall, hands resting on his hips, stood near her left foot, staring up at her.

"You wouldn't happen to be a fairy princess would you?" he said.

"Come again?" Good lord, was she really talking to a two-inch naked man? It had been a long day at work, not to mention the disappointing and anger filled evening. But still...

"I need to be kissed by a fairy princess," he paused. "Oh yeah, and I have to nuzzle her neck, too, so I can grow back to my regular size."

Shaking her head again, Camille hoped to toss aside the effects of the red wine, if that was possible.

"It's pretty damn cold out here."

"Well...um...that's because you're naked."

"I don't remember Tom Thumb running around naked," he grumbled.

Tom Thumb, the fairy tale? It had been years since she'd read that book. And it *had* been a fairy tale. She was firmly rooted in reality with her job as an accountant at a local bank and a no good boyfriend. Correction. Ex-boyfriend.

"Do you have any clothes that would fit me?"

That manly voice...

Geez, even her old Barbie doll's clothes would be too big for this little guy. "No, not really."

Camille kept expecting him to disappear because stress had to be responsible for causing this episode. Episode of what, she wasn't sure. She had leaped off her rocker literally. "Are you for real?"

He held up his hands and circled around. "Do I look real?"

"You know, I have to be honest here. You're about two inches tall, so no, you don't look real."

"Jeremy cast a spell on me."

For a smidgen of a thing, he had a voice that could seduce and tempt a woman. "And who might Jeremy be?"

"My five-year-old nephew."

"Your five-year-old nephew cast a spell on you? Yeah, right. And I'm really Cindy Crawford."

"You kind of look like her, but no way as tall. Your hair's about the same color, but shorter," he paused. "And you're more curvy."

Oh, now she felt positively certifiable because it sounded like the little man was coming onto her. Had she conjured him up because of Todd's thoughtlessness and insensitivity over the past several months? If that was the case, why couldn't her imagination at least get the guy up to normal size?

"I'm going to bed." Practical was her middle name. Engaged in a conversation with a runt of a guy that had a deep, intoxicating voice didn't fit into the parameters of her practicality.

"Are you going to leave me out here to freeze to death?"

Chewing on her bottom lip, she stared down at him. Dark, midnight colored hair covered his teeny, tiny head. And it looked like the same black hair covered his chest and his...*uh, oh*. Bending forward from the waist, she saw that he had all of his man equipment, only in miniature.

Camille considered calling the local mental hospital and begging them to come and cart her off.

"Touch me," he said.

So the bogus Tom Thumb was a pervert to boot. "Sorry, no can do."

"If you touch me, you'll see I'm a real man. All flesh and blood."

True, the measure of man wasn't determined by his size, but this was pushing the envelope a tad too far.

"Come on," he coaxed in a husky voice. "Then you'll know I'm for real."

Why the hell not? Her evening had already turned out to be a wash out, she might as well play along. She crouched down and slowly reached out, letting her hand hover over his head. Working up the nerve to actually touch Mr. Tom Thumb, she gently poked him in the chest with her forefinger.

A mixture of fear and confusion raced through her because he actually felt like a man of flesh and blood. Camille leaped up. "I'm losing it. I mean, big time losing it."

Spinning around, she padded across the porch.

"You just can't find it in your heart to put a guy up for the night?"

Camille stopped and glanced over her shoulder. She wanted her practical life back. A practical man, and a practical picket fence to go along with it.

The voice that boomed out of him did things to her. If a naked man had to show up suddenly on her porch, why couldn't he be a tall, muscular hottie? If he really was a man. Because if he was a normal sized man, that voice of his could get her to do things. Impractical things. Sexy things.

In the morning, she'd wake up and realize this had all been some cock-eyed, twisted, insane dream. "Sure. Why not? Follow me."

"With pleasure."

Still looking over her shoulder, she could have sworn his gaze focused in on her butt in her snug, faded jeans. Why did an unexpected wave of heat roll through her? Gawd...now she was turning into a pervert like little Mr. Bogus Tom Thumb.

From now on out, she would never skip dinner before a glass of wine and she would never date losers again either. Dating losers for the majority of her adult life had apparently brought on some kind of strange breakdown. One that hadn't been documented in any psychiatric journals as of yet.

She'd be fine in the morning. Camille opened the door, feeling Tom Thumb following her inside. *Just fine.*

As she walked through the house to her bedroom, she kept peeking over her shoulder. Tom Thumb jogged to keep up with her. It really hadn't been some kind of mini mental lapse on her porch. In the morning, he'd be gone and everything would be back to normal. She walked into her bedroom, and unbuttoned her blouse but quickly remembered she had company. The little guy leaned one shoulder against the doorframe and looked up at her.

Camille pulled her blouse together to cover her black, lace bra. She had no intention of stripping in front of him. *If there really was a him.* As far as she knew this could be a dream. With her thumb, she pointed over her shoulder. "There's the bed." Circling around, she headed for the bathroom.

* * * *

Tanner shoved away from the doorframe and strode over to the bed. A ladder sure as hell would be handy. The inside of his head felt swollen like he'd taken a hard punch to his face. He grabbed onto the drawer handles of the nightstand and climbed up to the top until he stood next to the digital clock. Feeling slightly dizzy after his climb, he rubbed his temples. Since his head wouldn't clear, he decided a good night's sleep would fix everything. With a lot of muscle, cursing, and determination, he managed to push back the comforter and slide under it.

The woman returned wearing a pair of pink flannel pajamas. Suspicion glinted in her eyes when she spotted him reclining on her bed. The hard peaks of her nipples under her pajama top made his cock swell. He might be two inches tall, but nevertheless, he felt a swift rush to his groin causing another wave of dizziness to wash through him.

Now he remembered. He had to kiss her and nuzzle her neck. Impatience grated on his nerves while waiting for her climb into bed.

She pulled back the blankets. "Just for the record. You're not real. I'm having a break down. Tomorrow I'll be back to normal."

Tanner heard the doubt laced in her voice. Hell, maybe he'd had a break down, too. All he knew was he had to kiss her and nuzzle her neck, which in spite of his physical state and groggy brain he looked forward to with a combination of lust and anticipation.

When she lay down and pulled the blankets up to her neck, Tanner frowned. He studied her neck, which had a nice line to it, not to mention that it looked soft to the touch.

Turning her head, she narrowed her eyes at him. "Don't go getting any ideas. For some reason, I don't trust you."

"Hey, I'm stand up kind of guy." So much for making a move on her. He would have to wait until she fell asleep. He hoped like hell he could stay awake that long because his brain felt fuzzier with each passing minute.

"I'm just sure you are."

She rolled onto her side, putting her back to him before she turned off the lamp on the nightstand.

Teeth clenched together, he stared up at the ceiling, forcing himself to stay awake. Once he completed his mission, he could get the hell out of here and be on his way home. *Home?* Damn, he brain was all screwed up because he couldn't remember where home was. Shit. Jaw tightening, Tanner waited for the shapely woman next to him to drift off into dreamland.

After a long time, he listened to her steady breathing, which signaled she'd fallen asleep. Tanner inched over to her pillow, careful not to wake her. He stood up, bent over her and kissed her cheek. Her skin tasted like some sweet flowery fragrance. She sighed. Fighting back the urge to kiss her again, he lowered his lips to her neck. He rubbed his cheek against her soft and satiny skin.

His eyelids suddenly felt heavy like weights were attached to them...

Chapter 2

A large, calloused hand massaged her breast. Sighing with pleasure, Camille arched her back. When a tongue raked across her nipple, tendrils of heat coasted through her. And when that same tongue drew her hardened nipple into his mouth to suckle it, languid heat slowly rippled throughout her body.

The supple lips moved away a moment. "Mmmm....you taste good."

That deep seductive voice wiggled through her brain, still foggy with sleep, and sparked a vague memory. A hand wedged between her thighs spreading them open. Blunt fingertips caressed her clit.

"You feel good, too," he whispered.

The voice that belonged to the hand seduced her senses. *Todd?* No...his voice had a nasal tone to it. The fingers trailed lower, slipping inside of her, causing her to not care who the voice belonged to. Unable to stop the moan that tumbled from her lips, she moved her hips as his finger slowly moved in and out of her pussy. Red hot sensations shot from her head to her toes.

Those yielding lips closed around her nipple again while a bare, muscled thigh slid across her knees. His fingers pumped faster into her. Camille, on the periphery of sleep, not wanting to wake up, felt her body coming alive with a burning need. When his lips found hers in the murky darkness, she wrapped her arms around a strong, broad back. She opened her lips for more of him as his tongue drove inside of her. His husky groan rumbled into her mouth, causing more erotic heat to wash through her.

His finger diving into her pushed her closer and closer until a sudden exquisite orgasm fragmented her mind from her body. She wasn't sure how much time passed before the tip of his cock nudged against her pussy.

And then he plunged inside of her. Her nails dug into the muscled flesh of his shoulders as he filled her. His body hovered over her as he thrust himself hard into her again.

"Damn, woman," be whispered harshly. "You feel better than good."

The scent of their sex and his male sweat drifted around her, mixing with that rich voice of his. She pulled his head down for another kiss, but first she rubbed her cheek against his stubbled jaw and neck. He came willingly, his tongue thrusting as hard into her mouth as he drove himself deeper into her sex.

His cock was big and bulging inside of her. When he pulled out for a moment, she heard herself whimper, but he quickly pushed himself into her again. Their movements combined into a perfect rhythm. Oh, she'd never had dream like this before, so passionate, so hot that every inch of this large man felt real. Camille tore her lips from him, needing air, needing to breathe. His groans increased in volume as he pounded his cock roughly into her pussy. Another orgasm rocketed through her leaving her boneless beneath him before one final groan rumbled from his lips.

Chapter 3

Tanner felt a shapely, warm female rump pressed against his dick. What a dream. He slipped his hand over a soft hip until his fingers tangled in crisp, curly pubic hair. A soft lock of hair tickled his nose, and he lowered his head and nipped at the nape of her neck. A sleepy, womanly sigh fell from her lips.

As his fingers trailed lowered, barely grazing her clit, the woman in his dream let go with a scream so loud and piercing he was damned near positive both of his eardrums had just been busted.

With the scream still echoing inside his head, an elbow jabbed him hard in the ribs. "Shit."

The woman kicked and clawed at the blankets before she tumbled out of bed, landing on the floor with a thud. Tanner quickly scooted to the edge and looked down at her. He'd never had a woman kick and claw her way out of bed before. "Are you okay?"

"Okay?" Her eyes widened in fear and shock. "You're asking if I'm okay?"

Her voice had only lowered a few decibels. Damn, she was a screamer. Her hazel eyes glowed with fear as she stared up at him. Her glossy, mahogany colored hair was tangled around her face, while her lips, which looked like they had a permanent pout to them, were pressed together in a tight line. "Yeah. Are you okay?" He held out a hand to her, but she shrank back from him. Frowning, Tanner let his hand drop.

She looked fine to him as his gaze took in her small, but firm breasts with rosy, hardened nipples. Sitting on her butt, her hips were slightly spread, showing her pubic hair where his fingers had lingered just a few minutes ago. He'd been hard, when she'd let go with that wild scream but he was even harder now.

"You were two inches tall last night." The tone of her voice bordered on hysteria.

His frown deepened, wondering what kind of woman he'd gotten involved with. His brain struggled to get a hold of the situation, but his head felt all scratchy like it was stuffed full of straw. "I don't think so."

"Don't you play with me." She scrambled into a kneeling position.

What a pose. Obviously unaware of her nakedness, she waved her hand in front of her, making her breasts jiggle. "Just go away."

"Why don't you come back to bed," Tanner coaxed, "and we'll talk about this?"

"In your dreams, Mister."

Leaning forward, she poked him in the chest with her forefinger. He tried to grab her hand but she snatched it away.

Covering her face with her hands, she slowly opened her fingers enough to peek at him. "Ohmigod...ohmigod....ohmigod..."

Was that some kind of ritualistic chant? Had he by chance, fallen into bed with one of those Goth women? Or whatever they were called?

"Ohmigod..." Lowering her hands, she stared at him.

She stared at him so long and hard, with fear and total confusion etched across her face, he wondered if had transformed into some kind of hideous monster during the night.

Maybe he should get the hell out of here, but something held him back. The sexy woman kneeling by the side of the bed seemed to be in some kind of mental shock. Even if he didn't know who the hell she was, he just couldn't leave her. "What's your name?"

She came out of her trance long enough to glare at him.

Bad move on his part. He always made a point of remembering a woman's name the next morning. "I'm," he paused. Shit, he must have really tied one on last night because he couldn't remember his own frigging name. *Tanner.* "I'm Tanner." Was he suffering from some kind of amnesia? "Clinton."

"No you're not. You're Tom Thumb."

"What the hell?"

"You were two inches tall last when you just turned up out of nowhere on my porch last night. And you were naked."

For that matter, he was still naked. Like a light flickering to life in her head, he watched her expression change as she slowly looked down at herself.

"Stop staring at me." The woman scrambled to her feet, scrabbling to get a blanket off the bed. When she yanked at a blanket, the motion rolled him onto his back. He slid a glance in her direction as she wrapped the pink blanket around her like a toga. He might be in a mental state himself this morning, but unfortunately for him, she'd just covered up a body that could make any man want to do things to it. Sexy, erotic things.

"I'm calling the local mental hospital." Spinning around, she marched out of the room, the blanket trailing behind her like the train of a wedding gown.

Was she planning on calling for her, himself, or the both of them?

"Damn." Why couldn't he remember how he got here last night? And why didn't he know her name and why could he barely remember his own name? And why in the blazes did she think he was Tom Thumb? That was a kid's book.

Maybe this was some Looney Tunes dream he couldn't wake up from. He looked around the room, which was all decorated in soft blues and pinks from the curtains to the comforter. Not seeing any vials of blood hanging from the walls, he figured it was safe to assume she wasn't a vampire or wanna-be vamp.

Some where along the way, she'd lost the blanket because when she walked back into the room. She had changed into a sunshine yellow robe, cinched tight around her narrow waist.

"You need to go," she said, pausing to comb her fingers through her hair. "Before I lose my freaking mind."

"Are you sure you're okay?" She now appeared slightly calmer, but the lady was out there. Where, he wasn't sure.

A crying shame. She was attractive with a sultry sounding voice that had his cock twitching again. "Did you have too much to drink last night?"

Stomping over to the bed, she planted her hands on her hips, causing her robe to open a slit. A hint of her bare breasts showed.

"For your information, Mr. Tom Thumb, I had one glass of wine. One lousy glass of wine."

Tanner held up his hands. "Okay, okay, I get the picture." No, he really didn't get the picture but he had to admit she didn't look hung over. Her eyes were sleepy, but not bloodshot.

Tossing the blankets back, he stood up.

She gasped.

He flicked her a quick glanced before he looked down at his body. Everything looked as it should to him. Even his hard-on looked normal. His eyes scanned the room in search of his clothes. When he didn't spot them in a heap anywhere, he turned to face her. "Where are my clothes?"

"I told you, you were naked."

Tanner shook his head. "There is no way I turned up on your porch buck naked last night."

"I should have got my digital camera out, but I was too much in shock."

"I don't know what the hell is going on here. I'm more than willing to get out of your house, but I need my clothes first."

Irritation flashing in her eyes, she said, "You do not have any clothes."

He plopped his ass back down on the bed, and plowed his hands through his hair. "Talk about a crazy dream."

"Tell me."

"Okay. I came naked, but I sure as hell can't leave naked. Do you have some clothes I could borrow?"

She spread her hands in front of her. "Do my clothes look like they would fit you?"

She was maybe five- foot six, not slender, just padded in all the right places. No way in hell would her clothes fit him. "How about I borrow a towel or something?"

"Hmmph." She spun around and disappeared.

Walking back into the room, she tossed a large folded pink towel at him.

"You wouldn't happen to have another color, would you?" Damn, he at least needed a manly color to make a dash for his truck and get the hell out of here. Since the curtains were closed, he didn't know if he was in town or the country.

"Oh, for God's sakes." She snatched the towel from him, and stormed out of the room.

A minute or so later, she returned with a navy blue towel. Navel blue he could handle. He caught it when she tossed it at him again. Standing, he wrapped it around his waist, making sure it was knotted tight. "Is there a white Ford truck parked out front?"

"Not that I noticed."

"Wait one cotton picking minute." If he didn't have any clothes, where were his wallet and keys? He advanced toward her, wondering if he'd just been fleeced. She backed up a few steps. "Where are my wallet and keys?"

Lifting her chin, she stopped. "I'm telling you for the last time, you were naked when you got here. And," she stabbed a finger in the air. "You were two inches tall. There was no way you could have toted a man's wallet and set of keys around."

Jesus, why did she keep insisting he'd been two inches tall last night?

"Supposedly your nephew cast a spell on you." She rolled her eyes. "Yeah, right."

He moved towards her again, but she stood her ground. "How do you know I have a nephew?"

"Because you told me. Jason? Jeffrey? Now I remember. Jeremy."

Not liking that she knew his one and only nephew's name, Tanner scowled at her. "Why won't you tell me your name?"

"Oh hell, call me Cindy."

"Cindy, huh?" The look in her eye dared him to challenge her name. "Here's the deal, Cindy. I need to get out of here. Can I use your phone?"

Without a word, she pointed at the nightstand next to her bed. He angled around it and reached for the phone. He hoped like hell his right hand man, Luke, picked up and fast. "Luke, it's me Tanner."

"Where the hell are you? A bunch of heifers broke through the fence and I need your help rounding them up."

"Forget about the cows. Let them wander for now. I need you to come pick me up." Pausing, he glanced over at Cindy. She stood in the exact spot he'd left her, tapping her bare foot on the carpet. By the look on her face, she either wanted to strangle him or suck his blood right out of him. "Is my truck there?"

"Course, it's here. It's parked in front of your house. What's going on?"

"Grab some clothes for me and get into town."

"Did you tie one on last night?"

"No. Just get into town."

"It would help if I knew where you are."

"Hold on." Tucking the phone under his chin, he turned back to Cindy. Judging by the expression on her face and the fire blazing in her eyes, oh, she definitely wanted to suck the blood right out of him. "What's your address?"

"Two forty-six Fulton Street."

Tanner nodded. "What color is your house?"

"Light brown."

"Ah...thanks." He recited the address to Luke. Lowering his voice to a whisper, he said, "Just get here fast."

"What kind of woman did you tangle with now?"

"Never mind. Just get here." He dropped the phone back into its cradle. Rubbing the back of his neck, he glanced over his shoulder at Cindy. She stared down at her bare feet, her nails painted with hot pink polish. He'd never noticed her toes until now. She might be wacky as hell, but she had sex appeal in spades.

Raising her eyes, she caught him watching her. Their gazes locked for one hot, sizzling moment. Bits and pieces of being in her bed started floating through his mind. Oh yeah, they'd done the nasty together. A blush crept up her cheeks, which meant she remembered, too. He circled around to face her. "My friend, Luke, is on his way to pick me up. He should be here soon."

"Good."

According to Luke, his truck was parked back at his ranch, which offered him some relief about this whole convoluted mess. He vaguely remembered talking to Jeremy last night, but what they covered in the conversation escaped him at the moment.

A strange, uncomfortable silence filled the room. The morning after a one-night stand had a tendency to be uncomfortable at times, but that depended on the woman. He caught her eye again, but she quickly looked down at her feet.

Rubbing the back of his neck for the second time, he considered apologizing to her. For what, he wasn't sure. "You wouldn't happen to have any coffee brewing, would you?" Right now, he'd kill for a hot, scalding cup of fresh coffee.

"I suppose I could make a pot."

"Thanks. I'd sure appreciate it."

Cindy leveled a long, distrustful look on him before she spun around and sashayed out of the room. After she left, he knelt down, searching under the bed on the off chance his clothes might have gotten kicked under it. A pink pair of ladies pajamas was scrunched up under the bed. One or both of them had stripped of her pajamas last night. Normally, he loved taking off a woman's clothes, but this particular time he didn't have the pleasure of reflecting back on that sexy pleasure.

Brows knitting together, he frowned, then he stood up and slowly circled around. He still didn't see his clothes. Damn, he didn't even remember what he might have been wearing. A sense of uneasiness raked at his nerves. Baffled by the entire situation, he wandered out of the bedroom in search of the kitchen, and hoped some caffeine might clear his foggy and scratchy feeling brain.

Cindy stood at the counter, her back to him. The bright yellow robe clung to her ass.

Wheeling around, she caught him staring at her. "You did the same thing last night."

He leaned a shoulder against the doorframe. "And what was that?" He'd obviously done a lot of things last night...

"You ogled my...my butt."

Crossing his arms over his chest, he said, "My apologies, but you have a noteworthy butt." When a pink flush stained her cheeks, the blood in his veins heated.

She mimicked his gesture by crossing her arms over her chest, and leaned back against the counter. "You don't believe me, do you?"

"That I appeared here in inches instead of feet or that we got down and dirty?"

The flush deepened before she circled around, and grabbed two mugs out of a cupboard. What he did remember was the feel of her lips pressed against his and the feel of his cock inside of her.

She carried a mug with steam rising from it over to him.

His fingers brushed against hers as he took the mug from her hand. She jumped back like she'd been stung by a bee. "I don't bite."

Cindy narrowed her eyes a fraction before circled around, her robe billowing around her. He caught a flash of bare thigh before she walked back to the counter and picked up a mug. Since she didn't offer him a chair, he drank his coffee from where he stood.

He'd only taken a couple of drinks sips when the doorbell rang. "Must be Luke."

Pushing away from the doorframe, he walked to the front door. When he opened it, Luke stood there with his folded clothes under an arm and his boots dangling from one hand.

Luke eyed him from under the brim of his straw cowboy hat. A devilish gleam twinkled in his green eyes.

"Good. Clothes." Tanner snatched a pair of jeans and light flannel shirt from his friend. "Where's my underwear?"

"If you think I'm going to paw through another man's drawers, you're one shy of six pack, pardner."

Luke took a step forward, but Tanner flattened his hand against his chest, and stopped him. "Wait for me in the truck."

"I was hoping to meet this woman. If you lost your clothes somewhere, and can't remember where you left your truck, she's gotta be worth seeing."

"Forget it. I'll be ready in a minute." Before he closed the door, he heard Luke muttering to himself.

He took another quick drink sip of coffee before he set it on a small table near the door. Since he couldn't see Cindy from where he stood, he dressed right there. Stuffing one foot into a boot, he swore under his breath. Luke must have tossed his boots in the bed of truck. The inside leather felt frozen. It might be spring in Montana, but the mornings were still chilly. Buttoning his shirt, he worked his jaw while he stared over at the kitchen.

He couldn't just leave without saying something to her. He walked into the kitchen and found Cindy still leaning against the counter, with a mug cradled in her hands.

"I'll be on my way now." When he looked into her eyes, he saw traces of vulnerability, which got to him, which in turn surprised the hell out of him. "Thanks for the coffee and..."

"No problem."

"Okay, then." One last lingering look at her before he wheeled around and strode out of Cindy's house.

Once he was off the porch, he jogged across the lawn to Luke's truck where he climbed inside, and slammed the door behind him.

Luke gassed it and pulled away from the curb. "You got some explaining to do. Why wouldn't you let me meet Camille?"

He jerked his head so fast to the left, it almost felt like he'd thrown it out of alignment. "Camille? Her name's Cindy."

"The name on her mailbox is Camille Barton."

"Maybe she has a roommate." He hadn't seen any signs of a roommate.

"She might be a fugitive from justice," Luke said.

"No way." She might be slightly confused, but no more than he was. Tanner couldn't get the look in her eyes out of his head as Luke cruised down the residential streets. First, she'd been terrified of him, followed by angry. She'd acted like she'd wanted him out of her hair and fast. The vulnerability he'd noticed in her eyes before he left her house nagged at him.

"So how did you end up in town with a woman you don't know, naked as the day you were born?"

After he scrubbed a hand down his face, he glanced over at his friend. "Your guess is as good as mine."

Maybe she'd wanted him out of her house, but she had given him coffee and a manly colored towel. He wondered what Camille or Cindy as she called herself was really like. He couldn't shake the image of how willing and passionate she'd been while they'd made love. All warm and soft while molded against him.

She'd made it abundantly clear that it was a one night that she wanted to forget.

He'd had some memorable one-night stands in his time. There was something about the woman he'd woken up with this morning, which made it damned hard for him to just walk away.

Images and sexy fragments floated back to him about their lovemaking. He remembered enough of last night to know it had been good, damned good.

Chapter 4

With a trembling hand trembling, Camille set her mug on the counter. Her house yawned with a big emptiness after Tom Thumb, aka Tanner Clinton, walked out. Raking her fingers through her hair, she shook her head in disbelief.

What happened just couldn't have happened. She pinched the back of her left hand. "Ouch." She really was wide awake and not snared in some wild, crazy dream. The two-inch man she'd found on her back porch last time night had morphed into a six-foot hunk of burning love sometime while they slept.

Hot Technicolor images surfaced of the things they had done. His finger giving her delicious pleasure. The feel of him filling her. And lordy, the man could kiss. The doorbell rang, jolting her from her reverie. Heart pounding, she wondered if he had returned. Not possible. There was nothing he could have forgotten, since he'd arrived with nothing. She had to admit, he'd been polite and concerned about her when she'd tumbled out of bed.

Struggling to compose herself, she walked to the door and opened it.

"You're not ready?"

Amanda, her best friend, stood across the threshold dressed in tight jeans, knee high black boots, and a red pullover sweater.

Amanda hiked her purse higher on her shoulder. "I can't believe you're not ready."

Camille blinked. "Ready for what?"

"You're not going to tell me you and Todd had all night marathon sex and you forgot about going shopping." Amanda shook her head. "No way. That's not possible."

"Todd and I broke up."

Amanda raised her arms in the air and did a little jig. Neatly jelled into place, her short, spiked blond hair jelled into place never moved. "Hallelujah." Brushing past Camille, she walked inside and kicked the door closed with her boot. "This calls for a celebration. I'll buy you lunch."

"I don't want lunch, and I don't feel like going shopping. Sorry, I forgot."

Her friend tilted her head. "Are you really that heartbroken? You've been threatening to break up with him for the past month.

Funny, but Todd had been the farthest thing from her mind since she'd woken up this morning in bed with the six-foot man. Besides, the no good s.o.b. hadn't even bothered to call. "Really, I'm fine with it."

"Then what gives?"

If she told Amanda about her adventure or episode or hallucination, she knew her friend would die of laughter. "Let's have some coffee."

Amanda followed her into the kitchen and poured her own coffee before dropping her purse on the counter. Camille took her mug and sat down at the table.

Amanda joined her. "You've got me worried? Did you pick up a bug or something?"

Fever could make a person delusional, but she didn't have a cold or the flu. Drawing in a deep breath, she worked to get her thoughts in order. "Okay, here goes. You have to promise not to laugh your butt off. And to at least consider what I'm going to tell you."

Amanda leaned forward. "You didn't off Todd, did you? Do you need me to help you stuff his body in your trunk so we can drive to the river and dump it?"

Murdering an insensitive jerk of a boyfriend was at least real. Trying to cover it up, would be real, too. Camille shook her head. "I'm sure he's alive and breathing, probably in some other woman's bed." She had no proof that he'd ever cheated on her, but the countless times he'd stood her up, made her question his faithfulness.

Amanda snorted. "I'd say that's doubtful."

Todd hadn't been that bad, but then again he hadn't been that good, either. "A naked, two-inch man, the size of Tom Thumb, turned up on my porch last night."

Camille had no idea how Amanda's perfectly plucked blonde brows could raise so high so fast.

"Did you drink an entire bottle of wine by yourself last night when Todd went missing in action?"

"I had one glass." She watched as her friend struggled not to laugh. "No laughing."

Amanda made a stab at a straight face. "Go on."

Her hands tightened around her mug. "Some time during the night he morphed into a six- foot hunk of man."

"Oh...gawd, what a dream."

"It wasn't a dream."

"Did you and the hunk partake in the pleasures of the flesh?"

Camille nodded, watching Amanda still fighting back laughter. "Just go ahead and laugh. Get it out of your system."

Impatience threading through her, she waited while Amanda had a gut busting laugh at her expense.

Amanda wiped her eyes. "Now you've gone and ruined my eye makeup."

"His friend brought him some clothes and picked him up this morning. In fact, he just left a few minutes before you got here."

"Uh...huh. Tell me more."

"I knew you wouldn't believe me."

"Come on, girl. It's a really off the wall story."

Off the wall didn't even begin to explain it.

"What's his name and what did he look like?"

"He said his name is Tanner Clinton and–

"Clinton, that name sounds familiar."

"Ex-president."

"No. Clintons have been around Missoula for years in the ranching business."

Amanda had grown up in the Missoula area, while she had only moved to town a few years ago from Billings. Because of that, she didn't know the history of the residents. "You're serious?"

"They're like third or fourth generation ranchers. There's still some hold outs these days." Amanda paused and took another drink of her coffee. "So what did he look like?"

"Shiny black short hair, deep blue eyes, all hard muscles and wide shoulders." Describing him got her all hot and bothered, which in turn, made her frown. "Do you know him?"

Amanda shook her head. "We went to different schools, but I think he's older than us, probably mid-thirties. He dated a coworker of mine a few years ago. I met him once." She tapped a long, black-polished fingernail against her lips. "As I recall, he was quite yummy."

Yummy. That one word definitely described Tanner Clinton.

Amanda jumped up and grabbed Camille's hand, dragging her to her feet. "Hurry, take a shower so we can shop."

She glared at her friend. "I can't just forget about last night or what...what happened between us." Tanner Clinton seemed like a genuinely nice guy, not to mention nice on the eyes.

Amanda tilted her head, studying Camille. "Are you sure you didn't hit a bar last night, hon?"

"No. I did not hit a bar. I spent the entire evening stewing and simmering and cursing Todd. I poured one." She held up a finger. "*One* glass of wine and went and sat on the back porch. Damn, I didn't even get a chance to finish it before Tom Thumb, I mean Tanner Clinton, showed up on my porch. Poof." She snapped her fingers. "Magic."

Amanda was thoughtful for a moment. "Is it possible you met him at the bank?"

If she had met that man at the bank, she would have remembered. Men like Tanner Clinton didn't happen along every day. Camille shook her head.

"Maybe he came by and asked to use your phone because his truck or car broke down." Amanda grinned. "I know what happened. You two looked at each other, instant attraction and well...the rest is history."

"Ha-ha. At that height, he couldn't have driven."

Amanda laid her hand on Camille's forehead. "You don't seem to have a fever."

She batted Amanda's hand away. "I don't have a fever. I'm not sick."

"Okay then, why don't we talk about it on the way to the mall? We'll see if we can figure this out. We do know you had sex with a red-blooded American male. As far as the size of Tom Thumb..."

"It really happened."

Amanda gave her a shove. "Like I said, we'll sort it out while shopping. There has to be a logical explanation for this."

Logical? Logic had disappeared as quickly as Tom Thumb had appeared. Reluctantly Camille headed for the bathroom. According to Amanda, Tanner Clinton really did exist, but that didn't explain his two-inch height last night or anything else for that matter.

Remembering the skill of his big, rough hands and the taste of his lips made her face warm with heat. Oh...he was better than good. And there was something about his dark blue eyes. They weren't just sexy, but trustworthy and honorable, too. Picking up her pace, she hurried into the bathroom, desperate to wash away the burning memories.

* * * *

Luke rolled his truck to a stop next to Tanner's truck. "Give me forty-five minutes," he said. "I need a quick shower and some food in me."

"Those damn cows are probably halfway to Wyoming by now all because you had some kind of wild night with a woman."

Wild didn't even come close to explaining it. "I'll catch up with you." He stretched himself out of the truck, then bent down. "Thanks for rescuing me."

"Are you sure you needed rescuing?"

Luke's question made him pause. "Why would you say that?"

"Because a woman who can make a man look like he just got struck by a bolt of lightning has to be special."

His brows knitting together, he shut the door. Well, yeah, he needed rescuing. What in the blazes was Luke talking about? He walked up to his house, let himself in the back door, and headed straight for his bedroom. Food and a shower would have to wait.

Striding into his room, he went straight to his tall, oak chest of drawers. "I'll be damned." His wallet, keys, and loose change were scattered across the top, just like always. He picked up his wallet and thumbed through the cash. One hundred and thirty eight dollars. He never carried more than a couple of hundred on him, so that was about right.

Circling around, he spotted his jeans and briefs piled in a heap near his bed. His temples throbbed slightly as he struggled to remember last night before he ended up at Cindy or Camille's house. He'd peeled off his clothes and crawled into bed. He always slept in the buff no matter what the season.

Tanner walked across the hall to the bathroom, digging around in the clothes hamper until he found the red plaid shirt he'd worn yesterday. He'd tossed it in the hamper right before Jeremy called. Everything inside his house was normal. Then why in the hell didn't he feel normal?

After he turned on the shower, he stripped off his clothes and stepped under the hot spray of water. *Her scent still lingered on him. Their scent.* Scowling at the bar of soap he'd just picked up, he quickly scrubbed away any reminders of her.

Ten minutes later, dressed and ready to track down renegade cattle, he picked up his cell phone off the counter in the kitchen and hit speed dial.

"Hello."

"Hey, sis, it's me. Is Jeremy around?"

"Bob took him to the hardware store with him," Ann said. "The kitchen faucet is leaking."

He wedged the phone between his ear and shoulder so he could start a pot of coffee. "Did you happen to overhear our conversation last night?"

"Yeah, I was sitting on the couch next to him. Jeremy laughed all the way to bed because he turned his great big uncle into Tom Thumb. By the way, did you kiss a fairy princess last night?"

As it turned out, he had more than kissed a fairy princess, but his sister didn't need that info. He almost said, the little tyke's hocus-pocus worked.

"Yoo hoo, Tanner, are you still there?"

"A...yeah." He turned on the coffee maker. "So Jeremy is really into casting spells?" Shit, he couldn't believe he was trying to ferret information out of his sister about her kid.

"The other day he turned me into the Wicked Witch of the West. Only because I had to rush to pick him up from kindergarten and take him to the dentist. Then we had to grocery shop. By the time we got home, I felt like the Wicked Witch of the West."

"Hmmm."

"And last week he turned Bob into Superman because his dad helped him fit the last four pieces into a jigsaw puzzle." His sister laughed. "Bob as Superman?"

Bob was a great guy, but no way did he fit the Superman profile. "Okay, then..."

"Are you okay?"

"I'm a little tired. Luke and I have to go chase down some wandering cows that broke through the fence. Say hi to my little buddy for me."

"Sure, bye."

He slid the phone on the counter and felt his jaw tighten. His nephew was into casting spells on his family, but he was just a kid and spells only happened in fairy tales. Then why did Camille, or Cindy as she called herself, know Jeremy's name? She'd kept insisting he was only two inches tall, just like Tom Thumb, when she'd seen him. And how had he ended up in her bed making love with her?

Tanner filled a glass with water and grabbed the aspirin bottle off the cupboard shelf. The slight pounding at his temples had turned into full-fledged headache.

After he wolfed down a quick breakfast, he settled his black cowboy hat on his head and left the house. Walking toward the barn, he saw that Luke had saddled his horse, Bourbon, and left him tethered to the hitching post.

When he mounted his horse, saddle leather creaking underneath him, he struggled to forget about the events of the last twelve hours, but Camille's or Cindy's face kept scrolling through his mind. The feel of her body pressed under his, the sound of her throaty moans as she'd came beneath him.

His headache still throbbing, he tightened the reins, and steered his horse to the left. He still battled to clear his head and get that woman out of his mind. Yeah, the sex had been damned good. He should be satisfied with that. Instead, he had a crazy urge to get to know her better, to find out what she was about. As it stood, he didn't even know her real name. After spending the night with a woman, he never made empty promises. Saying he would call with no intention of ever doing that, had never sat well with him.

By the time he caught up with Luke in the south pasture, his head pounded harder. And his thoughts wouldn't let go of Cindy or Camille or whatever the hell her name was.

Chapter 5

Camille pointed the remote at the television, flipping through the channels and wished she had picked up a movie to watch. Instead, she had an ex-boyfriend that hadn't even bothered to call and beg her forgiveness. Not that she planned to forgive him for his sins. And she had the memory of a fairy tale of a man that had walked out of her house this morning. Sighing, she finally settled on a cop show.

For once in her life, she'd actually been with an attractive, desirable man, rugged in the Wild West kind of way, and it had turned out to be some kind of nonsensical dream.

While shopping and over lunch, she and Amanda hadn't come up with a logical explanation. Because there wasn't a logical explanation for what happened.

She had crawled into bed with a two-inch man and had woken up with the real deal this morning. The man knew how to use his hands. His large, rough palms had been sure, confident, and provocative as they had explored her body.

For the most part, he conducted himself like a gentleman, except for those few tense moments when he'd believed she'd ripped him off or rolled him. She'd seen it in his eyes. He'd been just as confused as she was about the whole convoluted situation.

Tanner could have walked out on her this morning after his friend came to pick him up. He'd been enough of a gentleman to walk back into the kitchen and thank her. True, it had been awkward when he'd said good-by, but the entire morning had turned out to be awkward and unsettling. Not paying any attention to the television, she let herself wonder what Tanner Clinton, the man, was really like. She found it hard to believe he wasn't married unless he liked to play the field. She'd had a taste of what he was like in bed. Oh...he definitely knew how to please a woman. Picking up a magazine off the coffee table, she fanned herself.

An unexpected longing grew inside of her to know the real man. Yeah, right. Like she would ever see him again. No doubt he'd been overcome with relief when his friend had arrived.

Camille frowned when the doorbell rang several minutes later. Since she wasn't expecting any company, she wondered who it could be. Amanda had tried to sweet talk her into a party at one of her friend's, but she wasn't in the mood for socializing. If she didn't answer, maybe whoever was out there would go away. The way her luck was running lately, she didn't believe that for a second.

With the second ring, annoyance pecked at her nerves. She stood up, and hit the mute button on the remote before dropping it on the coffee table. Camille walked to the door and flipped on the porch light. When she opened the door, she immediately tried to slam it closed, but a man's hand stopped her.

The long lost boyfriend finally returned. Good old-fashioned irritation shot through her. "Go away."

"Come on, Camille," Todd pleaded.

"I left you a message last night. We have nothing to talk about."

"The last half of your message got cut off."

She figured she might have been talking into dead air, since she'd carried on for so long. "If you didn't get my drift in the first part, then that's your problem."

Todd's sandy colored hair looked freshly cut, and he was dressed for a night on the town. Not with her. Not by a long shot. He shifted on the balls of his feet and grinned at her. "Save it," she said.

"How about a late dinner?"

Crossing her arms over her chest, she glared at him. "We're finished. End of story."

"Don't you even want to know why I didn't show?"

"No, I really don't. Just leave me alone."

"Is there a problem here?"

The deep seductive voice shot projectiles of heat through her bloodstream. Camille poked her head around Todd who had wheeled around at the sound of the man's voice. Tanner walked up the porch steps wearing sinfully faded jeans, a black tee shirt, and a chocolate-brown, waist-length leather jacket. The brim of his coal-black cowboy hat was pulled low over his brow, giving him both a dangerous and sexy look. She merely stared at him while her heart sounded like a jackhammer doing its work at a construction sight.

"Who the hell are you?" Todd asked.

"Are you okay, Camille?" Tanner regarded her with a steady, even gaze.

How did he know her name? She'd thrown out Cindy this morning because he'd said she reminded him of Cindy Crawford. Caught off guard by his sudden and unexpected appearance at her house again, she found her brain refusing to cooperate.

"Camille?" he repeated.

The way he said her name had her wanting to elbow Todd out of her way.

"If you don't mind," Todd said. "Camille and I are having a private conversation."

Tanner leaned a shoulder against the porch pillar. "Is that right? I heard the lady ask you to leave."

She finally found her voice, and did elbow Todd in the ribs to get him to move out of her way. He cursed, but she ignored him and spoke to Tanner instead. "He's my ex-boyfriend, but he's having a hard time comprehending that simple fact."

Tanner rubbed his jaw. "You could call the cops or I can escort him off your property."

"Oh, please, give me a break," Todd said.

Tanner cocked his head and his eyes locked on her. "How do you want to play this?"

Turning to face Todd, she said. "Please just leave. It's over. It should have been over a long time of ago."

"Give me another chance." A hint of irritation glowed in his eyes. "I can explain about last night."

"I don't want to hear about last night. I just want you to go."

"You heard the lady," Tanner said.

Before he directed his anger at Tanner, first, Todd leveled an angry look at her. Without another word, Todd brushed past Tanner and stomped down the steps. Why wasn't she surprised that Todd hadn't even made a stab at fighting for her? Several seconds later she heard him gas the engine of his car and peel away from the curb.

Her gaze moved to Tanner again. They simply looked into each other's eyes for what seemed like forever to her.

"Do you want me to leave, too, Camille?"

"How do you know my real name?"

He pointed a thumb over his shoulder. "It's on your mailbox."

Stuffing her hands in the back pocket of her jeans, she glanced away from him for a moment. "Oh yeah." So much for her alias.

"Why did you say it was Cindy?"

"Because last night on my porch you said I reminded you of Cindy Crawford. You probably don't even remember saying that."

His eyes narrowed a fraction. "Now that you mention it, I do remember. And you do remind me of her."

He did remember. And why did that make her feel so darned good? Especially since there was a strong possibility she still floated in la-la land somewhere.

The cowboy pushed away from the pillar and angled over to her. His blue eyes darkened, filling with unreadable emotions. "I think we need to talk. That's why I came over."

"I agree. Come in." She planned to keep her distance from him because the six-foot man package was just too tempting.

Tanner followed her inside, closing the door behind.

"Sit down." She circled around the coffee table and sat down at one end of her couch.

He shrugged off his leather jacket, then plucked off his hat, dropping them on a chair near the couch. She'd been hoping he'd sit on that chair instead of parking himself only a foot from her. His aftershave wafted toward her, some kind of spicy scent. This morning, black stubble had covered his face. Now he was clean shaven. Either way he looked too good.

Dropping both hands onto his thighs, he stared straight ahead for a few seconds. "This is how everything went down for me last night." He shifted on the couch, turning his attention on her. "I talked to Jeremy, my nephew, last night on the phone about ten. According to my sister, Ann, he's really into casting spells on everybody and turning them into some fictional character. Last night he believed he turned me into Tom Thumb and I played along."

"But he really did turn you into Tom Thumb. I swear to God."

His expression still said he didn't believe her. She huffed out a big sigh. "Okay, go on. Tell me what else you remember."

"Jeremy told me I had to kiss a fairy princess and nuzzle her neck before I'd be six feet tall again. After I finished talking to him." He drummed his fingers on his thigh. "I went straight to bed and fell asleep. And the next thing I know I'm standing on your porch." He shook his head. "Unbelievable."

Camille rolled her eyes. "No kidding."

"I waited for you to fall asleep so I could kiss you and nuzzle your neck." Tanner scratched his jaw. "Then I could barely keep my eyes open."

So by kissing her and nuzzling her neck, the spell his nephew cast over him vanished. "Okay, now that we've shed light on the whole crazy thing, we can go our separate ways." From the corner of her, she caught him watching her. Camille fought to ignore her beating pulse.

"Hey, not so fast."

She tilted her head in his direction. "What do you mean not so fast? We've explained it as best as we can. What else is there to say?"

"I could say this, that I really do believe I did kiss a fairy princess last night."

The tone of his seductive voice felt like a warm summer breeze whispering across her senses. Feeling a blush creep into her cheeks, she clasped her hands together in her lap. "Hardly."

"You're even sexier when you blush. And your lips..." He reached out and outlined them with the pad of his thumb.

A delicious ring of heat formed in her belly with his touch, making her feel like she *was* under some kind of spell. "Are you trying to seduce me?" Because if he was, Camille doubted he would have to put out much effort. Minutes earlier, she'd given Todd his walking papers and now she hovered on the edge of doing something totally insane. Like making love with Tanner.

He traced his thumb over her lips again. "I don't know. Maybe I am. You're a woman that should be seduced."

She wasn't sure what he meant by that, but it sounded good.

"How did I get in your bed last night?"

His thumb continued doing luscious things to her lips. "Um...let's see." Thinking was nearly impossible with him touching her. "I haven't the foggiest. After I finished changing you were in my bed."

His voice lowered a notch. "That was thoughtful of you to offer to let me stay for the night."

Look where it had gotten her. Under some kind of unbelievable, crazy, provocative spell.

"What about your boyfriend?"

"He's history. He should have been history a long time ago."

"He doesn't think so."

Looking into his eyes, she whispered, "I guess that's his problem." At this moment, she felt mesmerized by Tanner's touch and the dark depths of his blue eyes.

He lowered his thumb and lifted up her chin. "I don't know what the hell happened last night. Looks like it might remain one of those mysteries of life that never gets solved. But," he paused. "Right now, I'm glad it happened."

A raw desire burned in his gaze. She couldn't nod because he held her chin and she couldn't speak because her throat had suddenly turned bone dry. Last night had felt like a dream when they'd made love, but now they were both wide awake. The electrically charged air surrounding them proved that.

Tanner slanted his head, brushing his lips across hers. Oh, his lips tasted just as delectable as last night. When she parted her lips, his tongue slithered inside, slow and easy in an exploring way. She let him probe to his heart's content, savoring the feel of his touch.

A moment later, his hand covered her breast. She cupped his face with her hands pulling him closer while his hand lowered, and slid under her top. His rough hand pushed up and gently squeezed her breast.

Tanner ended the kiss, nibbling at the corner of her lips. "I'd like to return the favor."

While his hand massaged her breast, she struggled to clear her sex filled brain. "Pardon me?"

"You let me sleep in your bed. Now I want to carry you to your bed." He nipped her bottom lip this time. "Lay you down and let your pretty hair spread out on your pillow."

Circling his tongue around the outline of her lips, his hand traveled to her other aching breast, where this time he fondled her nipple.

"Camille?"

Blinking a couple of times, she fought to break the spell he'd cast on her. Looking into his hooded eyes, she realized it was impossible to run from Tanner's magic charm. Eyes locked with his, she managed to nod.

He kissed her quick and hard, before he stood up and offered his hands to her. She placed her hands in his while he hoisted her to her feet.

In one quick swoop, she was in his strong arms, her breath momentarily stolen away.

Tanner carried her from the living room to her bedroom, while her house passed by her like in a blur. Expecting him to lay her on the bed, he stood her on her feet instead, next to the bed.

"First, we get naked." He peeled her black pull over top off in seconds, dropping it to the floor.

He stared at her black, lacy bra. "So sexy."

And then he unsnapped her jeans, pushing them down over her hips.

"I couldn't stop thinking about you today." Bending down, he kissed the tender skin above her bikini panty line. "No matter how hard I tried."

She'd suffered from the same problem. Tanner overload.

After he helped her step out of her jeans, he skimmed her black panties down her thighs, to the floor. She reached behind her to unhook her bra, but he slipped his hands behind her back, stopping her.

"I want the pleasure." Skimming the tip of his tongue down the nape of her neck, he unclasped her bra.

* * * *

Camille held out her arms so he could skim off her bra. His eyes feasted on her small, plump breasts. Her hard nipples pointed straight at him. Rubbing his fingers over her nipples, she moaned low and deep in her throat. A woman who he only knew in the biblical sense, but a woman he wanted to know everything about. Tanner stepped back, so he could enjoy her body.

A tiny smile played at her lips.

"I want to look at you." Although, he'd seen her naked this morning, she'd been terrified and so confused. Now, her body was flushed with sexual heat, her eyes dreamy.

He skimmed his fingers down her body, starting at the undersides of her breasts. His hard cock strained against his snug jeans. He slid one hand between her legs, rubbing his palm down her slick pussy. Camille moaned again for him. Clenching his teeth, he removed his hand and with breakneck speed peeled off his clothes and boots.

As he she reached for him, he swung her up into his arms again and laid her down on the bed.

She smiled at him, those pouty lips curving into this sexiest smile he'd ever seen. "Jesus." He came down hard on her lips, forcing them open, feeling her arms twine around his neck.

With one knee, he spread her legs, pressing his thigh against her warm, wet pussy. Tightening her arms around him, she clamped her legs around his thigh. He ended the kiss as abruptly as he started it. Listening to her little moan of displeasure, made him all even hotter. He scooted down until he was eye level with her breasts and drew one hardened peak into his mouth. He groaned at the salty taste of her between his teeth.

Tanner felt Camille's fingers tangle in his hair, pushing his head against her. When he had his fill, he moved onto the next while his hand slid back between her legs, searching out her clit.

She gasped when he pressed his fingers against her. Rolling her over, with her now on top of him, Tanner looked up at her, holding her gaze. "I want you to sit on my face, babe."

Her eyes widened, while the sexual flush deepened on her cheeks. "Please." His voice came out as a harsh whisper.

She stared at him for several moments before she scooted up his chest, while he lowered his body. When her thighs framed his head and her musky scent surrounded him, he grabbed her hips and started to lave her clit. Above him, her hips moved in perfect rhythm with the movements of his tongue. With broad strokes, he licked her clit, her opening. Above his own muffled groans, he listened to her sharp gasps of breath and throaty moans, which turned him on as much as his head buried between her legs.

Letting go of her hips, he reached up to fondle her breasts, pinching her nipples between his fingers. Way too soon, her thighs tightened around his head while her body convulsed and jerked as she came.

Camille leaned back with her eyes closed and her body limp. Gently, he pushed her back until her pussy touched the head of his cock. And then he rammed himself up high into her. She gasped, her eyes flying open.

"Ride me, Camille honey." He ground the words out through tight jaws.

"Oh....oh...."

His hands latched onto her hips, working her pussy up and down over his cock. Through half closed eyes, he watched her plump, small breasts bounce and jiggle, loving the sight of her. Not sure how much longer he could hold out, he increased his hard thrusts, wanting her to come first, so he could feel and see her pleasure.

"Camille, baby, come on. You gotta come for me."

Opening her eyes, she stared at him, her hair tangled and tossed around her face, her lips pressed tight together. Tanner knew the moment she came, by the look of pure surprise spreading across her face. With one last thrust of his cock into her, his own body shuddered in release.

She collapsed on top of him, while his arms slid around her back.

After his breathing had evened out, he whispered in her ear, "Tell me about yourself."

She raised her head. Tanner brushed the hair back from her cheeks. "What do you do? How old are you?"

A small smile curled up her lips. "Now you ask."

He grinned back at her. "Better late than never."

"I'm thirty two and I'm the senior accountant at First Federal Savings and Loan."

"Senior accountant, huh? That sounds impressive."

She kissed him softly on the lips first before answering. "I'm not doing too bad in my career, if I do say so myself." She kissed him again. "You're a rancher."

"My cowboy hat gave me away?"

"No. I heard it through the grapevine today. That's how I learned you were a real live person."

One of his brows lifted. "My family has been around these parts for generations."

"What do you ranch?"

"Mostly cattle, and grow a lot of alfalfa hay."

Their eyes locked and Tanner slipped his hand behind her neck, dragging her down for another kiss. This one, slow and easy. "How about we start over?"

"Start over?"

"Yeah. I want to get to know you. I'd like to take you out to dinner tomorrow night."

Another one of her sexy smiles was his answer.

"I'd like that, but..."

An uneasy feeling moved through him. "But what?"

"I'd like to meet your nephew and thank him for casting a spell on you."

Surprised at how good he felt with at the relief filtering through him, the corners of his lips kicked up into a grin. While he'd made love with her, he'd completely forgotten about Jeremy's spell and how he'd met her in the first place. "He lives in Seattle."

"Oh, darn."

"I could call him, I wouldn't mind thanking him myself."

"Really?"

"Yeah, I'll introduce him to you."

Camille giggled and climbed off of him. He grabbed her for a quick kiss before he reached for the phone on her nightstand. Tangled together, he dialed his sister's cell phone number.

"Hey, sis." Too much static on the phone made it hard for him to hear her. "Ann, are you there?"

"Tanner, yeah, I'm here."

He had to raise his voice because of the high amount of interference over the lines. "Where's Jeremy? I want to talk to him." He caught Camille staring at him so he mouthed the word. *Static.*

Ann raised her voice, too. "He's at a sleep over."

Disappointed that he couldn't talk to his nephew, he said, "Why is there so much interference? Did you forget to charge yeah battery?"

"No, it's because Bob and I are flying?"

A frown furrowed his brows together. Bob and Ann weren't exactly rolling in dough. And they would never leave Jeremy while they flew off somewhere. "Where are you going?"

"We're just out for a cruise."

"What the hell? What's going on, Ann?"

"Jeremy turned Bob into superman. He's holding me in his arms."

He could have sworn his heart stopped beat for one full second. "Pull my leg, if you want."

"Really, we are. Bob, honey, watch out for the Space Needle."

"Sorry, my pretty, I'm taking a sharp right," He heard Bob holler.

"Tanner, I'll call you tomorrow. Bye." The line went dead.

Camille shook his shoulder. "What's going on? You look like you just saw a ghost. Is Jeremy okay? Your sister?"

Struggling to digest the conversation between himself and Ann, he didn't answer her as he replaced the phone. He rolled onto his back and looked at Camille. "You're not going to believe this."

"I'll believe anything after last night."

He wondered since Ann and Bob had a free night if they weren't having some kind of fun together with Jeremy out of the house.

"Tanner, talk to me."

"Okay, here goes. Supposedly Jeremy turned his dad, Bob, into Superman, last week." He paused. Damn, was his entire family nuts? "Ann said they were flying and Bob was carrying her in his arms. Then she told him to watch out for the Space Needle."

Camille's hand flew to her mouth. "Ohmigod."

Tanner shook his head. "It can't be. Ann was playing some kind of practical joke on me."

She lowered her hand, a serious expression on her face. "You don't know that for sure."

He supposed she did have a point. There was no way to know that for sure. "I guess I don't."

"I mean, look what happened to you. To us."

"Are you going to tell me you believe in fairy tales?"

Pursing her lips together, she was quiet for a time. "Up until last night, I would have said no. But now..." She lifted a shoulder.

Wrapping his arms around her, he pulled her closer. "So Ms. Fairy Princess, maybe it was fate that brought us together."

Her eyes twinkled with mischief. "Or magic."

"I have to admit I'm a practical guy, but it could definitely be magic." Tanner kissed her, feeling the magic of Camille's sweet lips.

UNDER TANNER'S THUMB

THE END

WWW.SAGEBURNETT.COM

SIREN ADULT FAIRY TALE
Little Red Rides the Wolf
Lara Santiago

Little Red Rides the Wolf

Erotic Sci-Fi Fairy Tale (Shape-shifting)

Against her mother's final dying wish, Cheri Amaranth travels across the galaxy to the planet Selenia to meet her ailing Grampa for the first time.

Caine Wolver eagerly awaits her arrival to explain his intentions for their intertwined future.

However, Hunter spoils their first meeting and guides Cheri through the woods to Grampa's house, taking her on a different path than Caine planned.

Long bitter rivals, one man wants her heart, but the other only wants her goodies bag.

Will Cheri make it to her Grampa's house in time to give him the goodies she's brought from so far away? And which man can Cheri ultimately trust, the man she met first or the one who drives her crazy with passion?

LITTLE RED RIDES THE WOLF

The Fairy Tale Collection

Lara Santiago

Chapter 1

"You must come alone..."

Cheri Amaranth leaned closer to the console of her spacecraft communications device as if it would help her see the garbled holographic vid-phone message better. It didn't.

"…main platform is dangerous…use alternate landing site…" the miniaturized figure of her recently located grandfather pleaded.

"Roger, that. Setting coordinates for alternate landing platform." Nothing but static greeted her. "Send your coordinate location."

"…sending a guide…not safe…the woods alone…follow… path…" The vid-message degraded further.

"Say again. What path?"

"…watch out for the w…wolf!" Her grandfather's urgent tone on the last word came through clearly, then the image disappeared. Communications went dead as her ship entered the misty atmosphere of the small planet Selenia.

"Did he just say watch out for the werewolf?" Rex, her co-pilot, asked.

"Very funny." Cheri gave Rex an eye roll and flipped the switch to end transmission.

"That's what it sounded like. Are you sure we want to land on a planet named Selenia with a fresh werewolf warning?"

"Why wouldn't we?"

"Selenia means dweller of the moon. Moon dwellers added to a werewolf warning is trouble with a capital T."

Cheri scrunched her brows in disbelief. "Remind me to send you on a long vacation really soon."

Rex huffed. "I don't like this sudden trip to visit someone you've never met."

"Noted. Now prepare us to land at the new coordinates." Cheri didn't believe in the boogieman—or werewolves either—and Rex knew it.

They landed without incident in the thick wooded forest. The alternate landing site was on the opposite side of the planet from the primary port. Selenia had little substantial population anyway. She imagined the alternate port would be deserted.

Rex powered the craft down. "Are you sure you want to traipse alone through the woods to visit a man you've never even met?"

"Sure. Why not? I'm doing a good deed. Grampa was very glad to hear from me. He asked me to come right away when I contacted him."

"Grampa? You don't even know this guy and you're already calling him Grampa?"

"I realize he's a stranger, Mr. Mother-Hen, but he is also the only link I have to my father's people. I was born here, you know." Cheri paused before adding, "I'd probably still live here if my mother hadn't moved us when my father died."

Cheri wondered if she'd still have wanderlust if she'd grown up here. Since her earliest memory, she'd looked to the twinkling night sky as a place she wanted to explore.

"Why contact 'Grampa' now?"

She heaved a deep sigh. "Curiosity, I guess. I didn't know anything about my dad until Mom died. She left me a letter to be opened on my twenty-fifth birthday."

"Your twenty-fifth birthday isn't until next month." Rex gave her an accusatory glare.

She shrugged, refusing to feel guilty about ignoring the warning emblazoned on the letter her mother had left. "You should know me by now. I was filled with raging curiosity, Rex. I've always wanted to know more about my father and his family. Now is my chance."

"Curiosity killed the cat, you know."

Cheri shrugged again, grinned and added, "But not the werewolf."

Rex sent his surly gaze upward. "I'm going on the record that this is very strange."

"Right. Again, noted. Now please go get my goodie bag for Grampa ready. I'll be outside checking the hull for damage until the guide gets here."

"Watch out for werewolves," he warned.

Cheri responded with a deep sigh and stepped into the airlock to exit the ship. Outside she walked around her pride and joy, the small transport ship called Scarlet's Legacy, named for her mother. A few dings here and there. Seeing no serious damage, she headed to the hatch. Pushing her collar button to radio Rex as she approached the ship's entrance, she halted in her tracks, then released the button without speaking.

The largest wolf she'd ever seen blocked her way back to the hatch.

Her instincts, always attuned to animals of all kinds, told her this great beast was not a danger. Even with fresh werewolf warnings dancing in her mind, the uncontrollable urge to stroke the wolf's beautiful fur to determine if it was as soft as it looked raged inside her.

Sensing no threat, Cheri took a step closer.

"Holy shit, Cheri," Rex whispered in her ear breaking her calm. "There's a big fuckin' wolf by the hatch door."

"Yeah, I *see* him," she muttered sarcastically. "He's blocking the door." The wolf regarded her with the most stunning blue eyes. On his haunches with front paws resting forward, tail wrapped around his paws, mouth open slightly as he panted, revealing lots of white teeth, he was the most beautiful creature she'd ever seen. His coat was deep space black minus the stars.

"Don't move. I'll try to angle the cannon around and get a shot," Rex whispered in her ear.

"No," Cheri shouted into her radio. "Don't shoot him." She moved closer to the wolf, putting herself between the ship's gun mount and her visitor. The beautiful wolf didn't budge except for his gentle panting.

"What's wrong with you? That beast is two seconds away from ripping your throat out." Rex's flair for the dramatic emerged in full force.

Cheri glanced at the wolf and couldn't help but smile. The wolf in turn tilted his head to the side and his tongue lolled out. Her smile changed into a huge grin.

She crept forward to an arm's length away. The wolf watched. His eyes blinked slowly as if sizing her up and finding her acceptable.

"Are you crazy, Cheri?"

"Relax. He won't hurt me. I can sense it."

"Oh? You're a wolf whisperer, now?"

Reaching out with thumb and fingers tucked inside her palm to be less threatening, Cheri let the wolf sniff her hand. After bumping his long nose against her fist, he licked her knuckles. A girly giggle bubbled out as his rough textured tongue tickled her skin. She stroked his nose and scratched behind his ears. His fur was kitten belly soft.

"See, Rex. He's harmless."

Her sentiment changed in the next second when the black wolf's ears went straight up. He turned his big furry head toward the forest and a deep growl resonated from his throat.

"Someone's coming..." Rex shouted. The wolf sprang up on hind legs, towering over her. Sucking in a breath, Cheri almost peed on herself when the animal's great front paws landed on her shoulders and pushed her to the ground. A couple hundred pounds of canine landed on top of her as the sound of a sonic laser blast rang out.

The wolf yelped when she hit the ground with a thump. His paw brushed her neck, scratching her. The warm sting of the wound registered as her head struck the dirt. She fought the blackness of unconsciousness. Something wet caressed her cheek. The wolf licked her? She didn't have time to analyze the gesture before dropping out.

* * * *

The wolf scrambled off of the landing platform favoring his hind leg and disappeared into the vast forest covering Selenia. His leg hurt. A lot. He hated leaving her behind, but he could barely walk. He couldn't go back until his wound healed. Changing to his human form was the fastest way to heal.

Transforming from wolf to man before Cheri's eyes moments after she landed on this planet, or letting her see his rapid recovery, wouldn't facilitate his plan.

Out of sight of the space craft, the wolf tucked away his beast and became human again. Glancing down at his thigh, he watched the skin knitting over the laser blast as if it had never happened.

His leg wound completely healed, he sprinted, picking up speed as he traveled. The man soon shifted back into his wolf form. Leaping over a pile of dead branches, he raced back through the woods towards Scarlet's Legacy ready to fulfill his destiny. And hers.

Chapter 2

When she opened her eyes, Rex hovered over her his face pinched in worry. Behind him, a stranger wearing a satisfied smirk held a big sonic blaster gun.

"Who the hell are you?" Cheri asked the newcomer, rising to her elbows.

"I'm Hunter."

She glanced at the gun. "If you were trying to kill me, you missed."

"I wasn't aiming for you. I was trying to kill the wolf. He was about to eat you." The sincerity of his expression moved her.

Cheri nodded, but she was unconvinced the wolf was anything but intriguing. She had a sudden flash of wrestling with that big wolf in a meadow of fragrant flowers, but she kept her opinions and visions to herself. Now that she was waking up, the idea was ludicrous.

Standing up, Cheri brushed dirt off of her clothes. She glanced surreptitiously at Hunter and sized him up. He was attractive. His hair was so blond it was nearly white. His eyes were an unusual amber color and watching *her* closely as well.

Rex broke the silence. "Did Cheri's grampa send you as a guide?"

Shifting his gun to the other hand, Hunter paused a moment before answering. "Yes. He sent me to guide her through the woods to his house." Turning his complete attention on Cheri, he asked, "You're bringing something to him, yes?"

She stared at Hunter without answering. She'd rather find the wolf and ask for directions, but she remained silent. Shifting her gaze to the ground, she noticed a small puddle of blood, presumably from the wolf. Concern for the friendly beast enveloped her and she hoped he wasn't seriously hurt.

"Goodies," Rex's amused voice answered for her when she neglected to respond. "She's bringing a satchel of goodies to him."

Hunter's mouth lifted on one side as if in scornful amusement. Cheri wished Rex would shut up.

"Go get my stuff, Rex. Don't forget my coat."

"Sure thing." Rex grinned and ducked into the hatch. When he returned, he carried the coat her mother had treasured and the satchel with the goodies.

"You aren't wearing that coat, are you?" Hunter asked.

"I most certainly am." Cheri slipped the hip length jacket on and slung the satchel over one shoulder.

"Red marks you. It's not safe. Take it off."

"No. Lead me or don't. I don't care, but I'm wearing the coat." Cheri hitched the durable micron-fiber knapsack higher on one shoulder. The strap, made of the same indestructible fabric, was hooked under one thumb.

Hunter didn't argue further about her coat. Lifting one hand, he tilted his head shielding his eyes from the mid-morning sun peeking through the clouds. Turning back to her, Hunter grazed her body with his stare. "Time wastes. Let's be on our way. We have miles to go."

* * * *

The wolf hadn't meant to mark her. The nick from his claw on her throat had been accidental. Before leaving to heal his own wound, he'd licked her face to apologize, inhaled her scent to commit it to memory, and moved away to avoid detection. More than anything, he wanted to discover the shooter's identity.

Scenting her on the wind, he knew she'd already moved into the woods, but another smell crossed his nose in tandem with hers.

The rank stench forced an automatic growl low in his chest. Her scent, which dominated his being, was tainted by the smell of…the other. His enemy. His rival.

Who had the shooter aimed for? Him…or her?

Senses acute, the wolf sniffed the air once more and moved silently through the woods toward the woman he'd marked.

* * * *

"Are you mated with anyone?" Hunter asked.

"Do you mean married?" At his curt nod, Cheri responded, "No. I'm not married."

"Why not? Don't you wish to bear children?"

Cheri wanted to tell him to mind his own business but decided it might be part of his job as guide to extract information for her grandfather. "Perhaps one day, but for now I'm content with my supply transport business."

"A man would be foolish to turn you down as a mate." Hunter perused her form. His gaze was decidedly dispassionate. Why did he want to know about her marital status and parental aspirations since he was so obviously not interested?

Was her grandfather trying to set her up with this man? Cheri hoped not. She wasn't exactly looking to snag a husband and *bear* children any time soon.

"Foolish perhaps, but it hasn't ever come up. Anyway, I'm not ready to settle down yet. I have plenty of time."

Hunter didn't respond, but he picked up the pace. They walked a well-marked path deeper into the dark forest. The misty dreamy quality of the air around them put her in an odd mood. Her heart rate sped with each step. The landscape wasn't familiar, but it called to her. It was frightening and beautiful at the same time.

Unease replaced the anticipation of meeting her father's family, which had pounded in her brain all the way here. She was uncomfortable for a reason she couldn't name and glanced at Hunter to see if he was disturbed. He marched forward without looking around as if on an urgent mission. As their pace increased, the trees overhead soon blocked most of the meager sun light leaving only a few shafts of light to offer direction.

Hunter didn't speak or ask her anymore questions, so they marched in silence.

After twenty minutes, the path forked. To the right, the way was wider and easier to navigate. To the left, the trail was narrow and dark. Limbs encroached on the space and tree roots jutted up through the mat of leaves.

Cheri paused to stare down the lonely left side path in consideration. As derelict as it looked, Cheri thought they should traverse left. The dark path called to her on some subliminal and unexplainable level.

Hunter marched to the right without noticing her hesitation.

"What's to the left?" Cheri called out to his back.

Hunter turned quickly, clutching his gun close as if he'd forgotten she was along for the trip and was surprised to hear someone speak.

His brows creased in puzzlement. Suspicious eyes glanced at the other path and then back at her. "Nothing. It's an ancient path not used any more. Derelict. We need to go this way." He motioned for her to follow and turned as if she were an obedient dog that should trail behind its master without question. She wasn't.

Cheri remained rooted and looked down the neglected path again. Once more the dark, twisty lane called to her like a siren song. Cheri frowned. She was a scientist. She didn't believe in magic or werewolves or the like, but right now her sixth sense told her she should go left.

An indefinable pull from her instinctual side had lodged in her soul the second she had landed on this planet. She was loath to admit relying on her gut instinct, but she had done so a time or two with excellent results. Something about this planet heightened her instincts and changed her attitude.

"I'm going left."

Turning back with a flash of anger that radiated all the way to his glowing amber eyes, Hunter growled. "Who's the guide here? We're going right."

Cheri heaved a sigh. "Taking the path less traveled makes all the difference, I hear." She crossed her arms, ready to be difficult. She did difficult very well.

A wolf howled from the direction of the abandoned path, a lonely, eerie wail. They both turned their heads in the direction of the sound. The haunting cry calmed Cheri. It confirmed her gut instinct on which path she should travel. Perhaps her beautiful wolf waited at the end of the trail she wanted to follow.

Hunter, on the other hand, became distinctly agitated. "Enough. We need to go. Now!" He grabbed her arm and took off down the right lane, dragging her along and bruising her flesh with every step. Another wolf howled as if in angry agony. The sound definitely more irritated than the first.

Cheri wrenched her arm from Hunter's grasp. "I'm not going anywhere with you." She turned toward where her soul directed.

Behind her another growl erupted. Hunter aimed his gun at her, but before he could level it completely, a huge black wolf jumped from the thick woods and knocked Hunter to the ground. He dropped his weapon when he hit the dirt trail, but Cheri saw the flash of a knife in his hand.

"No," she screamed when Hunter reared back to strike her wolf.

Chapter 3

The wolf rolled to the side and Hunter's knife missed. Sinking his teeth into Hunter's hand, the wolf caused him to drop the knife. Wrapping his arms around the beast, Hunter clinched him close so the wolf couldn't bite again. They wrestled, moving closer to the gun.

Watching the fight, Cheri shuffled back and forth on the balls of her feet wondering what to do. A growled voice called, "Run!"

Uncertain where the command had come from, she turned and ran anyway. She headed for the derelict path, running for all she was worth and clutching the satchel close.

The new path was difficult to follow, but fear motivated her.

She'd had an unsettled feeling about Hunter from the moment she'd met him. After having him pull his gun on her for the second time, it was weak relief that her gut instinct was vindicated.

Her greater concern lay with the beautiful black wolf wrestling with Hunter. She hadn't seen his eyes but suspected they were cerulean blue. Their ability to make her throw caution to the wind and approach was uncanny, but there was something else in the way the lovely beast looked at her, lolling his tongue out that made her feel safe.

Cheri didn't know how far she'd run along this new trail, but the hitch in her side begged her to stop moving. She ignored it and pressed on, dodging hanging branches around every sharp twist of the path.

The trail was fast losing shape and becoming more deep woods than a marked pathway leading anywhere.

Cheri looked behind her for anyone following and tripped on a root sticking out of the ground. She fell to her knees and hands. The satchel slid to the ground with a thud.

Scrambling to her feet, Cheri yanked the bag into her arms and turned to the direction she'd come from. Branches snapped and broke behind her. Something moved toward her through the dense forest.

Finding no options for a hiding place, she stepped further into the dark trees, seeking haven from unseen danger.

She needed time to assess her options. Time she didn't have. Her usually great sense of direction might not get her back to her own ship at this point. She needed help.

Hunter, wherever he was now, wasn't trustworthy enough to provide it. She'd rather try to communicate with the wolf and see if he could lead her back to her spacecraft or forward to her Grampa's house.

As if she'd conjured him up from her mind, her black wolf appeared between the trees in a clearing near where she hid. Cheri moved as quietly as possible to the clearing's edge for a better look. The black wolf with the incredible blue eyes sat as serenely as he had before when he'd blocked the door to her ship. This time his mouth was closed. No big white teeth or lolling pink tongue.

"Hello," Cheri whispered, feeling slightly foolish to be talking to an animal. Speaking in a low tone made it easier.

She scanned his coat for wounds but saw none. He didn't look any worse for wear from the gun battle back at her ship, or the more recent one on the trail.

"Are you okay?" Cheri squinted and searched his fur again quickly for fresh wounds.

The wolf's ears perked up. He tilted his head to one side as if puzzled by her presence as well as her question. His great jaws snapped open. Cheri sucked in a surprised breath. But the wolf only yawned, a big deep one showing all those beautiful white teeth. His jaws snapped shut again and he returned to his tilted head stare.

"I'm lost," Cheri whispered. "Will you help me find a safe place?"

The wolf woofed once in response, rose to all fours and left the clearing. He turned his mighty head back as if to see if she followed. Cheri took a deep breath and crossed the clearing after him hoping he'd lead her to her grampa's house. Or at least to someone besides Hunter for the information.

She wouldn't normally take such risks to see a man she'd never met if it weren't for the letter her mother had left upon her death.

I know you're a good girl, Cheri. I wouldn't ask you to do this if it weren't important. I know I was the one who kept you from visiting your father's people. I was so devastated by his unneeded death. I couldn't deal with it. I left and turned my back on them, but you need to visit there eventually and meet your grampa. If I die before your twenty-fifth birthday, then you're reading this letter and they'll have to explain.

There is a remote possibility you carry a genetic anomaly, sweetie. The only way to test for it is to visit your father's people. I ask only that you wait until after you turn twenty-five. I want you to have every chance to live as you wish. I want you to have choices. I know it sounds melodramatic, but please listen to me in this one matter.

Cheri couldn't wait. She loved her mother, but Scarlet tended to be overly dramatic. Of the two women, Cheri was the sensible one. She had contacted her grampa with her mother's warning letter still clutched in her fist.

Visiting her father's side of the family shouldn't be constrained by a silly superstitious notion of her mother's. Before or after her twenty-fifth birthday didn't matter. At least Cheri hoped not. She knew for a fact she couldn't wait a moment longer or her brain would explode with curiosity.

Her heart had slowed its furious pounding since she departed the ancient trail. Now completely lost in the woods of Selenia, Cheri forged ahead, brushing branches out of her face trying to keep the black wolf in sight. Several minutes in, she lost him and decided it was beyond foolish to follow an animal through a strange and misty forest in the first place.

Finding a large elm tree beside another small clearing, she crouched by it to listen for anyone following. Nothing. She might be lost, but she was safe.

Tucking a piece of hair behind her ear, she closed her eyes to listen to the forest sounds around her. Plans to set off in another direction and locate the trail were quickly discarded. What was she going to do? How would she find her grampa now? Or the ancient trail, for that matter? Her gut instinct remained silent.

Strangely, she wasn't scared. Not like she should be.

"Are you okay?" a voice queried from behind.

Opening her eyes, Cheri twisted to see a stranger towering above her.

Slapping a hand to her chest, she huffed out, "Lord above, you scared me. Where did you come from?"

Why hadn't she heard him?

"I'm sorry."

Cheri stood, slinging the satchel over one shoulder as she assessed the attractive man standing before her. The top of her head didn't come level with his very muscular shoulders.

Black, shaggy hair and three days growth of beard gracing his jaw, highlighting the most amazing blue eyes she'd ever seen on a man. The impact of his presence shot her libido off the charts.

Mesmerized by the blue depths of his eyes, she continued to stare while wicked thoughts of him naked slid through her mind. After several seconds, the corners of his eyes crinkled in amusement and she was distracted by the straight white teeth revealed by his grin. Dazzling. Had he read her mind?

He laughed.

"What are you laughing at?" His amusement puzzled her. She hoped he couldn't read her thoughts.

"What are you staring at?" he responded and she realized how rude she was being.

"Sorry. I've never seen eyes the color of yours before." *And in my recent daydreams, you have a great body.*

His laughter changed to a chuckle. "You've never seen blue eyes before? I find that hard to believe."

Cheri broke the gaze and searched for something intelligent to say without divulging her true thoughts. "Did you see a wolf run through here a minute ago?"

The blue-eyed Adonis stepped closer and caught her stare again. "You're looking for a wolf?"

Cheri sucked in a breath. Lord above, he was gorgeous. "Kind of."

Another step closer. The wind picked up at that moment and blew his scent into her face. He smelled like the woods around them. A hint of campfire smoke and pine trees melded with his unique musk. She inhaled the enticing scent deeply and a buzz of sensation centered in her core, dampening her.

"Either you are or you aren't." He grinned again.

Cheri knew she didn't sound the least bit intelligent. "I am." She nodded partly to convince herself. "I followed a wolf through the woods."

The man tilted his head to one side. "What were you going to do with him once you caught him?"

Cheri couldn't find her voice to answer, but the rush of blood to her cheeks made her curse the fact that embarrassment showed so easily on her face. It wasn't like she could say, "Gee, after running for my life from the guide my grampa sent, I was hoping the wolf could lead me to his house so I could give him some goodies." She shrugged and remained silent. Probably the first intelligent move she's made.

"Lucky wolf." He grinned. His gaze swept up and down her body with seeming interest. Cheri's gut instinct kicked in. Finding this man was even better than finding the wolf.

Chapter 4

Caine resisted the virulent urge to bury his face in her throat, sniff her skin's unique fragrance and lick her. Focused so intently on the lovely span of her neck, he noticed the puncture mark.

"You're hurt." He reached out, not thinking beyond the fact that she was wounded, but halted his hand inches from her throat. Caine didn't quite trust himself to touch her yet. She was more beautiful than he'd imagined. He didn't want to scare her.

Eyes widening, she brushed her fingers over the injury on her neck, hiding the mark briefly. "It's nothing."

Caine glanced from her neck to her face. "You're bleeding." He wiped a drop of blood from her cheek, ignoring his previous worry. She shivered the moment he touched her. Caine eased closer, to within an arm's length away.

Her skin was rose petal soft. A vision of his hands stroking her naked body skated through his mind.

Premonition or merely wishful desire? He didn't know.

Her eyes lifted to his. Mesmerized by her appraisal, he brushed a strand of strawberry blonde hair off of her face avoiding the scratches.

"What happened to you?" Caine tucked the errant strand of her hair behind one ear.

She lifted her small shoulders in another shrug. "I was running through the woods because…I thought someone was chasing me." Her low soft voice caressed him until the words registered.

He frowned. "Who chased you?"

"I'm not sure." She smiled suddenly and added, "He didn't catch me though."

Caine wanted to catch her. "Nobody caught you. Until me."

"You haven't really caught me." Her gaze darted from his eyes to his chest to his hands and back up. What was she thinking about?

"Not yet anyway. May I offer you a place to clean up?" he asked. "My lodge is tucked away over this hill."

A falling tree crashed thorough the foliage. The racket startled her. She twisted toward the direction of the sound. While she was turned away, he closed the distance between them, leaving only inches.

Her scent pounded though his veins. The vision of them writhing together in a frenzied sexual fervor pervaded his mind. He took a deep breath to calm himself, but the delicious perfume of her arousal tightened around his lust. He blew out the breath. Focus. He wouldn't gain her trust if he yanked her pants down and mounted her right here in the clearing. Beautiful aroused scent or not, he needed to calm down. She was so important. He'd waited endlessly for her to arrive.

Caine lowered his lips to her ear and whispered, "I don't mean to sound dramatic, but it isn't safe here. We should go."

If she was troubled by his proximity when she turned to face him, she didn't show it.

Her head tipped back until their gaze met. "I haven't seen safe on this planet yet."

"I'll keep you safe." His hand grazed her shoulder gently. She held his piercing stare as he ran fingertips down her arm, stroking her wrist. So soft. He tugged her closer. "Trust me."

"Why I should trust you?" she whispered.

"I won't hurt you. I'll mend your scratches. And besides, you're already entranced by my blue eyes."

She grinned and his heart melted a little further.

"What's your name?" she asked.

"Caine Wolver."

Cheri nodded. "I'm Cheri Amaranth."

"I know."

Her brows quirked. "How?"

"There aren't many visitors to these woods. Besides, your grandfather mentioned you were coming. I expected you, eventually." It was beyond fortunate that she'd arrived here before her twenty-fifth birthday.

"Can you take me to him?"

"Sure. But first let me take you to my lodge and tend your wounds. Your grampa would be concerned to see you bleeding. Let me clean you up and I'll take you to his cabin myself."

"Okay. Thanks."

Caine pulled her hand to lead her to his cabin until she said, "The guide my grampa sent was scary."

"Guide?" Caine stopped and turned to her. "What guide was scary?" The wolf had arrived first. Had she been frightened of him?

"Said his name was Hunter." She shivered.

Caine stiffened at the mention of the other man's name.

"Hunter wasn't sent by your Grampa." Caine started walking again. "They don't get along."

"Figures." Cheri huffed.

Caine led her carefully through the thick forest, holding limbs back for her to pass. Each time he paused, Cheri slid so close he fought grabbing her to inhale her delicious scent and nibble on her neck. The longer she stayed in his immediate presence, the more desperately he wanted her.

They traversed the dense woods as quietly as possible. Around a copse of flowering red bushes and through a stand of trees, the corner of his log cabin came into view.

Once past the trees, he said, “Here we are.”

As they walked up the stone path to his door, he vowed to keep a civil distance once they were alone inside. He’d patch her up and take her to see her grandfather straight away.

Unless she wanted a kiss. He would gladly oblige. Caine glanced at her luscious mouth and cursed under his breath.

If they kissed, it was likely he wouldn’t want to stop at just one. If he tasted her, it was likely he wouldn’t stop at merely a kiss.

* * * *

Cheri followed Caine inside. The rustic cabin charmed her on several levels. The stone fireplace, which took up the entire back wall, made it homey. She easily pictured a huge roaring fire in the dark space. The huge bed in one corner made her want Mr. Gorgeous on a visceral sexual level. She slid the pack between her feet and shrugged off her jacket, never taking her eyes off the bed. It was huge. A homemade quilt covered the mattress. The four poster frame lacked a canopy, but that would make it look too girly. She preferred its masculine appeal.

Caine slid close behind her and took her jacket. He hung it on the wooden peg by the door. Picking her satchel off the floor, she handed that to him, too. Grazing her fingers with his electric touch as he took the bag, he added it to the peg holding her jacket. She fought the urge to throw her arms around him and hug his neck.

Stroking a sleeve, he smiled and said, “I like your coat.”

“Thanks. It was my mother’s. I think my granny made it for her as a wedding gift.”

“Red is definitely your color.” He crossed the room and pulled out a chair at the small dining table in the center of the space. “Have a seat.”

Cheri eyed the bed again and smiled as she seated herself on the edge of the simple wooden chair he held for her. Legs spread wide with her hands resting on her thighs, she glanced around the room. It was welcoming and comfortable.

Next to the peg with her coat and satchel was a bookshelf filled with titles. Even squinting, Cheri couldn’t read any of the titles in the small library from where she sat. She wondered what a sexy man about the forest read in his spare time when he wasn't rescuing damsels in distress.

Meanwhile, her sexual senses were already on high alert. She'd been off-balance since landing on this fantasy planet, but never more than right now in the company of the man about to tend her wounds.

Caine busied himself at a side table gathering things. Cheri watched his muscular backside as vivid images slid deliciously into her mind. Tall and well-built, she wondered if his body looked as muscled as she imagined underneath his simple clothing.

Glancing over at the bed intensified her visions. Cheri knew one other thing she wanted before heading to Grampa's house. Seducing the stranger was out of character for her, but she couldn't think of anything else. She shifted in her chair as her clitoris twitched with impatient need. Sliding her hands to her sensitive inner thighs, she resisted the urge to rub herself to end the torment.

Caine turned and carried a tray with supplies across the room to her now wiggling, anxious form. "Is that bed comfortable?" Her heart pounded at the audacious thoughts pummeling her brain.

His low-lidded gaze pierced all the way to her clit, but he didn't seem too surprised by her question. "Yes, it is." He pulled out a chair and stuck it directly in front of hers. "After I patch you up, you can try it out."

Perhaps he had the same salacious visions running through his head. Cheri pulsed with sexual desire.

"Excellent." She planned her seduction. Her gaze slid to his wickedly seductive mouth. That was exactly where she would start. A lip-smacking, tonsil-tickling kiss.

Caine glanced across the room at her satchel hanging on the peg. "So, what's in the bag, if you don't mind my asking?"

Cheri smiled. "I'm bringing some goodies to my grampa."

"Goodies?" He grinned and wiped her face with a damp cloth. "Like chocolate?"

He leaned closer, holding the cloth in place against her neck where the wound from the black wolf itched but didn't sting. His luscious woodsy scent penetrated to her core. She leaned closer, wanting desperately to kiss him as he wiped blood away from her cheek and neck.

She grinned and pretended to be coy about her goodies. “Something like that. Grampa asked for some things. I’m just the carrier.”

“I see.” He dabbed a wad of cotton on the wounds with something that stung a little at first but quickly stopped when he blew on it.

His warm breath floating across her flesh did nothing to stop the heat rushing across every inch of her skin. He ignited her senses to the point she was fast becoming unable to control herself. She glanced at his face.

Caine looked at her like...well, like a man who was interested in...goodies. Her goodies. Cheri wanted to touch him. Wanted to run her hands underneath his thick shirt and caress what she suspected was mouthwateringly lean muscular flesh. Wanted to follow her fingertips with her tongue.

She blinked once. Lust overwhelmed her.

In one smooth move, she leaned up and pressed her lips to his. The moment their mouths touched, something wicked and carnal unleashed inside her. She licked his bottom lip as they kissed.

Cheri moaned and Caine responded with a low growl. He slanted his mouth across hers and deepened their first intoxicating kiss, licking his way through her parted lips.

Chapter 5

Cheri hungered for Caine’s touch as his tongue penetrated her mouth. Hovering over him, she squeezed his shoulder once before sliding her hand to the back of his neck.

She straddled his legs and sat on his lap. Rubbing her breasts, complete with sensitive peaked nipples, against his muscular chest inflamed her ardor to an irrational proportion. His arms slid around her back and held her loosely.

Breaking the kiss, she trailed her lips across his rough whiskered face to whisper in his ear, “Are you finished patching me up yet?”

He either groaned or cleared his throat, she wasn’t certain, but he didn’t respond. His fingers traced the length of her spine. His touch sent a spasm of desire straight to her clit. Wet and vibrating with a longing she could barely control, Cheri stepped up her seduction.

After a lengthy silence, she whispered, "Because if you are…" Cheri brushed her mouth along his jaw and continued, "I'd love for you to join me on the very comfortable bed."

She leaned away from his warmth to ascertain her chances of getting him to scratch the strident itch now pervading her clit.

Caine's eyes fairly glowed with desire. "I'm done." His gravelly voice betrayed the calm exterior he expressed. She scooted her hips closer and bumped into a huge ridge beneath the front of his pants.

Grinning, she lifted her wet and wanting body off of his lap and replaced it with her hand on his thigh. She ran her fingertips all the way to his hip and said, "Let's go then."

"Right now?"

"Yes, please." Cheri ran her hand over his cock. He sucked in a breath at her bold touch. She stroked him. Under the rough texture of his slacks, he enlarged even further with her attention.

"My, what a big cock you have!" Cheri couldn't seem to help her attitude. It was as if she was under a spell, a spell she didn't want to break. She'd stroked a cock or two in her past, but none which made her so hot and bothered before. A shot of moisture coated the sensitive lips between her legs. She was drenched and ready.

Caine kissed her cheek. His lips slid to her mouth. He licked the corner and nibbled her bottom lip. Cheri twisted her mouth over his and devoured him.

The subtle buzz of arousal upon entering the cabin had developed into full blown lust. She couldn't think past gratification. Her feminine parts retracted in pleasure, further soaking her core.

Breaking the sensuous kiss, Cheri murmured, "I really want you." She grabbed two fistfuls of shirt and hauled him up to prove her point.

"I have no doubt." He pulled away, grabbing her arms before they could circle his neck. "You need to know something first."

Cheri paused in mid launch. "What?"

"I don't usually fall into bed with women I've only known for ten minutes."

"Seems like longer."

Wait a minute. She didn't normally attack men she'd only known ten minutes, either. What was wrong with her? She backed away sitting in her chair but didn't release his arms.

"I'm not usually so aggressive. Have you put me under a spell?" She couldn't believe she'd said that out loud. She extracted herself from touching his delicious body but remained close. Her breasts tingled with the desire to rub against him.

"I haven't put any enchantment on you…that I remember anyway." Towering over her, he sighed deeply and watched her eyes.

She grinned. "I wouldn't mind."

Caine sat back down. He placed his hands on her hips. Gazing into her eyes, he lured her with his hypnotic stare. "I know this sounds like a line, but have we met before? I feel like…maybe I know you or that I've seen you before. Have you been on this planet recently?"

Cheri shook her head. "I haven't been on this planet since I was an infant." She knew her mother hadn't wanted her to come here until after she'd turned twenty-five. But Cheri was drawn here as if she'd been merely waiting for a destination in her riotous search of the galaxies. Now, she was inexplicably drawn to this man. Was he the reason she was here?

"What about you? Do you live here?"

He nodded. "I was also born here. This is my primary domain, but I do travel quite a bit" He rubbed his hands up and down her arms and the tingly warmth reminded her she was still unsatisfied.

"Why?" Cheri didn't really care why he traveled. She wanted to peel his clothes off.

"I'm a doctor. I travel as a part of my practice."

Cheri shook her head in disbelief. "You're a doctor?" The sexiest, most gorgeous man she'd ever seen was a doctor, too. What were the odds?

He grinned. "Didn't my medical training show when I cleaned you up?

"I guess. Honestly, I wasn't paying attention." She'd been focused on his mouth. As a matter of fact, she wanted to kiss him again. Will power already dissolved, she straddled one of his legs and sat on his thigh. Her nipples brushed his torso and hardened. Pushing her hands along his muscular chest, she said, "Maybe you could kiss me again and make it all better."

Caine slid his fingers to her head. Grabbing her face between his large hands, he pressed his mouth to hers without hesitation.

His firm lips rubbing across hers sent another gush of moisture through her pussy. Cheri scooted even closer. He slid his arms around her and crushed her to his chest. His tongue slipped inside her mouth, a warm, wonderful invasion. Cheri moaned as their tongues danced. Her body pulsed with desire with each thrust and lick.

In the distance, a wolf howled. Cheri paused breaking their ardent kiss to listen.

"Are there a lot of wolves on this planet?"

"Yes."

"Any of them friendly?"

He chuckled. "Many of them are very friendly." He hugged her tight and nuzzled her neck.

"I saw a beautiful black wolf when I landed." She pulled away and gazed deeply into Caine's eyes. "He also had blue eyes."

Caine laughed. "Wolves can have blue eyes."

"Do they?" Cheri smiled and asked another question burning in her brain. "Is it true they mate for life?"

* * * *

Caine was speechless. Her question about mating for life took him completely off guard. His rampant desire to mate with Cheri for eternity danced in his soul, screaming, "Yes. Yes. Yes."

"My mom told me that once. She never remarried after my father died. She told me she was like a wolf. She never wanted anyone else but my father." Cheri's thoughtful expression as she reminisced about her parents touched him.

"Wolves do mate for life." *So do I,* the additional three words Caine wanted to say out loud, but he didn't.

Instead, he shifted her off of his lap and back into her own chair. Resting his elbows on his knees, he drilled a gaze her way and said, "If we carry this any further, prepare to have me in your life."

Cheri nodded, leaned forward and kissed his mouth. "I think I belong with you. Or you've enchanted me with your blue eyes. Either way, I'd like to check out that bed." In a flash, she shifted to his lap again, straddling his legs, and threw her arms around his neck.

He hugged her close. "You're right. We belong together." His self-control disappearing, Caine kissed the space below her ear, earning a sensual moan. His cock throbbed in response. Iron willpower was what he needed desperately and lacked entirely.

Hands beneath her thighs, Caine stood and took her with him across the room. Cheri remained wrapped around him, locking her feet behind his back. She clenched him tight on the short journey. He carried her to the foot of the bed, kissing her slowly and methodically. She moaned again, stoking his passion, which was already at a volcanic level. He couldn't resist her. If she didn't choose him as a mate, he'd be devastated. Caine vowed not to carry things so far as to leave her without choices. He'd concentrate on pleasuring her until she was left with only one choice. Him.

Caine removed his hands from underneath her legs. She slid down his body until her feet touched the floor as they kissed. And kissed. And kissed.

Slowly undressing each other, a trail of shed clothing dotted the floor from the foot of the bed to the edge of the quilt on one side. Caine hugged her naked body close and lifted her onto the tall mattress. Standing by the bed, his mouth aligned with hers perfectly, so he kissed her. His hands found their way to her thighs. He pulled her knees apart and stepped between them.

Kissing a path down her throat, Cheri arched her neck, exposing the lovely flesh to his mouth. Her subsequent moan of approval sent an electric pulse to his cock.

Unable to resist, Caine trailed kisses to her chest. Once there, he paused to lick her breasts. He sucked a nipple into his mouth and was rewarded with another seductive whimper. Trailing his hands from her knees to her thighs, he couldn't resist slipping his fingers into her body to assess her level of readiness.

Fingers parting her soft lower lips, he slid his longest one deeply inside her pussy and shuddered, realizing she was drenched and ready. His cocked throbbed in anticipation. Time to pleasure her.

Caine kissed a path down her belly on a trajectory to her clit. He couldn't wait to taste her.

* * * *

Cheri fairly vibrated with the need to release when he pumped his finger inside her, hitting a sensitive spot. It only heightened her passion. She moaned. His mouth trailed to her lap and attached to her clit before she took her next breath. When his tongue flickered over the sensitive flesh of her clitoris with feather light pressure, Cheri slid her fingers into his hair and arched back until her shoulders met the bed. A moan escaped her lips.

Sinking into the mattress, she noted that it was indeed very comfortable, but with Caine's head between her legs, blinding ecstasy overtook her thoughts. He sucked her clit and licked her until she was on the edge of release. The rough texture of his whiskered face added delicious friction on her thighs.

She wanted to climax but knew that if she did, an invisible line would be crossed. There would be no going back to her ordinary life after sex with this fascinating man. In her heart, she knew this to be true. She hesitated only a moment before allowing the sensations he wrought to envelope her. He sucked harder on her clit, the tempo of the pleasure almost too much to bear. His fingers eased in and out of her drenched pussy with a pulse-driven rhythm. A pressure of monumental proportion was moments away from releasing a primal response in her core.

"Caine. Ohmigod." Cheri heard her desire-laced moan.

Her nipples tingled. She reached up to caress and pinch the hardened tips herself as Caine strummed her clit with his tongue and penetrated her pussy with his talented fingers.

His tongue slid over her with light strokes, driving her insane with the desire to shoot over the edge of orgasm. She hesitated only a moment more. He sucked her clit between his lips, licking her with his firm tongue, and the pressure sent her into unfathomable bliss. Her hips bucked as the delicious climax gripped her body.

Cheri screamed his name as waves of pleasure rode across her heated flesh. She quivered in utter delight.

Caine released her clit with a final lick, kissed his way to her bellybutton, and rested his head on her stomach. His hands skimmed her thighs, and her pussy clenched with the need to copulate. She rose to her elbows, body sated and satisfied.

"Take me. I want to feel you inside me. Please."

"If we make love…it will bind us permanently." Caine nibbled her tummy and sighed. "I won't deny I want you, but make no mistake. Once I penetrate you, you're mine forever."

"I'm already yours. I just hope forever is long enough."

He laughed against the tender skin of her belly. "I hope so, too."

Caine climbed onto the bed beside her, snuggling up close. His cock brushed her thigh, and it was all she could do not to pounce on him.

"Let me hold you for a little while." He gathered her in his arms, resting his head on her shoulder.

Cheri didn't want to wait. She twisted in his embrace. "I need more. I want you inside me." She rolled him over onto his back. "I have the most enthusiastic desire to ride you."

She straddled his hips. Caine's thick cock nestled at her slick entrance.

"Wait." He grabbed her thighs, keeping her from impaling herself on his cock.

"What?" Shifting her legs apart, the tip of his dick glanced across her clit and made her shudder. "Please."

"Look at me," Caine's husky voice commanded. His eyes had deepened in color to an azure blue deeper than any ocean hue.

"You're mine. I claim you." And with those simple words, he released his hold on her legs. Cheri sank down over his wide cock. It pierced her slick pussy, penetrating to the hilt.

Beneath her, Caine's eyes drifted shut and he groaned.

Cheri clenched on him, unable to stop the shiver of her body. "I'm yours," she whispered. Grabbing his face, she leaned to kiss his mouth once, tasting herself on his lips. She straightened to ride him. As she raised and lowered herself on his magnificent cock, his eyes drifted open. He watched her with something akin to awe. His gaze dipped to where their bodies joined in carnal abandon.

In and out. In and out. The magnificent sensation of skin sliding across skin made the anticipation of climax unbearable.

His fingertips danced on her responsive thighs before skimming up past her belly to cup her breasts. Cheri's pussy clenched hard when his clever fingers pinched her nipples. Electric arcs sizzled a path from peak to clit.

His thick cock stretched her with each plunge. He scratched an insistent fiery thirst Cheri wanted desperately to quench. She was on the brink of climax again. His movement teased her clit, almost touching her but not quite enough.

Reaching her hand between them, she stroked herself.

Caine broke their gaze and watched her touch her clit for a few seconds before he uttered a deep groan and thrust his cock so deep Cheri came instantly. Dizzying waves of pleasure rode over her flesh and through her body. She threw her head back and screamed.

Unable to hold herself upright any longer, she slumped over his chest, brushing his shoulder with her lips. She stopped moving, but Caine continued to pump his cock inside her with gentle strokes.

The urge to bite came when she kissed his skin. She tasted the salt on his smooth flesh before sinking her teeth into his shoulder. The indescribably perfect climax still clenched her pussy around his embedded cock as she licked his shoulder where she'd nipped him.

Caine wrapped his arms around her and twisted them until she was beneath him, never breaking their intimate contact. He kissed her mouth and pumped his shaft inside her with a tenderness she wouldn't have expected.

The reverence of his movement touched her on some primal level. He took his time as if savoring the experience of this continued mating with her. Never before had lovemaking been so sweet or so perfect.

Cheri lifted her hips to meet each deep stroke of his cock inside her slick walls. The slow, steady rhythm compelled her legs to open wider. His penetration went deeper. He moaned, increasing the speed of his thrusts.

Three strokes later, he released a positively satanic growl and grabbed her face. His gaze penetrated to her soul as surely as his cock penetrated her body. Cheri watched his climax wash down his face. His eyes drifted shut, and his teeth clamped down.

A moment later, he slumped against her spent body, breathing deeply. His head dipped to the scratch from the wolf earlier. He kissed the spot and rested his cheek on it, burrowing his head into her shoulder.

Cheri wrapped her arms and legs around his body, trapping his cock snugly inside and his lips against her throat. Together they panted until a serene calm descended. It didn't last long. Her heightened and recently satisfied libido wasn't through yet.

His cock, amazingly enough, was still stiff within her. Wiggling her hips, she asked, "Don't you ever go soft?"

The deep rumble of his laugh made her smile.

"Not with you, it seems."

"Whose turn is it to be on top?"

"Ladies choice, love."

"Am I really your love, or do you say that to all the girls you bring here?"

"You are my only love. No other woman has graced the inside of this cabin who wasn't related to me. You're the first and only girl I've brought here. You'll be the last."

"Promise?"

"Yes." He nudged her with his hips, his cock hard, thick and heavy inside her. "So what's it going to be? I'm ready."

Cheri took a deep breath and rolled him to his back. Her nipples tingled with desire to be sucked. Caine slipped an arm around her back, bent at the waist, and scooted across the bed to rest against the headboard. Intimately connected as they faced each other, Caine eyed her nipples and smiled.

She lowered one tip to his mouth and he clamped it between his lips. A zing of pleasure went straight to her clit as he sucked on her. Shifting her pussy halfway off his cock, she sank down again until he was deep. He slid his hand between her legs to rub her clit as she rode him softly. The insatiable itch for release was back as if she hadn't just climaxed twice before. She wondered if she'd ever get enough.

Riding Caine as he sucked on her nipples and played with her clit proved to be the most gratifying experience of all. Her pussy clenched his cock repeatedly when she came. Caine thrust up from beneath her as she impaled him. Cheri's head flipped back and her eyes shut as a groan of enthusiastic release escaped her lips.

The third orgasm was the most powerful, as if the first two were merely trial attempts to whet her voracious appetite. Caine grabbed her hips, thrusting deep and sure until he thundered a growl, unmistakable for anything but climax.

Moments later, Caine held her tight as she slumped against him. He maneuvered them between the sheets and snuggled her close. Sleepy and sated, her mind drifted as her body relaxed enough to fall asleep.

She fought the urge to doze in the arms of her lover. A stranger. He wasn't really a stranger, was he? After sharing this most intimate of acts, she was convinced she belonged exactly here.

Moments before she dropped into misty dreams of satisfaction, she heard the howl of a wolf outside in the distance.

Caine lifted his head from her shoulder and Cheri promptly fell into a deep gratified sleep.

Chapter 6

Caine slid from beneath the covers, doing his best not to disturb his beauty. His focus remained on her lovely body as his feet touched the cabin's cold floorboards. Cheri. His mate. The One he'd waited so long to meet. And love. He bent over and kissed her soft cheek. She sighed but didn't wake.

Pure providence brought her to this planet before he had to seek another. Fate put them in each other's arms with a little help from Cheri's ardent passion. As he stood by the bed watching her sleep, Caine's chest filled with emotion akin to gratitude and relief. He swiped a hand down his face. For the first time in years, he was hopeful for the future of his family.

He'd meant to bring her to the cabin to explain, to tell her the history of his family and hers. Instead, the pull of sexual craving long denied encompassed them. She was feisty. The thought of her passionate nature brought a smile.

The wail of a wolf interrupted his reverie. The air in the room was cold, but he barely registered the chill. Taking his gaze from Cheri, Caine glanced at the satchel hanging on the hook over her coat. The contents were so important.

Caine tread silently to the satchel and removed it from the hook. Shifting his gaze back to Cheri to ensure she still slept, he carried the bag out. Once he secured it, Caine went to gather wood for a fire. When she woke up, they'd have much to talk about. He hoped she would be receptive to his long-range plans.

He exited the cabin and strolled to the woodpile, lost in thought over his future.

Carrying several pieces of firewood to the back door of his cabin, Caine nearly dropped them when the urgent call of a lone wolf beckoned him into the woods with news. Bad news. He dropped the load he carried and ran into the stand of trees behind his place. Glancing back at the cabin before he disappeared through the trees to respond, he sent a prayer up that he would return before Cheri woke all alone.

* * * *

Cheri stirred awake and stretched, trying to remember where she was. Yawning, she rolled over on the soft bed and realized it wasn't the narrow cot on her ship. Sitting up in a blind panic, searching her memories for an explanation, a worse realization occurred.

She was completely naked under a homespun quilt. A darting glance around the rustic cabin found her jacket on the peg where Caine had hung it up. Caine.

The memories of him, and all they'd done together, flooded in all at once. She put a hand to her cheek. *Oh, my.*

What had she been thinking? And where was he? Cheri vaguely remembered hearing a wolf howl after they'd made love that last time. She'd only noted it because Caine reacted, lifting his head as if the wolf's call had meaning.

He'd left the bed as she'd rolled over in sated slumber. He'd also brushed a kiss on her cheek. Cheri touched fingertips to the spot. Silly. It wasn't as if she could feel the kiss. Her fingers unerringly slid to the wound on her neck. She rubbed the scratch lightly. It didn't hurt but was beginning to itch. Didn't that mean it was healing? Could a scratch she received only hours ago heal that fast?

Glancing around the room again, she knew she was alone. Where had he gone? Another awful thought finally made its way through her murky mind. Cheri shifted her gaze to a disturbing sight. Her coat hung alone. The satchel was gone from the peg.

Scooting to the side of the bed clutching the sheet to her chest, she looked over the edge. Caine's clothes were no longer strewn on the floor with hers.

Where was he? Had he taken her bag? And if so, why?

The front door burst open, and Hunter crowded his large frame into the doorway. He stared her down, eyes narrowing as he scanned her body. His free hand clenched into a fist; the other held his blaster.

Cheri clutched the quilt tighter to her naked body, eyes wide, as Hunter entered the room.

"I've looked everywhere for you," he snarled. "What were you doing here with him?"

"None of your business. Get out." Cheri wished she had her gun. She'd left it on her space craft.

Hunter spied her coat on the peg. Turning his head first left then right, he searched the space urgently before he asked, "Where is the satchel?" Not waiting for an answer, he shouted, "Did you let him take it?"

"Stop screaming at me. Get out of here. I mean it." Cheri didn't know what to threaten him with, so she just glared. A pillow seemed like an inadequate projectile and the only thing surrounding her.

Hunter deflated a little and seemed to notice she wasn't dressed or attempting to get that way with him in the room.

"I'll wait outside. Get dressed. We'll have to go after your lover. I can track him. We must get the satchel."

"Why?"

"It carries something important for your grandfather."

"What?"

Hunter cleared his throat. "Your grandfather is dying. The item he asked you to bring will save his life."

Cheri shook her head. "But he didn't tell me it was life or death."

"Undoubtedly he didn't want you to worry." Hunter gave her a once over as if he wanted to see through the quilt.

Cheri pulled the blanket higher on her neck. "I'll meet you outside."

Hunter retreated out the door, closing it behind him, and left her alone. Cheri gathered her clothing, wondering what she'd done. Why would she sleep with a stranger? *Because you belong with him*, said a voice in her subconscious. She brushed her hands over the quilt.

You're mine. I claim you. Caine's declaration rang in her memory.

Spell or not, she sensed in her bones that Caine was important to her and didn't regret their tryst.

Cheri didn't completely trust Hunter, but unease colored her judgment as she wondered why Caine would take her satchel.

She'd been mesmerized somehow. Perhaps Caine *had* cast a spell on her after all. Oddly enough, she didn't have any regrets about what had happened. It seemed natural.

Cheri shook her head and donned her red coat. Securing the buttons, she took a deep breath, preparing herself to confront Hunter. She couldn't figure out what it was about him that troubled her. Once outside, she shivered, but not from the chill in the air.

"Why did you pull a gun on me back on the path?" Cheri asked without preamble.

"I didn't pull it on you. I heard the wolf coming. Didn't you see him jump on me?" Hunter's eyes widened as if persecuted unfairly.

Cheri nodded as if his answer had satisfied her, but she didn't believe him. "Take me to my grandfather, then."

"We need to get the satchel first."

Hands gripping the hem of her jacket, she asked, "What would Caine do with it?"

Hunter pondered her question, eyes shifting back and forth as if trying to think up a plausible explanation. "He would probably take it to your grandfather's house to taunt him."

Cheri crossed her arms. "Why would he do that? He's not the monster you paint him to be."

"How do you know? Sleeping with him only proves my point. He has bewitched you. You trust him, but not me. Why is that, I wonder?"

Cheri shrugged. "I don't know." She directed her eyes to the ground to avoid his close scrutiny. But she *did* know. It was because Hunter unnerved her. His eyes were dead. Frosty yellow in color and dead. Even glowing in anger didn't make the windows to his soul appealing.

"Are we going to grandfather's house after all?"

Hunter nodded. "Let's hope we make it in time to save him from your lover."

* * * *

Caine rushed through the woods toward his cabin. His gut told him he'd been gone too long. The information regarding the declining health of Cheri's grandfather spurred him to run faster. New plans would have to be made and put in place if her grandfather died before the pack alpha transfer ceremony. Ignoring the pile of firewood he'd dropped earlier, Caine burst through the back door.

Hunter's foul odor assaulted him first. A growl erupted from his throat without warning. Cheri was gone. Caine glanced around, looking for a struggle and finding none. His relief was short-lived when he noticed her coat gone from the peg.

Launching out the front door, he sniffed the air. Catching her scent, Caine took a step in the direction of the ancient trail that led to her grandfather's house, but stopped. Indecision gripped him for only a moment. Scraping his hands through his hair in frustration, he turned from the scent of Cheri's trail and went back into his cabin.

He rushed to the hidden compartment in the floor where he'd hidden the satchel expecting it to be gone. Thankfully, it was exactly where he'd left it.

Caine slung the bag over one shoulder and ran out the back. He knew a short cut through the woods, which would hopefully put him at Cheri's grandfather's house before she and Hunter arrived.

With the 'goodies' from Cheri's pack, the future of her grandfather's life would change dramatically. Caine would die before allowing Hunter to impede his ultimate goal.

With Cheri as his mate, he would assume leadership as the pack's next alpha without a contest.

Chapter 7

Cheri followed Hunter as they tromped through the woods, arriving at the derelict path quickly. Hunter stopped to show her an occasional broken branch as a sign that they were on the right path and following Caine. She dearly wanted to mention that they were on the path she'd wanted to follow in the first place but held her tongue. Her snarky attitude would no doubt make an appearance soon enough.

The further they traveled together, the less Cheri trusted him. His surly demeanor didn't help. Hunter led her along, but Cheri waited for an opportunity to ditch him and look for Caine on her own. She was convinced that she'd find him if she only listened to the voice inside her heart. The lovelorn one still pining for him.

A short time later, the path straightened and became easier to navigate. She and Hunter strolled along in silence. Staying slightly behind him, Cheri watched for any sign or signal from Caine. Not a bird or cricket sounded as they walked along.

The unnatural quiet put Cheri's nerves on edge.

Near a forested hill Hunter stopped suddenly and stepped off the path a few feet. He pulled back a branch and pointed to a tidy little cottage at the base of the incline.

He motioned her to remain silent with a finger to his lips. Together they watched. Only a few moments later, Caine emerged from the bank of trees on the opposite side of the clearing where they hid.

Caine paused and looked in their direction, but after only a second, he continued to the door and entered as if he lived there.

"Why is he going inside?" Cheri whispered.

"Probably to harass your grandfather. Trust me, he's up to no good. You'll have to go in and get the satchel."

"Why me?"

"He'll give it to you, now that you've become so intimately acquainted." He sneered.

"That's none of your business." Cheri narrowed her gaze. "Why were we on the wrong path earlier if the one I chose led us directly to my grandfather's cottage?"

Hunter's eyes widened a moment, but then he calmed. "I moved your grandfather to a hidden location. He's not inside the cabin."

"You have an answer for everything, don't you?"

Hunter pressed his lips flat. "Go get the satchel so we can take it to him. Your grandfather doesn't have much time left."

Cheri wasn't convinced Hunter was telling the truth, but she didn't know why Caine had taken her satchel, either. Her trust in this planet's men flagged.

"I'll get it. Then you'll take me to my grandfather so we can give him what he needs, right?"

"Of course. Now go."

Cheri crept down the hill. Curiosity compelled her to discover what Caine was doing with the satchel. Was he actually taunting her grandfather? She doubted it, since he was a doctor. Doctors didn't taunt people. But then again was he really a doctor?

Entering the cottage, she heard Hunter rustling around on the hill behind her, but she closed the door as soon as she slid through.

Straight down a short hallway, a large room opened up with a beautiful stone fireplace centered against the far wall. Next to the fireplace rested a large brass bed. In it was a very large gray wolf with kindly brown eyes and spectacles perched on his long nose. He wore a brown homespun dressing jacket exactly like the one her grandfather had worn in the vid-phone message sent to her ship.

Trying to understand the scene before her, she spun as the door to the cottage burst in behind her.

Hunter stormed inside, his gun aimed at Cheri. She pushed out a breath. "Are you telling me that you aren't pointing your gun at me this time? Because if you are…I don't believe you."

"The gun is for the wolf."

When Cheri turned back, her grandfather was no longer a wolf but the man she'd seen on the vid-phone. He looked old, ailing and very frail.

Hunter leveled the gun at her grandfather, but Cheri stepped in the path. "I won't let you shoot a helpless old man."

"He's not a helpless old man. He's a rabid werewolf. Remember the wolf at your spacecraft? That's him. He's just shape-shifted to fool you." Hunter nodded once in the direction of the bed, pointed the gun at her head, and motioned for her to move.

Cheri turned to look over her shoulder and saw the gray wolf once again. Twisting back before Hunter could fire off a round, she said, "I don't believe you. He's not the wolf I first saw." The wolf from earlier had been black.

"He's tricking you, Cheri. We must kill him." Hunter lunged forward with the gun cocked.

"No." Cheri shot a spiteful glare in his direction. She grabbed for the gun but he pulled it back out of her reach. She placed her body into the path of Hunter's blaster again and raised her hands in the air. "Put your gun down. You're not shooting anyone."

"Hunter, stop this nonsense." The frail voice of her grandfather came from behind her.

Hunter tightened his hold on the gun and closed his eyes as if trying to decide whether to pull the trigger or not.

"Where is Caine, old man? Did he desert you?"

Cheri kept her body in front of the gun but twisted her head enough to watch behind her. Her grampa sat taller in his bed. "No. Caine isn't a coward like you."

"I know he hasn't cured you yet or you'd have your shifting under control."

"I don't know what you mean." Her grampa clamped his lips tight.

"Caine!" Hunter called out loudly. "Where are you? I have your bitch out here. Bring the satchel or I'll shoot her."

Cheri was sick and tired of Hunter pointing that big honking laser canon at her. Arms still raised over her head, she took a deep breath, leveled another insolent expression and yelled, "Stop pointing your gun at me!"

"Sorry. I can't allow you to give the goodies in your satchel to your grandfather like you gave 'your' goodies to your mangy werewolf lover."

Cheri squinted her eyes in question. "Werewolf lover? What is wrong with you?"

"Didn't you know? You're part werewolf, too, Cheri. When you turn twenty-five, you'll find out whether you'll spend the rest of your life howling at the moon."

A door next to the fireplace opened and Caine entered, carrying her satchel. "Shut up, Hunter. Lower your damned weapon."

The black strap rested over one beefy shoulder. In his hand, he carried a fragile tea cup too small for his big fingers to the bedside night stand. Her grandfather was a wolf again. Caine turned to Cheri. "As you can see, he's lying to you. I haven't shape-shifted into your grampa."

"However, you *are* a werewolf," Hunter growled. "Give me the satchel or I shoot her.

The gun barrel poked her temple. "He's not a werewolf." She shot a look to Caine. "Are you?"

"Once you bear his litter of pups from your tryst in the woods, you'll sing a different tune." Hunter tapped the side of her head with his gun again.

Caine rolled his eyes. "Shut up, Hunter. You know that's not true."

Cheri looked over her shoulder and sent Hunter a malicious glare. "Stop jabbing me," she uttered between gritted teeth.

"I see you marked her as yours, Caine." Hunter glanced at the scratch on her neck, ignoring her snarled demand.

"You marked my granddaughter as yours?" Her grampa was back in human form. The switching back and forth from man to wolf made her dizzy. Her grampa turned a questioning glance to Caine.

Caine didn't respond. He tilted his head to one side and raked a possessive glare down her body. She was his all right. Cheri longed for his hands to stroke her skin.

"Shotgun marriage later. Satchel now or I start shooting," Hunter said.

Cheri held Caine's intense stare and asked, "Does he need what he asked me to bring, or is that a lie, too?"

Caine focused his searing gaze on her face. "He needs it. He has a virus that prevents him staying in his human form. If he doesn't get a dose soon, he won't be able to stop it…permanently."

Cheri turned to her grandfather. "Why didn't you tell me it was life of death?"

Her grampa sighed. "I didn't want you to think it was the only reason I wanted you to visit."

She turned back to Caine. "If he's a werewolf, what am I?"

"Mine," Caine responded leveling a malevolent gaze toward Hunter.

"The satchel or I blow her head off, Caine," Hunter barked. "This is the last time I ask."

Chapter 8

Caine stuck a thumb under the strap at his shoulder and lifted the bag off. He tossed it one-handed at Hunter's feet.

Hunter smiled but didn't look down. Instead, he gave Cheri a blatantly sexual stare from head to toes.

"Shouldn't have left her behind, Caine. I was tempted to overlay your mark with my own. Anyone with ambition will sniff after her until you become the alpha," Hunter taunted. "Or should I say *if* you become the alpha."

Caine glanced at Cheri. "I'll be the alpha."

"You won't if 'Grampa' dies without overseeing the official transfer ceremony." Hunter pressed the gun to Cheri's torso and squatted to grab the bag at his feet. Slinging it over his shoulder, he added, "Now that I have the satchel and the cure, we'll fight to the death for the title of alpha." A sneer shaped Hunter's lips. "And make no mistake. I'll annihilate you in battle."

Caine growled, "Trust me, that won't happen."

Shaking his head, Hunter grinned. "All this could have been avoided."

"No, it couldn't."

"If you had agreed to my terms, he'd already be healed." Hunter gripped the gun tighter.

"Your 'terms' went against our laws. Extortion isn't the way to endear yourself, Hunter. You don't deserve to be the alpha in this pack."

"What pack?" Cheri asked. Arching a brow at Caine, she was lightheaded at what their conversation implied, not to mention the disturbing vision of her grampa morphing from man into a wolf every few moments.

"Tell her, Caine. Tell her how you spend the first night of each and every full moon."

Caine stared at Cheri first then glanced at her grandfather. Cheri returned a searing gaze. She smelled his seductive woodsy scent from where she stood. She *was* like a bitch in heat. Was her grampa really a werewolf? Was Caine? Was she?

"Put the gun down, Hunter. There is no need for any violence." Caine's voice was calm. The deep tone resonated to her already aching core. What was wrong with her? This was not the time to want to leap on Caine's frame and suck his tongue into her mouth, but she found herself gravitating towards him.

Hunter yanked on her shoulder to halt her drift. Caine's eyes narrowed the second Hunter's hand touched her.

Caine leveled his gaze at Hunter. "Take your hand off her or we'll do more than a ceremonial fight for the position of alpha."

Hunter stiffened. "I'm not afraid of you."

"You should be." Caine's hands fisted at his sides. "Touch her again and I'll show you why."

Hunter retreated a step and patted the satchel. "I have what I came for. I'll be back to fight you as soon as the old one expires."

Caine launched forward. Hunter shoved Cheri into his arms.

In an inhuman flash, Hunter escaped out the door, changing into a large white wolf right before her disbelieving eyes. He leapt through the door frame and dropped the satchel outside.

Arms wrapped securely around her waist, Caine clenched her close, fingers digging into her sides. He rested his chin on her shoulder and released a sigh. "I'm sorry."

Through the open front door Cheri watched the newly formed Hunter. Transformation complete, the white wolf picked up the satchel in its teeth and loped off into the woods.

Cheri could have sworn the beast was grinning.

She twisted her head back to focus on being wrapped in Caine's arms. "Did you see that?"

Caine shrugged. "I've seen him change before."

Inhaling a deep lungful of his wonderful scent, she sighed when her grampa changed from a wolf to a man again.

"Damn it, Caine. Release her and go after Hunter."

"There's no need." Caine pulled her away from his chest. "I checked the satchel. The cure wasn't in there."

The deep sigh from Grampa was the only sound in the room. "I guess that settles it then. Call the council. We'll try to get through the ceremony while I can. If not, you'll have to fight—"

"No, wait," Cheri said grasping Caine's shirt. "You don't have to fight to the death."

Grampa huffed, "I don't understand. Did you bring the vial of cure or not?"

"I brought it."

Caine gripped her shoulders. "It wasn't in the satchel."

Cheri leaned in and kissed Caine on the mouth. She couldn't resist. "I know." She reluctantly disengaged herself long enough to open one side of her red jacket.

"I didn't put the cure in the knapsack. I kept it close. It was so difficult to find, I figured it must be important."

"Clever girl." Caine's relieved smile touched her heart.

"Sometimes." Cheri retrieved a small vial of blue liquid from her inside pocket and crossed the room to Grampa's bedside.

Uncorking the vial, she emptied the contents into Grampa's tea cup and handed it to him. "Cheers."

"Thank you." He smiled and sipped his tea with the cure. "I thought I told you to beware of the white wolf."

Cheri smiled and turned to Caine. "It sounded like you said beware of the werewolf. Guess that would have worked too. Everyone is a werewolf. Even me."

Her grandfather finished his tea and placed the cup on the nightstand. "Cheri, I need to explain a few more things to you."

"I'll explain everything she needs to know." Caine enfolded her in his arms.

"Why didn't you wait for Caine at your ship?" Her grandfather crossed his arms. "I told you I'd send a guide."

Cheri laughed. "I wasn't expecting a big black wolf as a guide."

Brows furrowed, Grampa shifted his stare to Caine and huffed, "I wasn't either. Why didn't you go to her in your human form?"

"I had my reasons." Caine led Cheri to the door next to the fireplace where he'd emerged earlier with the teacup. "We'll be back in a few minutes."

Grampa nodded as a smile played on his lips.

In the rustic kitchen, Cheri asked, "Why did you show up as a wolf?"

"I wanted to see how you'd react."

"Oh? A test to see if I was scared of the big, bad wolf?"

"Something like that." He grinned. "You passed when you rubbed my nose and patted me on the head."

"You licked my fingers. It tickled."

Caine leaned closer and whispered in her ear, "For the record, that wasn't the only thing I licked." He chuckled and moved away. "I'm not going to forget that you marked me when you bit my shoulder."

"I'm sorry. I couldn't seem to help myself." Her fingertips brushed over her lips in memory of kissing his shoulder before she sank her teeth lightly into his firm flesh.

"Don't be sorry. I liked it" He tipped her chin up with a finger to gaze deeply into her eyes, his lips shaped into a wicked smile. "Besides that little bite mated us."

She sobered. "Mated sounds very permanent."

He squinted. "Is that a problem?"

"Why did you leave me alone at your cabin?" Cheri changed the subject to avoid answering his question.

Caine rolled his shoulders back. "I'm sorry. I didn't mean to leave you for so long. I went to get firewood, but there was a message about your grandfather getting worse. When I came back, you were already gone."

"Why did you take my satchel? I woke up and thought you'd deserted me."

His hands came up between them as if gesturing capitulation. "I didn't take it. I hid it. The satchel was still in the cabin when you left with Hunter. I grabbed it after you'd already gone. I took a shortcut to beat you here."

"About what we did in your cabin…" Cheri didn't mean to sound so melodramatic.

Caine's spine snapped straight. "Yes?"

"All those things you said about claiming me...does that mean I'm required to be your mate?"

A blank expression washed down his face. "Technically, yes." He exhaled and his body deflated. "Are you sorry?" He picked up his cup and turned toward the sink.

Cheri grabbed his shoulder before he could turn away. "No. I'm not sorry. I just never planned on a permanent relationship. It isn't because I don't care for you."

Caine eased into her personal space. "What is it then?"

"What if I don't want to stay here? I like piloting my own ship and flying through space."

His brows quirked. "No one is asking you to give up your life."

Cheri rolled her eyes upward. "What will happen now?"

He shrugged. "Your grampa will survive, and when he's ready to relinquish his alpha status, we'll go through an official pack ceremony. No one knows this, but he named me his successor regardless of whether you came back in time."

"In time for what?"

"We were promised to each other as children. However, if your twenty-fifth birthday had passed without word from you, I would have been forced to select another female in your bloodline as my mate."

Cheri's eyebrows rose to her hairline in jealousy. "Why?"

"You're a direct blood line to the alpha clan. I'm not. Even though we were informally matched when you were born, the alpha female must be available to accept. After your father died, your mother left the planet with you and no trace of her could be found. In order to qualify as pack alpha, I needed to mate with a member of your bloodline."

"Who else was in the running?"

"In my mind? No one."

"That doesn't answer my question."

Caine's eyes lifted to the ceiling. "You have a couple of distant female cousins here on the planet."

She crossed her arms. "You would have mated with them if I hadn't shown up?"

He pushed out a deep breath. "Eventually or else I would have had to relinquish the title of alpha to Hunter."

"I don't like thinking about you with anyone else."

"And as my permanent mate, you no longer have to worry about it."

"How long will I have to stay?"

"You only have to be present during the ceremony the one time." He pushed a heavy breath out. "Then you'll be free to go." This time he didn't let her stop him from turning around. He stared out a small window over the sink and didn't speak.

Cheri studied his back and released her own sigh. "I have one more question."

"What?"

She stared at his luscious backside. "Why can't I resist you?"

Caine laughed and turned to face her again. "I accidentally marked you when I pushed you down. During the initial few weeks of mating, feelings can be intense."

"I'll say. What if we weren't meant for each other?"

"If you hadn't been attracted to me, it wouldn't have worked. Instead of enhancing your attraction, it would have fueled your distaste. You instinctively made your choice."

"Oh? By ravishing you in your bed?" She grinned.

"No. You chose me when you bit my shoulder and marked me as yours."

"So Hunter knew that at the cabin." Cheri moved closer.

"Yes. Once we were mated, he had to keep you from getting the cure to your grampa. He obviously thought, as we all did, that it was in the satchel."

"And if Grampa wasn't cured to designate a new leader in the ceremony, then you'd have to fight for the position of alpha?"

"Yes."

She nodded. "Would you have to fight as wolves or men?"

"Both."

Cheri pressed her lips flat. "There's another problem..."

"There's no problem." Caine crossed his arms and leaned against the sink.

"What if I don't want to settle down and raise a litter of pups? I have a business. I like what I do."

"You don't have to settle down or raise pups. I'm a doctor. I travel, too. Perhaps we could work out a schedule and travel together."

"A schedule? Travel together?"

"Yes. Will you try to make it work?"

"I guess so. For a price." Cheri smiled and crossed her arms mirroring him.

"What price?"

"Will you let me see you change into a wolf?"

He grinned. "If you'd like."

"Will I ever change into a wolf?"

He shrugged. "We'll know when you turn twenty-five."

Cheri pursed her lips. “Will you still love me if I can’t turn?”

“Of course. Will you still love me when I do?”

“Yes.” Cheri tilted her head to one side. “When you’re the wolf, can you understand me?”

He nodded. “It’s instinctual.”

“Can you speak?”

“Sometimes a word or two if it’s necessary.”

“Like the word ‘run’ when you’re battling an enemy?”

“You’ve asked more than one question.” Caine arched one eyebrow. “I want something.”

“What do you want?”

“My price is a kiss.” He dropped his arms and closed the distance between them. Cheri didn’t stop him when he took her into his arms and pressed his mouth to hers. She couldn’t resist him.

After several lip-licking minutes, Cheri broke the luscious kiss. “Did you say we were promised to each other as children? Like an arranged marriage or something?”

“Yes. I even remember visiting you with my parents a few months after you were born.” He pressed his mouth to hers, swiped his tongue across her lips once and then retreated. He glanced at the top of her head. “Back then you had bright red hair just like your mother’s. I believe I called you Little Red.”

Cheri pulled away slightly and narrowed her eyelids. “If you ever want to see me naked again, I believe you won’t call me that in the future.”

He burrowed his face in her neck. “No problem. I was five, I can certainly let that nickname go for the sake of seeing you naked again.”

Epilogue

Caine became alpha so Grampa could retire. Cheri turned twenty-five, but she never became a wolf.

As promised, Caine loved Cheri anyway just as she loved him.

LITTLE RED RIDES THE WOLF

THE END

WWW.LARASANTIAGO.COM

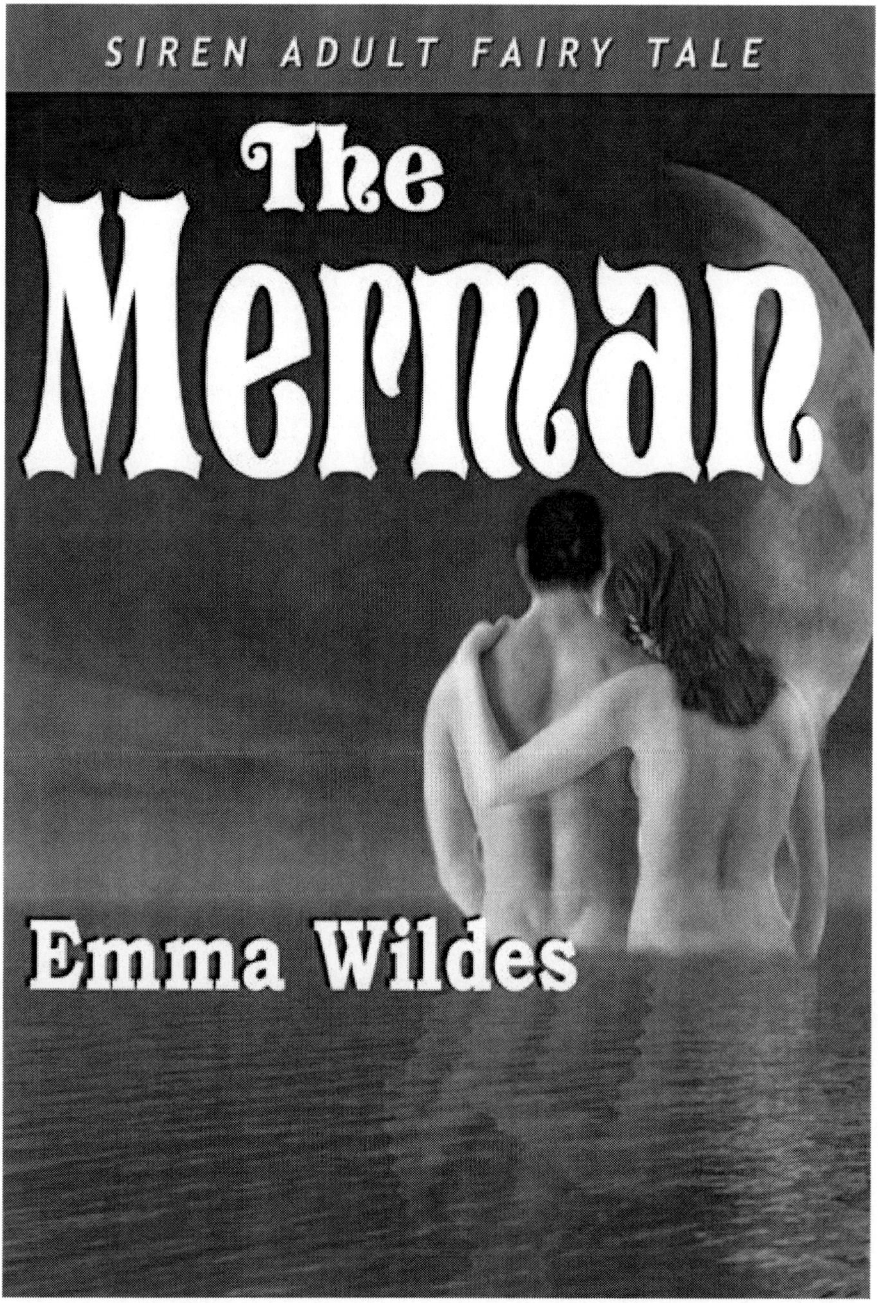
SIREN ADULT FAIRY TALE
The Merman
Emma Wildes

The Merman

Regency Fairy Tale

Is she just lonely or does Lady Cynthia Lucas really hear a phantom voice calling to her in the night? True, the Cornish coast is infamous for stories of the supernatural, but this seems different somehow…and so real.

Or is this a game, waiting to drown her in watery empire where she would find a hollow-hung ocean green, and moss beds under the sea…and the virile lover who waits for her in a hazy, splendid dream?

Prince Armand has no use for poetic words, but he does need a human bride. Destiny has stepped in and he is helpless against the rush of the tide. If he can pull off acting the gentleman and lure the lady into his arms—and the sea—the prophecy will be fulfilled and the merman will find his one true love…

THE MERMAN

The Fairy Tale Collection

EMMA WILDES

Chapter 1

The sound rose, as soft and beckoning as the seductive whisper of the restless sea. Lady Cynthia Lucas sat up in bed, listening, not certain she wasn't still dreaming.

As odd as it seemed in the middle of the night, it sounded like someone outside was singing.

"Come to me, my love…"

Bright moonlight spilled in blocks across the floor and illuminated the room. She slid out from under the coverlet and went to the window, pushing it open a little more. Curious, she stared out over the shadowed formal gardens below. Beyond that the grounds gave to a grassy knoll and the cliffs above the water. Nothing moved, but that melodic song continued, fading and then swelling, the words unintelligible. It was beautiful, if a little haunting, and she felt an almost unwilling fascination.

"*…across oceans blue and deep silver seas…*"

It was a male voice, and so resonant she could not help but feel the echo.

On impulse, she slid over the sill like she had so many times as a mischievous child and began to climb down. The ivy had grown on the walls on the manor house for well over a century and some of the vines were as thick around as her arm, making for an easy descent. Even hampered by her long nightdress, she reached the ground quickly. A little breathless, she glanced around. It was a lovely night, warm and still, and the deserted gardens were fragrant with the scent of overblown roses and moist soil.

And always, always, the ever present tang of the sea.

"...you lure me in..."

In fact, she discerned, the sound seemed to be coming from that direction. Lifting her skirts, she hurried through the formal paths until she reached the gate and quietly opened it. With the familiarity of a lifetime, she skirted the edge of a small wood and sought the path to the cove below, following the sound.

It grew louder, she thought triumphantly, though an inward glimmer of trepidation told her she was being extraordinarily reckless. Somehow she doubted her parents would approve of her dashing off, clad in nothing but a thin gown, to investigate a mysterious noise, no matter how lovely.

Yes, reckless definitely described it, she decided wryly as she ran, but it was a gorgeous night, she loved the sea, and somehow she felt she *had* to find out who was singing so beautifully to her.

To her? Where had that notion come from?

With in inward shake of her head at that romantic flight of fancy, she descended the steep, well-worn way, aided by the brilliant light of the full moon. The cove was a sheltered inlet, cradled by rocky outcroppings on either side, with a small sandy beach and clear deep water. It was a perfect place to swim, and she had learned there at her father's insistence. It might be unfashionable for young ladies to have that particular skill, but early on he had come to the resigned conclusion that in her case it was prudent. She adored the water, and almost from the time she could walk, had escaped—rather like at this moment—to play on the beach and in the waves.

To her dismay, even as she felt the cool sand beneath her bare feet and ran out onto the beach, the singing stopped. In fact, she realized as she looked around, maybe she *was* dreaming. Or sleepwalking, for the cove appeared to be utterly deserted. Besides, it was a ludicrous assumption that she could hear in her bedroom the sound of a person's voice from this far away.

A night bird's call, she wondered, inexplicably disappointed, feeling the light breeze off the glimmering water tug at her loose hair. Or even just the sighing wind whistling through the rocks. It was possible, of course, no, more than that, much more *probable* than some musical human voice in the middle of the night.

Well, that was that.

Feeling a little foolish, Cynthia turned to climb back up to the cliff and the way to the house, when she spied something white sitting a on small jumble of rock near the edge of the water. She picked her way toward it, realizing that it was a man's linen shirt. A pair of boots sat there also, and some dark breeches, the clothing folded into a neat pile.

It was natural to turn and look at the water. She saw nothing break the shimmering surface of the sea and wondered uneasily if the owner of the garments next to her had somehow drowned in such a short amount of time. Surely he would have made some sort of cry if he was in distress? Walking to the very edge, so close she had to lift her skirts as the water lapped around her bare ankles, Cynthia scanned the entire cove for any sign of movement.

A small gasp escaped her lips as suddenly a figure rose from the water not but a few yards away. Waves lapped around his waist, and the moonlit glow reflected from the water gleamed off a muscular torso. More than a little startled at such an abrupt materialization of her quarry, she stumbled a little as she stepped backwards and retreated out of the water.

"Hello," she stammered stupidly.

Though she had expected to see someone, presumably he had not. Still, he didn't seem to be terribly astonished to find some strange young woman in a nightdress on the beach in the middle of the night.

"Hello," he said in obvious amusement, for there was a brief gleam of white teeth and she heard a small laugh.

As usual, she had not thoroughly thought things through. Unfortunately, she had an adventurous nature that her father often pointed out sternly, landed her in trouble now and again. A flush grew in her cheeks as she wondered what on earth to say next to this naked stranger. "I heard singing."

That sounds more stupid than hello. Oh, Lord.

"Did you?" His voice was smooth, cultured, with a singular unique richness recognizable even in just those two words.

In that instant, she knew with full certainty in *had* been him. Her lips parted in surprise as she stared. Dark hair, sleek and long, streamed over his wide shoulders, and his features were aristocratic: straight nose, high elegant cheekbones, and a beautifully modeled mouth that curved upward just slightly in a mesmerizing smile.

The man bowed, which was a little ridiculous under the circumstances and considering he was half in the ocean, but it somehow managed to be a very courtly gesture. "I am Prince Armand, Lady Cynthia, and I believe I am trespassing on your father's property. However, when it was explained to me that this was the best place to swim for miles, I could not resist. Please forgive me."

"You know who I am?" Not certain she had ever been so flustered, Cynthia was hard pressed to be equally polite, all social graces apparently have flown away when he appeared like some mythical creature.

"Slender, with beautiful auburn hair, and exceptionally fair of face. My hostess, Lady Fry, described you very well."

Well, that explained part of it anyway. Lord and Lady Fry resided on the next estate, only a few miles away, and yes, now that she thought of it, there had been some sort of local furor over the fact that an exalted foreign prince would be their guest.

Finally finding some of shred of dignity, she murmured, "Thank you. I believe I heard you were coming, Your Highness. My father and Lord Fry are very good friends. And you need not apologize, for I believe I am the one intruding on your swim."

"No, indeed you are not. In fact, the water is marvelous. Would you care to join me?"

If she had thought she was flustered before, that invitation left her utterly speechless. Did he honestly think she would agree? When she did find her voice, she mumbled, "I couldn't."

"Ah, a pity, but maybe another time. In that case I hope you do not mind if I get dressed?" Without waiting for a reply, he waded out of the water in two long strides.

Entirely nude and apparently indifferent to it.

Though she was certainly stricken with horrified embarrassment, Cynthia found that it didn't override her overt fascination. Rivulets of seawater streamed over the bulge of impressive muscles, his belly was flat and tight, and his legs long and sinewy. He was very tall, she realized, and so beautifully male she suddenly could not breathe. Most certainly she had seen sketches of Greek statues, but that was closest she had ever come to being able to imagine a naked man.

Beyond her will, she let her gaze drop to below his waist. Riveted, she felt her lips part in surprise as she stared.

Good God. Are all men so large?

He stopped in front of her, staring down with an enigmatic expression on his face. With one long finger he caught her chin and tipped it up, so that she had no choice but to look into his eyes. They were unusually clear, almost crystalline—she couldn't tell exactly the color in the moonlight—and thickly framed by dark wet lashes. He said softly, "I have traveled a long way to find you."

* * * *

Her skin felt so infinitely smooth, so warm and alive under the very slight pressure of his fingers. Armand could see the wild beat of her pulse in the column of her slim throat, and the almost panicked reaction to his words in her lovely face. A halo of gleaming reddish brown hair framed her delicate features in alluring disarray, the contrast of the vibrant color and her pale skin striking. The drape of white fabric of what was obviously a sleeping gown did little to conceal her graceful feminine figure.

Lady Cynthia said breathlessly, "I…I beg your pardon?"

Arousal tightened his lower body and she had been shocked enough for one evening. The last thing he wanted was to frighten her. On the contrary, he had come halfway across the world to seduce her. Dropping his hand, he quickly reached for his breeches and slid them on over his growing erection, pleased she had come to him so easily. He gave her a quixotic smile, having no intention of explaining anything quite yet. "I insist upon escorting you home safely."

It was almost amusing how relieved she looked over the fact he had covered himself, but he was worldly and knew she had been more intrigued than affronted. In fact, she had seemed delightfully curious. Lady Cynthia shook her head. "I am quite capable of going alone. There is no need."

"My honor requires I insist." He put on his shirt and fastened it, tucking it into his breeches. His boots he would carry for he refused to fill them with the sand from his wet feet. He offered his arm and lifted a brow ironically. "Unless you have changed your mind about a swim?"

"No," she said hastily and placed her hand tentatively in the crook of his arm. There were two splotches of high color on her cheekbones.

"Very well." He found her chagrin amusing, and even more than that, her innocent but instinctive interest in his body very promising.

The path was a little steep and he led the way with care, relishing the supple sway of her full breasts under the thin gown, and the hesitant and curious glances she sent him under her long lashes. She finally asked him formally, "Will you be staying in Cornwall long, Your Highness?"

"That depends," he answered truthfully. *On you*, he added silently. *How long will it take until you fall into my arms and my bed?*

"Oh."

His evasive reply seemed to rob her of the desire to stir him into further polite conversation, and he sensed she was belatedly realizing that their unorthodox meeting was completely lacking in propriety. From what he'd heard about the very lovely Lady Cynthia—and he had subtly questioned his hostess at every opportunity—she was somewhat impetuous in nature. Certainly running around in the middle of the night in one's nightdress qualified, but then again, he had beckoned her deliberately.

There was a gate in an ornate fence, unlatched and still ajar. Beyond it he could see the looming outline of the big house, all the windows dark at this very late—or very early—hour. His companion slipped her hand from his arm and murmured, "Thank you very much for the escort, I—"

"I must see you inside the house, my lady. I will not be satisfied until I am sure you are safe." He said it firmly, looking into her eyes. They were dark and wide and her cheeks still held a telltale flush.

She shook her head, her long hair moving sensuously across her slender shoulders. "I do not know the customs of your country, Your Highness, but here if we were seen together as we are…it..." she faltered slightly, "…it would be quite a scandal. I am not sure what prompted me to be so impulsive as to leave the house dressed like this."

Dryly he said, "In my country also, Lady Cynthia, a barely dressed woman and a man together in the middle of the night usually has a singular easily guessed implication. In our case however, we are so far completely innocent."

Her mouth was soft and enticingly pink, and her lips parted as she registered exactly what he said. "So far?" she repeated faintly.

Armand reached down and took her hand, gently entwining their fingers. "Come, there is no one about. Let me see you to the house. Tomorrow, I believe, we will be properly introduced, for there is to be a grand dinner party given by Lady Fry. I vow to do my utmost as a gentleman to pretend we have never met and protect your reputation. How is that?"

The warmth of her hand, so dainty and small compared to his, felt delightful. It was easy to see she did not know exactly how to handle his insistence, and when he led her through the gate, she went without any further protest. When they reached the house, she pointed upward and said in a resigned and embarrassed tone, "You will think this most unladylike, but I climbed out my window. I cannot imagine what kind of impression I have made on you."

"I think it is a very resourceful way to come and go as long as you do not break your pretty neck on the return trip." Armand fought a smile.

His beautiful companion tugged her hand free and he felt a small sense of loss. "It's quite easy, actually."

She certainly made it look like it was easy, climbing up the ivy-covered wall with athletic grace. It was his pleasure to watch also, for that activity showed him enticing glimpses of her shapely ankles and calves, and molded the thin material of her gown to her delectable bottom.

Inside his breeches, his cock stiffened, desire swirling through him and centering between his legs. In just the short time it took for her to shimmy over the windowsill in a flurry of lustrous hair and pale cloth, he had a full throbbing erection. For a long moment, he stood there, staring upward, rewarded when she leaned out slightly. He'd felt the unanswered question and wondered if she could contain asking it.

In fact, he wanted her to ask it.

"Was it you singing?" It was a light whisper, barely audible.

Inwardly he smiled and said just as quietly, "Yes."

Chapter 2

The formal parlor tended to get stuffy in late summer, and Cynthia was grateful that her mother had instead chosen the back terrace for afternoon tea. This way she could at least gaze out over the glittering ocean if the conversation bored her, which happened often enough. She really did not have the slightest use for tidbits about the latest fashions. Oh yes, she liked pretty gowns, but having in-depth discussions over them seemed superficial and a waste of intellect.

Though, she *was* agonizing over what to wear later. The prince had been correct. They were indeed invited to the neighboring estate for a celebration dinner given in his honor, and while normally she would have been only mildly enthusiastic, she felt an unusual delicious sense of anticipation.

"…from some place in the Aegean, I believe. It's an island principality and Vivian Fry says she can't even begin to pronounce the name."

Cynthia glanced up, suddenly interested. "Are we discussing their royal visitor?"

Her older sister, Camille, made a small face. She sat primly in a small chair at the glass-topped table, sipping from a porcelain cup. "I take it you were daydreaming again, Cyn. Yes, we were talking about Prince Armand. Word is he is almost too handsome, and a bit mysterious to add to his allure. One of their maids told one of ours that he has the most unusual eyes, the color hard to describe."

He certainly did have unusual eyes. Cynthia well remembered the startling intensity of his clear gaze.

She remembered other things, too. That very male, hard-sculpted body, the beauty of his deep voice, the clasp of his long-fingered hand, which had made her entire body tingle in a very odd way she had never felt before. Cynthia reached for a small lemon tart in what she hoped was an entirely casual movement. "How can a man be too handsome?"

Camille smiled, her pretty face lighting as she dimpled. "I am not sure I know the answer to that, but I am interested to find out."

Their mother lifted a brow, picking up the teapot from the trolley. "From what I have heard, Lord Fry met the Prince while on the Continent on business. I think they have the same banker, or something such as that. When his Highness expressed that he'd always had an interest in seeing Cornwall, Lord Fry immediately invited him. As I understand it, he is well-educated, beautifully polite, and besides his reputed good looks, immensely rich."

"He sounds like something from a mythic fable then," Cynthia interjected, feeling entirely unsettled. If her mother and sister knew that she had seen him completely naked, they would both faint dead away. If her mother knew she had actually stared at his cock instead of immediately looking away, she would stay in a permanent swoon. Yes, Cynthia had been embarrassed, but it hadn't overridden her curiosity. "No man is all those things."

Predictably, her mother ignored that somewhat petulant statement, stirring sugar into her cup with a thoughtful expression on her face. "He does have some peculiarities though. He always travels by water, even if it means days more, and has a self-confessed loathing for certain foods. I only know this because Vivian mentioned it. She said he imparted it in the most charming, diffident way possible, but it is a little odd just the same to not eat beefsteak."

"He's foreign," Camille said with a small languid wave of one pale hand, as if it explained everything and excused the prince his idiosyncrasies.

"Maybe there are no cows in the middle of Aegean," Cynthia remarked dryly.

Her mother looked comically horrified. "Do you think that's true?"

"No." She elevated her brows in patent exasperation. "Remember Crete and the Minoans? The legend of the Minotaur? He was half-bull, half man, so there must be…oh never mind," she broke off, both her sister and mother giving her the same blank look. "I was merely joking anyway."

"Hmm," Camille said as she took a third pastry. "Crete? Legends? You read too much, Cyn. Whatever are you talking about?"

Maybe it was true, for certainly she had some fairly odd notions when it came to the beautiful prince. For one thing, how had he lured her to the cove and why? That evocative song, in a language she had never heard, and his dramatic appearance straight out of the sea, both certainly reverberated with fictional elements. "Nothing," she muttered.

"Well, I for one, am looking forward to this evening," her mother said succinctly. "Vivian gives wonderful parties anyway and the prince will be a nice addition. He sounds fascinating."

Fascinating.

Uneasily, Cynthia wondered if that wasn't just too apt a word.

* * * *

The crowded room made him ill at ease and he hoped it didn't show. Armand was used to open vistas and clear crystal seas, not overdressed aristocrats and simpering young misses hanging all over him.

Where is she?

His gaze went to the doorway, spotted the gleam of lustrous reddish brown hair, and honed in as his eyes narrowed.

Oh, yes.

Absolutely stunning in pale rose silk, her creamy shoulders set off by the low cut bodice of her gown, Lady Cynthia's radiant beauty was unmistakable. Her shining hair was caught in a chignon at her nape, the simple style suiting her vibrant coloring. The older couple she arrived with must be her parents; her father distinguished, her mother still holding a fading loveliness. Another young woman, maybe her sister from the resemblance, chatted in her ear, but he had eyes only for the woman he had waited for all evening.

She was ravishing.

She was *his*.

"Excuse me," he said politely to the small crowd around him, probably interrupting the conversation for they all looked vaguely surprised. With a small bow, he left, making his way toward the arriving guests. Lady Fry, seeing him shoulder his way through the throng, gave a small enthusiastic wave. "Oh, Prince, please meet the earl, his wife, and lovely daughters."

Now *that* would be his pleasure.

Cynthia was introduced last, and when he took her proffered hand and bent over it, he noticed she blushed vividly. Apparently, the impetuous circumstances of their midnight meeting were also fresh in her mind. That was perfect, he thought as his mouth grazed her delicate fingers, for he wanted her to remember every moment. Luckily, the harried Lady Fry immediately had to hurry off to greet another arrival, and they were left relatively alone, even though they were surrounded by a sea of guests.

When Armand straightened, he gave her a lazy, teasing smile. "I am enchanted, my lady."

"To meet me, or just in general?" Auburn brows arched slightly over dark blue eyes, and she asked the question with a tart edge to her voice, though she said it quietly so only he would hear.

Armand could not help it, he laughed out loud. Not only was she strikingly beautiful, but also intelligent. He had wondered how she would feel once she realized that she had been lured out her window by his song on purpose. “Perhaps both,” he responded, still retaining his hold on her hand though he should have released it. “But most definitely I am delighted to be *formally* introduced to such a charming and lovely lady.”

She stared up at him, her cheeks still pink. “I think any credit for being charming is all yours, Prince.”

“If you find me such, that pleases me.”

“I am not sure what I find you.” There was a slight stammer in her words. “But for now, perhaps you should let go of my hand. People will notice.”

He didn’t oblige her, but kept his fingers clasped around hers. “I have very little regard for what others think, Lady Cynthia. For instance, if they come to the conclusion this evening that I find you irresistibly attractive in the way a man wants a woman, it will not bother me.”

Her eyes widened at that frank declaration.

Armand went on in the same almost conversational tone, kept to a level so that only she could hear the words. “As I told you last night, I have traveled a long way to find you.”

“You…you don’t even know me.”

“Ah, but there you are wrong, my lady. I know you in every single way but physically and that will come soon.”

“That isn’t possible. We just met last night.” She looked slightly shocked he would say such a thing, but he also caught a glimmer of excitement in the depths of her lovely eyes.

“It is possible,” he informed her gently. “Our world is a complex place and none of us understand it completely. Take last evening, for instance. I know you have thought about it and now wonder exactly who and what I am.”

Her fingers trembled suddenly in his grasp.

“I could not wait to see you, for I am impatient by nature,” he admitted. “A personal failing, I’m afraid, as you will discover. Come, let me get you a glass of champagne. You look a bit flushed and I accept total blame. Allow me to rectify it.”

* * * *

The evening had a surreal feel to it, as if she were having a peculiar dream. Cynthia took a small bite of fish and automatically chewed and swallowed. Directly across from her, Prince Armand listened very politely to Lady Chadwick's tedious description of her grandchildren, the candlelight playing over his perfect features.

Yes, a man could be unnaturally handsome, she thought as she sipped her wine, covertly studying him. In formal evening clothes, he was more than striking; he was unforgettable. Glossy dark hair fell to his shoulders unconstrained, the thick ebony strands emphasizing the stark masculine beauty of his features. He had absolutely superb bone structure, downy arched dark brows, and those glorious eyes which were the clear hue of a turquoise sea. The color was pure, so vivid, that she had never seen anything like it before, and she was most certainly not the only captivated female at the table. In fact, the prince seemed to have a similar impact on every woman in the room.

I know you in every single way but physically and that will come soon.

For about the hundredth time that evening, Cynthia could feel heat rising into her neck and face as she recalled that very frank declaration. It had been said with complete assurance that shook her a little. She was not unaware that men found her beautiful, and was very much looking forward to her debut in society, when she was expected to choose a husband. However, no one had prepared her for someone like the man across the table.

Instinctively, she knew she would not be able to resist him if he meant it. It wasn't a guess. It was a certainty, and it both frightened and exhilarated her.

Next to her, Mr. Dodds, the local vicar, waited politely for Lady Chadwick's list of progeny to run out, and asked in a lull, "So tell us, Your Highness, about your country. I am a bit of a historian and most curious about it."

Prince Armand looked a little relieved at the change in subject and he toyed with his wine glass, his long fingers graceful and as masculine as the rest of him. "It is small," he began with a deprecating smile on his well-shaped mouth, "but very ancient. The island is populated by the descendants of my ancestors. We live mostly from the bounty of the sea. She is our goddess, and we worship her."

"Interesting," the vicar murmured. "In a true Pagan sense?"

The prince laughed lightly, the melodic sound ringing out. "Well, no. There is no formal religion, actually. Our proximity to Greece, and also to the influences of places such as Constantinople, has left us with an abundance of mixed beliefs. Ships from all over the world pass by, and for time out of mind, it has been that way."

"You have no accent," Cynthia couldn't resist interjecting, for it was something she had noticed, "and speak perfect English."

"No accent?" He looked at her with that crystal gaze she found so disconcerting. "Perhaps that is because I studied both in Paris and at Cambridge in my youth."

Lady Chadwick gave him a playful look. "In your youth? You are still young as far as I can tell."

"I am over thirty," he murmured, still looking at Cynthia. "The men of my kind wait until they are fully mature to take a wife."

It wasn't fair how with just a look, she could react so drastically. Her breasts actually tightened, and between her legs she felt warm. It was both embarrassing and pleasurable.

"Are *you* married?" she asked bluntly, both because she wanted to know and she was rattled. Out of the corner of her eye, she saw her mother's dismayed reaction at the way she blurted out such a personal question.

"Not yet," he answered softly, not looking offended in the least.

The subtle meaning in his voice and the way he looked at her did not go unnoticed. Cynthia saw her father shoot a glance at the prince and then look at her. She had an immediate interest in her wine glass, taking an unladylike gulp.

Thankfully, Mr. Dodds was still intent on finding out more about the history of the mysterious faraway island. "You come from an area of our world steeped in mythology, Your Highness. Do you have any particular legends you would care to share? I have been working here and there on a book about the subject. Old stories, fairy tales, and folklore fascinate me. Luckily, Cornwall has a wealth of such myths, but I want to include tales from all over the world."

The Prince smiled. "We have a unique one, actually, or at least I believe it to be so. Perhaps it came about because of where we live, perhaps because of our love of the sea, but it is a sort of variation of the legend of the lost city that sank so many centuries ago."

"Atlantis?" Cynthia asked, riveted by that compelling smile.

"Yes, indeed." Armand inclined his dark head. "Only in our version, though the city has still sunk beneath the water, it is occupied."

By this time, anyone at the table who could hear him speak was interested. Camille asked, "How is that possible?"

"The notion isn't new," he responded mildly. "For centuries—no even more than that—there have been tales of men and women who are both human and creatures of the sea. Mermaids have ever been in the dreams of sailors, have they not?"

Cynthia had seen the fanciful illustrations in books. "An underwater kingdom?"

"So the story goes." He quoted softly, "Who would be A merman bold, Sitting alone, Singing alone, Under the sea, With a crown of gold, On a throne."

Singing.

Vicar Dodds looked intrigued. "It sounds like poetry."

"It is." Armand picked up his glass and took a small drink.

"I confess I don't know it. Who wrote it?"

"It hasn't been written yet."

Nonplussed, the vicar seemed stymied. Cynthia felt again that almost magical thrill, the sense of touching something unknown and wonderful. "Then how can you recite it?" she asked carefully.

Armand didn't answer but instead merely looked at her, his unique azure gaze amused and challenging.

It was the vicar who finally broke through again. "Prince, I simply must ask you more questions. Would you mind if we met one day during your stay? I need the details of the legend for my book, and to hear it from you is above any research I could possibly do from books. Atlantis! Mermaids! This is wonderful. How long will you be here?"

The night before, Cynthia had asked the same question, she realized with a small quiver. He answered it the same way, not looking at the man who asked it, but at her.

"That depends," he said meaningfully and finished his wine.

Chapter 3

The time had come. It was not just that he felt it either, because despite the late hour, there was still a light in Lady Cynthia's window.

She waited for him and Armand felt a rush of exhilaration coupled with the more intense and complex emotion that was desire. For the past week, he had courted her in all the traditional ways, calling each afternoon, politely conversing with her mother and sister, taking short strolls in the garden, and not so much as stealing a chaste kiss for they were dutifully chaperoned the entire time.

It was killing him, actually.

He simply could not wait any longer and it both intrigued and amused him to sense in her a similar impatience under that ladylike exterior. Cynthia might have been raised as any well-bred young lady, but under the polish of genteel manners and drawing room decorum, a real woman existed, sexually curious and eager to discover the world of passion. One of the things he admired most about her was the adventurous streak that she simply could not keep hidden, and he counted on it to bring her to him.

She also loved the sea. This had been a somewhat shy confession during one of their walks along the shore, and he'd seen the way she gazed out over the dancing waves, as if entranced by the majestic beauty of the scene. The ocean breeze had been brisk that day, and she lifted her face to it as if breathing the salty essence into her soul.

At that moment, he had been tempted to tell her he loved her but worried she wasn't ready to hear it yet. Besides, they had not been alone.

Tonight would be a much better time.

He stood in the garden path, gazing upward, and very softly began to sing in a language long forgotten by ordinary men. In a moment a shadow hovered by the window, and then the drapes were pulled back and he could see the gleam of her rich hair and the pale oval of her face. She listened, motionless, staring downward, until he finished and the last note faded away. For a moment, they simply gazed at each other and then Armand lifted a hand, beckoning her.

Without hesitation, she slipped over the sill and began to climb down. He held his breath until she was close enough he could grasp her slender waist and set her down safely on the ground. Luminous dark blue eyes framed by lush lashes looked up at him in open question, and he smiled and began to lead her toward the gate without saying a word.

It was not very far but it seemed a lifetime before they reached the cove. Armand could feel the beating of his heart in time with the roll of the waves against the rocks, and he already swelled in arousal, his cock filling his breeches uncomfortably. When Cynthia saw the blanket spread out on the sand, she faltered for a moment, for certainly it was a clear symbol of his intentions.

He turned, touching her smooth cheek, running his fingertips along her jaw and down the graceful curve of her throat. "Lie with me."

That persuasive whisper made her tremble slightly, but she said in a hushed voice, "I am ashamed to admit it, but I want to, though I certainly shouldn't." Her soft mouth twisted a little, and she added wryly, "But I have a feeling, Your Highness, you know that quite well. Obviously, you have high hopes of a successful seduction."

He did, but he had the advantage of both experience and foreknowledge. "There is a powerful attraction between us, I cannot deny that. It brought me a very long distance."

"How can that be?" The night sky was speckled with diamond stars and her fragile features were cast in glimmering light. "You have said it before, and I admit I don't understand. There is quite a lot about you I don't understand for that matter. Tell me this, do I have any hope of resisting you?"

Armand looked back at her steadily, noting how the pulse beat fast in her throat. She was more than ethereally lovely with her lustrous hair tumbled to her waist and her voluptuous body gilded by the thin illumination.

"No," he answered truthfully, reaching out to catch an errant auburn curl teased by the wind. He rubbed it between his fingers, feeling the fine silken texture. "But why would you wish to resist me? Do not worry about what is about to happen. Making love is a matter of trust, Cynthia, especially for a female. I vow that you will experience pleasure like you never have imagined when I am inside you." He smiled wickedly and released the lock of hair. "It is a gift of my kind that we are all superior lovers."

"That is a rather arrogant statement." Her voice sounded a little shaky.

"On the contrary, it is simple truth."

"Your kind." she repeated slowly. "I have heard you say it before and always attributed it to the different speech patterns of someone for whom English is not the first language. Most would say, my people, or my countrymen, but you do not."

She was just as bright as she was beautiful and he had anticipated having to explain himself, but he was just so aroused that his preference would be that they talk *afterwards*. His hands spanned her slim waist, feeling the womanly curve on her hips, and he pulled her into his arms with a small groan. The ache between his legs was incessant and desire rolled over him like the rippling tide. He needed to mate with her now.

"My kind," he whispered against her smooth temple, inhaling her fragrance. "That is what I said, and it is what I meant."

Cynthia rested willingly against him, her arms curling around his neck. As he lowered his head, she asked tremulously, "Armand…tell me, are you human?"

"Not entirely," he admitted, and captured her mouth in a searing kiss.

* * * *

His lips were as she had imagined, warm, firm, and the glide of his tongue in her mouth felt both deliciously forbidden and wonderful. It was beguiling, the taste and pleasure of his kiss almost overwhelming.

Lashes drifting lower, Cynthia sank into his embrace as if he hadn't just admitted such a shocking thing, for truthfully, she had come to that same conclusion herself in the past week. It wasn't that she thought he was precisely inhuman—that sounded awful and he was anything but awful—but there was an almost magical aura about the mysterious prince that was both unmistakable and gave the impression of another world.

Was she under a spell? she wondered when he broke the kiss and tugged free the ribbon on the bodice of her nightdress, smoothing the material over her shoulders so it pooled at her feet and left her nude. The way he stared at her bared breasts made her blush, but it also made her feel warm between her legs and a small thrill of excitement curled in her stomach.

One graceful long-fingered hand cupped her flesh, lifting it slightly. His thumb glided over the nipple, making it harden. “Beautiful,” he said in a voice that sounded so thick she knew he was as affected as she was by the caress. “So firm, yet satin smooth, look how it fills my hand. Lie down,” he commanded, indicating the blanket. “While I undress I want to look at you. My dreams did not do you justice.”

She did as she was bid, reclining on her back and feeling the soft embrace of the sand through the wool. Armand undressed in swift efficient movements, taking off his shirt to expose his well-muscled chest and taut abdomen, then his boots, and lastly his breeches. She had seen him naked that first night, but this was different entirely. His cock rose stiffly against the flat plane of his stomach, blatantly announcing his full sexual arousal. She had thought it looked big before but never imagined such a transformation. A little alarmed by the sheer size of his erection, Cynthia tried to move away when he joined her, but laughing, he caught her and moved fluidly so he was on top of her body. Those unusual beautiful eyes held a tender, heavy light that took her breath away. “Do not ever be afraid of me. There is no need. I love you and would never cause you harm or pain.”

Why was she so drawn to him? Cynthia reached up and touched his cheek, very aware of the hot, hard length of his swollen penis pressed against her stomach and her furiously beating heart. “Why do I believe you? Why am I here now?”

“Because it is meant to be.”

Perhaps that simple explanation was true, for certainly it felt wondrous when he kissed her again, and the way his hands began to touch and caress her breasts made her sigh in unconcealed enjoyment as any resistance melted away. Midnight black hair, as soft as ebony satin, spilled across her skin as he trailed his warm mouth lower in a seductive slide that made her cry out when he took one nipple in his mouth, the sensation beyond anything she had ever experienced. Pleasure coursed in waves, small laps of exquisite enjoyment that made her feel almost dazed. He suckled gently, the adhesion of his mouth sparking a divine burst of blissful joy.

Everywhere he touched, her skin tingled, and Cynthia could not stifle the low moans coming from her throat. His hand drifted across her thigh, touching, exploring, and finding the wetness between her legs with deft skill.

"So hot, so womanly, so perfumed with your scent," he whispered in her ear as he began to stroke her sex, parting her labia. "You are ready for our joining, and so am I. My heart races and I am so hard it is almost painful. Can you feel how much I want you, my beautiful lady? I have waited almost two decades for this, most of my life. You have waited for me too, even if you did not realize it. Now, spread your legs and welcome me."

Mindless now, her quivering body needing something she didn't quite understand, Cynthia complied without shame, opening her thighs wide as he positioned himself between them, her hands imploring on his hard shoulders. "Armand," she breathed out in a gasp.

"An ordinary man would cause you pain your first time," he said, staring into her eyes intently. "I will not. Just enjoy, my love, for I am surely going to give as well as take. Pleasure for pleasure, and just the beginning for us."

My love.

He was right too, for as she felt the penetration of his rigid cock stretch her vaginal passage, there was no pain, but instead an almost excruciatingly wonderful sense of possession and physical joy. The loss of her virginity was nothing but a small twinge as he pushed past the barrier and the flooding bliss that held her entire body prisoner seemed to escalate into something completely beyond her control the instant he was embedded inside her. Cynthia arched wildly and gave a low scream of both surprise and ecstasy.

She clung to him as the force of her orgasm made the world go blank, the feeling so intensely marvelous that she couldn't breathe. Armand did nothing but simply hold her, lightly kissing her mouth in soft, tender touches of his lips until her body relaxed slightly.

"That was fast, my passionate lady. You like having me inside you," he said teasingly, his breath warm against her ear as he began to move slowly, sliding backwards until she feared he would slip free, and thrusting back inside so deep she could feel the swollen tip of his hard shaft against her womb.

Of course she liked it, for she never dreamed that sexual pleasure would be so wonderful. "Yes," she admitted, running her hands over the bunched muscles of his back, feeling his power and strength. "You feel…" she searched for the words that would suffice, intoxicated with the rapture of what he was doing to her body. Finally, she gasped out, "Like something from beyond my imagination. Nothing this wonderful can be real, Armand."

In the starlight, his clear eyes looked almost fierce. "It is real, and I am real." He spoke tersely, thrusting faster, holding her gaze. "I am your lover, Cynthia, not an imaginary creature from some fable, and you are mine."

The possessive note in his voice somehow escalated her blissful pleasure, and almost as if he willed it, she felt that peaking burst rise again, to crash over her like a towering wave. He rode this one with her, and as she felt the ripples of her inner muscles tighten around his glorious invasion, he went entirely still. As he climaxed, he whispered something in a language she did not recognize, the words beautiful as they echoed out, and she felt the liquid warm rush of his seed.

Slowly the stars came back into focus, and she could once again hear the low wash of the waves on the beach. Armand held her close, stroking her skin with one long-fingered hand, his face serene and a small smile hovering on his lips. He had shifted slightly to the side, but they were still nestled together intimately, their damp bodies entwined. "If you have questions for me," he said after a long silence in which they regained their breath after such a glorious moment, "I will do my best to answer them now. Before, I was a bit distracted." A low laugh punctuated the last statement. "And as I intend to become distracted again very soon, now seems the right time."

Cynthia wasn't even sure where to start. She rested her cheek against one hard shoulder and waited a moment before she murmured, "Do you really come from a small kingdom on an island in a distant sea?"

"Yes, indeed. I have never lied to you. There are not many of us any longer, but what there are live there together. It is a beautiful place, and you will love it."

She lifted up a little so she could see his expression. “You plan to take me there?”

“Of course. You are my mate.” His smile glimmered. “Would I travel all this way to seduce you and then leave without you?”

His mate?

He answered the unspoken question in her eyes, apparently understanding. “Centuries ago my ancestors began to realize we were in danger as men became more bold and sailed to the corners of the world. There has always been a certain mutual fascination between us and humans, but we were different, and there are just so many more of you. Our females were prized by sailors, and the males hunted, we diminished and were in danger of ceasing to exist altogether.”

As always, the magnetic power of his voice held her spellbound. Cynthia stared at him in disbelief, but then again, the entire evening—her life actually, since his arrival—had held that same surreal impression. “Are you saying you are—”

“Part human, part sea creature, yes.” Propped on one elbow, nude and glorious in his sleek male beauty, he lifted a brow ironically. “But obviously since I look like a normal human male in almost every way, we have succeeded in breeding out one part of us almost entirely. It began when a merman prince fell in love with a beautiful human, rescuing her from a violent shipwreck. As he held her in his arms, he was entranced and determined to keep her. He carried her to our island and married her. It has become a tradition that every one of us take a human bride.” For a moment, his expression became distant. “Eventually one side of us will disappear altogether, but for now, we still hold some of the traits of our kind. For instance, I cannot be away from the water or I would sicken and die. I can stay underwater for hours, and spend a great deal of time in the sea, which feels like home to me. Some foods also, that you find entirely palatable, I cannot stomach, such as the flesh of animals that eat grass, for it is simply not part of my natural diet, which comes from the ocean.”

Surely he wasn’t serious, but on the other hand, she had always felt something different in him, right from the very moment she heard his lilting song. She said faintly, “It is an unbelievable tale.”

“Yet I sense you don’t doubt it.”

"I think maybe I am just losing my mind." She shook her head, not certain how to feel.

"Think of how easily I seduced you," he said in a low voice that made a shiver of longing run up her spine. "And how much you enjoyed it, my lady. My seed is inside you, and even now perhaps we have created a child to share."

That her life had suddenly turned upside down was not in doubt. Armand kissed her throat, and she shivered against him at that light, persuasive caress. Just the touch of his lips against her skin made all doubts over what he had just told her fade into oblivion, banished by potent desire.

"Love me again," she whispered, threading her fingers into his soft hair.

Crystalline eyes gleamed like the stars as he rose above her. "I plan on it, my beautiful lady."

* * * *

The sea whispered her eternal lullaby, the tune familiar and as old as time. Armand rose from the water and walked slowly across the sandy beach, feeling more content than ever before in his life. On the blanket, Cynthia slept peacefully on her side, her nude body both breathtaking and inviting. Her beautiful breasts, so full, and tipped with delicious pink nipples, lifted in a gentle rhythm as she breathed. Tangled auburn curls spilled over her ivory shoulders and down the graceful curve of her back, and the entrancing triangle at the juncture of her slim thighs promised paradise. It would be dawn soon, and he needed to see her safely home, but for a moment, he just stood there and took in her matchless beauty.

Soon, he promised himself, he would mate with her in the tradition of the ancient rite, in the water. Once he entered her in the sea, she was bound to him forever. There was no legal marriage ceremony for his kind but sexual intercourse between a male and female, usually done in the gentle embrace of waist-deep surf, more meaningful than any words or formal procedure could be in his opinion. It was a vow of the most primal kind, and if this evening was any indication, it would be infinitely pleasurable.

His English lady was as passionate as she was beautiful, innocent in the ways of love, but also eager and easily aroused. Standing there and gazing down at her slumbering form, he smiled, remembering how readily she had climaxed the moment he had penetrated her. Human females were susceptible sexually; he'd been taught that from the first time it had been made clear to him that it was his duty to take one as his bride. However, he felt a communion with the lovely Cynthia that wasn't just on the physical level, and for that he was grateful and happy. Like any healthy male, he craved sex, but sharing his life meant more than coupling with his mate for enjoyment and breeding. Luckily, the woman chosen for him was also charming and intelligent.

As he stood there, she murmured something in her sleep, shifting a little with a small sigh. Entranced, he heard her say his name.

Was she dreaming of him even now? That was only fair, considering he had been dreaming of her since the day she was born. It had come to him the first time then, a vision of the woman she would become, and he had waited what felt like a lifetime for her to mature to the point he could claim her.

He dreamed of how it would feel to move between those pale thighs, to thrust his rigid cock fully inside her wet, tight heat, to find that pinnacle of the ultimate pleasure and spill his semen against her womb.

As if they were in tune even as she slept, she rolled to her back and her thighs parted sweetly.

She would take him again, he knew that, and so did his unruly body.

It was almost dawn, he argued with his rising erection, and he shouldn't be greedy. She had already given him exquisite satisfaction several times.

Her lashes, lush and dark, fluttered and lifted. Dark blue eyes stared up at him and for a moment a flash of confusion crossed her face. Then she whispered, "Armand."

He sank down next to her, he could no more help it than breathing air when he was out of the water. "Yes, my love."

"Uhm…I was dreaming."

"I know." He lightly touched her cheek. "Tell me what it was about."

"I was in the water," she murmured, still looking adorably sleepy and tousled. "It was lovely and warm, and the sun was shining." She added huskily, "You were there."

She'd seen the ancient rite.

An indescribable sensation filled his chest. "What were we doing?"

"Making love." Even in the near dawn gloom, he could see her cheeks flush. "And people were *cheering.* What an odd notion."

"Not odd at all," he argued gently, but did not explain. Instead he eased over her so that he rested between her legs. His erection prodded her vaginal entrance with slight pressure as he kissed her. "Come for me quickly," he whispered against her lips, "for we don't have much time to get you home without the scandal you so fear."

"Is that a royal command?" Cynthia asked in an amused but breathless tone, and she ran her hands over his back.

"Absolutely." He pushed fully inside and closed his eyes in sheer pleasure.

"Oh, God." She arched back and took his whole length. "Then, I promise to obey."

She did, he found to his ultimate satisfaction, very swiftly. So did he.

In that moment of perfect sexual fulfillment he saw crystal blue waters in a hollow hung ocean, moss beds under the sea, and felt a joy he'd never known existed.

Chapter 4

Taking a deep breath, Cynthia knocked lightly on her father's study door and heard him bid her to enter. "You wanted to see me about..." she started to ask, but then trailed off when she saw Armand rise politely to his feet at her entrance.

God help her, she couldn't help but blush.

And so she should. She had done the most outrageous things with the man.

Well, no, not man.

Merman. That sounded ridiculous, but as she took in his handsome, perfect features and superb, athletic build, she felt once again the tremor of disbelief the average human could be so beautiful. Even dressed immaculately in a tailored jacket, fitted dark breeches, and polished Hessians, he did not look at all like a proper Englishman. The night before could have been a dream it was so wonderful, but she was sure it hadn't been, and in her heart, that wasn't what she wanted anyway. If her life had dissolved into some sort of bizarre fairy tale, at least it was one of the most pleasurable sort imaginable.

It was true. She had fallen in love with a magical prince.

Her father had also stood, and he motioned her to a chair. His face was a little stiff, and he looked decidedly disconcerted. "Hello, my dear. There is something apparently we need to discuss."

Oh Lord, did he know about her indiscretion? Well, she should face it. It was several indiscretions. Wonderful, erotic indiscretions, but nonetheless she knew her proper father would not understand.

Taking a seat, she said faintly, "Oh?"

"The Prince," he murmured as he also sat, "has petitioned me for your hand in marriage. I pointed out, of course, that you have known each other little more than a week, but he was adamant we should ask you how you would feel about such an arrangement. I decided to bow to his confidence."

She gazed into Armand's clear azure eyes and felt her mouth curve into a soft smile. "The Prince has a great deal of self-assurance, but then again, he is unusual in every way."

Armand inclined his dark head, his mouth twitching in amusement. "One needs a bit of daring to court a spirited woman."

"One needs a bit of daring to contemplate marrying a foreign prince and going halfway around the world," she countered quietly, though they both knew her answer would be yes.

"I understand that." His expression softened. "It is a matter of trust."

That was exactly what he had said to her about their lovemaking. "But some things are meant to be," Cynthia murmured, remembering rapturous pleasure and tenderness.

"Exactly."

Her father cleared his throat. "My enthusiasm over having my daughter live so far away is limited, Your Highness. I am sure you understand that."

"Yes, Lord Hughes, I do understand." Armand cocked a brow. "When my own children leave, I am certain I will feel the loss very keenly, but it happens, doesn't it? Eventually, they mature and find their destiny."

Was this her destiny? A life more fable than reality? Cynthia wasn't sure, but she was certain of one thing, if she were to never see Armand again, she would be utterly desolate and lost. She was also sure that never would she find such pleasure, such fulfillment, in the arms of any other man.

Well, any *man*, she acknowledged with an inner grimace. Good heavens, the whole idea was so hard to get used to, but he didn't exactly fit into that neat category.

Mermaids? Beautiful half-women who swam in the sea? Gloriously good-looking half-men who were also part of another world and traveled great distances to claim human brides?

Preposterous.

Or was it?

"Yes, I want to marry him." The words came out almost involuntarily because truthfully, she had made her decision the night before when she had lain beneath him on the beach. Or maybe it had never even been up to her, but if that was the case, she wasn't arguing with the outcome.

Her father looked resigned. He muttered, "I had the oddest feeling you would say that after this past week of watching the way the two of you look at each other. I suppose, then, I should offer my congratulations to you both. Denying my blessing seems like a futile cause."

"Thank you." Armand smiled, but looked only at her.

Warmth shot through her body, centering between her thighs. She'd seen that provocative look before.

"Is the legend true?" she asked, forgetting her father for a moment and looking at her lover. "Is the city under the sea inhabited?"

"I will show it to you and you can judge the legend for yourself."

Cynthia felt flushed at once, but he had that predictable effect on her. "I cannot wait to see it."

Her prince lifted his brows, and his voice was full of meaning. "We will swim in the clear water together…and everyone will cheer, knowing I have brought home my bride."

Her dream. Soft gentle waves, and his body joining with hers, pleasure flooding her senses as they became one…

"Cheer?" she repeated with a tremor in her voice.

"It is our custom," he explained, lounging in his chair with cultured royal nonchalance, looking relaxed and impossibly handsome.

"I suppose my new life will take some getting used to," she managed to say in a reasonable tone, the idea of sexual consummation in front of a crowd more than a little daunting.

"I will do my very best to make sure every moment is memorable." He rose and came over to take her hand. The moment his lips brushed her knuckles, she felt a small thrill of physical pleasure.

Mythical sunken cities, sunlit islands…and Armand. Yes, she was sure it would be memorable.

THE MERMAN

THE END

WWW.EMMAWILDES.COM

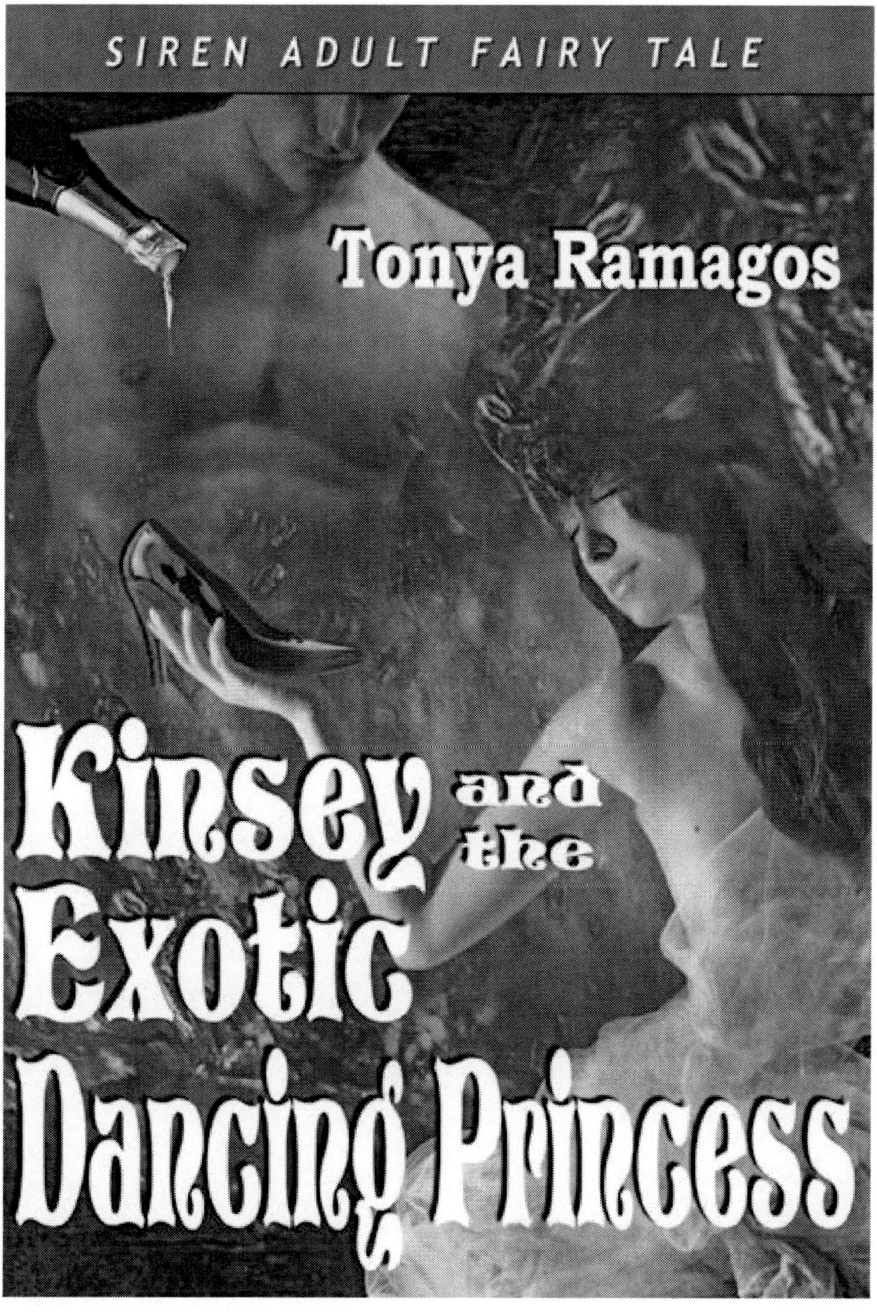
SIREN ADULT FAIRY TALE
Tonya Ramagos
Kinsey and the Exotic Dancing Princess

Kinsey & the Exotic Dancing Princess

Contemporary Fantasy / Erotic Fairy Tale

Being a princess isn't all it's cracked up to be. Even as she reaches adulthood, Princess Damita feels suffocated by the king and queen. Damita longs to experience life as a normal woman. She sneaks from her room at night and finds her way to the neighboring village.

Soon the king discovers that Damita is up to something and issues a proclamation.

All Kinsey must do is discover where Princess Damita spends her nights and he will be rich, but will he be richer with Damita as his lover?

KINSEY AND THE EXOTIC DANCING PRINCESS

The Fairy Tale Collection

TONYA RAMAGOS

Chapter 1

The king's anger pierced the air like a razor sharp dart. Princess Damita crept to the partially open door of her parents' bedchamber and listened with bated breath. She could just see her mother, the queen, through the crack in the doorway. Though she couldn't see her father, she heard his voice loud and clear.

"She has been leaving her room at night," the king raged.

"How can she when you lock her door from the outside every evening at dusk and do not unlock it until just before dawn each morning?" the queen asked in the reasonable voice Damita heard so often from her.

"I know not but I assure you I will find out. You defend her, yet how do you explain *these*?" A hand shot out, thrusting a pair of shiny black heels into the queen's arms. "Look at the soles so worn, the heels scuffed. Look at the toes scratched beyond polish. Explain to me how this can be if she is truly remaining locked in her room all night."

The queen's gaze darted almost imperceptivity to where Damita eavesdropped in the hall. "I cannot."

"She has found a way out of that room," the king insisted. "I will find out how. I will find out what she does by the light of the moon."

"What do you intend to do, my King? Surely you can not keep watch over her throughout every night."

"No. I will not."

Damita saw his tall, robust figure pass the slightly open doorway then disappear from sight only to pass once again mere seconds later. His chin tucked in his hand, head down as he paced, he didn't look toward the door where he surely would have spotted her listening. Her heart pounded hard in her chest, and her pulse was almost deafening in her ears. Fear blossomed deep in her stomach even as her mind rebelled further against her father's heavy rule. She would not give up her nocturnal life.

"I will send a messenger to the village," the king said in a contemplative tone. "Yes. Yes. He will spread the word."

Again the queen shot a fleeting glance at the doorway. "What word, my King?"

"I shall offer a bounty. The man who can tell me what our daughter does each night when she is trusted to be safely asleep behind her bed curtains will be rewarded with his weight in gold."

"You are to have men spy on our daughter?" The queen sounded appalled by the idea.

"Three nights should do it." The king passed the doorway and Damita shrunk back but not before she saw the determination in his walk, the confidence in the set of his shoulders. "Any man who wishes to try will be given three nights in which to solve this little mystery."

"And if he should fail at the end of those three nights?"

The king fell silent but only for a moment before he replied, "He shall become my slave until such time as he has worked off an amount equal to his weight. I should think one week per pound should do."

Damita thought about her father's plan with a growing dread. If a two hundred pound man decided to attempt the quest and succeeded, he would gain two hundred pounds of gold. To any man in the land aside from the king himself, that amount of gold would set the man and his entire family for life. And if he failed? She did the quick calculations in her head. Well, at one week per pound even a two hundred pound man would only be forced to spend three years and eighty-four days as the king's servant. Not so much to risk when one looked at what he could gain should he accomplish the task.

Silently, Damita crept away from the door and returned to her bedchamber in the north tower of the castle. She encountered no one on her short journey there so she needn't worry about questions arising as to her goings on near the king and queen's quarters. Once inside the sanctuary of her room, she began to pace much like she had seen her father do. Her mind reeled, and different scenarios played out in her head, some good and some bad, as she attempted to figure out what to do.

The shoes. How could they not have thought about the shoes? It seemed so obvious now. Though, in their defense, neither she nor her mother ever expected her father to inspect her shoes. She guessed that's what she got for underestimating the king. She would do good not to let that happen again.

She stopped before a full-length mirror and stared at her reflection as she glided one finger alongside an obscured button on the wall to the right. Ingenious really, that button, she thought. No one, not even the king, knew that bump in the stone wall was really a trigger that when pushed would cause the mirror to swing away from the wall to reveal the narrow, secret passageway it concealed. Even she had not known about the tunnel that lead underground and she lived her entire life, her nights virtually as a prisoner, in this bedchamber.

But the queen knew of it. When Damita came of age, her mother told her of the passage. It became a secret between Queen and Princess, mother and daughter. Her mother didn't know exactly what she did outside the castle walls nor where she went and never asked. The mere fact that Damita left the castle grounds each night was one of the few secrets they were ever able to share and keep. Now their secret was in danger. What to do? How could they keep the secret now?

A knock sounded outside the heavy bedroom door and Damita spun from the mirror. Before she could say anything, the queen hurried into the room and shut the door behind her.

"Mom," Damita cried and rushed to the queen, threw her arms around her neck. She didn't care that it was a childish gesture. She only wanted to feel close to her mother at that moment, to be comforted.

"I only have a minute, my sweet princess," the queen said softly. She brushed her lips in a chaste kiss over Damita's forehead and stepped back, the better to see her daughter. "You heard everything." It was a statement and not a question for the queen knew Damita had in fact heard it all.

Damita nodded. Her eyes grew warm with a rush of tears, and she blinked them away, unwilling to show her weakness. "Leave it to him to find the one detail we overlooked."

"He only has the best in his heart for you, Damita. You know that."

She did know. The king loved her implicitly. Making sure she was watched over by day, leaving her in a locked bedchamber by night…everything he did was merely his way of protecting his Princess. If she felt smothered by his affection, she simply hadn't reached the mature age of understanding. Lucky for Damita, the queen disagreed.

"Please don't tell me I must stop going out at night," Damita pleaded. "I will find different shoes so he won't get suspicious anymore. I'll go barefoot if I have to."

"No. You mustn't change a thing. If you stop wearing the shoes now your father will become even more suspicious."

"But he intends to have me followed!"

"He is giving the messenger his orders even as we speak."

Damita hung her head. A feeling of hopelessness too powerful for words tightened her throat. "Then I must stop going out."

"And make you father look like an absolute fool to the whole kingdom? No. I say again Damita, you must not change a thing."

"Then how are we to continue to keep our secret? Once he posts the first man outside my door all night, he will learn I have found another way out. I will not be hard to follow after that."

"My darling, Damita. Have you lost all faith in your mother?" the queen asked, her tone more mocking than sympathetic by the thought.

"Of course not!" Damita had all the faith in her mother a girl could have. The queen was her only ally in a castle of controlling love, the only one who understood a girl's need to grow and explore, to have a few secrets all her own. She also possessed a conniving mind that deserved envy and admiration. "You have a plan."

"It won't take long for the first hopeful man to respond to the king's challenge. A few years as servant in this castle is nothing to risk when there is so much to be gained. I expect your first stalker to arrive tonight, tomorrow evening at the latest."

"Stalker?" Damita raised a brow and couldn't stop the grin that came to her lips.

"He will be looking after his own well being, not yours. He will care not what happens to you should he report the truth of your mischief to the king. It is for that reason," she lifted a hand, glided the back of her fingers down

Damita's cheek, "and my love for you, that I will help you escape his eye and any that come after him each night."

“You speak as though you know where I go, what I do each night.”

The queen smirked. “You do underestimate your mother, Damita.”

She didn't bother to ask how her mother found out. Instead, she asked, "But how am I to escape the watchful eye of my stalkers?"

"Sleep is a very peaceful and freeing thing, my dear Princess."

And so it began. The very next evening the first stalker, as the queen termed him, was shown to the chamber next to the one where the princess lay. Damita had a moment to study him. *Pure skin and bones*, she mused in pity. When did the man eat last? She relaxed in the thought that even if he did somehow manage to follow her, his lack of nourishment and apparent weakness would prevent him from getting far.

Sure enough. Not long after the queen delivered the stalker's meal for the evening, Damita heard him snoring loudly in his bedchamber. She didn't question why the queen herself chose to deliver the man's food, couldn't find an ounce of compassion for the years he would spend as servant in the castle should his next two nights on guard duty turn out as this one would.

Then again, it could be exactly what the man needs, she thought as she slid her arms into the long cloak she had taken to wearing over her dance clothes and clipped her feet into the latest set of brand new heels. At least if her stalker became a servant in the castle he would be guaranteed three square meals a day. No one went hungry under the king's roof.

With one final glance at the sleeping, would-be stalker, she hurried on tip-toed across her bedchamber to the full-length glass. A light push of the concealed button, a quick step to the side as the mirror swung open to reveal the dark passage and she was off for her nightly journey to the village where she would dance the hours away.

Chapter 2

Kinsey tugged on his horse's reigns and muttered a few soothing words of encouragement. How ironic, he thought, that he was the one injured, the one who might very well walk with a limp for the rest of his life and yet he was the one doing the pampering and gentle prodding. Waldo needed new shoes and Kinsey couldn't remember exactly when either of them last ate a complete meal. Unfortunately for both, neither shoes nor food came free and Kinsey's pocket that once jingled loudly with silver had gone silent long ago. He had but one silver piece left and, injured as he was, no real prospect of replenishing his pockets until the news of the king's challenge reached his ears.

Solve the mystery of what the princess does at night, where she goes. How hard could that be? he mused as he and Waldo trampled through the forest toward the king's castle grounds. It surprised him that so many had befallen to slavery rather than lining their pockets with gold from such a simple task. If word through the kingdom rang true, a dozen men attempted the quest thus far, each falling asleep on their three nights only to awake with nothing to report to the king come morning. The king now had a dozen new servants but still no answer to his mystery.

A dozen men, Kinsey thought again. He found something odd about that, for it seemed far too coincidental that twelve men would all sleep through the night and never once hear the princess as she got up to her mischief.

"Unless they were tricked," he muttered. He stopped in the middle of a small clearing. One hand idly smoothed Waldo's head while the other massaged his knee in a gesture so common now that he hardly realized he did it.

"You think that's it?" he absently asked Waldo. The horse whinnied. "Yeah, me too. But how? Maybe the princess promised not to do anything while the man took a short nap," he considered. His hand moved to Waldo's reigns, gripped them tightly and they began their slow walk through the forest once more.

"Naw," Kinsey continued to think aloud. "Only a fool would believe such a promise." Yet, hadn't all twelve men been fools of some caliber? To have fallen asleep three nights in a row, each surely aware of the fate that befell his predecessor. Could the princess really be that sneaky, that patient? To wait it out until her pursuer became so exhausted he could no longer fight the sleep and then to sneak out of the castle, off the grounds without ever causing him to wake?

He ignored his stomach when it grumbled, intent on pinning down the princess's trick before he reached the castle grounds. She was no dammed magician, he knew. She couldn't simply vanish from a locked bedchamber at the snap of her fingers or the wiggle of her nose and appear miles away somewhere. So how did she do it?

He fell into an almost meditative state as he limped along, careful of holes and thorny branches. When his stomach growled a second time he merely pushed the hunger from his mind once more. He didn't have time to worry about something he could do nothing about. Surely once he reached the castle, faced the king and accepted the challenge he would be fed. The king was known by all to be quite generous to those under his roof after all.

Kinsey stopped so abruptly that Waldo walked into his back even as a low hanging branch slapped him in the face. His cheek burned immediately, a sure sign the branch had given him at least a surface scratch, but he merely covered it with his palm, his mind elsewhere. Food was the key, the trick. He would be served food all right, but that food would be tainted with something sure to put him in a peaceful, oblivious slumber right through the night and into the morning.

"Looks like there isn't any food around the bend after all," he said to Waldo. "At least not until we can buy it with our own gold awarded once we report the princess's goings on to the king."

And he would, he thought with a growing determination. Before his injury, he had been a solider, one of the best. A man didn't gain that reputation, didn’t survive battle after battle by being a naïve fool. It may have been days since he last ate well but his mass remained heavy, his muscles solid. Muscle, after all, weighed more than flesh. He *would* reveal the princess' secret. He wouldn't allow himself to think about why the king locked her away each night, why she chose to deceive her father by sneaking out. All he would think about was how she pulled it off, where she went. He would tell the king and collect his weight in gold as promised.

He wasn't surprised when he reached the castle just before dusk to be so well received. He informed the servant who opened the door of his business and moments later found himself facing the king. A plump man, Kinsey thought as he surveyed the king and couldn't help but wonder how many years of slavery his weight would equal. Certainly far more than Kinsey even with his hardened muscles and considerable height.

That height had Kinsey looking down at the king. Not good to look down on royalty, he thought but until offered a chair he hadn't much choice. The king didn't seem to mind though and actually beamed—his plump cheeks reminding Kinsey of two freshly ripened strawberries—as he craned his neck to look up at Kinsey.

"You have arrived just in time," the king said with a noticeable nod toward a nearby window. The last golden glimmers of the sun were barely visible as the darkness overtook them.

"A long journey, your majesty, and not an easy one." Kinsey glanced down at his injured knee. It hurt like hellfire and would likely be dammed near immobile by morning after he followed the princess. Yet, such pain and temporary handicap would be a small price to pay once he received his reward.

"Your knee soldier, were you injured in battle?" Kinsey focused his attention on the voice, the woman…the queen. Surprise made him stare impolitely for a long moment. He had heard of her beauty in his travels through the neighboring villages to the castle, but no words seemed to do her justice. Hair long and glimmering black, eyes as blue as the sea, and a figure that made the mouth run dry. He looked back at the king before he could catch himself and thought of just how blind love could truly be.

Not love you idiot, he thought, *but money, power*. One look at the odd couple the king and queen made and he knew he had to be right. *And what of the princess*? he wondered. Had she gotten her looks from her plump and rosy father or her striking mother? Few in the villages ever saw the princess for she rarely left the castle grounds, and when she did it was under heavy guard and disguise. He didn't know why the need for such mystery. Apparently, Princess Damita's whole life was a mystery.

"A battle, yes, my lady. A very vicious battle in the far kingdom."

"You arrived with a horse yet you chose to walk with an injured leg rather than ride. Why?"

"The journey was not easy on my horse either, my lady. His shoes have worn thin. Better that I endure a bit of pain rather than destroy his hoofs and legs by making him carry me."

"Your concern for your horse is admirable, soldier. I will see to it that Waldo is given a sound meal and new shoes."

"Many thanks, my lady," Kinsey bowed.

The queen seemed to study him, her gaze scrutinizing. "You have been hurt before soldier."

"Yes my lady, many times."

"Yet you return to battle at the first opportunity."

"I am a solider. I am sure you know what they say about men such as I. All muscle and no wits."

The queen's lips twitched but she didn't smile. "And you will fight again when healed."

"If the Gods see that I am able." Kinsey nodded, suspicion growing inside him like a slowly inflating balloon.

"He will have no need to fight come morning for he will have enough gold to start his own war." The king grinned and dimples appeared in his plump cheeks.

"Your confidence is inspiring, my lord."

"I hope that it is. I grow tired of men failing at this task." The king sighed. "Because of this I have decided to up the reward. Should you report to me before the end of the three allotted days with the answer I am looking for, you will receive double your weight in gold."

"Double, sir?" Kinsey repeated, awestruck. His weight in gold was already more than he thought the opportunity to earn in a lifetime. The idea of double his weight in gold left him completely flabbergasted.

"But," the king held up a heavily jeweled finger, "should you fail, you will spend the rest of your life as my servant."

Kinsey barely heard the consequence over the roar of excitement in his ears. "I will not fail, my lord," he said confidently and looked to the window again. The land was now fully dark. "If the king and queen would be so kind…"

"Yes, yes. You shall be shown to your chamber now." The king gestured for a waiting servant with one gallant flourish of his arm.

The man stepped to Kinsey's side, assumed a parade rest stance—hands behind his back and feet shoulder width apart. Was this one of the dozen who attempted the quest and failed?

"You shall dine on a feast brought to your chamber while you await your task to begin."

Chapter 3

Damita just managed to convince herself that she would get an evening without worry or concern when she heard heavy footsteps pass outside her door and enter the chamber to the right of her own. She waited until his tray of food was delivered, until all voices ceased, until she heard the soft rap outside her door—her mother's signal that all ran smooth—then she hurried to the wall that separated the two chambers.

Intrigue and curiosity made her peek through the small, secret hole bore some time ago through the stone. It was through that hole that she watched twelve men arrive in three-day intervals in the past months, held her breath as they ate their fill of the tray her mother brought to them, smiled when they curled up on the canopy bed and fell fast asleep.

Tonight, she looked in on number thirteen and felt her stomach dance with desire. Beauty and sheer male exquisiteness met her vision. Not looks like that of the pretty boy, she mused and thought of the rather handsome man who had actually believed that one look at him would actually cause her to reveal all her secrets and even possibly pledge her undying love. Men could be such idiots.

But this man…Well, this man might be worth a secret or two. Not her biggest secret, of course. Not the one secret that every man in the land seemed hell bent on attempting to find out—and failing miserably, she smirked. But surely she could come up with a couple of other secrets she could share.

She lost herself in the entertainment of long legs and lean hips, trim waist, wide back, and broad shoulders. She stifled a moan of appreciation when he removed his shirt, treating her to a bare view of that back, those shoulders. His skin had the deep tan of a man who labored in the sun and the faint scars she could just see only added character. Her fingertip itched to trace those scars—the long, thin line that looked to be made by a sharp tool or blade maybe. The rounded, jagged edged patch just below his shoulder blade that appeared to be a bullet wound.

No, this man was no pretty boy, she decided as he turned and finally afforded her a view of his front. The rippling muscles in his back continued in his biceps, his chest and abs, as did the scars. His face had a chiseled, rugged appearance even with his rounded chin, heart-shaped lips and predominate cheekbones. Through the tiny hole in the wall, she couldn't tell the color of his eyes but she guessed they were dark...chocolate brown or even ebony to match his hair.

She wondered briefly what it would feel like to run her fingers through his hair, skim her hands over his chest. She fantasized about him brushing those lips over her flesh, kissing her, and licking her everywhere his tongue could reach. Then she brought her daydreaming to an abrupt halt because even her standing as princess couldn't make those dreams a reality. Not unless she wished to give up all that she had become, all that she wanted, and face her father's wrath. A quick roll with a man—even one who made her panties wet simply by removing his shirt—wasn't worth such a price.

But love...Yes, love would be worth any price. She sighed wistfully and stepped away from the hole. It was no use going there either. That man wasn't out for love. He looked for money and nothing more. In a matter of minutes he would eat the tainted food the queen served him and fall fast asleep like all the others. Then she would be on her way and in three nights her father would have another servant to add to his quickly growing collection.

* * * *

Kinsey knew she watched him. He felt her gaze on him, felt the hairs on the back of his neck stand on end not long after he entered the bedchamber. He knew her chamber to be next door, guessed she must have a peephole somewhere in the adjoining wall. Because he knew, he carefully kept his back to that wall as much as possible.

He considered giving her a real show. Especially when he thought he heard a soft moan as he took off his shirt. He had been tempted to remove the rest of his clothes then turn to face the wall, to face her. The idea to jerk off for her even crossed his mind, but he resisted the urge. Something like that was not a show fit for the eyes of a princess.

He nearly decided to attempt to talk to her but he heard her shuffle, heard her wistful sigh as she stepped away from the wall just as he turned, opened his mouth to speak. He figured she waited for him to settle down and eat. If he possessed any doubts about the food being used to put the quest-seekers to sleep, all suspicions were confirmed when the queen herself delivered his dinner tray. How often, he wondered, did the queen play servant?

He didn't eat, of course, though he badly wanted to. The meal he had been served was one fit for the king. Yet, instead of indulging on a single bite, he moved the tray across the room and out of sight of the peephole should the princess decide to steal another look. He waited what he figured to be the right amount of time for a sleeping potion to absorb in a body his size, then sprawled across the canopy bed and pretended to sleep.

* * * *

Damita fell into a bit of a rhythm—pace to the mirror, over to the wall to glance at handsome number thirteen, then stomp to the mirror once more because he hadn't yet fallen asleep. By the time she finally heard him begin to snore, she'd nearly worn a permanent trail in her bedchamber floor.

"About dammed time," she muttered and rushed to her armoire, reached in and pulled her dance clothes from the hiding spot beneath old dresses. She changed quickly, covered herself with the traveling cloak then peeked one final time through the hole to be sure all remained safe.

His hardened features relaxed in sleep, he looked peaceful and harmless. He hadn't put his shirt back on before climbing into the bed. The sight of his bare chest once more made her mouth water, her juices flow. It could have been worse, she guessed, he could have chosen to sleep naked.

She let her gaze skim his body. Not that she would mind if he slept naked, she decided. The man did have one hell of a body. Her gaze stopped on the rise of his crouch and she nearly let out a low whistle before she caught herself. She had been too distracted by his chest and all his gloriously hard, toned muscles to notice and, looking now, it didn't seem possible that she missed it.

Her pussy contracted as she studied his sizeable bulge and she thought of how it would feel plunged inside her. By the time she tore her gaze away, her pussy lips were slick with her warm juices, her nipples taught and throbbing and she was running late for her journey. She took a half step back, blew a kiss to her sexy, sleeping stalker and promised herself she could take out her sexual frustrations on the stage.

* * * *

She moved with the grace of an angel and the seductiveness of a harlot. He hid in the shadows, watched and knew he found trouble when he began to want. He wondered in awed astonishment where she learned such moves. Where had a woman, a *princess*, learned to tease in such a way? The music that played was an interesting mix of horns and drums, the beat fast yet oddly melodic. She knew the music, the tempo and never missed a step as she glided across the stage.

She stomped, slid, dipped and twirled and left no doubt as to how she ruined each pair of shoes that led to her father's suspicion. Her legs carried her steady and sure with each move. Her hips swayed, gyrated and fell into a hypnotic rhythm that put Kinsey into a trance.

She wore a strapless dress of virgin white lace. The bodice fit snugly to her small but perfectly rounded breasts and her dark erect nipples were clearly visible through the sheer material. The skirt hung freely, billowing out when she turned, and clinging to her curves when she grasped the sides in her hands and pulled it tight. When she danced to a pole at the center of the stage and wrapped one leg around it, he saw that she wore only the thinnest strip of white satin for panties.

Wet satin, he realized and watched with a growing pain in his cock at how that satin formed to her pussy lips. His hands itched to touch. His tongue longed to lick, eat, devour. Her beauty was far more powerful than he could ever dream, her body far more alluring and inviting than what was good for him.

He watched as she slid down the pole, spun herself around it, and gyrated her hips against it. Men of varying stations from the poorest peasant to the most well dressed of the land short of the king surrounded the stage, their gazes transfixed with the hottest of erotic fantasies showing in their eyes as they gaped at Princess Damita.

Kinsey wondered how they did not recognize her as the princess. Then in the next heartbeat he figured he would not recognize her either had he not first followed her from the castle. No one would expect to find the princess masquerading as an exotic dancer by the light of the moon in a village far from the castle grounds.

The song ended and a slower, more seductive tune began. Damita abandoned the pole for this song, choosing instead to pretend she danced with a partner. Her hands held palms out in front of her as though they rested on a man's shoulders, she followed the lead of her imaginary partner around the edge of the circular stage. Her feet shuffled gracefully with each step. He thought he might like to dance with her at a ball. He could be pretty light on his feet too, after all. When his knee wasn't paining him, that was.

He sunk deeper into the shadows as her dancing brought her closer. She saw him. He knew she could make out his silhouette in the darkness. For a moment, he held his breath, worried that she would recognize more than his outline. How well had she been able to see him through that peephole of hers back at the castle? Had she seen him well enough to recognize him now in a place she wouldn't expect to find him? She thought him to be back at the castle sound asleep after all.

He knew he should make his way back to the castle. He had solved the mystery, discovered where the princess spent her nights, what she did while there. He could take a souvenir from this pub as proof, return to the castle and come morning he would report his news to the king and collect his riches.

She slithered to her knees on the stage before him like a silk ribbon dropped from high altitude. Her skirt rode at her hips and her legs spread wide affording him a close up view of sopping wet satin and dark pubic curls.

Kinsey gulped, stared and barely restrained himself from whimpering. He was in more trouble than he had ever been on a battlefield. No doubt he should hightail his ass back to the castle and lock himself in his bedchamber. He had no business staying here, nothing to gain by wishing to bed the princess. Yet, he risked everything. His future, his welfare, Waldo's well-being and that of any family he may ever have depended on the gold he would get come morning.

That realization compelled him to rise, careful to remain in the shadows. He paused only briefly when the princess skimmed a finger down her throat, delved in the cleft between her breasts and moved to trace a circle around one taut nipple. With her free hand, she blew a kiss goodbye into the air.

Though he wasn't sure she could see it, he returned her airy kiss and rushed off into the night.

He would return to his bedchamber and eat the food that waited for him there. It mattered not if he took a potion-induced nap now. He knew all he needed...more even. But he barely made it to the line of trees outside the pub when his knee buckled. He managed to catch himself on one of those trees, limped and maneuvered until he bathed himself in the shadow of its trunk to rest before continuing his journey. Apparently, it was a night for hiding in the darkness.

Chapter 4

Damita was always careful when she left the pub in the wee hours just before morning. No one ever recognized her, never put her face to the story of the rebellious princess. They saw her as a showgirl, a harlot. Because of this, a few men attempted to follow her, most likely hoping to get lucky. A woman who would dance nearly completely naked for them, spread her legs on stage and allow them to admire her body would be an easy fuck after all, right?

Wrong, she thought. The thrill of knowing what she did to a man was enough. She glanced over her shoulder, looked to her right and then her left before starting to make her way to the forest. Her feet ached as they so often did after a night of dancing and she limped a little as she disappeared into the trees.

"My but aren't we a pair."

Damita stopped so fast she teetered on her heels. A scream bubbled in her throat as she whirled around and spotted the silhouette that leaned against a tree just behind her. How had she not seen such an imposing figure when she passed?

"There is no need to scream. I will not harm you."

"Who—who are you?" Her voice trembled and even as she asked the question she knew the answer. The man from the pub who hid in the darkness. She had flirted with him, blew him a kiss as he stood to leave but even so had been unable to make out his features.

He shifted his weight on his left leg, his right knee bent at a somewhat odd angle as though he favored it, but he didn't move from the tree. "Let's just say that I'm an admirer."

"You're the man from the pub. I don't sleep with men who come to see me dance."

"Who said anything about sleeping?"

Damita's lips twitched and she relaxed a little. A wise ass, this man was. She did love a man with attitude. She bit the inside of her lip to hold back the smile but couldn't completely hide amusement in her tone. "Got me there, soldier." He stiffened at that and her eyes narrowed. "I don't have sex with men from the pub. Is that precise enough for you?"

"Yes, it will do I suppose." He pushed himself away from the tree and walked toward her with only the slightest limp in his step. Yet, in the darkness of the night, she still couldn't make out more than an outline of his body. He didn't stop until he stood beside her, his chest nearly brushing her arm.

"W—what are you doing?"

"Relax." He spoke that single word in such a way, in such a voice, that made her want to obey, to give him anything.

"You're too close." She could feel the heat radiating from his body and, when he leaned in, his warm breath against the sensitized flesh of her neck gave her goose pimples all over her body.

"I told you I would not hurt you."

"And I told you—"

"That you don't have sex with men from the pub," he finished for her and his tone wasn't mocking but understanding, soothing. "I won't do anything you don't want me to."

And that could present a problem, Damita thought, because she could think of all sorts of things she *wanted* this man to do to her. If she let him touch her, gave in to her own desires to be touched, she would break a personal rule she set the first night she danced at the pub. She would dance for men, allow them to look but never touch. She felt his palm glide down her spine, settle at the small of her back and could almost hear her rule shatter like glass.

"Your dancing," he whispered. His lips brushed the skin just below her ear. "It turns you on as much as the men who watch you, doesn't it?"

Breathless, she nodded. "Yes."

"And do you touch yourself when you get back to your cabin through these trees?"

Cabin? Yes, she would let him continue to believe she lived in a cabin in the next village. Forget that one could probably fit a dozen or more of those tiny cabins in one wing of the castle.

She didn't answer, couldn't. Her heart pounded loudly in her chest as he moved behind her. His arms encircled her waist. She should run, she thought. She should kick, scream, do something, *anything* rather than simply stand here and wait for what he would do next. Yet, she stood still, her knees trembling, fireworks exploding in her belly and waited.

"Do you lay in your bed alone in the hour just before dawn and cup your breasts?" His hands pushed the lapels of her cloak aside, moved the slide under her breasts, hold them. "Do you rub your thumbs over your sweet nipples until they harden for you?" Again, his actions mirrored his words. The callused pads of his thumbs grazed back and forth over her nipples until they became so erect they hurt. Then his forefingers joined his thumbs and he rolled her nipples as though they were marbles between his fingers.

Damita let out a strangled cry as her head fell back to rest on his chest. "Oh God!"

He folded himself around her, leaned in to lick and nip her ear as he continued to fondle her breasts. He applied just enough pressure to her nipples, squeezed just hard enough to pull a sound from her that was half scream of pain and half moan of pleasure. "Do you caress your body?" He whispered it in her ear as his right hand abandoned her breast to graze down the flat plane of her abs, her stomach. "Pull up your skirt for me the way you did on stage tonight."

"I—" She didn't know what she meant to say. Had she gone crazy? She let this man, this complete *stranger*, put his hands on her. She snuck out of the castle and went to the pub nearly on a nightly basis for some time now. Yet, she didn't lie when she said she never had sex with the men, never let them touch her. Until tonight. Until this man. With hands that shook, she lifted her skirt.

"You were wet on stage. So wet your panties were soaked with it. I wonder, are you wet now?"

She was. More wet now than she ever got on stage…because of him. Her panties felt as though she put them on straight from the wash bin without giving them a moment to dry, and when he palmed her mound through those panties, she felt still more juices seep out of her.

"Ah yes. Is that for me?"

Since she couldn't seem to find her voice, she simply nodded. She knew he would feel the movement of her head on his chest.

"Pull your panties down for me."

This request…No, not a request but more of an order, made an excitement more visceral than any she ever felt rush through her. Even as nervousness and indecision mixed with that excitement, she did as ordered. Would she really let this stranger have his way with her? she wondered even as she tugged at her panties and let them fall to the ground around her heels. Hadn't she gone too far to turn back now? When his finger slipped into her pubic hair, wiggled between her pussy lips, she knew she wouldn't stop him.

"By the Gods, you are wet," he whispered and she heard the evidence of his own arousal in the huskiness of his voice, felt it in the rigidity of his cock against her back. "And so hot. I bet you taste sweet too. Shall we find out?"

His finger seemed to take on the attributes of a spoon. It curved even as it slid from a point just behind her opening forward to delve quickly inside her before it pulled out again, skimmed over her clit then withdrew from between her pussy lips. He held the finger up and in the moonlight she could just see it drowned in her juices. Though she didn't see him do it, she knew he brought that finger to his mouth, heard him lick and suck until he dried it of her cum.

"Hmmm, so thick and sweet." His finger returned to her pussy to repeat the action. "Have you ever tasted yourself?"

"No." Because she suspected he couldn't hear her whispered reply, she shook her head.

"Lick my finger, dancer," he said and brought the finger once more covered in her cum to her lips. "Taste yourself."

He traced her lips with his fingertip, left a trail of her cum where he touched then prodded her lips to open for him. She sucked his finger into her mouth, pretended it was his dick she sucked as she licked it, circled it with her tongue, and nibbled it with her teeth.

"You like that, don't you? You like the way you taste."

"Yes." And to her surprise, it didn't shame her to admit it.

He growled low in his throat, a hopeless and frustrated sound. "I want to fuck you." His hand found her pussy yet again as his other hand kneaded her breast. "I want to shove my dick deep inside you, feel your hot juices slide down my balls."

His blunt words combined with his finger now moving slowly in and out of her sopping wet hole drove her mad. She wanted it too, everything he spoke of and more.

"Meet me here tomorrow night."

She nodded because she knew she would. To feel this again, to experience this sense of sheer euphoria, she would meet this stranger at the edge of the earth.

"Know this, dancer," he said and plunged two fingers side by side deep into her pussy.

"Oh Goddess! Yes!" Her cry was breathless, mindless as he picked up pace, began to fuck her hard and fast with those fingers.

"If you show tomorrow night, I will fuck you," he told her and she heard the conviction in his tone, didn't doubt that he meant what he said. "Now, come for me, dancer. Let me feel your hot, sweet juices fill my hand. Let me hear how good it feels, how badly you want me to fuck you tomorrow night."

He found her clit with the pad of his thumb on the inward thrust of his fingers and she writhed against him. With his other hand, he squeezed her breast, flicked his thumb over her nipple. In seconds she was coming. It exploded from her, rocked her back and made her putty in his hands. She would have crumpled to the ground had he not been behind her, holding her. Instead, she melted against him as her body jerked, convulsed.

"Not bad," he whispered and slowly pulled his fingers from her pussy. "Your moans have the sweetest sound. I'll be hearing them in my dreams tonight."

Damita didn't remember making a sound. She had been too lost in the pleasure to pay attention to anything else.

"Tomorrow night I'll make you moan some more." He shifted behind her, gripped her waist and stepped sideways. The moon seemed brighter now yet he still managed to remain shadowed as he moved beside her, leaned her back against a tree for support. He leaned in, nibbled her ear. "And when I push my cock inside you tomorrow night I want to hear you scream."

Damita closed her eyes as anticipation coursed through her veins. He would do it, she knew. He could do it. Tomorrow night he would hear her screaming in mindless pleasure. Tomorrow night.

Why wait? She no longer wanted to wait. She opened her eyes to tell him she wanted him now, reached for him and saw only thick darkness, grabbed nothing but air.

Chapter 5

Kinsey thought of nothing but the princess the following day. When the servant came to him just after sunrise to take him to the king, he sent the squire on his way with word that his first night on watch of the princess had been a failure. In truth, it had been nothing of the sort. The only failure he faced last night had been his inability to keep his hands off her. That delicate, curvaceous body and smooth, sweet scented flesh, her hot juices that filled his hand when he made her cum…

He should go straight to the king, he knew, but couldn't resist the opportunity to give himself one more night. He liked watching her dance, understood her need to do something completely unexpected of a princess. A woman as hot and sexy and exotic as the princess couldn't be counted on to remain behind locked doors for eternity. She should be allowed to blossom, to grow, to experience and he believed she would be a better queen for it when it became her turn to take the throne. Never mind that when his time ended and he reported the truth of her whereabouts to the king, she would likely wither like a dying flower no longer able to bloom and grow.

He would not think of that now, he told himself. The princess's fate was not of his concern. However, his own fate did concern him and because it did he averted his gaze when the queen entered his bedchamber with a tray loaded with more food than he could eat in a month. His stomach grumbled but he ignored the pesky sound.

She walked into the room with her head held high, confidence oozing from her pores. Like mother, like daughter, he thought as he watched her and wondered how rebellious the queen had been at the princess's age. Strange, but he could almost picture the queen dancing on a stage just as he watched the princess last night.

The queen glided past him to sit the tray on a small table in the corner. She hesitated a moment and then turned, pinned him with a serious and steady look. "You didn't eat last night."

"How—"

"A soldier such as yourself must keep up his strength. Please know that no harm will befall you tonight. The food and drink are safe to consume. I give you my solemn word as Queen."

Kinsey gaped at the queen for a long moment before he recovered. "You know?" He couldn't disguise the astonishment in his voice. He hid a large portion of the tainted food and poured out the wine after returning from his adventure with the princess in the forest. As a soldier, he learned long ago how to move in stealth and speed even when injured and he put that knowledge to good use last night. He left the princess leaning against the tree, hurried back down the trail through the forest and the secret passage and made it to his bedchamber with ample time to spare before her return. He used that time to set the stage of a man stuffed to the gills with spectacular tasting drugged food who slept soundlessly through the night.

"You proved yourself very clever." The queen lowered herself to perch on the edge of the chair at the table. Her gaze never wavered from Kinsey. "Then you made an error in judgment that cold cost you dearly."

Not a woman to play games, Kinsey decided as he watched the queen. "And what will it cost the princess if I tell the king what I discovered last night?"

"Her freedom." The answer came without hesitation but her eyes became clouded, despondent.

"You call having no privacy, being surrounded by the king's guards by day and locked in a bedchamber at night freedom?"

"He loves her. Damita is our only daughter, will be the only child we ever have, the only heir to the throne. He wants to protect her. If he is strict, smothering, it is only because he looks out for her."

"Yet, you know how she sneaks out at night, where she goes and what she does. You have known all along." When the queen's gaze fell to the stone floor he knew he assumed correctly. "You have been protecting her and when the king found out she was up to mischief you started putting a sleeping potion in the food served to the men to further protect her."

"She is my daughter," the queen said in that way had only by a mother with a deep love for her child.

"You let her dance for men. Have you seen what she wears when she dances?"

The queen's lips twitched. "I have."

"And you approve?" Kinsey asked, unable to hide the surprise in his voice.

"I do not necessarily approve of her choice to dance for men," the queen admitted. "I permit it because I feel she should be allowed to make her own decisions. Her father holds her back from enough. I know from personal experience, from my own childhood, how that can detriment a woman's soul, her heart. I wish better for my daughter. Happiness above all else."

"Your love for her has no bounds."

"No, as it shouldn't. Why did you lie, soldier? Why did you not report the princess's mischief to the king straight upon returning to the castle?"

Though he expected the question, waited for it, he didn't have an answer ready. *Because I want to fuck you daughter tonight before I betray her in the morning.* Though true, he couldn't very well say that to the queen. *Because I wish to remain a guest of the king's for as long as I am able.* Yes, having a warm and dry bedchamber to himself without worry of thieves or poachers for a couple of days would be a nice advantage he had not considered until now. Yet, he couldn't bring himself to use it as an excuse for his silence either.

"You are taken with her."

Kinsey's head whipped around. No way could he miss the look of pleased satisfaction in the smile that tilted the queen's lips, in the look that glistened like diamonds in her eyes. "She is very beautiful," he found himself saying.

"You are protecting her as well. That is why you did not report what you know to the king."

"I will," Kinsey said quickly and hardened his expression, let her see that the words he spoke were not a lie. "I don't intend to spend the next several years as a slave to the king simply because the princess is not woman enough to stand up to her father."

"So it is the gold you want after all." The queen's voice became small and rang of disappointment.

"Of course it's the gold. Why else do you think I came here?" He said the words, meant them, so why did they leave such a bitter taste in his mouth? Angry now, he threw his hands in the air and spun around, turning his back on the queen.

"I think you came looking to collect the gold, but now you want more. I would not sleep well at night if I did not warn you. The king will see you beheaded if he discovers you know and have not reported to him."

Kinsey felt his blood turn to ice. Beheaded! He would protect the princess for a night, maybe two, and risk decapitation? "Will you tell him I know?"

"Of course not. I do not know you, soldier, but already I like you. Your concern for my daughter is enough to buy my silence."

He heard the rustle of the queen's gown as she stood, the click of her heels on the stone floor as she walked to the door, but he didn't turn.

"You can have it all, everything you want and more. You need do little more than ask for her hand." The heavy door to the bedchamber opened with a loud creek. Then the queen said, "She is not to know of our conversation. You would be wise to pretend again as you did last night."

Chapter 6

Damita saw him in the shadows of the pub. She never felt nervous when she danced…not since the first night. But she felt it tonight, the constant flutter of butterflies low in her tummy, the slightly accelerated heartbeat. She did her best to ignore it, to ignore him. At the end of the night she even considered taking a different path back to the castle. But memories of the night before, of the promise in his voice, of the confidence in his touch, had her going down her normal trail, going to him.

Tonight was brighter than last, the moon fuller and higher in the sky. Harder for him to hide in the shadows, she mused but when she reached their meeting spot by the huge forked willow tree she saw he could still find a shadow even in the brightest of moonlight.

"You came."

It was the voice from her memory, from her dreams, deep and full of sugar and spice. She walked to him and boldly slid her palms up his chest, over his shoulders, locked her hands behind his neck. "You thought I wouldn't?"

"I confess I wasn't sure." His arms found their way to circle her waist and he pulled her against him, held her tight.

"You're always in shadow. Step forward. I want to see you."

"Not yet, dancer. The shadow adds to the mystery, the excitement." His hands slid down to cup her butt cheeks as he spoke.

"It's—"

"Isn't that what you want, what you look for?" He squeezed her ass and drew her to her tiptoes.

"I—" Dear Goddess, she had been about to tell him her name. He kept calling her dancer. He called her that last night as well. While the anonymity further added to the mystery, she thought she would really like to hear her name spoken in his deep, husky baritone. But she couldn't tell him her name. He may not recognize her face but her name… No one else in the kingdom held the name of Damita.

"Yes," she hissed instead. She did look for mystery and excitement. She looked for passion and satisfaction too, both of which this man already gave her once.

"Then do not fret. Let me give it to you." He leaned in, captured her mouth with his. He tasted sweet, hot and utterly male. His tongue moved skillfully between her parted lips, inside her mouth, over her own tongue in a dance that made her breathless, week-kneed and mindless before she knew what hit her.

His hands abandoned her rear to glide up her back. When he reached the strips of material that held up her dress, he untied them and the dress slowly fluttered down. Her breasts fell free and his hands were magically there to catch them.

She threw her head back and moaned as he began to caress her breasts, squeeze and knead them. She had missed his touch, battled with the memory of it all day. This time, she wanted to touch too. She let her hands slide over his shoulders, down his biceps. She felt hard, warm flesh beneath his shirt and wanted to feel the skin-to-skin contact more. Her hands moved to his stomach, his waist. She found the bottom his shirt, snaked her hands under it and began a slow climb back up.

With a speed that made her breath catch in surprise, he caught her hands, yanked them from beneath his shirt and twisted her arms behind her back, held her wrist together in one of his large hands. He spun her around so fast, pulled her back against him with such quick force that she let out a little squeak.

"Mystery, remember?" he whispered and nipped at the side of her neck. He took a wrist in each of his hands, raised her arms in front of her until her palms rested on the trunk of the willow tree. "Keep them there."

Then his hands returned to her flesh. His callused fingers and palms lit a fire within her everywhere he touched. He skimmed over her breasts, her abs, and her stomach. He glided over her hips, pushed at the dress that caught there when he'd untied it until it fell completely from her body.

"Ah, another set for my new collection," he said of the satiny thin strip of panties he quickly removed along with the dress.

She stood with her hands splayed on the tree, her feet shoulders-width apart, back arched and ass in the air. It was a very undignified position for a princess, she thought. Yet, she didn't feel shamed in the least. Especially when his hand reached around her, found the mound of curls between her legs and delved inside.

"Are you wet for me tonight, dancer?" Rather than wait for her answer, he plunged a finger inside her.

Damita cried out, rocked into his hand to draw the finger deeper. "Yes," she hissed. "Yes, yes!"

"Yes you are." He withdrew the finger as quickly as it entered her. "I think we enjoyed enough foreplay last night, don't you?" And before she could answer, he thrust his dick inside her.

This time, she screamed at the intrusion. Not in pain, though his thick shaft stretched her tender inner flesh, but in a pleasure the likes of which she never before felt. Her fingers gripped at the tree trunk, scratched as he pounded into her.

The slow tenderness of the night before gone, he fucked her as he said he wanted to. His hand fisted in her hair, pulled as if tugging on a horse's reigns. His other hand smoothed her ass, one finger slipping between her ass cheeks to graze over her anus.

She made an indecipherable sound at that and involuntarily flexed her butt muscles. She tried to convince herself he touched it by accident. Surely he didn't mean to play there. But he did mean to, she realized in the next heartbeat as she felt his finger move over her anus again, slowly inch just inside the rim.

"Relax," he whispered and slowed his thrusts. "You'll like it. I promise. The orgasm you'll get will be unlike any you've ever had. Now relax that sweet ass for me, dancer."

Her heart pounded in anticipation as much as fear, but Damita forced herself to relax. She felt her anus open, spread. It didn't give as easily to the probing as her vagina and hurt more because of it. But it was a pleasurable pain, an exotic pain that sent her juices flowing and made her clit throb.

"That's it, baby. See, I told you that you would like it. You do like it, don't you?" As he asked the question he slid his dick out of her pussy until only the head remained inside her, pulled his finger nearly completely from her anus before plunging both as deeply as he could in one fast and hard thrust.

"Yes!" The word screamed out of her in both answer and plea for more. He was right. The orgasm would be like nothing she ever had. She could feel it now, that burning flame tangling with the sensations and darts of pain as he plunged inside her, cock and finger. His double penetration filled her completely, left no room for her body to give. She could only take and take she did.

She leaned onto the tree trunk, nails digging into the bark, and let him ride her. She took him inside her with vicious thrusts until the world exploded in a riot of colors before her eyes. The orgasm ripped through her, tore the scream from her throat and in the deep recesses of sound she heard his grunt as he came inside her.

Neither moved, neither spoke for minutes that seemed like hours as both waited for their pulse to slow, for breathing to return to normal. Finally, he slowly eased himself out of her but still did not move away.

Damita remained propped on the tree to spent to be worried or ashamed by her position or nakedness. A soft breeze rippled the air and she shivered from the sudden chill. A palm slid down her back, caressed with smoothness and affection.

"Are you cold, Damita?"

"A little," she admitted and gradually began to stand upright. "The breeze in the air, it's getting a bit..." She froze, the full impact of his question, each of his words finally penetrating the foggy sexual afterglow that remained in her mind. "What did you call me?" she asked carefully, her breath measured even as her pulse began to drum in her ears. When he didn't answer she slowly began to turn. Part of her didn't want to. Part of her wanted to forget what she just heard and walk away secure in the knowledge that she just had amazing sex with an anonymous stranger. Yet, she couldn't do that. She had to know.

Instinctively, her arms folded to cover her breasts as she glared at his silhouette in the darkness. "H—how do you know my name?" Her voice shook, dammit. Now more than ever she needed to sound strong, superior, like a princess. "Who are you?"

He took the smallest step backward, but it was enough. Moonlight streamed across his face, bathed his features in the pale white light.

Damita sucked in a breath. "You!"

He nodded once, his expression unreadable. "Me."

"But how? The food...You were...When I left..."

"I didn't eat, pretended to sleep, followed you when you left." He didn't bother to explain the queen left tonight's food untainted. Best to let her believe he simply hadn't eaten rather than to get her pissed at her mother.

"You followed me." Her voice rang with shock. Her eyes glimmered in disbelief. "And last night..."

"I followed you then too," Kinsey confirmed the obvious. He wished he could rewind time. A few minutes, ten at most, and they wouldn't be having this conversation. She wouldn't be looking at him as though her world just ended because he would not have called her by name. He got caught in the moment, or the after moment as it was, lost himself and her name slipped out.

"My father…" She shook her head, brushed at a stray lock of dark hair that curled at her cheek while careful to keep her breasts covered with her other arm.

"Doesn't know."

She eyed him suspiciously. "You didn't tell him. This morning. I heard you. You told the servant you found nothing. Why? Why not tell the truth, collect your gold and be on your way?"

Good question, Kinsey thought, *one I have yet to quite figure out an answer to myself.* He opened his mouth to speak but closed it again when no response came to mind.. Then he saw a heat rise in her eyes and wanted to step back, run for dear life.

"You thought you would fuck me first."

Hurt moved behind the heat and he found that harder than her anger. Feeling the need to comfort her, he reached for her. "Damita, please."

"Don't touch me, you son-of-a-bitch!" She jerked away, turned her back to him.

Though he knew it wasn't the time to notice such things, he couldn't help but admire her heart-shaped ass and the two small dimples just above each cheek, couldn't help but remember only moments before when he'd had that ass in the air in front of him as he fucked her. "We need to talk," he said patiently.

"I have nothing to say to you." Venom laced her words. "Leave me alone."

"Damita—"

"I said leave, dammit!"

Kinsey rocked back on his heels. He didn't want to leave her like this, somewhere between an explosion of temper and a river of tears. Yet, staying would do him no good. "I'll go," he said finally. "But we need to talk about this, about what we are going to do. We *have* to talk."

Chapter 7

Damita thought she knew what Kinsey had in mind. He figured he would fuck her again before he betrayed her to the king. He had one more night before his time ran out. Why waste it?

Torn between a boring evening alone locked in her bedchamber and one final night dancing on the stage at the pub, Damita paced. Like her father, she was good at pacing and often did so when she pondered a problem. Unlike her father, she had never been so quick at thinking of a solution to said problem. No matter how she spent her night, come morning he…

She stopped pacing and shoved her fingers through her hair. She teased him while on stage, met him in the dark, fucked him, let him do unspeakable yet wonderful things to her and she didn't even know his name. Still, no matter his name, come morning he would tell the king everything.

Maybe she should go tonight, let him follow her again, let him fuck her one more time before she lost what little bit of freedom she managed to sneak. She walked to her four-poster bed, flung herself down and stared at the ceiling. He had knocked on her door twice since last night and once even tried to talk to her through her peephole in the wall. She ignored him, of course. What could they have to talk about? Would he apologize? *I'm sorry Damita but I have to tell your father what a bad girl you've been so he will let me leave the castle and pay me tons of gold.*

Funny, even as she thought it, she could hear his deep, seductive voice saying such words. He had been so gentle with her. Even when he took control of her last night, put her in an uncompromising position and fucked her until she felt thoroughly used and sated, he had still been gentle.

You're a fool, Damita, she told herself and closed her eyes. *He played you, seduced you, and you fell for it. To bad too,* she mused as a clear picture of him formed in the darkness behind her lids. She saw him as she had that first evening through the peephole when she watched him undress. She remembered how she admired his physique just before leaving that night when she thought him to be asleep. Yes, she could have fallen for that man, nearly did fall for him. His voice, his touch, the feel of his body against hers, of his cock so deep inside her all opened a place in her heart she hadn't known she wanted to fill.

Thoughts of what could have been twisted with fears of what would happen tomorrow. Tears filled her eyes and blurred the picture in her dreams of the one man she ever met that she could have loved.

* * * *

Kinsey fingered the straps of material he made by tearing the skirt of one of Damita's most worn-looking gowns and stared down at the sleeping princess. She wore the cloak she used when traveling the forest path to the pub and nothing else. He guessed she tossed it on earlier after bathing as a simple means to cover herself. The sides of the cloak had parted in her slumber and the pale rounded edges of her breasts teased him now.

She'd cried herself to sleep. He hated watching that but knew she would only balk at any attempt to comfort her. So he watched, waited, and plotted. It came to him in the darkest of night hours, a whisper in his ear and a sudden understanding. *You need do nothing more than ask for her hand*, the queen had told him.

Ask for her hand, he thought and nearly laughed. She would give him her hand all right, right upside his face. So he came up with a better plan, one certain to protect his face and leave her no choice but to listen.

* * * *

"Damita."

She stirred, the voice penetrating the deep realm of darkness in her sleep.

"Damita, wake up. It's time for us to talk."

She didn't want to wake, didn't want to face the impending doom of the daylight hours. *Best to sleep*, she thought in her unconscious haze. She wanted to roll onto her side, to pull her knees to her chest and make a protective ball of herself but she couldn't. Why couldn't she move her legs? she wondered feebly and attempted to reach for her ankles.

Fear made her eyes pop open when she discovered she couldn't move her hands either. She blinked rapidly, forced her mind to do a fast climb from the grogginess of first waking. Alertness came quick with fury fast at its heels.

"Untie me, you son-of-a-bitch."

"Whoa! Such poetic language from a princess."

She growled at the mocking tone of his voice. "There's more where that came from. Now untie me!"

"No."

"What do you mean, no?" His calm demeanor only made her fury deepen. "I'll scream."

He shrugged. "If you must. You should know that it is unlikely you will be heard."

It galled her that he was right. Worse, that he knew it. They would be the only two in her wing of the castle at this time of night. When she wanted to, she could be a loud screamer but no one could wail loud enough to be heard through the twenty-plus room and four floors of solid stone and wood between them and any other occupants of the castle.

"You should know," she began, turning his own words around on him, "that when I do get free of these ties, I am going to cut off your dick and feed it to you."

He laughed. "A creative idea." He walked around the bed and perched on the edge. "I can see I am going to thoroughly love being married to you, Damita."

"Married to me! What the hell are you talking about?"

"The perfect solution to both of our problems," he told her, his voice full of certainty and confidence. He lifted a hand, brushed the backs of his fingers over her cheek.

Though she didn't want to feel it, desire sprang to life inside her at his simple touch. She turned her head away from him, from his hand and quashed any warm fuzzies he awoke in her. "How is my agreeing to marry you going to solve my problems? And what makes you think I would want to marry you? I don't even want you to touch me!"

"Yes, you do. You crave my touch as badly as I crave to do the touching." He turned more toward her on the edge of the bed, settled a bit. "But first, we will talk."

"We have nothing to talk about," Damita said through gritted teeth.

"Sure we do. I can't marry a woman I don't know now, can I? What's your favorite color?"

"I am not—" She glared at him as his question cut through the fog of anger in her mind. “What?"

Amusement sparkled in his eyes. "My favorite color is brown. What's yours?"

She wrinkled her nose. "Brown? But brown is so…blah."

"There are lots of beautiful things that are brown. Deer are brown, some rabbits and dogs. Tree trunks are brown." He grinned just a little and she knew he was remembering last night in the forest.

"So is mud and shit," she countered but felt herself starting to weaken. He saw beauty in things most simply took for granted, she realized, and even knowing that small bit about him tugged at her heartstrings.

"I can't say much for shit," he said, his grin growing wide, "but mud can be quite fun. Ever had a mud bath or even a mud fight?"

"No, but give me some mud and I will be happy to throw it at you."

He chuckled. "I bet you would, princess. You never answered me. Your favorite color is…"

"Red," she finally answered. "Deep, dark red."

"Like a rose." He nodded. "It suits you. Strong and beautiful yet delicate with a sweet scent that overwhelms the senses like a seductive caress."

"I thought you said you were a soldier." She looked at him through narrowed eyes.

"I am."

"Soldiers are not usually so poetic."

"Princesses are not usually so moody and cynical."

"Touché," she said with a sneer. "I was thinking more of the color of blood, not some silly rose."

"Princess, you are breaking my little red heart."

She almost smiled but caught herself.

"Why red? Why not pink?"

"Pink is too soft. Red is the color of fire, of passion, of…"

"You can say it. Red is the color of love. What do you love to do most in the world, Damita?"

"Dance," she answered automatically, her tone wistful.

"Is that why you go to the pub?"

"Part of it. The pub is the only place I can go at night to dance for people. When I'm on stage I feel so…alive. I'm not Princess Damita on that stage. I'm someone else, someone free and exotic, mysterious and sought after. I'm so much more, can be so much more there than I can held prisoner in this dammed castle." To her horror, a single tear slid down her cheek. She moved to wipe it away and only then remembered Kinsey had yet to untie her. "Are you going to let me loose?"

"I'm not done with you yet."

To her mortification, he brushed the tear from her cheek.

"I told you I don't want you to touch me."

"You are full of surprises, princess, and varying moods as well. I like that about you." He smiled at her and her heart tripped. He had a great smile, warm and seductive and full of heated promise. His hand left her cheek to trail down her neck, over her collarbone and down further still to sneak beneath the material of the cloak she still wore. "Why bother to lie about something you know you want so badly?" His fingers brushed over her nipple already taut with need. "Tell me again that you don't want me to touch you."

She closed her eyes, attempted to focus on anything but the heat forming in her breast, the tingling in her clit. "I—" She stopped, swallowed, then barely held back a moan when she felt his lips close around her breast. His tongue licked circles around her nipple then he drew it between his teeth for a gentle bite.

"What was that, princess?" he asked as he released her right breast, licked his way to her left and covered it with his mouth.

"I don't want you to touch me," she managed on a whoosh of air. But it sounded half-hearted, even to her own ears.

"Then I won't touch you," he said and she felt his hands move away from her, but his mouth stayed to lick, kiss and tease. He bathed her breasts, her abs, her belly in a shower of wet kisses that made her writhe on the bed. Her hands pulled at the restraints on her wrists, her legs tugged at the materials that held her ankles. Each gave from her strength but only enough to allow her room to squirm.

Her eyes popped open when he stopped kissing her and stood but before she could say anything he climbed onto the bed between her legs. The mattress gave on either side of her where he placed his hands, rested his weight and leaned in. His lips grazed her flesh, heated even as goose pimples rose to the surface of her shin, her knee, and her inner thigh.

She shivered and he lifted his head, the expression of his face as steamy and consumed with need as her body felt. "Is that better? I'm not touching." A ghost of a smile toyed with the corners of his lips.

"Smart ass," Damita muttered and would have come off the bed in the next heartbeat if she hadn't been tied down. He covered her pussy with his mouth, sucked her pussy lips between his teeth, and licked her clit until she writhed, panted, begged for release.

He didn't touch her, not with his hands. He didn't need to. He worked the tender flesh of her pussy with his lips and tongue, sucked her sensitive clit until it felt swollen and fit to burst. Tied as she was, she could do nothing but squirm, moan and curse her restraints. When she came, it gushed out of her with such force she screamed from the relief of it and was silently grateful after all that her wing of the castle was deserted.

Her body still shook with the after effects of her release when her eyes fluttered open and she found him hovering over her, gazing down at her. "Are you ready to marry me yet?"

She nearly laughed at his nerve. "You don't give up, do you?"

"I'm a soldier at heart." He shrugged as if that explained it all. "A good soldier doesn't surrender but fights his battles until they are won."

"Well, this is a battle you aren't likely to win, soldier."

"Oh, I think I am already over half way to victory." His hands skimmed down her sides. "I'm going to touch you now and when you cum this time I want to hear you screaming my name." He hitched up her hips and prepared to slide inside her.

How could a man make her so hot yet so angry at the same time, she wondered. Juices flowed wildly through her even as her blood simmered, but she hid both reactions well. "You never told me your name."

A slow, boyish grin unfolded on his lips. "Kinsey."

"Kinsey," she repeated. "What kind of a name is that?"

He entered her, stopped when just the head of his cock was inside her. "The name you will be screaming for the rest of your life, princess." He plunged inside her, one vicious and rapid thrust that drove his cock to the end of her womb. It wasn't until his hands slid down her thighs and he pulled one leg to drape over his shoulder that she realized at some point he'd untied her legs. The new position made each thrust deeper, harder, more mind-blowing and satisfying.

"Marry me, Damita," he growled as he continued to pound, to fuck.

She heard him though he sounded distant somehow, her concentration focused more on the pleasure he gave her and the frustration over her hands still being tied. "I want to touch you," she panted.

"Marry me," he repeated.

"Untie me," she countered.

"Not yet." His thrusts slowed. His eyes softened. "Not until you listen to me."

"I'm listening for Christ's sake, Kinsey. Untie me!"

He stopped. His dick buried impossibly deep inside her, his thrusts ceased and he stared into her eyes. "Marry me, Damita, and you will not have to give up anything."

"Except my freedom," Damita said dryly.

"And what freedom do you have now? You spend your days under guard, your nights locked in this room. Even the time you manage to steal isn't truly free for you are constantly looking over your shoulder."

Damita looked away and blinked back tears. He was right. She was never truly free from her father's guard. "So I marry you, and what? You become my keeper instead of my father?"

"I would not become your keeper, Damita. I would not rule you, nor would I attempt to put you under lock and key."

Damita snorted at that. It sounded too good to be true. To be truly free, able to do her heart's desire without fear or consequence.

Kinsey hooked a finger under her chin, pulled until she had no choice but to look at him or close her eyes. She looked at him. "Marry me and you can have the freedom you desire. You can even continue to dance at the pub if you wish."

She raised a brow at that. "You would let me dance for other men?"

That boyishly sly grin returned to his lips and she felt him flex his cock still buried deep inside her. "As long as you save the best dances for me." The grin faded, his expression turning serious. "I would not take from you something that means so much, although I do hope that you would decide instead to spend your evenings with me. We can make up our own special dance if you want."

Damita stared into his eyes and nearly allowed herself to drown in the promises she saw there. Then something in her head snapped, a string on her reality she supposed, and she shook her head. "This is crazy. Why would you marry me? Why give up your bachelorhood when you could leave tomorrow a single man wealthy beyond imagination?"

The answer came to her in a rush of realization, and fury wasn't far behind. She welcomed the fury because it was better than the alternative, better than what she felt behind it, better than the pain. Still, when she spoke her voice sounded small, hurt. "You will have it anyway."

"Have what?"

"Untie me Kinsey." She didn't scream it this time, barely managed to keep it from sounding like a plea. But this time it got his attention.

He didn't pull his cock out of her, didn't need to adjust his body in any way to reach the restraints on her wrists. With an easy tug on the material, her wrists sprang free. It did her no good with his body still pinning her to the bed and though she was no longer tied it took him only a half a heartbeat to catch her hands in his, hold them on the pillow on either side of her head.

"You're upset again. Why? What did you mean I would have it anyway?"

"Riches." She all but snarled the word. "Oh, you won't have so much to yourself right off but that's not what you're after anyway. You want it all and marrying me will ensure that you get it."

"Damita, what are you talking about?" He actually looked genuinely confused.

"Don't play coy with me, Kinsey. I may be a sheltered princess but I'm not stupid."

"All right. Then let's pretend I am for the moment and tell me what you are talking about."

His patience was waning. She could hear it in his voice but she didn't care. She wanted him to feel something more than the control and confidence that never seemed to leave him. Irritation would do for now.

"Why have just a little gold when one day you can have the whole kingdom?" She saw when understanding dawned in his eyes, watched as it faded away leaving only anger in its wake.

"You think I want to marry you so that I will someday be king?" Somehow, when he said it, even in a voice laced with fury, the idea sounded preposterous.

"You act as if the thought never crossed your mind."

"It didn't," he said and sounded so sincere she laughed in his face.

"Ha! You really do think I'm stupid, don't you?"

"I am not royalty, Damita," he said slowly, as if he were reeling in the string on his patience. "I'm a soldier. To rule a kingdom has never been an option for me. Hell," he let out a short laugh, "I don't even know if I would want to be king."

"Then why marry me? If the gold is all you want, why not take it and go? Why tie yourself to the castle, to my family, to me?"

He cupped her cheek in the palm of his hand, leaned down until his lips were but a mere breath from hers. "Because the gold isn't all I want." He kissed her, softly at first but with more passion and intensity when she responded.

She tried not to react, not to respond with such needy urgency to his kiss, to his touch but her body betrayed her. She opened her lips for him, met his tongue with her own stroke for stroke in a dance that was now becoming familiar with this man. She felt him shift between her legs, ease his cock out until he nearly fell out of her then slowly, so agonizingly slowly, he pushed himself back in.

"I want you, Damita," he whispered against her chin, her neck. "I want to marry you because I love you."

Disbelief twisted with sheer glee inside her at his words. Love her. How could he love her when they only met two days ago? Could he be lying, saying what he thought she would want to hear to get her to agree to marriage? Her eyes were closed, her head turned away from him. She was afraid to look at him, afraid to believe, afraid to hope.

"Look at me, Damita."

She shook her head.

"Please, baby," Kinsey whispered.

It was his tone of voice, so soft and pleading, more than the endearment that made her meet his gaze. This time she allowed herself to see deep into his chocolate brown eyes, let herself see the truth of his words.

"I love you, Damita. Marry me, princess. Be my wife."

She stared at him, let his proposal glide through her. She thought she needed time to think, to decide, to search for her own feelings. It was time she didn't have. Hadn't she thought him to be the first man she met that she could love? Yes, she could love him. She could spend her life with this man and she believed, whether he wished to rule or not, he would make a great king someday.

She opened her mouth, acceptance on the tip of her tongue, but something entirely different spilled out. "It will never work. My father will never allow us to marry."

Kinsey caressed the side of her face with his thumb and did that slow, agonizing out/in slide with his dick that made her squirm on the mattress beneath him. "You let me handle the king. Say yes and I will take care of everything else."

Damita dug her right heel and elbow into the mattress, used them for leverage as she twisted the left side of her body off the mattress, built the momentum and rolled them until she was on top. She straddled his hips, splayed her hands on his chest and grinned down at him.

"Yes," she said and began to ride his cock until, this time, it was he who screamed her name.

* * * *

"I want children," Damita said later. She lay with Kinsey on her bed, her head on his shoulder, one leg draped over his. Idly, her fingers doodled pictures on his bare chest.

"Of course. We will have a dozen if you wish." He brushed his lips over the top of her head, a head that sprang up a half a second later with an expression of pure horror.

"Twelve kids! Have you lost your mind?"

Goddess, I do love this woman, he thought and tucked his tongue in his cheek to keep from laughing at her. "I expected you would want many children with as many servants for we alone would not be able to keep our eyes on them all of the time."

"We won't," she said in a tone full of conviction. "Our children will be allowed to run, to grow, to peruse the castle grounds and the kingdom without guard or disguise."

Kinsey skimmed his hand up and down her arm, hoping to sooth, to comfort. "Yes but they will still need supervision, guidance, not shelter or imprisonment but a more open kind of love."

Damita sighed. "I suppose you are right." She lifted her head again, looked at him. "I *could* have a dozen kids with you."

"Pregnancy would interfere with your dancing."

"Who said pregnant women can't dance?" she asked with a raised eyebrow. "You and I will simply have to adjust the dance we make up to accommodate me with a large belly."

He knew what she was telling him, understood it was her way of letting him know she would give up dancing at the pub. "Do not give it up just for me, Damita. Do what makes you happy."

"You make me happy."

Kinsey felt his heart swell with more love than he ever hoped to feel. Yet, even through his own happiness, he felt a sense of dread. "We need to decide what to do about your father."

"We tell him we want to get married," Damita said easily.

"I want it to be that simple, but there is something you should—" Before he could finish the sentence, tell her about the queen's belief that he would be beheaded if he didn't confess his knowledge to the king, the door to the bedchamber burst open.

Chapter 8

They took him. Damita wrung her hands as she paced. Two squires came into her bedchamber with little regard to her or Kinsey's state of undress and all but yanked Kinsey from her bed, took him away. She saw her mother standing in the hallway just before the door to her chamber was slammed in her face and locked tight. She pounded on the door, screamed until she could hardly feel her throat or her hands through the numbness.

Her mother, she thought. How could her mother betray her this way, and where had they taken Kinsey? What would they do to him?

"Damita."

She heard the soft, whispered voice and spun around, her gaze landing on the peephole in the stone wall. Her mother's voice, her mind registered a second later. Anger mixed with hurt and began to boil just below the surface of her skin. "How could you?" she demanded and stalked to the peephole.

"Please, baby, keep your voice down. Someone may hear."

"I don't care if the king in the next land hears."

"Damita, you must listen to me," the queen pleaded.

"You turned on me," Damita shouted. "You told daddy. You—"

"Kinsey will be beheaded come first light," the queen spoke over her.

That stopped her. Fear slid over her like a blanket of ice. "Beheaded?" she whispered and felt her eyes burn with instant tears. "Buy why? Is it because we made love?"

"Is that what it was, sweetheart? Do you love him?"

"Yes. Oh, mom, yes. I love him. He asked me to marry him." She heard her mother take a quick intake of breath.

"Baby, that is wonderful, but your father…he has found out that Kinsey lied to him, that Kinsey knew what you were doing, where you were going and did not report to the king."

"How—"

"There is no time to explain," the queen said, her voice sounding urgent. "It will be light soon. Damita, I do not know how to save Kinsey."

"I know what to do." Damita kissed the tips of her first two fingers, placed them over the peephole. "Thank you, mother. I love you," she whispered and bolted for the secret passage.

* * * *

"Prepare the prisoner," the king bellowed. "We execute at first light."

"Leave him be," Damita said in an authoritative tone that mirrored her father's. She walked into the Great Room, careful to keep her steps even, her posture confident and regal. She bit back a smile of satisfaction when the servants stopped, looked from her to the king and back again as if unsure which order to obey.

The king whirled on her. "How dare you contradict an order I give to my men? You are supposed to be locked in your bedchamber. How did you get out?"

Damita stopped a full arm's length from her father. He never hit her before, never so much as raised a threatening hand, but she never stood up to him like she did now. She would keep her distance, not take any unnecessary chances. "I dare, father, because it is *my* man that you have ordered your men to prepare for execution." Though her voice sounded steady, defiant, her heart hammered in her chest. "I got out of my bedchamber the same way I do every night. Isn't that what this is all about, how I've been sneaking out of my room each night?"

"Damita."

She turned to see the queen enter the room, her cheeks a bit red, breaths a bit ragged as though she ran most of the way there. "It's okay, mother. I will do what I have to do to save Kinsey." She turned back to her father and told him of the secret passage.

"How did you find out about this passage?" the king asked, but his gaze was on the queen.

"You have ordered me locked in my chamber at night nearly my whole life, father. I got bored," she lied with a shrug. "At one point I was certain I knew every crack, every dent, every bump in that room. Until one night, I spotted one I hadn't noticed before. The button to open the passage."

"And where has this passage taken you each night?"

Time to play hardball. "Release Kinsey and I will tell you."

The king raised an eyebrow. "You dare bargain with me, daughter?"

Damita took a deep breath, tried a different track. "He has asked me to marry him."

The king raised both brows at that. Surprise overtook the anger in his expression.

"He will make a good king when it comes our turn to rule," she continued, knowing what mattered most to her father. "He is a soldier, a hero. He is strong with both muscle and knowledge. Come to think of it, father, he is a lot like you in many ways," she added almost as an afterthought and hoped he would take it as a compliment.

"You intend to marry him?"

"I do," Damita nodded, her heart suddenly in her throat. "With your blessings, of course. But I can not very well marry a man without a head now, can I?"

The king turned his attention to the servants. "Bring the prisoner to me. We will dine on an early breakfast."

* * * *

"You wish to marry the princess." The king studied Kinsey over his glass. "Why?"

Kinsey didn't flinch under the king's penetrating gaze but merely looked back, his own gaze steady and confident. He opened his mouth to answer but the queen spoke instead.

"What dose it matter the why, my lord? Look at them." She gestured across the table at Kinsey and Damita. "Damita has stood up to you for the first time in her life, risked an unknown punishment to spare this man's life, to give him her life. They have obviously fallen in love."

"It this true, Damita?" The king turned prying eyes on his daughter. "Are you in love with this man?"

Kinsey turned his attention to Damita, eager for her answer. Though he professed his love for her—something he never said to any other woman—she had not returned his declaration. She agreed to marry him, confronted her father for him, but would she return his love? He suddenly realized the answer to that single question was worth more to him than any amount of gold. *She* was worth more to him.

Damita reached for him, took his hand, gazed into his eyes and smiled. "I do father. I do love this man."

Kinsey's heart filled and he grinned like an idiot.

The king nodded slowly. He coughed, cleared his throat. He made a noise that sounded suspiciously as though he were attempting to cover the fact that his voice was thick with joyous tears when he spoke. "Then you shall be married with my blessing."

Slow, mirrored smiles of delight spread over the princess and queen's faces, proving just how much mother and daughter looked alike. For a moment, he fell speechless in the presence of such beauty and realized this is how it would be now for all time.

"You have my blessing," the king repeated. "However, you still owe me an explanation, soldier. You have escaped execution for your deceit, yet you still have not told me where it is that you discovered the princess spent her nights when she was believed to be locked in her bed chamber."

Beside him, Kinsey heard Damita suck in a breath even as he glanced at the queen whose face had gone pale. Neither woman expected the king to pursue his quest in the face of the marriage proposal.

Kinsey wondered how the king would react now if he told the truth. More, what would he do if he discovered Damita lied as well? That it had been the queen who showed her the secret passage and knew all along where Damita spent her nights? That the queen even helped Damita by putting a sleeping potion in the guard's food?

He looked from mother to daughter and back again, realized both waited with bated breath to hear his answer. Then he addressed the king. He had a sneaky suspicion the king already knew more than he pretended. "I believe some secrets should remain between husband and wife. Don't you, your majesty? Damita will not be sneaking anywhere anymore for she will be spending her nights and her days with me."

KINSEY AND THE EXOTIC DANCING PRINCESS

THE END

WWW.TONYARAMAGOS.COM

SIREN ADULT FAIRY TALE
Tower of Secrets
Samantha Lucas

Tower of Secrets

Contemporary Erotic Fairy Tale

After one look, Sebastian wants Marina , but can their love overcome a tower of secrets?

Sebastian Montclaire is used to getting what he wants, from women to business. What he wants now is the patent on a revolutionary computer code. One look at the inventor's daughter has him questioning which he wants more.

He has no idea Marina Bennett is a proverbial princess in a tower and only true love can ever free her.

TOWER OF SECRETS

The Fairy Tale Collection

SAMANTHA LUCAS

Chapter 1

Marina slid her hand over her breast. Her nipple stiffened and the ache to be touched grew until she almost couldn't handle it.

S: *Marina? Would you like that?*

She could almost hear his voice, as if he were in the room with her, not just some words in a box on her monitor. Before she chickened out, she typed the one word he wanted to hear. Knowing it was true embarrassed her. She felt herself blushing in the flickering light from the computer screen.

Bennett: *Yes*

She waited, nervous, and vulnerable, unsure how she'd handle his rejection at this point. She wanted him. It was nearly unbelievable. In twenty-six years, she'd never wanted anyone. Although, to be fair, the only men she'd met were either servants or business associates of her father, both types with one foot in the grave. Good God, the last man who visited here must have been a hundred and fifty. She'd expected him to cough up a lung any second.

S: *Mmmm. Good girl. Do you have any idea how much you turn me on, Marina?*

A giddy swell flowed through her and a smile bloomed. Suddenly shy in the darkened study, she bit the sensitive flesh of her lower lip and typed.

Bennett: *No.*

S: *I'm hard, dripping pre-cum and want you so bad I'm imagining ways I can rip you right through my screen.*

S: *If I were there, Marina, in this shape, my cock hard and weeping for you, what would you do?*

A quiet, hysterical bubble of laughter purged itself. She had no fucking idea and was tempted to type that. Instead, she thought of a book she'd been reading and typed.

Bennett: *Wrap my fingers around you, squeezing, pulling. Take the finger of my other hand and spread the cum over your tip. Then suck on my finger, taste you for the first time.*

Despite being secretly horrified with her boldness, she was also a little thrilled and a lot turned on.

S: *Good Lord, Marina, I'll cum if you say things like that. Are you touching yourself?*

Her breath tripped. Could she? It was four in the morning. No one was around, but still...If she got caught, forget being embarrassed. If her father found out, he'd lock her in her room for a decade this time. All the same, she *wanted* to touch herself, to pretend it was him touching her. She knew they'd never meet in real life, but in her fantasies, he came to her every night, made love to her and let her sleep in the safety of his arms. He was her prince, riding to her rescue and together they'd live happily ever after.

Pushing away guilt and shame, she slid her hand beneath her robe and ran it along her inner thigh.

S: *Marina?*

Her other hand hesitated over the keyboard. Could she tell him she'd just brushed her fingers over her folds, finding them *very* wet?

S: *Don't go shy on me now, princess. I'm touching myself. Stroking my cock, wishing I was inside you. Wishing I could kiss you, hold you. Wishing when I came, which is inevitable, btw, that my cum would fill you. Marina, tell me you're wet, that you need me.*

S: *Please, love.*

His words squeezed her heart and for reasons more than he was the first to say anything like this to her, more than all the childhood dreams she'd had of Prince Charming—it was *him*. Somehow he reached through the computer and touched her soul.

She drew a deep breath, closed one eye...and typed.

Bennett: *I'm touching myself. I'm wet. I want you, need you. Please, Sebastian, please touch me.*

Feeling the familiar swirl of butterflies in her stomach, she dipped her finger inside herself and spread her juices over her clit.

S: *Oh, love, you have no idea how I wish I could touch you. How deeply I desire to lay you in a bed of silk and velvet, watch the candlelight spill over your naked body while I run my hands over your skin, feeling every inch of you.*

S: *I want to taste you. The sweetness of your lips, the saltiness of your skin, the tangy nectar of your pussy.*

S: *I want it all, Marina. I want all of you.*

Her heart cracked, a rough jagged fracture that split the organ directly in two. She knew none of these fantasies would come true. They'd never meet. She'd never feel his lips on hers his hands on her skin. They'd never get closer than this and yet, she lived for the nights when Sebastian found her on-line and made love to her with his words.

S: *Tell me you want me, my love.*

She closed her eyes. Those words stung more than he could understand, because she longed for him in a way she couldn't have imagined three short months ago when she accidentally opened an IM meant for her father.

Bennett: *I want you, Sebastian.*

S: *How much, my darling? Tell me what you want me to do to you.*

Her breath went shallow, her inner muscles clenched hard; she would come very soon. In the heated haze of pre-orgasmic bliss, she seemed to lose all her inhibitions.

Bennett: *I want you to suck on my clit, Sebastian. I want you to make me come with your mouth, then slide your cock deep inside me, make us one. I want to ride you, clenching you with my pussy. I want to make you cum, Sebastian. Is that okay?*

She waited breathless for the next words to appear.

S: *Mmmm, love, I am coming. Hard. Oh, God...*

The thought of him, cock in hand, cum spurting, pushed her over the edge into her own orgasm. She held her breath, not making a sound as the waves of pleasure rolled over her. She wanted this moment to never end, in part because she knew once her hormones leveled, the loneliness would swarm back in, taking her prisoner once more.

S: *Marina?*

In the dim flicker of light from the monitor, she cringed, knowing what he was about to say—knowing she had to deny him again. Her heart still pounding hard, she waited breathlessly.

S: *I want to meet you.*

She smiled sadly. Five words she'd come to dread. They could never meet, but the desire was so strong some nights it overwhelmed her. She was glad she'd never told him who she really was, that she was Claude's daughter. He probably thought she was a servant or something, but there was safety in that. He couldn't find her if he didn't know her secret and some nights she thought he would search the planet for her.

Bennett: *I can't. You know that.*

That crack in her heart widened.

S: *No. I know you say that every fucking night. Marina, I'm falling in love with you.*

Her eyes closed against the pain of longing that tore through her. Recovering, quickly, she typed.

Bennett: *You know nothing about me. You can't possibly love me.*

S: *I know you're indescribably thoughtful, intelligent, giving, fair, sexy as hell and extraordinarily loving. Favorite color: aquamarine, favorite food: turtle cheesecake, favorite song: Austin by Blake Shelton. You also like to rock out to Def Leppard and Bon Jovi. Long chestnut hair I'm dying to run my fingers through. Eyes the color of emeralds I'm dying to stare into. You're lonely as hell, and for whatever reason, you share your nights with me.*

S: *Let me meet you.*

A tear rolled down her cheek and splashed on the deep mahogany of the desktop. This man touched her so deeply she could barely resist him. Ultimately, however, she had no choice.

Bennett: *No.*

She disconnected and ran to her room in tears.

* * * *

In his study, Sebastian shoved his still half-erect cock back into his pants. That girl had him wrapped around her finger like no woman ever had been able to do.

He picked up the small photo his detective had given him and traced the outline of her face. He imagined he could have fifty pictures of Marina Bennett and she'd be smiling in none of them. He wanted to make her smile.

A wicked smile crept across his face. *I want to make her come, and using more than my damn words.*

He paced to the full-length windows lining one wall. Open tonight, they allowed the summer air to float in and caress him.

"I'm coming for you, Marina. Like it or not…you are *mine* and I will possess you."

Chapter 2

Sebastian Montclair never played games—unless he knew he would win. This one was already over even if that fool Claude Bennett didn't realize it. He agitatedly checked his watch again. Men—and women—in many circles respected and feared him for his numerous achievements and attributes, but patience was not among them. Sebastian fumed. This trip might just push him beyond his limits. It was taking so fucking long to reach Bennett's refuge.

Nothing since he'd arrived at the airport had gone his way. Now, even the damned weather schemed against him. Hugging the mountainside, the storm-borne darkness forced his driver to go slow around the curves, adding to his edginess. Vivid, explicit images of Marina assaulting him at inopportune moments failed to improve his mood.

The air around him tasted stale. He tugged on his tie, shifting in the plush leather interior, grateful for the shelter. Nevertheless, part of him wanted to be out in the storm, feeling the rain prick his skin as it fell upon him in sharp beads. He wanted to inhale deeply of wet earth and pine, but it was an impulse he contained—as always.

Images of himself in his study every night for the past three months—desperately waiting for Marina to appear—prompted bitter laughter.

"Way to keep your feelings on lockdown."

This woman's pull spelled danger, in more ways than one. Yet, just like a siren's song, he followed it, despite his gut intuition that it could mean the end of him.

Wind tossed sheets of rain against the darkened windows, occasionally giving his driver the need to correct the vehicle's position on the narrow road. The uncomfortable expedition, the storm, the narrow road littered with sharp turns, all disrupted his concentration, making work a waste of time. Finally, shoving the report into his attaché, he poured himself a straight shot of vodka. Even without those petty distractions, not the least of which had hair like a fairly-tale princess, his mind was ultimately on Bennett himself. The man would not expect him, giving Sebastian a perverse sense of bliss. He often relied upon advantages gained from acting outside the others' expectations.

This would be no different. He needed that patent and he'd damn well get it, Marina was a side benefit he hadn't planned on. He knew her well enough now to know she'd resist him, but there wasn't anything he could not, or *did not*, get, that he wanted badly enough.

Moonlight broke through the trees as the car finally crested the cliff. Sebastian swirled the contents of his glass. Watching the moonlight sparkle off the clear liquid, he felt a deep sense of satisfaction at that moment in being Sebastian Montclair.

The Bennetts don't stand a chance.

* * * *

Marina's loneliness and misery oppressed her. Having spent a great deal of her life that way, she tried not to want things she would never have. Tonight, though, the restlessness had taken another form. Unused to feeling quite this way, she didn't think the storm or Sebastian's apparent desertion had caused it. Something else loomed out there—something that would bring change. She could feel it.

For the hundredth time she walked from her bed to the French doors and peered out into the blackness. Lightning lit the countryside. Perched atop the mountain, she could see forever when the lightning flashed. Flat meadows and open fields to the horizon in one direction, sheer cliffs and a steep drop to churning waters below in the other.

Opening the door, she immediately heard the angry surf crash upon the rocks far below and inhaled deeply of the rain-drenched air. Some nights when she felt particularly lonely, she thought about throwing herself into the sea. Only thoughts of her poor father's resulting heartbreak stopped her. He'd already lost the love of his life when her mother died; she knew he couldn't bear to lose her, too.

Leaning against the door, watching the storm in all its glory, she wondered again what went wrong with Sebastian.

It wasn't like he owed her anything. Maybe he'd just gotten fed up with her constant refusal to meet in real life. Nearly two weeks had passed since she'd heard from him. It had never been more than a few days before, and even then she'd gotten the impression he'd been there even when she couldn't get to the computer.

So what happened?

She refused to admit to herself how deeply her heart ached, how much she missed him. She'd only wanted a little fun. Nothing could ever come from it.

Lights crested the hill approaching the driveway.

Company?

Her heart raced. Unexpected visitors *never* came, not once in all the years she could remember. She knew they didn't expect anyone because her father hadn't locked her in. Fingernails pierced soft wood as she gripped the open door, standing on tiptoe as if she could somehow see into the vehicle that way.

As a rule, she didn't complain or whine. Her father treated her well, trying to give her everything she desired. Sadly, he seemed to completely overlook companionship and she longed for it desperately.

The car pulled right up to the house. Excitement overriding anxiety, she stepped onto the stone balcony, immediately drenched, but not caring. She watched the driver get out and run around to the back. She held her breath as he opened the door.

The young man who stepped from the back of the car looked nothing like any of her father's usual visitors. Jet-black hair slicked back from his face picked up a silver sparkle from the moonlight. Thunder cracked, startling Marina, but couldn't make her look away. However, her small yelp drew his attention. Before she could retreat, his gaze pinned her where she stood.

* * * *

Sebastian looked up without knowing why. A feeling, he supposed, like someone watching him. The last thing he expected was a half-naked woman, sheer white gown gone transparent in the rain, now outlining every seductive curve of her body.

My Marina. At last.

Chapter 3

Within a heartbeat, Sebastian went hard. His all-too-familiar animal instincts took over. He'd known it would be like this with her. For whatever reason, she had an inexplicable hold on him. He'd never had an internet-based relationship before. All the women he dated he'd met through work or friends, but the night Marina Bennett opened her father's IM by mistake, all fluster and apologies, he'd felt as if she reached right through his screen and latched onto the least-used organ in his body—his heart.

He stood there, gaze locked with hers, refusing to make the necessary adjustment to his pants to allow for his now fully-erect cock. Instead, he stared up at her, not releasing her from his stare until she felt half as uncomfortable as she'd made him. Not that he actually blamed her for her allure. Still, he felt a need to dish out some of what she did to him. He exulted to see her as powerless to this attraction as he felt.

"Mr. Montclair?"

Shaking his head, never breaking eye contact with Marina, he replied, "Ring the bell."

He had no intentions of explaining himself. His eyes traveled the length of her body, what he could see of it past the stone and iron building, more castle than any other type of structure.

Crazy bastard, Claude is.

Vines clung to the stone as if drawing life from it, and the balcony three floors up made it difficult to see her well. Tilting his head all the way back, he could see her clutching a stone pillar. Unfortunately for him, she decided in that moment to step behind the pillar, hiding her body.

He had a good mind to toss out that he could still see her, but he couldn't imagine that she'd ever hear him, not even on a clear day. So he said nothing, simply allowing his hungry gaze to feast. Six-thousand-dollar suit ruined, he stood in the wind and the rain, staring down a vision of such seduction he knew he would never recover completely from this interlude.

She didn't exactly fit what he'd expected. That first night, they'd talked for hours, about everything and nothing in particular. He still had no idea why he did it, only that he didn't want to let her go. He knew she didn't think him serious about talking again the following night, or the one after that, or the one after.

He found her shyness endearing, and himself drawn back to his computer night after night, inexplicably angry when she didn't appear some nights. Unaccountably jealous, he wondered who she spent time with when she didn't spend it with him. A grin slowly spread. For the next few nights, he knew exactly who she'd be with, because it would be *him*.

She moved slightly, coming more into focus. In the moonlight, he imagined he could see the outline of one breast clearly, saw the areola and peaked nipple. His tongue ran the length of his bottom lip, reflecting his need to suckle on the ripe flesh before him, to entwine their hot naked bodies for a good long time,

Then she smiled.

If the darkness and the rain hadn't blurred his vision so, he'd have sworn she blushed. That smile had the odd effect of wrapping a fist around his cock and his heart at the same time, something he'd never felt before her. In fact, the first time it had happened, it scared the shit out of him. Even now, his body flinched as if she'd hit him with that smile.

She sucked in her lower lip. He swore he could see it clearly, straight white teeth biting into the tender flesh. He knew his cock was weeping pre-cum by now.

Good God, woman.

Originally he'd planned on business first, seducing the lovely Marina second. Standing in the pouring rain watching her, he knew he was lost. He'd have his cock inside her within the next hour. *Then* he could focus on business.

* * * *

Marina tossed the soaked nightdress to the floor and grabbed her robe. She had no idea why, but he had come to *her* home and she intended to find out. Bare feet treading over the slate floor, she ignored the cold that always permeated the place. Quickly she traversed the back stairwell that led from her sanctuary, gliding silently through the second floor hallways until she came to the edge of the main foyer and the grand staircase.

She held back in the shadows, not wanting to be seen. Her father would be furious if he knew, but her heart—in fact, every cell in her body—insisted she take the chance. It didn't take long before he came into view. The butler, Stedman, handed out towels, gushing as he tended to do. The driver was drying off, but the visitor…

He stood like a hunter, keenly aware of his environment, completely ignoring anything of little consequence. Watching from the darkness, she saw his eyes scanning, gaining familiarity.

Her heart sat in her throat as she waited to be discovered. She had the oddest feeling that if he truly knew her thoughts, he'd simply laugh at her, pat her on the head and tell her to go play with her dolls. She bristled. Her father always treated her like a child, but good God, she was twenty-six years old.

She watched as he seemed to relax. Maybe it was his shoulders, or just the manner of him, but for whatever reason, he didn't seem quite so intimidating all of a sudden. She leaned closer to the banister, bottom lip snugly tucked between her teeth and got her first real look at him in the soft light from below.

She knew she didn't have the frame of reference most girls her age had, but she had spent one particularly long, lonely night on a website that would have sent her father to an early grave if he'd known. At the time, she'd thought the men offered up as the epitome of the species were…cold, forbidding. They seemed removed, untouchable—ultimately fine by her, because she'd also found them lacking.

But *this* man was different. This man she definitely did not find lacking. She was determined to find out who he was. Something inside her wept at the sight of him. Several wet locks of hair dangled over his forehead, releasing drops of clear rainwater onto his cheeks. Even from this distance, she could see the fire flash in his dark eyes, his rain-soaked suit clinging nicely to every muscle in his body. He was definitely handsome—if a little dark and brooding—but he had something more, something indefinable. That something told Marina this man would be hers.

Chapter 4

Sebastian did not relish the coming confrontation. He had been, until the encounter outside. Now he felt an animalistic need to mate, the likes of which he'd never felt and, in all honesty, didn't appreciate. Even as he heard Claude's angry tone, ninety percent bluster as it rolled over all the damn stone in this place, he couldn't quite release her from his memory. He'd expected the attraction, but not the primal gut-level need to pull her to him and never let her leave.

"Why are you here, Montclair? I've told you repeatedly in every way imaginable and even in several languages, that I'm not selling it to you."

Sebastian drew a deep breath and leveled his glare on the smaller, rounder, older man with the nerve to behave as if *he* had the advantage here. He smiled, feeling a lot more like baring his teeth, one junkyard dog to another.

"What are you going to do with it, old man? I've offered you ninety million dollars at last count, but your stubborn ass is too proud to take it." He took a step forward. "I'm wet, damn tired, and on the whole, in no mood to discuss this tonight. Direct me to a shower and a bed. We'll talk tomorrow."

"You are *not* welcome here."

The low, threatening tone of Bennett's voice drove Sebastian to take another step closer.

"And what are your plans? Send me back to the limo for the night? I'm not leaving until I have that patent, Claude, whether you extend hospitality or not."

Sebastian was tired, wet and horny. He had no intention of letting a man he had little use—and even less respect—for, give him the runaround. He wanted a hot shower, a bed, and…

He glanced up at the balcony, sensing her presence before he spied her. Not wanting to give away that he'd seen her, he kept his gaze on Claude, but all the rest of his senses converged on her.

She'd been watching. He wondered how long she'd been there but refused to let his male ego cause him to preen for her. Damn, but he wanted to, though.

He wanted her wet, naked and writhing atop him, but that wasn't why he'd come here. Well, not entirely, anyway. Keeping his lustful urges in check, he focused on the business at hand.

"So what is it, Claude? Do I find my own bed?"

He saw the flicker of agitation and guilt in the old man's eyes. He loved games and figuring people out, excelling at both. Old Claude thought he had a secret, but Sebastian knew the only secrets here were his.

"You'll stay where I tell you, Montclair. I don't like guests and I like you even less. I find you wandering about my home..."

He didn't finish. Sebastian almost laughed, amused at Claude's obvious realization that he had nothing to threaten with.

"You can stay until morning. Your welcome ends then."

Sebastian saw no point in responding; he'd stay as long as he damn well liked. He moved past Claude for the stairs.

"The third floor tower is off limits, Montclair. Go near it and I'll kill you with my bare hands."

Again, Sebastian made no response. His body ached and had begun to shiver. Hitting the second floor landing, he scanned the perimeter, catching the last of long strands of hair disappearing behind a column.

He continued down the hall to the first door he found that led to a bedroom. Once he'd showered, dried and slipped into casual slacks and a silk shirt, he couldn't stop thinking about that tower and Marina and a need that had been building for three long months. It was past time to fulfill it.

He headed for the stairwell, intent on seeking out the third floor tower and the woman who'd captivated every free thought for months. He wanted that silken mane of hair to slide over his fingers, brush against his skin, cover his cock. He wanted to bury himself deep inside her, possess her, imprint himself on her so completely she'd never forget him.

Unfortunately, he found no stairwell to another floor. From where he stood, he saw no evidence of anything above the first two. He paced the landing, descended the stairs and climbed back up. Nothing.

Eyes narrowed, he slowly circled the landing, then moved to where he'd seen Marina earlier, recalling how she had seemed to disappear into the wall. Running his hands over smooth stone and rough plaster, he explored the varying textures, but nothing seemed out of place. Standing back, he studied the wall. His gut told him it must be right in front of his eyes, but where?

Pacing the landing, he studied the artwork on the walls. Tapestries and landscapes, an oil painting of young lovers—which, in his opinion seemed very unlike Claude Bennett. Nonetheless, he moved along until he came to a portrait of a young woman resembling Marina, but with longer, darker hair. Though he'd only ever seen a portrait of Marina's eyes, they held a warmth this woman's didn't.

A satisfied smile crossed his face as he moved closer.

"Well, Sophia Bennett. Hadn't expected to see you here."

He reached to touch the woman's cheek, but his foot stumbled on something as he got close. An unexpected draft chilled him, drawing his attention to a tapestry on the far wall. Moving closer, he pushed back the tapestry in time to find the hidden wall closing. He slipped through quickly, only to be greeted with pitch darkness as the wall closed behind him.

"Fucking brilliant."

Running his hand along the sidewall, he traveled the steps slowly until he reached a landing, where soft light illuminated three doors. He chose the one directly ahead. Turning the knob, he pushed open the door as anticipation churned in his gut. Moonlight spilled through large French doors to greet him, illuminating the small, sparsely furnished room. A large canopy bed dominated the space and on the bed…

Sebastian felt a sense of completion wash over him. His tower princess at last. Now the question remained, what the hell to do with her?

She moved in the moonlight, turning onto her back. Sebastian took a step closer, anxious to see the face of this seductress who'd bewitched him so thoroughly.

She moaned. Wrinkles etched her brow. He reached to touch them, stopping just short of her satiny perfect skin. She confused him, as she had since that first night. He'd never had this sort of feelings for anyone. Not for man, woman, friends, dates, family. No one. However, for *this* woman his heart filled with messages he couldn't entirely translate.

He touched her. Sitting on the bed, he ran his fingers over the long hair spread out all around her. She turned into his touch, sighing softly. His heart contracted. Before he could control the impulse, he lay beside her, tucking her into his side. She snuggled close with another sigh, hand curled against his chest.

Sebastian rested his head against hers, completely blindsided by the feelings taking him hostage. She entwined herself into his soul the way the vines outside had captured the stone tower.

He would stay just a while, then leave. Marina posed more of a problem than he'd bargained for. He'd never expected to feel this deep, this fast. He thought of his neatly ordered world and decided, then and there, that not telling her he was coming had been a good idea. Come the dawn, he would leave. Forget the patent. Forget Marina. Return to his life the way it had always been. Never look back.

Chapter 5

Marina woke as sunlight began to flicker through the windows into her sanctuary. As long as it had taken her to fall asleep last night, she couldn't believe how well she'd slept. She even had a faint recollection of a dream. She *never* dreamt. Most nights she was restless. Many nights she wandered the halls, investigating the rooms of what she called home, though it had never felt that way. Last night, however, had been, different—*good.*

Consciousness seeped into her mind, along with a warn scent of musk. She supposed any woman in her right mind would be terrified, waking to find a strange man in her bed. For some reason, though, she felt peace rather than fear. Though she knew with certainty she'd never met him before, she felt an inexplicable connection to him in her soul.

Why he had come to her room and held her while she slept, she had no idea. Still, she wasn't about to refuse it.

She couldn't remember the last time she'd been held, hugged, even touched at all. This horrible existence left every inch of her skin aching for human contact. She wondered how he'd found her. Had he tried or had it been an accident? In fact, she had about a million questions, but they could wait. Something she'd never felt before tugged at her heart. She went with her gut and snuggled in closer.

Burrowing into his arms, pressing her nose into the chest hairs exposed in the opening of his shirt, flashes of the chats she'd had with Sebastian flooded her mind. For a second she ached again, wanting this to be him, but then she shoved all thoughts of Sebastian away and focused on the moment, on the sensations of actually being held, as opposed to *virtually* being held.

"You could get yourself into trouble with a maneuver like that, my darling."

Marina looked up into deep brown eyes so dark they were nearly black. He took her breath away. Even last night, at the distance she'd observed him, he'd been stunningly handsome. Up close, there simply weren't words. His voice was rough with sleep and his use of the words "my darling" struck the very center of her heart.

"Why are you here?"

He smiled then, a small smile. She touched his cheek, wondering why he seemed startled by the action. After all, he'd snuck into her bed in the night. She brazenly ran her thumb over his full lower lip.

"You haven't answered me."

"There isn't enough blood left in my brain to answer."

He smirked then and caught her wrist, pulling her hand away from his face.

"Be. Careful."

She met his stare. He didn't frighten her, though she wondered if he meant to. She ran her bare toes over his calf, batted her lashes and asked, "Or what?"

His strangled laugh made her feel feminine and decidedly naughty.

"You're a wicked princess locked away for the good of mankind then, hmm?" He ran his hand across her cheek before taking a long strand of her hair and rubbing it between his fingers. As she watched him, he studied her hair with an air of fascination. "I wondered why that old fool had you secured like a state secret."

His smile left her breathless. She felt quite certain no one else had ever smiled quite like that in the history of the universe. Then again, her father always called her a hopeless romantic.

"You haven't answered me. Should I call for Stedman and have you thrown out, or will you tell me what you think you're doing in my bed?"

His eyes sparked with mischief as he responded. "Is it often Stedman has to throw strange men from your bed?" His smile grew wicked. "It wouldn't surprise me if he did."

Marina liked this game; it left her feeling a bit giddy. She smiled coyly, "You're the first. However, I think I like waking in the arms of a man. Perhaps I will find others."

He tugged her possessively against his body, the look in his eyes feral.

"There will be no others. Only me."

Before she could draw breath, he captured her lips in a complete assault that didn't bear fighting. She sighed, went limp in his arms and enjoyed every warm sensation shooting through her body. As his tongue slowed and gently brushed over hers, she wiggled closer. She wanted to get so close she'd be a part of him. His tongue took her by surprise, but she proved to be a quick study and soon began twirling hers with his. When he suckled gently on it, it pulled in her womb and she arched against him instinctively.

When he moaned into her mouth, she felt the vibrations against her lips, and as he moved his fingers beneath the thin fabric of her gown, she felt herself growing wet. Pulling her mouth from his, she nuzzled into his neck, giving soft kisses, and in moments of daring, small bites. When he growled in response, she thrilled in delight.

"Good God, woman, where on earth did you come from?"

He rolled her beneath him, pulling her body closer still. Lost in her feelings, she couldn't coherently answer him. His finger brushed her nipple, sending a burst of greater need through her body.

"Kiss me, there." She tugged aside the gown with a frantic edge, and heard it tear, but simply didn't care. "Now. Please, now."

He rewarded her with another growl and a wicked, lethal smile. Squeezing her thighs closer together in the hopes of stemming the need and moisture steadily growing, she knew all hope of keeping her wits was lost the second she felt the warm moisture of his mouth as he softly touched his tongue to her nipple. With all hope of regaining her senses fleeing fast, she abandoned herself to the moment, the yearning, the aching.

Sebastian had more warning bells going off in his head than a firehouse during high winds, but God help him, he couldn't stop. Every taste of her supple skin burnt into his soul, every touch of his lips to hers set him on fire like he'd never experienced. Poets immortalized moments like this one, the poets he mocked with his own personal disbelief that indeed moments like these were possible. Right now, if his life depended on it, he knew he couldn't walk away from this woman.

Chapter 6

Hormones.

As Sebastian sucked on her nipple, his fingers twitching with need to submerge in her wet heat, he determined hormones must be the answer. No need to worry.

Her scent and taste permeated his every fiber as his need grew out of control. His mouth hungrily sought hers. She met him with a fire equally intense. Her tongue, once shy, now battled for supremacy as her hands innocently clutched at his shoulders.

He pushed away from her to rip his shirt over his head. Her eyes darkened with lust and approval as she gazed at him. He grew painfully hard. His skin missed the contact with hers. Laying his body atop her, he tugged at her gown, worsening the initial tear. His hands moved along her sides, making her shiver.

He reached for the bottom of the gown, pushing it up until he found the supple skin of her thigh. His hand moved upward, cupping her ass. Her nails dug into his shoulders, clawed down his back. She bit him. God, he couldn't remember being so fucking hot.

Concerned only with having her, he tossed back the covers, straddled her body and tore her gown from neckline to waist. Pushing away the fabric, he bared her beauty for his pleasure. Slowly, his gaze took in her body, naked and breathless beneath him. Nothing he'd ever experienced compared. God help him if he survived it.

* * * *

Marina was crazy with desire. She ached from it. She was so wet and needy she could barely control her urges.

Fuck me.

She could think the word, but she'd never said it before and couldn't force it past her throat. Sebastian said it to her—repeatedly some nights. She'd never brought herself to type the words back, but that's all she could think right now. She arched off the bed, pressing her breasts toward his touch, needing him, moaning from that need. Her gaze locked with his, sensing how badly he wanted her. It shone in his eyes. So why didn't he just fuck her?

His hands ran the length of her body. She closed her eyes as he roamed from her shoulders, over her breasts. He touched her nipple and she felt contractions begin in her womb, arched wildly, but it wasn't enough. She wanted...*needed*, so much more.

"Please. *Please.*"

Thrashing wildly against the bed, crazed with passion, she didn't realize at first he'd begun to move away from her. As he slid down her body, she whimpered from the loss of his touch, his heat. She missed the hard press of his cock. Even through his pants she'd felt it, undeniably wanting her.

"No, don't leave me."

"I'm not, princess. Shhh."

His low tone calmed her fervor. She watched as his gaze took in all of her. No man had ever seen her naked before. For *this* man, she wanted desperately to be appealing. His tongue ran across his lips. She moaned.

"Touch me."

His growl sent shivers along her skin. He lowered himself between her legs, pressing her thighs wider. She swallowed hard, watching him. For the longest time, he just looked, just examined her, eyes full of lust and raw need. She wanted to squirm, but couldn't move, couldn't breathe. When she could no longer bear it, she closed her eyes, felt his hot breath on her labia.

"*Please.*"

She hated him for making her beg, hated the throaty need in her voice, hated that she was so lost to the moment that she didn't give a fuck what happened after.

She felt his finger first. She pressed deeper into the mattress to keep from flying off it while his fingers brushed her soft wet folds, separating them, tantalizing her. Feeling she would die from this, she laughed, so thrilled to finally be having these feelings, this experience.

When his mouth closed over her labia, his tongue now moving between her folds, she moaned deep in her throat, bit on the heel of her palm to keep from screaming out in raw pleasure. It was like being outside her own body, the intense pleasure he brought her almost too much, but if he stopped she'd never forgive him.

She moved her leg along his arm, hooking it over his shoulder, feeling his nails bite into the soft flesh of her ass as he pulled her closer to his mouth and ate her voraciously until she couldn't see any longer.

Behind her closed lids she saw patterns of white and black. Her head began to spin. Her thighs spasmed with every pass of his tongue until finally she crested the enormous wave, screaming out in sheer ecstasy that nothing ever prepared her for—not even Sebastian's patient explanations about how relations between man and woman worked. After experiencing this, she began to wonder if maybe Sebastian's inexperience matched hers, because nothing he'd ever told her came close to this.

Wave after wave of pleasure rolled over her, slowly ebbing, leaving her unable to move, barely able to breathe. She lay on the bed, limp. Emotions rose, cresting, reeling from everything he'd done to her body. Her heart ached for this man she didn't even know.

He knelt above her, unfastening his pants. She smiled weakly, not entirely sure how she was going to participate in this part. She reached for him. His gaze locked with hers. She wished he'd say something, anything that would make her feel a bit less vulnerable, but the hunger in his eyes spoke volumes and comforted her soul.

"You are the most incredibly passionate woman I've ever known." He reached for her hand, kissing the palm. "I'm going to love you so completely, you won't be able to remember your own name." He came down atop her, his face an inch from her own. "I'm going to leave my presence on you so thoroughly, you won't find another man to ever satisfy the way I can." He kissed her near senseless. "The way I *will*."

Her breath still not entirely recovered, she lay waiting for his claim on her body to become permanent. He kissed her mouth, re-igniting a flame that hadn't really waned. At first she thought the pounding on the door was merely the pounding of her own heartbeat. Until…

"Marina, open the goddamned door this minute, you ungrateful bitch!"

Chapter 7

The angry voice of her father barreled through the door, forcing consciousness to invade her senses. Guilt and shame pounding in her veins, she tore herself from her lover's arms.

"One moment, Father."

Gathering her torn gown around herself once more, she reached for the velvet robe that lay across the settee, mouthed the words "get out" frantically to the man still lying in her bed as if nothing in the world was wrong.

Overwhelming fear engulfed her. She made a lot of excuses for her father's behavior. It was the only way she knew how to survive her captivity, but deep down, she knew he could be a very dangerous man. She grabbed his arm, pleading with her eyes and saw the moment when he took her seriously. He reached out to touch her cheek, pulling her closer to him. She wanted to melt into his arms forever but she wouldn't risk his life. Her father *would* kill him, and possibly her, if he found this man in her bedroom.

"Marina, why do you fear him?"

Even though his words were so quiet they barely registered on her, she imagined her father had heard them. His continued pounding on the door accompanied by the occasional slur unnerved her.

He finally got out of her bed, grabbed for his clothes then strode towards the door, but she grabbed his arm hard. Even though she knew she would never have the strength to stop him, her nails biting into his bicep at least seemed to make him realize she needed him to listen.

"No!" Though barely more than a whisper, her voice held all the alarm she felt.

Unexpectedly, he turned to growl at her. "No one speaks to my woman like that. I'll fucking kill him!"

"No. No. No."

Her brain wasn't functioning properly. Panic sapped her strength, but she had to get him out of there. She tugged him toward the secret door. He went with her, glancing back several times. She felt the tension in his body, different from the sexual tension of before, but just as powerful.

Finally reaching the large curtain, she tried to shove him behind when he grabbed her face in a tender assault and captured her mouth so she hadn't time to react.

Feelings of lust and safety and arousal invaded her every cell, pushing out fear and panic, making her tingle head to toe. She melted into the kiss, welcoming his tongue into her mouth as if he'd been gone a lifetime.

Before his kiss could consume her, she shoved hard against his shoulders, torn between relief and bereavement when he released her.

"Go. Down the stairs, you'll be in the south corridor."

He brushed her cheek.

"I won't leave you here with him like that, but I'll stay hidden and quiet unless you need me."

"He's my *father*. He has his moods, but he would never hurt me."

His eyes hardened. He repeated himself even more fervently, "I'm *not* leaving"

Knowing she had no time left, she pulled away, made certain the curtain covered the opening and went to open the door to her father. She would never admit to another soul how frightened she was, but she held firm to her belief that he would not hurt her. She pulled open the door.

"What took you so damn long? I have more important things to do than stand in that alcove waiting for her royal highness to grant me an appearance."

Marina blinked twice at her father's angry tone as he pushed past her into the room. The dramatic switch from the heightened state of arousal she'd been in moments before threatened to overwhelm her. As Claude neared the hidden stairs, blood pounded in her ears. She pulled the robe sash tight around her. Swallowing back a strange sense of fear, she forced herself to be assertive.

"Father, what is it you need?"

"Don't be impertinent."

Marina's breath froze in her chest as he pulled back the heavy tapestry curtain that she knew would reveal her lover.

"I have a guest." He dropped the fabric panel and turned towards her once more. "A very unwelcome guest. You are to stay up here until he's gone."

"But fath—"

"Shut up!" He stepped closer and for a split second Marina feared he would strike her. She flinched. "I've already had the south corridor blocked and since I know you can not be trusted…" he pulled a key from his wrinkled jacket, "…I intend to lock you in."

He moved past her again, obviously agitated and distracted, though at times Marina thought of that as his natural state.

"Sebastian Montclair is a treacherous man who cannot be trusted."

Marina swayed slightly, breathless and dizzy as the realization sunk in. Her father spun back around, looking at her as if she were utterly unworthy of his time and attention. She felt her cheeks warm under his intense stare, as if he could see Sebastian's fingerprints on her skin.

"*Especially* around women."

She wanted to tell him to stop acting crazy, but still clearly remembered the consequences of the last time she'd said something similar. She rubbed her cheek, still feeling the sharp bolt of pain that slid right through her cheekbone, making her feel as if her eye would explode.

Claude grabbed for the door and stepped through. She wasn't sure which was greater at that moment, her fear for Sebastian, her anger over his deception, or her sadness in realizing she would *never* have a real life. Not one of her dreams would ever come true.

How can they, when I'm locked in a tower like some damned fairytale princess?

"And stay off the balcony. The last thing I need is for that hound to know the likes of you is around. He'd probably climb the damn tower to get to you. I won't have it, Marina! You understand me?"

"Yes, Father."

A single tear slipped her guard as her voice trembled.

"Good. I'll have Stedman bring your meals."

The heavy wood door closed solidly and Marina flinched as she heard the key in the lock. Moments later, she felt Sebastian's hands at her elbows, gently pulling her body against his, wrapping her in his arms.

"He has no right, Marina."

She shook her head, knowing if she tried to utter a single word, the tears she was fighting against would swamp her.

Sebastian turned her, cupping her face he tilted her head up until she had no choice but to look into his eyes.

"Marina. He. Has. No. Right."

She looked into his eyes for the longest time, a million questions racing through her mind.

* * * *

Sebastian flicked away a tear from her cheek, pulling her body close to his. He had no idea how to fix this, an unfamiliar feeling. He held her close, tucking her head beneath his chin. He couldn't remember a time when he'd felt so protective of another living being. Yet it felt perfectly natural and right, as if he were born for just this.

"There's no way for you to get out. He's going to find you here."

Well, he hadn't thought that far yet. He kissed the top of her head, moving away from her to the tapestry-covered entry.

"Is there a secret panel at the bottom of this or anything?"

"No. They move a heavy armoire in front of it. It's immovable from this side."

Sebastian took a slow breath hoping to restrain his temper before he spoke again.

"Does he lock you in often?"

Impressed with how level his voice sounded when he fucking seethed with fury, he watched her straighten. Even seeing the flash of anger in her eyes, he was unprepared for her assault.

"He does the best he can. After my mother died, he nearly died with her, then he was left with me to raise alone. I've never needed for anything. He may have some strange…*quirks*, but he loves me. Why the hell didn't you tell me who you were?"

Sebastian took a step back, realizing she'd learned his identity the worst possible way. He felt like an ass.

"Marina, I…have no defense."

He dropped his gaze to the floor, feeling real shame for maybe the first time in his life. Pulling on his reserve of strength, he took a step forward and took her hand.

"I hurt you."

She impressed him as no one ever had with her reply, chin tipped defiantly in the air. "You did."

He tugged her closer. "It won't happen again."

Chapter 8

She held his stare for a long moment. Sebastian steadied himself for whatever hoops she'd demand to make this right. She drew a long, slow breath, closed her eyes for a moment, then nailed him with her incredible beauty, the emerald depths of her eyes asking for things and yet promising in return.

"It better not. I haven't had many people in my life. Something tells me I don't want to lose you."

He cupped her cheek, tipping her head, bringing his lips close to hers.

"It will *never* happen again. I swear it, my darling."

It shocked him how much he meant that promise. As he brought his lips down on hers, the soft scent of magnolia clung to her skin. He hadn't noticed before. He ran his tongue along the seam of her lips, moving slowly inside as she opened them with a whimper.

He felt dizzy when he finished kissing her. His head clouded with thoughts of passion and sex and making her his own, but he knew all that would have to wait. They had another much more pressing issue here.

"Hold that thought for later, my love. In an effort to keep you out of trouble, how do I get out of here, princess?"

He felt like shit the second her eyes filled with tears.

"Oh lord, Marina, I'm sorry."

"No, I'm just overwhelmed. I can't believe you're here and you're so…so…" She waved her hand up and down in front of his body. "I've shared my heart with you, the depths of my soul. You know my every secret."

He brushed stray hairs from her face. "And just the other night you said I didn't know you well enough to be in love with you."

He laughed, though he hadn't meant to. She was just so damned adorable when she pouted. He suddenly thought if she'd have him, he'd be one lucky man. Those were thoughts for another time, however.

He moved to the French doors that led to the balcony. "How far down until I reach a landing?"

"You cannot go down the side of the house!"

He tried not to smile, knowing that would only aggravate her more. Instead he moved close, pulled her to him, capturing her mouth in a deep kiss laced with longing, a longing he needed to satisfy, and soon. For now, though, he needed to find out what that bastard Claude had up his sleeve.

Pulling back, he ran his thumb over her lower lip.

"I've never felt that way from a kiss in my life. You are an amazing woman. And now, I *am* going over the balcony."

She grabbed for his arm before he got too far away. "Sebastian, you cannot go over the balcony. Someone will bring me food. I'll sneak you out then."

He smiled. "You sort of like me, don't you, darling?"

Laughing at her indignant snort—and the way she dropped his arm as if it was covered in roaches—he decided he better get over that balcony rail before he fucked her senseless.

"My darling, I will be fine. Your father will *never* beat me."

He saw the look in her eyes change. He took a step back towards her, sensing the shift in her demeanor.

"Why do you hate my father, Sebastian? What did he do?"

"Marina." He put his hands on her forearms. For the first time she didn't melt away at his touch. "I don't want to get into that. What's between me and your father has nothing to do with you. Now I'm leaving." He smiled wickedly. "Will you kiss me before I plunge to my death?"

She gasped and pulled out of his hold. "I will *not*!"

Folding her arms over her chest, she turned away. He guessed she didn't want to weaken by looking into his eyes. He imagined he held much the same power over her that she did him.

"If you're determined to kill yourself, go ahead, but don't expect me to watch."

"Marina." Determinedly, he pulled her back into his arms, brushing his fingers along her cheek, debating whether or not to kiss her again. "I will be just fine. I have things that must be taken care of." She tried to look away, but he captured her chin in his fingers and forced her to look at him. "But I will be coming back here, tonight, so be ready for me, my darling. Tonight you will be mine."

Together they fell into another scorching kiss full of promises, but before she could argue with him again, he slipped over the balcony.

* * * *

"What, you didn't invite me to dinner?"

Sebastian contained his smile as the old man looked up and sneered. "I didn't invite you for anything, Montclair."

Sebastian laughed, then dropped a file on the marble dining table in front of Claude. "Sign."

The old man blustered, wiped his mouth with a napkin and pushed the papers away. "You're a fool. I won't sell this to a Montclair, not ever. You can all rot in hell for all I—"

Sebastian grabbed Claude by his shirtfront and pulled him partially out of the chair. He'd hated this man as long as he could remember, but right now, he forced himself to control his rage. Business was business.

"I know your secrets, old man. Are you truly prepared for your daughter to know them as well?" He dropped Claude back into his seat and pulled a pen from his jacket. Placing it on top of the files, he pushed the papers forward once more. "*Sign*."

"You can't get anywhere near my daughter. You're bluffing."

Sebastian smiled, revealing his cold, feral nature. "I was with her when you barged in this morning. Seductive young thing. No wonder you keep her locked up."

Sebastian watched Claude literally turn red. He tried to plan for all possibilities, but now wondered if he'd underestimated the man's propensity for physical violence.

"Just sign the damn papers and I'll leave here, your secrets intact. I won't return. It's a fair price, old man. I'm not trying to *steal* the fucking patent."

"Why should I believe anything you say? 'Like father, like son,' the saying goes."

Sebastian refused to visibly show how deep that wound cut. "I haven't seen my father since I was ten and you know why." He slammed his hand on top of the file, shoving it against Claude's plate of half-eaten salmon and Brussels sprouts, causing it to crash to the floor. "Sign the damn papers, or not only will I fuck your daughter senseless, but when I'm finished, I'll also tell her what you've done. Then I'll find my father and tell him as well."

The color drained from Claude's face. He pushed away from the table and walked, visibly shaken, to the bank of windows across the room. Sebastian nearly had a moment of doubt but shoved it aside. He'd waited for just this moment, the moment he always loved, when his opponent *knew* he'd been beaten, immediately before the surrender.

He'd lived the past fifteen years for it, pushing aside any warmth or happiness in his life, instead just living for the kill. Standing in Claude's dining room, seconds away from a victory he'd chased for eighteen months, he felt doubt for the first time in his life.

That night in his study, going over files and trying to find some way to get to Bennett without using his father, he'd never imagined how his life would change. Seeing Bennett's online logo pop up had given him a sensation much like a cat probably got when the mouse finally came out of hiding. However, he'd never bargained for a woman supposedly dead on the other end. Worse, he'd never bargained for a woman who could steal his heart.

"If I sign this, you'll leave here? Never come back?"

Claude's words broke into his consciousness. When he looked up, the man stood a mere foot in front of him, strands of white hair mussed from fingers savagely raking through it. For the briefest moment, Sebastian felt a flare of compassion. He ruthlessly shoved it aside, covered his moment of weakness with an evil smile that said he'd won, and agreed to Claude's terms.

"I'll leave tonight."

The sound of pen scratching along paper should have been glorious, but instead it sounded…*felt* hollow. He looked over the documents, folded them back in the folder and slipped the pen inside his jacket.

"You'll be hearing from my attorneys shortly. Good doing business with you, Bennett."

He heard the glass shatter against the wall, as he walked away, but didn't let it phase him. He had one more thing to claim before he left this goddamned castle. Regardless of what he'd told Claude, tonight Marina would be *his.*

Chapter 9

Marina paced in the moonlight. She hadn't been at peace for one second since Sebastian had left. She worried about his safety, worried about whatever it was between him and her father, worried over her father's strange behavior. Being locked in her room, able to do nothing, threatened to drive her mad.

Taking a breath, she smoothed the silk gown over her hips, then ran her fingers through the waves of hair that fell nearly to her waist.

Will he really come as he promised?

This was her own personal moment of truth. She would finally have the opportunity to be with a man intimately and she was *conflicted*, of all things. She half wanted him to be true to his word and claim her, half feared it. She'd dreamt about this for years, but now that her opportunity might actually be only moments away…well, she felt more than a little nervous.

A sound came from the direction of the balcony, drawing her attention. She closed her eyes, heart beating so fast she knew he'd be able to hear it. Pressing a hand against her chest as if that would help, she went to the French doors and threw them open.

"Rapunzel, Rapunzel, let down your hair."

It failed to amuse her. She narrowed her eyes as his hand came over the stone railing.

"Oh, you're hysterical."

"Well, maybe you could just come grab my hand, then?"

"Oh, God!"

She ran to him, took his hand and helped as much as she could getting his large frame over the railing. The second his feet were solidly planted on the balcony floor, he had her in his arms. She nearly wept for joy at being there again.

She'd tried not to think of him all day, but what else could she do? She'd been awaiting his return from the moment he left. As he pulled back, the mischief dancing in his eyes as he smiled down at her, told her he knew it.

"Did you miss me, my darling?"

Her breath stuttered at the mere sight of his smile. She felt herself growing wet, aching to be touched, but she liked the games they played and acted unaffected by his touch.

"Some."

She pushed from his arms, moving back inside, nervous heartbeat accompanying her every step. The room wasn't all that big, so she had little room to maneuver. As she moved near the bed, she felt his hand slide up her arm. She shivered.

"Only *some*, my love?"

Tucking her chin down, she smiled to herself.

"I thought of you once or twice."

His heat engulfed her as he stepped closer, his chest pressed against her back, his arm wrapped around her waist, his mouth at her ear. He whispered, "I will have to do far better tonight, then, my love, if I am to keep my promises." His mouth traveled down her neck, until he bit softly into her shoulder. "You will be mine, Marina."

"I d-don't belong to *any* m-man."

She couldn't think straight with his mouth on her skin, his hand cupping the underside of her breast. She was in so much trouble with this man. He turned her to face him, tipped her chin up and brought his mouth just barely against hers.

"Wrong, Marina. You belong to *me*."

As if to prove that to her, he captured her mouth in a gentle assault, making her knees buckle. As he caught her, he pulled her tight against him. Immediately, his cock pressed against her belly. She arched instinctively, wanting to touch it, taste it, feel it, wanting him inside her, wanting all the things she'd dreamt of so long.

She broke the kiss, forcing herself to be braver than she felt.

"Are we going to make love, then?"

His rich laughter made her womb contract.

"My precious Marina, I'm going to love you until the heavens weep."

He swept her from her feet and placed her on the bed. Removing his shirt, he lay beside her and kissed her again. His tongue swept over hers. Then he sucked on it, making her moan and whimper with a need she'd shoved aside for far too long.

"Sebastian, you do remember what I told you. Right?"

Breathless, she felt him rain tiny kisses on her neck, shoulders and along the opening of her gown. He looked up at her, the look in his eyes more tender than she'd seen so far. With one of his hands he captured both of hers and held them above her head as he maneuvered his body atop hers.

"About you being a virgin, princess?"

She swallowed and closed her eyes. Hearing him say it aloud felt far more embarrassing than being one. She felt his fingers against her cheek, his lips on her other cheek.

"I remember." His mouth moved close to her ear and he whispered, "Trust me." before nibbling her lobe.

She couldn't see how she had much choice. She was aching with want, trying to shove aside her nerves and worries. Sebastian's gentle touches and soft kisses were doing a wonderful job of relaxing her. Her breathing slowly returned to normal, even as his fingers stroked her breast through the silk.

"Do you want my kisses again, Marina?" He drew a light circle around her nipple, snagging her breath. "Here?"

Her first instincts screamed panic, denial, *run*, but she fought them all back. She wasn't a child. She wanted this. Her hands still captive in Sebastian's grip, she raised her head to meet his gaze.

"Yes."

Growling deep in his throat, he released her and stripped her before she could react. Now, naked on her bed in the moonlight, Sebastian's gaze feasting on every inch of her, she'd never felt so much a woman in her life. She captured his face, bringing his lips to hers and gently kissed him.

"Thank you."

He straddled her again, pressing his cock against her.

"I think we are mutually pleased here, my darling."

She smiled and laughed, then met his gaze again, batting her lashes in mock innocence. "Sadly, though, we are *not* mutually naked."

With a look that heated her blood, he rose off the bed and stripped off the rest of the clothes. "Better, princess?

She actually made a purring sound that she wasn't aware she *could* make, then smiled at him like the most experienced temptress that ever lived. "Much."

Raising her arms, she begged him to return. It took only seconds for him to comply. As they lay naked, legs entwined, their mouths and hands exploring and discovering, Marina realized she'd never had a better moment in all her life. Despite the churning butterflies in her stomach and the worry he might reject her...she told him so the only way she knew how.

"I love you, Sebastian."

Chapter 10

Sebastian closed his eyes as her words washed over him. He'd heard them before. In fact, he quite feared hearing them from any of the women he dated. He made it his guiding principle to break off a relationship before the woman in question could ever fall for him, but this time...

He cupped her face in his hands, placed a kiss to her forehead. A feeling very akin to joy welled in his heart.

"I love you, my darling Marina."

He pulled his face away far enough to see the tears glistening in her eyes. The thought that he would break her heart come the morning viciously invaded his thoughts Just as viciously, he shoved it back. Nothing would stop him from making love to her tonight. Come the cold light of day, he'd be branded a bastard, but tonight he planned to show her enough love to last a lifetime.

"No more words. Lie back. Let me pleasure you."

He knew the act of lovemaking would be painful for her this first time, but he intended to do everything possible to make it right. He slid down her body, kissing and nibbling every millimeter of tender flesh on his way. He rolled a nipple between his tongue and the roof of his mouth and loved when she arched into him with a seductive moan of desire.

His fingers dug gently into her thighs as he pushed her legs apart. Her heated folds were already slick with her nectar and her scent rose up to greet him, making him painfully hard. He moved between her legs, sitting back on his heels.

"Spread your legs for me, darling. I want to see you."

He watched her battle her own shyness. In the end, she spread her beautiful legs wide for him, revealing her pink, wet pussy. He growled in a mix of arousal and frustration for not being able to just plunge deep within her. He grabbed his cock, sliding his fist over it, pre-cum dripping from the tip. He reached forward to touch her with the other hand. She shivered.

When he looked up, her eyes were dark and huge as she watched him work his own cock.

"Touch yourself, Marina. Show me what you like."

Hesitantly her fingers moved over the folds of her pussy and dipped inside. Sebastian had to bite the inside of his jaw to keep from coming. He moved her hand, replaced it with his own and slid first one, then a second finger deep inside her. She was tight, but she was so very wet, he knew she was ready for him.

"Darling, if I don't get inside you very soon, you will have my cum on your body instead of inside. I'll go slowly, but I need to get inside you now."

She swallowed, nodded her consent and raised her ass off the bed, giving him an ever better view. He started thinking of finance charts and his next merger. Then, simply because he was the biggest fool on the planet with apparently no discipline, he leaned down and ran his tongue between her folds and then pressed it inside her. The taste of her flooded his mouth. He grazed her clit with his teeth gently before sitting up again and pressing the tip of his cock just inside her virginal opening.

"Are you ready?"

She nodded. He pressed slowly inside until he felt her barrier, then stopped. Her pussy was holding him so tight and the sight of his cock half embedded within her was pushing him to the edge very rapidly. He hated to do this to her, but it was a matter of urgency at this point.

Without warning, he pushed through the thin barrier and came down atop her, holding her tight, not moving while she rode out the pain. He planted soft kisses into her hairline and waited until he felt her body relax again.

"Okay?"

She nodded, but he could see the hint of fear back in her eyes and he hated that.

"I'll make it right, darling." He smiled with wicked assurance. "I promise you."

Slowly, he began to move inside her, thankful that simply holding her set back his own orgasm. He wanted this night to be memorable for her in a good way, not as the fastest she'd ever have.

The thought of her with other men suddenly gripped his heart so hard he lost his breath for a moment.

There is *no other way.*

Again, he shoved thoughts of leaving her aside. Her pussy was clenching at him so hard now, he couldn't think, anyway. He slipped out from inside her and loved it when she whimpered. He soothed the frown on her forehead and grabbed her around the waist, pulling her body close.

"Wrap your legs around me."

She did. Positioning himself again, he slid deep inside her. She wrapped her arms around him, pressed her breasts against him and purred into his ear. He held her as tight as he could, rocking them both slowly until the passion threatened to take him again. Then he lay down, placed her atop him and gently coaxed her to ride him.

Every time she rose up, her pussy clenched him hard. He started biting his jaw again and reached for her clit. He wasn't coming without her. A moment later, he flipped her to her stomach, hauled her ass into the air and readied himself to get back inside, but that perfectly pink swollen pussy was too much temptation for him.

He lowered his mouth to her. Smiling at her yelp of shock, he pushed his tongue inside. The taste of her sent shivers through his entire body. He licked and sucked while she moaned and wriggled, at times trying to pull away.

He'd never had so much fun playing with a woman in bed before. This went beyond any dream he'd ever had. She matched his adventurous side, trusting him completely, and that awed him.

Finally, he knew they were both too close to continue this. He rose up behind her, sank his cock deep inside her and exploded almost instantly. He fingered her clit as his thighs slapped hard against hers and within seconds she cried out and he felt her pussy grab him, milking him into the most powerful orgasm of his life.

Moments later, his legs began shaking so bad, they wouldn't support him. He dropped Marina to the bed and fell beside her, wrapping his arm around her waist and tucking her closely into his side. She snuggled close, burrowing her face against him, murmuring her contentment. Sebastian fell asleep wishing fervently that morning would never come.

Chapter 11

Marina stared out over the water, numb.

No, that wasn't true; her heart was raw, breaking. She was in so much pain, most days she would have been happy if it just stopped beating altogether.

"Why?"

It was the only question she kept coming back to over and over and over.

"Marina, your father is looking for you."

Shoving back the ambivalence, she nodded respectfully and allowed Stedman to escort her back to the house. She pulled the shawl she wore loosely over her shoulders around the gentle swell of her belly.

She'd have to tell her father eventually, but until she figured out what to do about the baby, she figured it was better to keep it a secret.

Her father's menacing presence filled the doorway as she and Stedman returned. He'd been in such a black mood ever since…for months. If she were truthful, she had to admit he had begun to scare her.

"What did you need, father?"

He stared right through her until Stedman disappeared into the house, then slapped her so suddenly she had no opportunity to react to it, hard enough to knock her to the stone porch floor.

Stunned, she sat motionless, trying to catch her breath.

"Did you think I would never find you out?"

Marina cautiously tilted her head until her gaze captured her father's menacing one.

"*Did you*?"

"I…"

She had no idea what this was about, had no idea what the right thing to say was, but it wasn't just her safety on the line anymore. She curled into a ball, trying to wrap her entire body somehow around the tiny life inside her.

"I should have let you die. You have been nothing but trouble. The pleasure I got from torturing your mother was worth it, but *this*, you goddamned bitch, *this* is too much. Get your things and get the fuck out of my house. I never want to see you again!"

She pushed herself against the wall, carefully standing, head spinning.

"What have I done?" Tears began to flow despite her efforts. "I've done nothing but love you."

She withstood the slap that time, though her cheek stung like hell. She closed her eyes to the pain.

"You think I'm a complete fool, don't you? You and Montclair have been working together to ruin me. You stole my patent, cost me millions and don't think I haven't noticed what's beneath that shawl. You're carrying his bastard! Get the fuck out of my house, Marina. You are no longer my daughter."

She watched him walk back towards the door, her world splintering along with her heart. She couldn't take any more. She was going to break; she felt it happening.

"Why?"

Her tear filled voice carried her pain, but he acted as if she'd said nothing, striding through the door and slamming it behind him.

Rage and fear filled her veins. How was she supposed to leave? Where was she supposed to go? She'd never been away from this fortress in all her life. She didn't know the first thing about the real world. The thought of being completely alone terrified her. She pulled open the door, running after the man her whole life was built around.

"Daddy, why? What did I do?"

He shook her off his arm, turning towards her with hatred, but she refused to fear him.

"I found your e-mails, your chats, you whore. The only thing I couldn't figure out was, did he find you, or did you find him?"

"I…I don't know…"

He slapped her again, but she forbid the tears.

"Don't lie to me now, Marina. I have all the proof I need on my computer."

She stood in shock, small twinges of pain splintering her womb. He laughed then, a cold heartless sound she remembered from when she was very small.

"Don't tell me you are so stupid that he used you and you didn't even know it. Don't tell me you let him fuck you—impregnate you—and you had no idea he just wanted to use you to get to me." His head dropped back with sharp bursts of laughter. His long white hair fell over his forehead when he straightened again. "You're a slut and a fool and I want you and that bastard out of my house, *now*, Marina. I will not support a Montclair or any woman who's fucked one."

Shock and disbelief pummeled her. Disoriented, she stumbled back against the nearest wall. Legs too weak to hold her, she slid to the floor, watching him walk away from her as if she was *nothing*. She grabbed her baby as the first sharp pain gripped her. Closing her eyes, she simply wished for death.

Chapter 12

The quiet of driving on pavement changed to the crunch of dirt and rocks as Marina took the turn onto the old road. The dust swirling up from beneath the tires blurred the vision in the rear view, but she figured it didn't really matter—she hadn't seen another soul for the past hour and a half, even on the main road.

As she drove, the cool air tempered the sun's heat. For the first time in three months, she smelled the scent of mussels and tasted the tang of salt in the air.

The ocean.

She smiled. Silly thing to miss, but she *had* missed it. Surprisingly, it was all she had missed. Her heart instantly reminded her with a sharp stab that the ocean was *not* the only thing she missed. She missed Sebastian, sometimes so much she still wished her heart would just stop beating altogether instead of limping along half-dead and hemorrhaging.

Finally, through the pines, she saw a glimmer of the ocean. The sun's reflection nearly blinded her, but the little bit of joy it brought was worth it. To the right, the house instantly came into view. Her nerves shot through the roof. This was it. After all these months, this was finally it. She swore what was left of her heart was going to give out with the stress she'd been under these past few months all culminating in this visit.

The car engine halted. She heard seagulls and waves rolling to shore in the distance. For whatever reason, though, she couldn't bring herself to get out of the car. She'd wanted this from the second Sebastian's letter had arrived. She laughed. It was almost the same as the night he took her virginity. She'd wanted that for years, too, and it had been the most wonderful experience of her life. She closed her eyes to the pain and drew a deep breath.

And look how that turned out.

Gathering her courage, she pushed open the car door and got out, just as a man with silver-streaked black hair appeared. Tall and muscular, he seemed…quiet, was the best description.

Marina's breath accelerated again.

A second later the woman she'd expected followed the man out the door. Her long dark hair pulled back in a single blue ribbon, she wore no make-up. Marina thought she looked happy. Really, truly happy. At peace.

Marina watched the man take the woman's hand to help her down the steps of the wooden deck. Her heart did that stupid pinchy thing again that it did any time she saw a happy couple. She drew a breath against tears she knew would well up next.

"Marina! Oh, child, you have no idea how much we've been looking forward to this."

She stood still as he looked her up and down with a strange almost paternal smile on his lips, lips that were a little too familiar.

"Neither of us slept last night, did we, darling?"

Marina smiled shyly as she locked eyes with a woman she had hoped would stir some memories in her but didn't.

"Hi."

Her throat shut down, or maybe it was her brain. She wasn't sure, but whatever the case, all the eloquent things she'd been planning to say flew out the window. The stupid tears welled up, slipping down her cheeks, regardless of how she tried to push them away.

"Marina, I'm sorry, I promised to be...oh, I don't even know. I just want to hug you."

The look in her mother's eyes broke the last barrier on her strained emotions. She flew into the arms of a woman she couldn't remember, but that her heart seemed to know all the same.

"Marina, I swear I never knew. He convinced me you were dead. I never knew."

Marina straightened out of her mother's embrace, wiped the tears from her cheeks with her fingertips, drew a breath against a wave of nausea, and did her best to smile.

"The whole thing was pretty screwed up. I don't blame you. I never even suspected."

Her mother's fingers gently touched her cheek.

"You were so little. How could you?"

The three of them stood for a few minutes in silence. Marina tried to take everything in. She couldn't believe this was her mother, alive and well and...*happy*.

When Sebastian had sent her the letter, with all the documents and information she needed to find her mother, she'd had a hard time wrapping her mind around the fact that her mother had in actuality left her father for Sebastian's. How weird does a world have to be for that to happen?

"Marina, you must be tired from the drive. Come inside. We have lunch ready. Or I can show you a room to lie down in for a while. Whatever you like."

She smiled at him. He looked so much like Sebastian. It would take her awhile to get used to him. She certainly hoped the pain she felt every time she looked at him would subside soon, anyway.

"Thank you Bernard. I think I would like to lie down for a while, so long as you both won't think me terribly rude."

Sophia smiled and placed an arm around her daughter's shoulders.

"Of course not. You've been through so much. I'm just so glad your doctor finally let you make the trip, although I do wish you'd let us come to you."

They started the walk back to the house. Marina wasn't sure how to respond to that. Finding out her mother was alive, and that Sebastian had indeed just used her to get to her father had been so much to handle, she needed the time to come to grips with it all. She knew though that both Sophia and Bernard never really understood why she didn't want them with her while she recovered and she knew it had hurt them, but the way she saw it, they all had a fresh start and years to grow into a real family now.

The A-frame structure set amongst the pines over looking the ocean felt incredibly welcoming as Marina stepped inside. It felt like a home. Wood and stucco and plants and light flooded through floor to ceiling windows. It was everything the fortress she'd shared with her father was not.

"Lie down and don't worry about anything. I'll bring in your bags and they'll be here when you wake up."

Bernard smiled at her again, she tried to smile back but at the moment, couldn't find it in her.

"Thank you."

Sophia had tears in her eyes and Marina was struck with how little she'd changed since the portrait that hung on the second floor landing had been painted. She didn't fight the impulse to hug her one more time. Then she pushed open the door to a beautiful guest room, flooded with sunlight and decorated in colors of mauve and cream.

Though exhausted, she couldn't resist a quick look out at the balcony off her room. As she opened the sliding glass door, the sound of the ocean filled the room. It made her smile, made her feel at home in a strange way.

"Marina."

She turned at the voice, a lump in her throat at how very much Bernard sounded like Sebastian. Placed a smile on her face and summoned the last of her strength to answer whatever it was.

Only the face she saw wasn't Bernard's. Dizziness swamped her, making her lean hard against the doorframe. Within a second, Sebastian had swept her from her feet and placed her on the bed, bringing back so many memories that had been wonderful and now were so painful she couldn't bear them.

The tears ran freely down her cheeks. She couldn't find any words; she only looked at him, her heart longing despite everything her head knew.

Sebastian looked down at Marina, more beautiful then he ever remembered. He touched her cheek, pushed back her hair, unable to resist touching her even in small ways. Every second of the past seven months had been excruciating torture. How he ever thought he'd be able to live without her was beyond him. She was a part of him, and without her he'd never be complete.

"'I'm sorry' doesn't begin to cover it, I realize, but if you'll just let me…"

She sat up and shoved his hand off her.

"Just let you what?"

He saw the pain he'd caused her etched on her face, in the set of her mouth, the depths of her eyes and for a second he doubted his father's well-meant advice.

When she moved, heading for the door, Sebastian knew this was the defining moment of his life. Everything he was, everything he would become hinged in this moment in time. He shoved away fear and doubt and grabbed her hand, pulling her back towards him, cupping her cheek in his hand, exuberant when she leaned into his touch.

"Marina, there is no excuse for what I did. I was weak. I was a coward. I do not deserve another chance and I won't blame you in the least if you refuse me, but…" He stepped back just an inch, moved his hand from her cheek to her belly. "For all of us, please…" He glanced at his hand resting on his child, remembering the pain he felt at learning of the child and how terrified he was when she nearly lost him. Raising his gaze back into the eyes of the only woman he would ever love, he knew he had to make this work. "Please, just hear me out."

He watched emotions flicker in her eyes. He saw fear, he saw anger and hurt, but more he saw hope and it was that he latched onto.

"I love you. I know I have a horrible way of showing you, but that was exactly what I was trying to do when I left, and when I sent you the information about your mother. I just…I was…fuck!"

He walked away, over to the glass doors and looked out over the water.

"I have no excuse. I have no reasons you should trust me again. I was a coward, Marina. I was terrified of you and what I felt for you and I…"

He turned back, met her gaze and this time he saw the crack in her anger and through the crack, he saw her love for him.

"I nearly lost the baby."

"I know." He moved back to her taking her hands. "I checked with your doctors every day, but I thought the last thing you needed was me. I was convinced I had nothing to offer you and that you were far better off without me.

"I've never loved anyone in my life, Marina. I have no idea what I'd be doing with you. And what if I screwed up our child? I'm a cold-hearted bastard, hardly father material. And you, you deserve so much more than my inadequate attempts to love you.

"I swore I wouldn't hurt you again, Marina, I can't imagine I'll do anything but."

Marina's brain was flashing through everything this man had put her through. The pain he caused her when he walked away. The fear she'd felt every day that he'd left her alone. She could walk away, heal eventually, but would she ever truly be whole without him?

Oh, she'd go on, have their baby and somehow find a way to make a life for them, but her heart…he owned a piece of it plain and simple.

"I love you, Sebastian. You've owned my heart from the first night we talked. I won't lie to you, I'm hurt and I'm scared to trust you again, but at the end of the day, I just don't want to do this without you."

She rubbed her belly where her son kicked his approval and laughed.

"What?"

She smiled, reached for his hand and placed it atop the tiny protruding foot.

"*We* don't want to do this without you."

He rested his forehead against hers. She was surprised to feel his tears drop on her cheeks. She wrapped her arms tight around him, pulling her large body as close as she could get it.

"I love you."

"Princess…" His voice cracked, she kissed his cheek and knew she'd made the right decision to trust him again.

"Please help me be a better man. I want to be everything you deserve."

He kissed her, the salty taste of his tears on his lips. Marina realized she probably wasn't signing up for an easy life loving Sebastian Montclair, but she knew it was the exact life she'd always dreamt of and that they would indeed live happily ever after.

TOWER OF SECRETS

THE END

WWW.SAMANTHALUCAS.COM

Siren Publishing, Inc.
www.SirenPublishing.com

Printed in the United States
217425BV00004B/114/P

9 781606 010365